# SALVAGE

ALEXANDRA DUNCAN

# SALVAGE

An Imprint of *HarperCollins*Publishers

This book is a work of fiction. References to real people, events, establishments, organizations, or locales are intended only to provide a sense of authenticity, and are used to advance the fictional narrative. All other characters, and all incidents and dialogue, are drawn from the author's imagination and are not to be construed as real.


For information address HarperCollins Children's Books,
a division of HarperCollins Publishers, 10 East 53rd Street,
New York, NY 10022.
www.epicreads.com
The text of this book is set in Caslon 540.
Book design by Sylvie Le Floc'h

Library of Congress Cataloging-in-Publication Data
Duncan, Alexandra.
Salvage / by Alexandra Duncan.
pages cm
Summary: "Ava, a teenage girl living aboard the male-dominated, conservative, deep space merchant ship *Parastrata*, faces betrayal, banishment, and death. Taking her fate into her own hands, she flees to the Gyre, a floating continent of garbage and scrap in the Pacific Ocean. How will she build a future on an Earth ravaged by climate change?"—Provided by publisher.
ISBN 978-0-06-222014-1 (hardback)
[1. Science fiction. 2. Self-reliance—Fiction. 3. Choice—Fiction.] I. Title.
PZ7.D8946Sal 2014 [Fic]—dc23 2013045267

14 15 16 17 18 CG/RRDH 10 9 8 7 6 5 4 3 2 1
First Edition

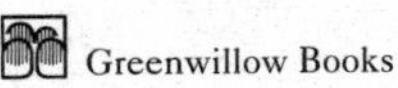

*For my sisters,*

*Rachel, Molly, and Nora*

# PART I

# CHAPTER • 1

The morning before our ship, *Parastrata*, docks at the skyport, I rise early. I climb over my littlest sister, Lifil, and the other smallgirls curled together like puppies on our bunk. Out in the common room, the rest of the women and girls lie sleeping in the dark, humid simulation of night. As I wind up my hair and bind it with a work rag, I mark how Modrie Reller's bunk is empty. My stepmother must have spent the night in my father's quarters, even some months gone with child again as she is.

I fasten the clasps of my shift at my shoulders, step first into my light skirts, then my quilted ones, and tie them all at my waist until they hang heavy around my hips. I lean forward to check their length. Only the barest hint of toe peeks out from beneath the hem.

*Right so.* I smile to myself in the dark. Today will be a good day. Everything balanced, everything raveled right.

I tuck my folding fan into my pocket and make my way to the hatch. Nan and Llell and some of the other grown girls stir on the mattresses cramping the floor as I punch in the pattern code to unlock the door—circle, bar, bar, slant. Only Modrie Reller and me know the pattern. Me, since I'm so girl of our ship, and her, since she's firstwife to the *Parastrata*'s captain, at least ever since a fever took my mother to the Void ten turns past. Nan tried to get me to tell the pattern one time, so she could sneak off to her cats in the livestock bay, but I told her no. My father can trust me and Modrie Reller, but it's hardly safe if all the women and girls know.

I heave the door open on its rollers and creep out into the hallway. The faint, moon-blue light of a biolume bowl washes the walls. I think on going back and hurrying the others along so I won't be caught alone out in the corridors, but I am the so girl and my father's eldest daughter, besides. No one would dare say anything to me. And a few minutes by myself is too choice to pass up when I spend near every minute of the day hemmed in by other people. I roll the door partway closed behind me.

I breathe deep. Without the heat and breath of so many

women pressed together in one room, the air is less close, almost cool. One of our canaries pipes a question at me from its cage in an alcove along the wall. I bend close and work the tip of my finger between the bars. The canary quirks its head at me, its eyes small, inky spots in the half light.

"Ava," Llell hisses behind me. She leans out of the hatch, still working the tie of her outer skirt. "Wait on us, huh?"

I pull my finger from the cage, straighten up, and fold my arms in feigned impatience.

Llell squints at me, uncertain.

"Hurry on, then," I say. Sometimes I forget Llell can't read my looks. I have to speak aloud if I want her to do what needs doing. Her eyes are bad, like her mother's and all her brothers' and sisters'.

Llell nods and ducks back into the sleeping quarters.

There's doctors on the waystations what can fix bad eyes, but Priority says it's only for those on Flight and Fixes duty. It's not worth the cost if you're only assigned to the kitchens or the nurseries, much less cleaning or the dyeworks. Maybe someday Llell and her mother can share a pair of glasses like my great-grandfather's widow Hannah has.

Across the corridor, a porthole looks out on the darkness of the Void, speckled bright with stars like a vast, black egg. A distant silver-gray moon hangs against it, and farther out, a blue planet mottled cloud white and brown-green slips into view, a bright halo circling it. *Earth, the seat of our woes.*

I step up to the glass. The skyport floats somewhere above the blue planet, still some far to be seen with the naked eye. But come endday, we'll dock our ship, and we'll join the other crewes for our first endrun meet in five turns. A nervy, electric thrill trips through my body at the sight of the moon and its world, so impossibly near and far at once. Sometimes I forget the true, endless scope of the Void and lull myself to thinking our ship is all the universe there is. But then we pass a moon or a world, hanging lonely and luminous in the dark, and it comes to me, the sheer stretch of the emptiness we live in. I touch my hand to the porthole's cool, scored surface, and trace the curve of the Earth.

*No.* I tamp out the thought, tuck my hands under my arms, and look away so I see only our ship. If I've taken to gazing out portholes like a silly, Earthstruck girl, I truly must be in need of marrying, as Modrie Reller's son Jerej teases. All the oldgirls say we younger ones are drawn to the Earth, even though its touch means our ruin. They say even Saeleas, our first patriarch's wife, fell weeping when our people departed some thousand turns past, and she had seen its desolation with her own eyes. They say ever since, our women have harbored a wanting for the Earth like a soft, rotten spot in our souls.

It is our men who risk to walk it when the need comes, our men who gird themselves and shield us from its pull, who must purify themselves with oil and water after suffering its weight. And in turn, all we need do is remember how our ship is life, the true world, the pure world. I whisper a piece from the Word of the Sky to keep me raveled.

"Clean the dust from our feet,
Our hair, our clothes.
Bring us oil, bring us water,
And in the heavens
We will make a world anew."

"Sorry, sorry." Nan finally emerges from the sleeping quarters, followed by Llell.

I stand back to inspect them. They've bound up their red hair in work rags, like mine, and their green skirts brush the floor. Well, Llell's do. Nan needs to let out the hem of her dress. She's grown again, and the bare tops of her feet show. If you weren't looking close, you'd think we were sisters, all dressed alike, except my skin is dull and dark, like my mother's was, whereas theirs holds a translucent pearl. Llell and all the boys used to tease me on my coloring before I became so girl, but not now. Everything is different now.

I nod my approval and sweep off in the direction of the livestock bay, the other girls in tow.

"Hurry on," I call over my shoulder. "We want to be done and out of the way for the docking, right so?"

"Right so," Llell mutters.

"Right so," Nan chirps, Llell's blithe echo.

The ship is still observing night, so the solar-fed lights are out. Strips of phosphorous lining the hallway bathe our bare feet in a dim blue glow, and the biolume bowls hanging from the ceiling at every turn keep us from descending into complete darkness. As we reach the bend before the gangway, the daylights buzz to life. Turrut, one of the boys near our age, barrels around the corner with an armful of dioxide canisters for the workrooms clutched to his chest. We shrink against the wall and duck our heads as one, waiting for him to pass. Sometimes Turrut will tease us, try to rouse some words out of us so he can hold it over our heads later, maybe make us do his chores, but today he's too busy. He flies by without a word.

As he disappears around the bend, Llell hurries forward and falls into step beside me. She keeps her neck bent so our heads are even and speaks down to her feet. "You right know you shouldn't walk out without us."

I don't answer. Llell's father may head the dyeworks, but her mother is only a fourthwife and a half-blind dyegirl, a nobody.

"What if you come on some trouble?" She doesn't look up at me. "What if Turrut or . . . or the captain catches you out alone?"

I stop in my tracks. Nan almost bumps into us.

"Llell," I say, pulling all the sternness of Modrie Reller's voice into my own. "I don't need you to tell me what's proper. Are you forgetting my place?"

Llell falls quiet. She scratches the inside arch of her foot with her big toe.

"If you and Nan and the others would rise with me, I wouldn't need to walk out alone, would I?"

Llell makes a face but doesn't say anything.

"How can we protect one another's honor if you're still asleep?"

Llell stares at the floor. "Right so," she says quietly.

A twinge of remorse nips at me. I want to reach out and squeeze her hand, as we did when we were younger and neither of us knew what our stations meant. But I am the so girl. I lift my head and continue along the corridor.

The warm, heavy stink of dung, synthetic hay, and animal bodies hits us as I activate the doors to the livestock bay. I leave the chickens to Llell. They're hateful and like to nip, but she doesn't mind them so much as the rest of us. I let Nan wander off in search of the cats, even though Llell and I both know she has her pockets full of leftover bean cake from the kitchens and she's going to spoil them for mousing. I start on the goats.

I unhook the coaxer from its peg on the bulkhead wall and lead the first of the nanny goats into the outer paddock for milking. Above me, Llell activates the pneumatic lift and rides it up to the chicken coop, filling the bay with an awful grinding sound. She *coo-coo*s softly to the birds as it comes to a stop. I strap the first goat into the coaxer, notch the dial to the yellow setting in the middle, and go back into the paddock for another goat to milk by hand while the coaxer does its work on the first. The second one is testy. She tries to step on my feet and kick over the pail as I pull milk from her udders, but I've been milking every day since I was a smallgirl near five turns. I know all the goats' tricks. I hitch in her lead and hold her back left leg still.

Beside me, the coaxer choke-rattle-grinds, and the

first goat bleats in fright. She tries to bolt, but the heavy machinery weighs her down. She rears. I jump up and pull the milking pail out of the way before the second goat can bolt and knock it over. The tang of too-hot metal floods the air.

"*Hshhh, hshhh.*" I lay a calming hand on the goat's neck and unstrap her. The second she's free, she runs for the far side of the paddock in a kick of hay, flaps her ears, and stamps in annoyance. I tap the regulator face on the coaxer's side. It's stuck on the low setting, and trying to rev itself to catch up. I check over both shoulders to see if Llell or Nan is lurking behind me. No one. I'm alone.

I pop off the faceplate. The coaxer's old, some turns older than me, and sometimes its belts slip. The last time this happened, we had to turn it in at the Fixes' workshop and it took deciturns to get it back, since the coaxer's not Priority. But now no one's watching, so I can try one of the fixes I learned from my friend Soli at the runend meet some five turns past. I slide the faceplate away. The interlocking cogs in the coaxer's innards have been stripped, ground completely smooth.

"No. Oh, no." I groan softly. I could fix it, but for that I'd need parts. And if I go to the requisitions master and tell him what I need, he'll ask how I know what the fix is.

And then it'll come out someone's taught me fixes. So girl or no, that's hardly proper.

Nan scurries up, brushing crumbs from her hands. I snap the faceplate back on the coaxer and drop it into my lap in one smooth movement.

"It's bust again?" Nan asks.

I nod. "I'll take it by the Fixes after we finish." I have no choice.

"How many more?" she asks.

"Thirteen." I point to the pen of waiting goats.

Nan leads out another goat, a spotted one, and we both bend our heads over our work. It's some peaceful, the rattle of milk as it hits the pail, my knees on the warm hay, knowing Nan is beside me and the ship is extending its solar arms to the sun to power up the grids and wake everyone for the last day of our journey. Maybe I could gut some of the other machines in the junk locker for parts, slip around the Fixes, and get our coaxer working again. . . .

"Ava," Nan whispers.

I glance up and see her eyes locked somewhere behind me. I look over my shoulder. Modrie Reller has crossed the gangway. She's bearing down on us like a hawkship, her long copper-shot gray hair coiled in braids at the base of her skull and her fan swinging from a cord around her wrist. She moves quick and practiced, despite the round of pregnancy at her waist, like a caravel accustomed to sailing under heavy cargo. Iri, my great-grandfather's youngest widow and Modrie Reller's constant shadow, trails in her wake. I jump to my feet and brush the hay from my skirts.

The pneumatic lift rumbles above us. Llell is coming down, a crate of fresh brown eggs in her arms. The noise from the lift drowns out any hope of talk, but the question is all over her face. *What's happening?*

"Ava," Modrie Reller says. Her words are clear, even over the lift's gears. "Come with us."

I look back at Llell and Nan. They both stare openly at me, straw and muck all over their skirts. I brush myself down one last time, step out of the pen, and let the gate's latch fall closed behind me.

Modrie Reller doesn't speak as she leads the way through the halls. Iri and I trail in her wake with our heads bent modestly, so we don't look on the faces of any men by mistake. We pass the open arched doorways of the main corridor, the kitchens, the hydroponic gardens, the men mixing a slurry of paste, dung, and fabric remnants for paper, the dyegirls heating urine and water in vats while the older women bend over their weaving. Along the way, the caged canaries stand sentry for bad matter in the air.

We move past the men's training room, with its walking machines and pressure chamber for keeping them strong enough to bear the Earth's weight, and through the sleeping quarters, now almost empty. Modrie Reller pushes aside a heavy woven tapestry picturing Saeleas, haloed in copper-point stars.

We duck into the tiled cleanroom on the other side, where Kamak sits rubbing oil into the stretched skin of her stomach. She is pregnant with her third child. Modrie Reller gives her a tight smile and a nod as we bustle past. We cut through the narrow service corridors and stop short in a small room with a utility sink, its drain limed with age. Iri pulls the door shut behind us.

Now I know why we're here. They're going to dye my hair.

When I was born, my hair was auburn like my mother's, not too far from my crewemates' heads of amber and rust. But it darkened as I grew, until it was black like a canary's eye, and the oldgirls started talking. They said it was the curse, the bad matter left on us when my grandmother married a man from Earth, a visiting so doctor who took my grandmother for his secondwife. Crewes take such marriages every few decades, like a tonic. It brings new blood into our line. The so doctor was good, the oldgirls say, took care of my grandmother and the girl that came from their union, my own mother.

But when he passed, the so doctor's daughter by his firstwife came meddling, sending messages and even booking passage to the skyport to find us. I was only a smallgirl then, but I remember the sight of her stalking down the gangways beside our old captain, my great-grandfather Harrah, her head swathed in dark cloth and her arms covered. The deep brown of her face, brown as paper, looking out at us. How tall she was, the same height as my great-grandfather, and how she stared into everyone's eyes—even the men—as if she were looking for someone. She walked so sure and steady, as if she weren't tracking the Earth's taint through our ship.

Hah and Turrut snuck into her room in the passengers' quarters while she rested and said they saw her head uncovered. They said her hair was black like mine and teased she was a bad spirit come up after me from the Earth. *Maybe she come an' snatch you away.*

I cried and ran to find Iri, who brought me to Modrie Reller. That was the day they began dyeing my hair.

Modrie Reller tugs on a pair of hide gloves, the kind we use in the dyeworks.

"So soon?" I ask. They've only just dyed my hair three

weeks ago. The Void black at my roots is no more than a thin line, unnoticeable unless you're looking for it. I turn to Iri. Iri may be my great-grandfather's widow, but she's younger even than Modrie Reller, having been bound to my great-grandfather when she younger than I am now and he only a turn or two from death. She's some like an older sister to me, telling the why of things in whispers when Modrie Reller's back is turned. She levels her gaze at me but doesn't speak. She flicks her eyes to Modrie Reller. *Not now. Not in front of your stepmother.*

"Kneel," Modrie Reller says.

I do.

Only then does she continue. "This is your father's order." She pulls a dye tube wrapped in oilskin from deep in her pockets and twists off the cap. "This runend meet, he's decreed you're to be a bride."

# CHAPTER . 2

"A bride?" I try to keep my face calm.

"Right so." Modrie Reller looks pointedly at my hair. "We don't want the other crewes thinking something's wrong with the *Parastrata*'s so girl."

Iri smiles at me, kind. "Or passing off some palsied goats or brittle old plasticine in exchange for our Ava."

I laugh, but nervously. A bride. I know from watching the girls who've gone before me that I ought to chirrup and gab at the news, or else flush pink and do a poor job of hiding my pleasure behind a demure smile. Instead all I feel is dizzy, like the gravity has failed. I've always known I would be a bride, and sometime around now, in my sixteenth turn. It's the Mercies' will, after all. But I was never one of those girls to play wedding when I was younger, like Nan, or run it over and over in my mind at night while I stared up at the bunk above me. Suddenly Jerej's teasing weighs heavy on me. Has he known all this time?

"Who . . ." My throat sticks. I glance up and see Iri watching me close. "Who will it be?"

Modrie Reller shakes her head. "No knowing. A man from the Æther crewe, most likely. Your father was talking on how it's time to reseal our trade contract with them. But don't think on it. Your father and my Jerej will have it raveled."

The Æther crewe. My heart skips a little faster. My friend Soli, my only friend in the whole Void beyond the *Parastrata*'s hull, and her birthbrother, Luck, both belong to the *Æther*. Soli and I met five turns past, when Æther Fortune brought all his wives and their smallones aboard our ship for trade talks.

The day they came aboard, Modrie Reller dragged me out of the kitchens and made me sit with my handloom in the sticky heat of the women's quarters, where she and my great-grandfather's widows were supposed to entertain the women of the Æther retinue. The whole room sweated in silence, perched on quilted floor pillows, fans flapping to stir the air. The men's rowdy singing bled through the walls.

Modrie Reller pushed me down beside a dark-haired Æther girl with cocked-out ears and the same blue-veined, lucent shimmer to her skin all the spacefaring crewes shared after generations on generations hidden away from the sun—all except me, of course. I peeked over my loom at her as I pushed the thread tight with my shuttle. She was what I might look like if my hair grew out in its true shade, if I were taller and all the color had been bred out of my skin. Her clothes looked machine made, all the stitches tight and even. I watched as she wove a strand of the Æther crewe's trademark red silk thread into her fabric.

She caught me staring and scowled. "What're you looking on?"

I ducked my head and crouched over my own knobby weaving. "Nothing," I said. "That's some pretty, is all."

"Oh," she said, as if that were natural. "Right so."

I swallowed and finished another row. I glanced at her again. "What's your name?"

"Solidarity with the Stars."

I blinked. "Come how?"

"Solidarity with the Stars," she repeated, a bit of miff in her voice.

"Don't you have a luckname?" I asked. On the *Parastrata*, all parents gave their children names that circled, so we could find our way if we were lost, they said.

"My name *is* a luckname," she said.

"Isn't."

"Is," she said, voice rising. "Don't you know the Word? Where it says, *Call to mind always what our ancestors desired; forget it not.* That's where it's from."

"Oh." I picked at a thick snarl of wool. "It's some long, isn't it?"

"No," Solidarity with the Stars said. "Least, not specially. We're all named that way. My brother's called Luck Be with Us on This Journey, only we call him Luck for short."

We fell quiet again. Our shuttles knocked against the sides of our looms.

"You can call me Soli, if you want," Solidarity with the Stars said, breaking the silence. "That's how my brother calls me."

She looked over and smiled, and it made me feel almost the same height. I smiled back.

"So, what's yours?" she asked.

"My what?" I said.

"Your luckname." She tilted her head and bugged out her eyes to show me she thought I was slow.

"Ava," I said.

"Are you on Fixes?" Soli said. "I'm on Fixes."

"No." On the *Parastrata*, women stuck to what we knew: cooking, weaving, dyeing, mending, and growing children. Everything would come unraveled if we started fixing the ship. *It's only a step from fixing to flying,* my father said. *And then where would we be? You can't nurse a baby and run a navigation program at the same time.*

She must be lying, I decided. Trying to puff herself up. I pushed another thread tight.

"What duties are you on, then?" Soli bumped me with her elbow.

"Kitchens," I said, and then wished I'd thought to lie. "Livestock, and sometimes dyeworks." Modrie Reller made me work the vats once a deciturn so I wouldn't forget what real labor was or where I could end up if I didn't work hard at my other duties.

"My brother Luck's on Livestock," Soli said. "He says he likes it." She wrinkled up her face, stuck out her tongue, and made a gagging noise.

I giggled, even though I didn't mind Livestock duty so much myself. Me and Llell would whisper over boys while we collected eggs and mucked the stalls. She had eyes for Jerej, and neither of us understood yet how unlikely a pairing that would be.

Soli's mother flicked her eyes up from her work and looked sharp at us. "*Hssh.*"

Soli and me bit our lips and went back to work. When her mother turned away, we grinned at each other over our frames.

From then to the end of the Æthers' trade visit, we kept tight. Soli tried to talk Modrie Reller into putting her on Fixes while the Æthers were aboard, but my stepmother gave her a sour smile and said she didn't think that could be managed. Soli ended up on Livestock with me and Llell instead.

Which I'm glad of, because if she hadn't, I never would have met Luck.

Soli, Llell, and me were coming around the corner into the livestock bay, milking pails banging against our knees, when I saw him, crouched beside one of our goats.

"Æther Luck, what're you doing here?" Soli barked and tramped toward him. "Don't you mind we switched duties?"

Llell and I exchanged a wide-eyed look—*Did Soli just shout down her brother?*—and hurried in her wake.

Luck shot to his feet. Bristles of hay still clung to the knees of his pants. He rose a half head taller than his sister, but blood flushed his cheeks at her tone. He hung his head so his dark bangs fell over his eyes. A quarter-full pail sat by the goat he'd been milking. My eyes went wide. It was Chinny, our most troublesome, hand-stamping goat. She'd broken one of Llell's fingers once and always found a way to overturn her pail, simply to spite whoever milked her.

Luck looked up and our eyes met. Blue like welding flame ringed his irises, growing darker as it moved in on his pupils, like the patches of deep ocean you see from close orbit. Nothing like the brown or muddy-green color we shared on the *Parastrata*. I knew I wasn't supposed to look on him like that. I never would have looked, except I couldn't help some of Soli's Soliness rubbing off on me.

Chinny chose that exact moment to knock over the pail. Milk gushed around Luck's shoes and swamped the hay.

"Outh!" Luck jumped back. I expected him to jerk Chinny's lead and twist her long, floppy ear, which is what I'd been shown to do when the goats got nasty. Instead, he sighed and rubbed his forehead so his hair stuck up sideways. "You don't have a coaxer, do you?"

I unhinged my gaze from his and looked down into the hay. "Right so," I said. "But it's always broke, and they say the fix isn't in it."

"Soli'll fix it," Luck said. "Won't you, Soli?"

"I'll take a look," Soli agreed.

"But you're . . . ," I started to say.

Luck and Soli's odd looks stopped me. Soli couldn't really do fixes, could she?

My face went hot. "I mean, you're a guest here." I hadn't truly believed Soli about her being on Fixes, but if her brother said so, maybe it was true.

"Plus, you're a girl," Llell butted in. "Girls can't do fixes."

"Can." Soli crossed her arms and turned to me. "Show it to me."

I led them to the back of the pens, clapping my hands to move the goats out of our way. Llell and me tried to keep our distance from Luck, but he walked so close his arm nearly brushed mine. I flipped up the lid of the junk locker, leaned inside, and rattled around until I brought up the coaxer, a foam-lined udder bowl sprouting brittle plastic tubes for milk. I handed it to Luck, and he tossed it to Soli.

"The regulator's all bust." I shot a nervous look at Llell. This was real now. What if someone came in and caught us with Luck, and doing fixes no less? I swallowed and looked back at Soli. "It either drips milk and takes forever, or it pulls too hard and burns out."

"You have my fixers?" Soli asked Luck.

He unsnapped a vinyl pack from his belt and tossed it to her. "I wish you'd keep them. Their head Fix keeps talking on how slow I am."

"It's only till the meet's over. Then you can go back to your precious sheep." Soli popped open the pack and unrolled it across the top of the junk locker. Dozens of shiny silver readers and tools glistened in its pockets. Soli selected one with a power jack and an amp reader and snapped it into the coaxer's line-in.

"This might take a minute, depending what's wrong," she said. She hopped onto the locker beside her tools and looked up at me. "I could show you the fix, if you want."

"No." Llell cut in. She shot a hard look at me and her voice went high. "I don't think we should be here, Ava."

I hesitated. They were all looking at me, Soli and Llell and Luck. The words snarled up in my throat, and all I could come up with was a high-pitched "Umm . . ."

Llell spun on her heel. "Hurry on, Ava. We're leaving."

Soli snorted and rolled her eyes. "What're you afraid of?"

I paused, darting my eyes from my old friend to the new.

Llell turned back. "Ava." It was one sharp word, but it said so much. *Come here*, and *obey*, and *choose*. I wasn't so girl then, not yet, and because of my odd skin, Llell was the one stooping to be my friend.

I shook my head. "I'm staying," I said quietly.

Llell's eyes shot wide. "Come how?"

"I'm staying."

Llell's face crumpled, and then went hard and cold. "Right so." She swept one last look at me and edged out of the bay. I chewed on my lower lip as I watched her go.

"You sure you don't want to learn?" Soli raised an eyebrow at me.

I backed up a step. "No, no."

Soli shrugged and set about prying the casing from the regulator.

"I should clean up Chinny's mess," I said.

"I'll help you," Luck said.

"Mmmn," Soli agreed, already bent over her work.

"No." I accidentally looked at Luck again and pushed my eyes down. This was going too far. "That's not men's work."

A twitch of confusion passed Luck's face. He frowned. "It is on the *Æther*. Besides, it's my fault. I wasn't s'posed to be on this duty firstways."

"Please." My voice rose. "Let me do it."

I grabbed a pitchfork and a mucking brush and pushed

my way through the goats. Chinny stood by herself near the gate, slowly chewing a mouthful of hay.

"Some bad matter, you." I aimed a halfhearted kick at her. "Shoo."

I started pitching the sopping hay into the big, boxy methane digester at the side of the paddock, studiously ignoring Luck. Modrie Reller said the methane digester would churn old hay and whatever else we slopped into it down to a tank in the ship's guts, where it would rot away. Then the methane coming off the rot would turn to fuel for powering lights or raising the pneumatic lift, whatever the ship needed. A footstep scuffed behind me in the hay. I froze.

"Here." Luck eased the brush from under my arm. "At least let me hold that while you're clearing up."

I nodded, face and arms hot, and went back to my work.

"Um . . ." Luck slapped the brush against his leg absentmindedly and looked up at the rafters, where a pair of sparrows nested. "How long's the coaxer been bust, then?"

I hefted another forkful of wet hay into the digester's mouth. "Half a turn." My words came out a grunt.

"And your Fixes don't have it up yet?"

"Nothing wrong with our Fixes." I stopped pitching

hay and glared at him. "It's not Priority, is all."

"I didn't mean it bad." He squatted next to me and pushed the mucking brush across the milk-damp floor. "Soli'll have it up. Don't worry."

"Will you stop cleaning!" My voice came out shrill. I slapped a hand over my mouth.

Luck looked at me as if I'd bitten him.

I dropped my head and my voice. "I'm sorry. I mean, please, so, don't trouble yourself with it."

Luck laughed. "Did you just call me so?"

I nodded and peeked up.

"You're some odd girl," he said. "You're the same age as Soli, right?"

I shrugged and nodded again.

"I'm only two turns older than you, then," he said. "What're you doing calling me so?"

I shook my head and wished a breach would open in the hull below me and suck me out into the Void. "I didn't mean any harm."

Luck started cleaning again. "All your crewe is odd."

I let myself look on him. His bangs swung back and forth over his eyes as he scrubbed the floor. His shoulders tensed and rounded with the motion. A strange, light tickle lifted my stomach, and my ears fizzled, as if I'd come too near the engine's electromagnet.

"Isn't it the same on your ship?" I asked.

Luck snorted. "No." He looked up and saw me watching him. "Well, some. Except we clean our own messes and Soli can be on Fixes."

I sat cross-legged in the hay and straightened my skirt over my knees. I looked over at Soli, sitting on top of the junk locker, eyes narrowed in concentration. "I could never do that."

"You could," Luck said. "You're on Livestock, right so?"

I nodded.

Luck went back to scrubbing. "Fixes is a lot like Livestock, except with less to muck and more figuring. You can do figuring, can't you?"

I could count, sure, and even do some addings and takings away. But Modrie Reller always told me not to be proud and flaunt, especially not in front of men. I started to shake my head but caught Luck's eye again. Something about how he was talking to me, how he was looking at me and not past me, made me want to step full into recklessness. I changed my shake into a slow nod.

Luck nodded with me. "You could do Fixes, then."

"But you have to read, right so?"

Luck frowned. "Can't you read?"

I hesitated. "Course," I lied. It sounded like what he'd want to hear.

Luck smiled. "You'd be good as Soli after a turn or two."

I put my hand on the hay between us and leaned forward, mouth open with the start of a question. Blood surged into Luck's cheeks, brightening them as red as Æther thread. Our eyes met again.

"It's up." Soli called. She wove through the goats, holding the coaxer aloft so its tubes didn't drag the ground. "Who wants to try it?"

Luck and I both stood. He held Chinny still while I strapped the coaxer to her and bunched the tubes into the neck of a jug.

"Try knocking that over," I said to the goat. She glared back at me.

I toggled the controls to green and flipped the regulator switch. The coaxer whirred to life. Chinny bleated unhappily at me, but she didn't cry out in pain or give me the smug look I knew meant the coaxer wasn't doing its job. Milk filled the tubes and trickled into the jar.

I clapped my hands. "It's up!" I grabbed Soli and danced her around. "You did it!"

"Told you she'd have the fix," Luck said, and grinned at his sister. He leaned over and slapped her on the back, the way I'd only ever seen men do with each other. Then he looked at me, and his blush crept back.

They stayed only a few more days while their father finished trade talks with my great-grandfather Harrah and our crewes sealed the agreement with a pair of marriages—two of our girls to two of their men. I let Soli show me a few fixes on the sly, 'specially some to do with the coaxer and the lift to the chicken coops, while Llell kept a cool distance.

I hardly saw Luck, except for across the room at meals, when the women stood waiting against the wall while the men ate. But he looked at me sometimes, twice at the weddings, and smiled at me once when he passed through the livestock bay with his father, on the way to inspect our copper bales. That was when I started daydreaming, in my slow moments waiting for bread to come out of the machine or lifting and agitating lengths of wool in the dye bath, about what it would be like to be Soli's sister, to learn fixes and real figuring, to talk on things with Luck and wear neat-trimmed clothes every day.

The chemical smell of dye cuts the air. Modrie Reller's fingers dig into my scalp. Now Luck will be going on nineteen turns, the right age for taking a firstwife, and me to be married. *To someone in the Æther crewe,* Modrie Reller said. Perhaps to someone in the captain's family, if my father matches our stations in the usual way.

"Will I be a firstwife?" I ask Modrie Reller. My heart beats so hard I can almost taste it. *Let it be Luck. Please let it be Luck.*

"Your father will have it raveled," she repeats. She pushes my head down over the sink again.

The dye burns. I close my eyes tight and grip the sides of the utility sink. To keep the pain at bay, I think on how it will be to be a bride. How the women will wash me with real, cool water, braid skeins of copper into my hair and slip bracelets over my wrists, fasten my birthright pendant around my neck, and solder coins to my bridal headdress. They will bind my hand to my husband's at the wrist, and then . . . my imagination falters. After that, they'll give me over to my husband's crewe, and I'll only ever see my ship and birthcrewe at runend meets. It's too much, like the thought of stepping purposefully from the airlock into the cold nothing of the Void. My half-formed fantasies about Luck and Soli turn to vapor. My legs tremble, half at the thought of leaving my crewe, half from the strain of kneeling over the sink so long.

"There," Modrie Reller says. She drops a cooling cloth over my head and neck. Iri helps me stand and wraps it in a turban. They have me sit and wait while the cloth does its work, taming the harshness of the dye and unbrittling my hair. When it's done, Iri unwraps the turban and my hair falls in rust-red waves to my waist. For a little while, at least, I am still one of my crewe.

# CHAPTER .3

Modrie Reller sends me off to oversee the smallgirls on kitchen duty. The narrow room is a bustle of hot pans and girls edging past one another with bowls of batter for the eggcakes we'll bring to the meet. I divvy up the cakes onto platters as they come out of the ovens. Kitchen duty is my favorite. It takes figuring and counting, which I am best at of all the women, better even than Modrie Reller, though I know enough not to say so.

"Careful," I call to Eme, a child of maybe seven turns, the daughter of my father's fourthwife. She smacks an egg against the side of the bowl, dripping sticky white all over the table and flecking the dough with shell.

"Here." I swallow my annoyance. Seven turns is plenty long to learn how to crack an egg. I take one, rap it sharply against the counter, hold it over the bowl, and use my thumbnail to finish the job. “Right so?”

Eme nods. I watch her take an egg, tap it more gently, and carefully empty its contents into the mixing bowl.

“How many did you put in?” I ask.

“Six, like always,” she says.

“But we’re tripling the recipe,” I say. “So you need . . .”

“Sixteen?” she guesses.

“No,” I say. “Try again.”

She counts silently to herself. “Eighteen?”

“Right so,” I say.

Modrie Reller appears in the doorway. “Ava,” she calls over the banging pans and sizzling oil. She looks sharp at me, and I know she’s seen me showing Eme figuring, which is dangerous close to flaunting. “Where are those cakes?”

“Near done,” I call back. “Ten cooling, two cooking, two to go.”

“Finish up and go clean yourself.” Modrie Reller snaps open her fan and beats the steaming air away from her face. “Your father wants you for the visiting party.”

The pan of eggcakes wobbles in my hands. *Me, on the visiting party?* In our crewe, it’s rare for an unwed girl to set foot outside the ship. I had thought the Æthers—or whoever my father and brother chose, but please let it be the Æthers—would come aboard to claim me when the time came, like they did for those girls at the meet five turns past.

I grip the pan more firmly so the cakes don't slide to the floor. "As you say, Modrie."

Eme and the other smallgirls make wide eyes at me. Modrie Reller turns to go, and I clap my hands at them so they won't spot my nerves. "Enough now. Hurry on."

I'm itchy with sweat and covered in flour by the time we finish the cakes. I gather my oil cask and strigil as I make my way to the women's cleanroom. I am reaching to pull aside the tapestry of Saeleas that covers the door when the shipwide alarm sounds. My heart jolts. I race back into the corridor. A group of men—Fixes—led by my brother Jerej thunders down the hall in the direction of the control room, leaving the few women about wide-eyed and flattened against the walls in their wake.

I pick up my skirts and hurry after Jerej, careful to keep far enough back so they won't spot me. I know I should leave it to them to fix what's gone wrong. I should keep to my own duties and be content to worry quietly with the other women. But I can't help myself. This ship is my home, too, and some small part of me thinks the Fixes might let me help if they were desperate enough. *Oh, Ava,* they would say. *If only we had known what a talent she had for fixes sooner . . .*

The alarm stops as Jerej and the others reach the control room door. I hover outside and listen.

". . . said you had fixed it." The voice of the head Fix, Balab, reaches me first.

"We did fix it," my brother says.

Balab snorts. "Not well enough."

"I told you, we need a new pressure seal on the piston." Frustration creeps into Jerej's voice, making him sound younger than his fifteen years. "I can patch it all you want, but that boom's never going to work proper unless it's got a new seal."

I sigh with relief. It's only the boom again, one of the arms that spreads and retracts our solar sails. The men must have been pulling it in to prepare for docking when it broke.

"You're the heir," Balab says. "You try convincing Cerrec the seal's Priority. See where you get."

"Maybe I will," Jerej snaps back.

"Do," Balab says. "But in the meantime, get down there and patch it up so the whole spar doesn't snap off when we dock. The rest of you, back to your duties."

I scurry away from the door and squeeze into one of the

canary alcoves just in time. Jerej stalks past me.

I slip out after him and shadow him down the hall, into the access stair to the *Parastrata*'s innards. We pass the reactor engines humming behind their lead barriers and cross a gangway suspended over the murky desalination pool. Whenever I'm on kitchen duty, I volunteer to run things down to the Fixes in this part of the ship. I used to hope I'd get to see the reactor, but then I heard some of the men say it can melt your skin if you get too close. Jerej disappears down the last flight of stairs, into the dim sail storage berth. He stops at the bottom and stares at the half-folded boom.

"I know you're there." His voice echoes in the bare room.

I freeze, heart racing.

He looks over his shoulder and frowns up at me, stopped halfway down the steps. "What are you skulking down here for, Ava?"

"I wasn't skulking," I say.

He rolls his eyes. "Sneaking, then. What is it you want?"

"I, um . . ." I fiddle with the fan in my skirt pocket. "I thought I could help."

"Help?" He laughs, and then looks down at the broken

boom and the mess of hydraulic fluid all over the floor. "All right, you can help."

I grin and start down the last flight of stairs, but Jerej stops me at the bottom.

He points to a bucket of rags beneath the steps. "You can sop all this up so I don't slip."

Of course. He would never let me help with the fix itself. Why should he? But I nod anyway and fetch the rags. At least I can watch Jerej at his work, see if I can pick up anything new. And then when I'm with Soli and Luck, the Æthers will see how good I am and let me on Fixes.

I watch Jerej from the corner of my eye as I clean. He pulls out the pins holding the boom's casing in place and lifts it away to show the arm's inner works. It looks some like a skinned goat's leg, only with metal rods and tensile wire where the bones and ligaments would be, and a piston for the knee. I can see how it should work, the hydraulics easing the boom along its path, but with no pressure, the whole operation is jammed.

Jerej removes the piston from its mount. The seal curls up on one end, blown open by the force of the hydraulics.

Jerej grunts in displeasure. "Hand me that adhesive, would you, Ava?"

I glance at the supply shelves behind me. Cans

and tubs of all sizes fill the levels, each with their own indecipherable label across the front. I could no more pick out the one he wants than fly the ship.

Jerej looks up and rolls his eyes. "The red can. Top shelf, on the right."

I fetch it to him and step back to watch.

Jerej coats the seal in sticky spray, fits it back onto the piston, and pulls a device with a wide muzzle from the fixes dangling at his belt. It buzzes softly as he moves it around the edges of the seal.

"What's that?" I say.

Jerej throws me a half-amused look. "A cold fuser. What else?"

"What's it do?" I ask, even though I can guess it's somehow meant to help the seal stick better.

Jerej raises his eyebrows. "It doesn't interrupt me when I'm working."

"Sorry." I drop my sodden rag into the bucket and grab a clean one. Learning fixes is well and good, but Jerej is right. His work is Priority. I shouldn't be pestering him.

Jerej fits the piston back into the arm, refills the hydraulic chamber, and snaps the casing around it once again.

"There. That should last us till we dock, at least." Jerej

wipes his hands on his trousers and buzzes up to the control room with the handheld hanging from his belt. “So Balab, are you there?”

“Right so.” The older man’s voice comes back.

“I’ve got it raveled,” Jerej says. “Start it up.”

An electric hum fills the air. The boom shudders to life and resumes its slide, folding itself gracefully into sections.

Jerej pockets his handheld and grins. “Told that oldboy I’d do it.” He looks at me, and for a moment, I see the smallboy he was when we were younger, the one who played chase with me in the hangar bay before we were old enough for our separate duties.

Behind him, the metal arm jams and a deafening bang rocks the air. The boom jerks and collapses on itself with a shriek I feel in my teeth.

“Outh!” Jerej jumps clear of the spar and holds out a hand to shield me. In the distance, the warning alarm starts up again.

His handheld crackles to life—Balab, cursing him blue and laying out his plans for my brother’s worthless hide.

“I hear you,” Jerej shouts into the handheld. “I’m on it.

The alarm cuts off.

“Outh,” he says again. He runs a hand through his

hair and kicks the boom. "Worthless. How am I supposed to do a proper fix with scrap for a seal?"

I bite my lip. "Maybe . . ."

Jerej frowns at me. "What?"

"What if you made it so it didn't push so hard?"

"You mean decrease the pressure?" Jerej shakes his head. "That seal's so bust, Lifil could break it."

I reach past him and finger the seal's frayed edge. It's not the center that's weak, only the outer rim. It's like trying to keep the top on a jar of preserves without a ring.

"What if you had something . . ." I trail off and hurry to the supply shelves. I rummage through until I find what I need—a round rubber belt with enough give to fit over the mouth of the piston.

Jerej makes a face. "What's that for?"

"To keep it in place," I explain. "You lower the pressure, see? Then you put the seal back on and put this over it, around the sides."

"I don't know." He takes the belt from me. "I guess . . . it might do. The casing wouldn't fit back over it, though."

A moment of doubt creeps up on me. "That won't hurt it, will it?"

Jerej frowns in thought. "Not in the short run. I s'pose no casing's better than no boom at all."

I hover near the stairs as Jerej tries my fix. When it's in place, he calls up to Balab again.

"You'd better have it this time," the head Fix grumbles.

The hum starts back up. Slowly the boom moves back on track, clicking as each section snaps into place. I hold my breath. It's slower this time with the pressure turned low, but the seal holds. The last length of the arm clicks home, and the machinery powers itself down with a sigh.

"It worked!" Jerej grabs my shoulder and lets out a short laugh.

I laugh with him, and for a span of breath, we are those children again, running free across the bay.

Then suspicion chills Jerej's features. He steps away from me and narrows his eyes. "How . . . how did you know what to do?"

"I didn't," I say. My mouth has gone dry. "Just a lucky guess."

We stare at each other in uncomfortable silence. The other Fixes would never let him hear the end of it if they found out a girl had made the fix for him.

"I only wanted to help," I say. "I won't tell anyone."

Jerej's mouth sharpens into a line. "No. You won't."

I catch my breath, stung. Jerej is right. He'd be teased, sure, but we both know I'd have more to lose if it came out I was the one to repair the boom. Even so, it hurts to hear him say it.

"You should go," he says. "You've got your own chores."

"Right so," I agree. And without another look at him, I flee up the stairs.

The girls my age are still off on their duties, so most of the women bathing themselves are wives, some only a few turns older than me, their bellies big with child. They smile on me and whisper to their neighbors as I kneel on the cleanroom tile beside them. The word I'm to be a bride must be making the rounds.

I cover my hands and arms with oil and try to ignore the leaden feeling in my stomach.

*Never let them see you doubt*, I hear Modrie Reller say. *A so girl is a beacon to her people. She is our mother Saeleas reborn in virgin glory.*

I lift my chin and concentrate on wicking away the day's flour and dirt with the dull, curved blade of my strigil. Let them talk. As gossip goes, it isn't the bad kind. Far better than any rumor about my unnatural interest in fixes. Maybe it's better to be remembered this way, the dutiful daughter, not anyone extraordinary. I will be like Saeleas. I will be a story my crewemates tell their smallones of how a woman may be raised high by virtue and obedience.

I find Modrie Reller waiting for me back in the women's quarters, Llell at her side. I stop dead. Llell's arms are full of copper bands and quilted cloth, her eyes fastened to the floor. By all rights, she should be the one being washed and prepared for betrothal, since she's near a full turn older than me, and we both know it. Modrie Reller knows it, too. It's pure cruelty to make her attend me. I flash a look at my stepmother, but her face is serene.

"You're leaving us a bride." Modrie Reller motions Llell forward with a clipped wave. "We have to be sure you arrive looking like one."

Llell and I can barely meet each other's eyes as she helps me into fresh skirts, my good, dark-green ones with tiny mirrors surrounded by pale green starbursts. Why is Modrie Reller doing this? Llell can't have wanted to be my handmaid. She tugs too hard at my skirt ties. The cords dig into my skin, but I bite my lip and keep my tongue still.

Llell finishes with my skirts and laces me into a sleeveless quilted shirt with inlaid copper disks. Afterward, she holds up a mirror while Modrie Reller carefully combs and braids my hair. The dye leaves it shiny, but still some brittle, even after the cooling cloth.

"Hold out your arms," Modrie Reller says when I am brushed and braided.

I do. She has Llell kneel and wind the copper wire around my ankles and forearms. I try to hold still as she wraps me with practiced, pinching efficiency, but I can tell from the flush along her hands and downturned cheeks that shame is burning her up inside. Meanwhile, the copper weighs heavy on me, making my every move graceful but achingly slow.

Llell narrows her eyes to see better as she doubles the last of the wire into a tiny loop and secures it in place.

"Heavens, Llell." Modrie Reller rolls her eyes. "Don't squint. No one wants a squint-eyed wife."

"Modrie," I mumble in protest.

"Modrie nothing." She waves a hand, dismissing me. She flicks out the tip of her fan at Llell. "Now the mirror."

I try to catch Llell's eye, but she lifts the heavy mirror again, hiding her own face behind the reflection of mine. Modrie Reller grips my chin as she paints pale shine onto my cheeks.

"There now," she says when she finishes. "At least you don't look so Earth bred."

I can't see myself, only some other girl. A bride in her thick green skirts and heavy copper wristlets, face shimmer-pale beside her deep red braids. Is that me? I feel as if I'm only a passenger in this body.

"That will do, Llell." My stepmother flaps open her fan and waves it to cool her neck. "Have your mother bring those tapestries to the bay, the ones for the bride gift."

Llell slinks from the room. Maybe I can find her before the visiting party leaves, explain how I didn't ask Modrie Reller to pull her from her duties, didn't want her forced into being my handmaid . . .

But then Modrie Reller takes my face in her hands and presses a rare kiss on my forehead. The shock of it sinks everything else to the back of my mind. The only other time I've ever seen Modrie Reller give a kiss was to my mother's head as the women dressed her body in her old bridal finery for burial.

"Aren't you coming with us on the visiting party?" I ask. It's custom for a girl's mother and modries to prepare her for her husband on her binding day.

Modrie Reller shakes her head. "Not with the smallone coming so soon."

"But I'm coming back before the binding, right so? I'll see you then."

She shakes her head again. "Iri's going in my place." She brushes a stray lock from my forehead and tucks it behind my ear. "She'll finish making you ready."

I duck my head. "Right so."

"One thing more." Modrie Reller pulls a leather cord from her pocket. A pearly white data pendant, thin as paper, large around as the pad of my thumb, dangles from it. Raised circuitry forms a spiral at its center, like the whorl of a fingerprint. I gasp. Every girl receives such a pendant on her binding. It stores a record of her ancestry, back to the time of Candor and Saeleas. She wears it from that day on, even into death.

"Now, when you leave the ship, you'll feel the Earth tugging at you, understand?" The pendant gleams in the low light as Modrie Reller knots it behind my neck. "You'll go heavy, and your breath will come hard, but don't fear. Your father and Jerej and all the men will keep you safe until you reach the other ship. You marking me?"

"Right so." I finger the pendant. It rests cool on my collarbone.

"There now." Modrie Reller smiles tightly. "You're ready."

I step forward to throw my arms around her, but she puts out a hand to stop me. She shakes her head and backs away through the arch to the women's quarters without looking at me again. She has already begun the work of forgetting me.

## CHAPTER • 4

My father, Parastrata Cerrec, captain of the *Parastrata*, walks at the head of our procession. His red hair has thinned and faded yellow-white. A hand-quilted patriarch's stole drapes over his shoulders and beneath it, his green robes hang heavy with embroidery. The stole fans out behind him as he leads us across the wide cargo bay of our ship. Jerej follows him, cradling the wooden letterbox that holds my marriage contract. More men trail them, carting bride gifts—one of our pregnant nanny goats, the weighty bales of copper wire and fiberoptic cable that are our stock-in-trade, and a fighting cockerel. I carry a wide copper platter laden with eggcakes. For the first time in five turns, we have come to Bhutto station for the runend meet, where all the crewe ships join up for trade talks and marriages and treaty drawing.

I stand at the back of our party with the other women, feeling terrified and righteous and brave and pure, all at once. The wives with their armfuls of gifts—green cloth and heavy, coarse-edged paper—surround me. I feel as if I'm walking inside a velvet-lined box, the jewel of our procession. I wish my mother were here, wish she could hold my hand, wish she could see me grown to be a bride.

Once, when I was a smallgirl, our ship hit a solar storm on the way to a runend meet. The men herded all us women and smallones into the baling room, near the heart of the ship, and locked us in tight. But even with all the hulls and floors and doors between us and the Void, the ship bucked and shivered under our feet. My mother was there, sick with the virus that would soon take her. Her face, like mine always some darker than our crewemates', had gone pale and gray, beaded with fever sweat. Modrie Reller wrapped Ma in a coarse homespun blanket. She left me and Jerej to watch over her, while she hurried off to help quiet the squalling infants. I hugged my knees and watched my mother's eyes opening and closing while the ship shuddered all around me.

A bang shook the whole room, and the solar-fed lights sputtered out. Darkness swallowed us. Everyone screamed. My mother grasped my hand.

"Ava." Her voice was raw. "Keep your eyes open."

I blinked in the dark. After a moment, the dim glow of the ship's phosphorous strips bloomed, edging everything in bluish-green. I made out the shadow of my mother. My breath quickened. She looked like a skull in the half light. I groped for Jerej's hand, and he yelped in blind fright when my fingers touched his. I cried out in turn, setting him off again.

"*Hsssh, hsssh.*" My mother squeezed my hand.

The hull shook again. A tooth-aching grind rent the air. Jerej and I grabbed each other, and I tightened my grip on my mother.

"Calm, loves," Ma said. "The Mercies will hold us. It'll be over soon."

Jerej's small, chubby hand sweated in mine. His eyes stared wide and unblinking.

"Do you want a story?" my mother asked.

We both nodded.

"What say Saeleas and the Mercies?" my mother said. "Do you want that one?"

We'd heard it reckoned many times before, spoken soft and secret in the dark of the sleeping quarters by our mothers and modries and other women lulling their smallones to rest. Our father chanted it aloud on the Day of Apogee once each turn. Still, we nodded.

My mother closed her eyes.

*Once, our greatmother Saeleas found herself alone aboard her husband Candor's ship. He had gone groundways to seek water with his men, and while they walked the Earth, a ripping storm struck and breached the hull. Saeleas was pulled out into the Void, where there is naught of air or warmth or light. Long she fell before the Mercies caught her in their hands. Curious, they carried her through the veils of nebulae and seated her on their footstool, a star-seeded lily, all aglow with the warmth of the softest sun, and breathing out its own air to sustain her.*

Please, *she begged.* Let me return to my husband's side. I am sore needed there.

*But the Mercies said,* Nay, you shall be our pet, pretty one, and give more use through joy than ever you could at your husband's beck.

Not so, *said Saeleas.* For who shall weave if I am gone?

Men may weave without you, *said the Mercies.*

But who shall feed the men and babes if I am gone? *said Saeleas.*

Men may feed themselves and babes without you, *said the Mercies.*

And who, *said Saeleas*, shall bear forth children if I am gone?

*At this the Mercies fell silent, for here was a thing no man could do. And they saw Saeleas carried in her womb the great Neren, father of our race. They took pity and breathed their own life into her lungs, and carried her from their starry thrones home to the arms of her husband. Thus our race was saved by the grace of the Mercies. So do we honor them, for our life is ever in their hands.*

"So you see," my mother said, her voice a whisper. "You see the worth of a woman, Ava." Her eyes rolled back and she let free a cant from our holy song, the Word of the Sky, up into the dark.

". . . like copper sails to trap the sun's heat.
Cover us all, she does . . ."

"Ma, please . . ."

". . . tame the stars' fury and channel life."

"*Hsssh*, Ma. Everyone will hear." I swung my head to make sure none of the other wives had heard her singing.

But no. They were too terrored by the storm to notice.

I pinned Jerej with a look. "You won't tell, will you?" I whispered. "You won't tell she sang?"

Jerej shook his head.

"Swear it?"

Jerej's pale cheeks flushed. He nodded.

I breathed out. Even small as I was, I knew my ma shouldn't be singing the Word out loud. She might call down ship strippers or some other bad matter on us, like Mikim the Wayward from our tales. Or worse, the Mercies might choose not to bring us through the storm after all.

My mother mumbled on, quieter, picking up the song further down the line. "Women of the air, stay aloft . . ."

I leaned close to my mother's ear. Fever heat moved off her skin in waves. "Please, Ma," I whispered. "You got to stop singing now, right so?"

Her eyes opened to glints deep in the shadow of her face. "Ava." She touched my cheek. I smelled the fever on her breath. "You are the sails, Ava. My girl. You are the sails."

And I could see. Even with the fever touching her mind, turning her words to a torrent, I could see what she meant. I felt the seed of it in me. That I could give life and comfort and peace, even in the harshest reaches of the Void. And in that moment, the lights whined to life. I squinted up into their glare, and when I looked back, my mother's eyes had closed again in sleep. Resolve filled me, small as I was, and I knew I would bend with the will of the Mercies to bear life into our crewe someday.

Now as I stand at the back of the procession, I run my mother's cant through my mind like piece of silk ribbon, *like copper sails to trap the sun's heat. . . .*

Ahead, I spot Iri. She glances back over her shoulder and gives me a tight smile. A rumbling *clack-clack-clack* fills the room as my father orders the big bay doors open, and a sweep of cold air rushes into our ship.

Our procession shuffles forward until we reach the lip of the ship's outer bay. Before I have time to think, I have put my foot over the threshold and onto the loading ramp, and like that, I am farther from my home than I have ever been in my life. As we step away from the *Parastrata*, our ship's gravity gives way, and suddenly everything—the eggcakes, the copper bands, my very legs—weighs heavier on me. I stagger but right myself. The other women slow along with me, but the men don't so much as flinch. How glad I am to have them circled round us, guarding us from the Earth's sway. Modrie Reller was right. Its pull is stronger here, outside the pure world of our ship.

The dock is empty, except for two silent vessels resting alongside ours. A bulkhead door separates us from the station proper. My father taps a code into the keypad wired to the door, and it slowly rolls open along the runners in the floor, revealing a long hallway. We push forward in step. A steady roar builds and builds as we near the far end, and then overtakes us when we break out onto the station's concourse.

People and animals and vendor carts cram the floor. Lights stream and flash in all colors. Men and women shout over one another. Handhelds blip at their owners, heartbeat-quick music shudders, and signs shimmer with fast-moving pictures—a school of fish, a man running, a woman with kohl around her eyes. Somewhere, a lamb's bleat surfaces above the din. My head goes numb.

The wall of wives presses in against me as we jostle through the packed concourse. Between their shoulders, I catch sight of a man with bread-crust brown skin tinkering on a handheld. Another, with darker skin and blue clothes that ripple and shine like oil, changes the symbols on the sign above the awning of a shop. And another, with pink-blushed pale skin and metal gauges embedded in the soft flesh of his ear, hands out little scraps of paper covered in print. There are women, too, near none of them wearing skirts long enough to cover their boots, and some in men's trousers. They lord over shops selling handhelds and painted birds and fish as big as my forearm. They shout and boss as loud as men, and smile with all their teeth.

It's too much. All I can do is hold the platter level, try to keep my feet, and concentrate on the long trail of hair hanging down Lannal's back in front of me. I pray for it to be over, for us to reach the safety of another crewe's ship and leave this pressing crowd behind.

*And in the heavens, we will make the world anew*, I repeat to myself. *We will make the world anew.*

The roar of voices dulls as we leave the main concourse. We file through a dim, narrow hall, and stop suddenly.

"Are we there?" I whisper to Lannal. "Is it the *Æther*?"

She gives me a tight-lipped look that means I should know better than to speak.

Ahead, the rumble of a bulkhead door breaks the silence. Our little parade starts forward and stops again almost immediately.

My father's greeting carries up the corridor. "So Brother Fortune."

"So Brother Cerrec."

Their voices drop so we can no longer hear. I shift from one foot to the other and wish I could lay down the tray of eggcakes. Sweat slicks my palms. The electric light grid above me snaps and clicks.

And then they are calling for me.

"Ava." My great-grandmother Hannah snaps her fingers. "Come." Her milky blue eyes magnify in the brittle pair of glasses she's had to herself since my great-grandmother Laral died.

The women guide me forward. Somehow I manage not to drop the tray, although I'm sure my eyes are wide and rolling like a frightened goat's. The men at the head of the procession part to let us through, and suddenly I am standing beside my father and Jerej, facing a man with black, laceless boots and a patriarch's stole. In the split second before I remember to look away, not to look on his face, I see he is sharp jawed and handsome for a silver-haired man, despite a pocked field of radiation burns across one cheek. But his mouth is hard. Behind him, I catch a glimpse of a ship docked, its cargo bay open and filled with members of a dark-haired crewe. The *Æther*. My heart lifts.

"My daughter, Parastrata Ava," my father says.

I dip my head and curtsy, holding out the platter in front of me as an offering. "Honored to come to your home, Æther Fortune."

I feel his hand beneath my chin and the cool metal of his many rings. "Let me look on the bride." He tilts my face up to his. I hold still as a stunned bird under his hand and cast my eyes to the side as he studies me.

A young man stands behind Æther Fortune. He is a head taller than me, with thick black hair cut close to his head and irises the blue of ozone burn. He keeps his hands clasped behind him. Like a magnet finding its match, his eyes lock on mine.

*Luck*. My heart skitters. Luck, grown, as I am. I would drop my gaze if I could. No proper so girl should stare at a man like this. But his look holds me as steadily as the hand beneath my chin.

Æther Fortune releases his grip. I fade gratefully down into a curtsy, the platter of eggcakes still held out in front of me. My fingers tremble.

"This is my eldest son, Æther Luck, heir to the captaincy," Fortune says to my father and brother.

I inch my eyes up above the stack of cakes. Luck executes a small bow. He flicks a brief smile at me, and I duck back behind the platter. My heart pumps heat into every corner of my body. It is in my breasts and my toes, and suddenly I am aware of hidden corners of myself I never knew existed. Luck, heir to the captaincy. And me, a bride.

# CHAPTER . 5

The *Æther* is vast compared to the *Parastrata*. Its ceilings rise a good meter above our heads and the rooms circle off one another in a labyrinth. But at least the gravity is back to bearable. The Æther crewe eats with men and women separate, like we do, but their galley is so large they don't need to eat in shifts, men and boys, then women and girls. Little bowls of real salt and oil rest in the center of the galley tables, and the Æthers make free with them.

"Luxury," Hannah sniffs, but I see her sprinkle a heaping pinch of salt over the sticky pearl rice the Æther crewe favors.

I look across the crowded galley and spot Luck at a table with a group of other young men. His friends are laughing over some joke, but he's staring straight at me, a small, warm smile playing at the corners of his mouth. A welcome fire runs through me. I duck my head, but the feel of his eyes on me is irresistible. I have to look again.

That smile of his tugs at my own lips and fills me with a glow. I imagine the smooth skin of his inner wrist flush with mine, the binding ribbon winding around and around, trapping and sanctifying the heat between us. After the rite, we'll be alone in the marriage chamber, and he'll comb my bride's braids loose with his fingers. His hand will travel from my neck to my shoulder, and then unsnap the clasps of my shift. . . .

A sharp rap from Hannah's fan lands on my knuckles. She doesn't have to say a word. I'm being undignified, smiling like an idiot for the whole galley to see. I rub my hand and wrestle my face back under control. But even the threat of my great-grandmother's fan doesn't keep me from stealing glances at Luck until it's time to clear the table.

I don't see Soli until after dinner, when the Æther women usher us into a visiting room piled thick with woven rugs. I kneel alongside them. Soli sits on the other side of the circle, but I only recognize her by the way her face lights up when she catches sight of me. She's near tall as her brother, but she's hidden her ears behind her long hair, done up in marriage braids. Her own pendant hangs around her neck—black, but with a shifting sheen that changes colors, like a drop of oil. She grins and mouths something. *We need to talk.*

Hannah and Iri and the Æther women produce collapsible looms from their inner pockets and begin setting up their weaving. A bubble of panic rises in my chest. Modrie Reller said nothing on bringing a loom, but of course now it seems clear she shouldn't have to say something so simple to me. I feel in my pockets, as if by some miracle one might appear. Nothing.

"Ava," Iri says lowly. She has been sitting beside me all this time, slowly unwinding a skein of algae-green wool.

I look up. Iri silently holds out the pieces of an extra loom for me. The tight feeling in my chest eases. I don't know why Iri looks out for me, except she never did have smallones of her own before my great-grandfather died, and none of the men aboard the *Parastrata* have tried to take her as a wife, maybe out of respect for my great-grandfather. I nod my thanks, quickly snap the frame together, and reach into the common thread basket for a skein of my own.

"Our colors please your eye, then, Parastrata Ava," Soli's mother says without looking up from her own weaving.

I glance down at the yarn in my hand. The thread is the

Æthers' smooth red silk. It shows bright against my dark green skirts. "Yes," I say. "It's . . . it's some beautiful."

"Beautiful, she says." Soli's mother smiles to the women beside her, then turns back to me, her face suddenly solemn. "But if you use it long enough, you might start to think it dull."

I recognize some kind of test in that, even if I don't know what it is exactly.

"Never." I lock my spine straight and look at her evenly, drawing on my imitation of Modrie Reller. "Firstwife Æther, I'm not some changing girl. I won't go shifting on you and yours."

She watches me with eyes half lidded. All around us the looms clack softly, and the other women peer sideways at us over their handwork.

Finally Soli's mother nods. "Right so, then."

I let the air out of my lungs. I've passed. The other women return their attention to their weaving and murmured conversations. Soli rises and picks her way to me. My jaw drops. Soli's long red skirt swells over a soft, rounded lump at her waist. She's gotten herself pregnant.

"Soli, when? Who?" I grab her hand as she eases down beside me. I want to throw my arms around her,

I've missed her so, but the older women wouldn't stand for such a display. I settle for squeezing her hand tighter. "Tell me everything."

"Let me hold your thread for you, sister," Soli says aloud, but her face is bright to bursting with news, her cheeks flush. She leans close as she unwinds the skein. "His name's Ready, the requisitions officer. We had our binding close on half a turn past."

I glance down. I've seen lots of women pregnant on the *Parastrata*, and even some births. Soli looks too far gone for half a turn. "That's some fast."

Soli giggles, sounding a moment like the smallgirl I remember. "But I got my pick, didn't I? *That* we have to talk on later, without all these stuffed-up oldgirls hanging round."

"He's nice?" I ask. I stop my weaving and look up. "He's not old, is he?"

"Nah." Soli shakes her head. "Only five turns older. Perfect."

"Oh." I look down.

Soli nudges me. "Don't chew on it. Talk I hear says you're getting an even younger one." Soli's eyes shine so I almost think they're wet.

"How'd you . . . ," I start to ask.

"Come, Ava, it's clear as empty you're still sweet on Luck," Soli says. "And he's sweet on you, too. Couldn't stop staring at you on the dock today."

That rush of heat sweeps through me again, and I fumble with my thread. If only my bridal bands weren't making me so slow and clumsy.

"Think, you'll be my sister and our babies can play together."

The warmth changes to pure fire in my cheeks. They say a baby makes a new, small world all your own, and then the Earth will stop calling to you. That's what I want, but . . . but I've only begun fixing the idea of being a wife in my head, trying on Luck's face as the man snapping the coins from my bridal veil, the inside of Luck's wrist bound to mine. And now babies. Of course I knew that would come. It's what my body is made for, but . . . Soli's belly stares at me. It's one more piece too real. And it makes me some uneasy the way things are raveling up exactly how I dreamed, and so fast. It makes me worry I've left something out.

Soli and me lie face-to-face on her bunk in the women's quarters. It's not something married girls usually do, but all the Æther women know we were friends as smallgirls, and what with me about to be married, they're willing to let us pretend we're children a few nights longer. The air blows cool and fresh through the vents, and the dimmers carry us gently into ship's night.

"Ready's some strong," Soli whispers under the blankets. She lies on her back with her head turned to me. "He can pick me up, even with the baby, and he's always slipping me nice things from requisitions. Like the other day, he gave Hydroponics some extra grams of nutrient soak, and they held back an orange for him, so he gave it to me."

I suck my bottom lip. My father gave me a slice of orange once when I was a smallgirl, and even now I can taste the sweet bite under my tongue. "Did your father pick him for you?" I ask.

Soli shakes her head and grins. "Ready and I picked each other."

I raise my eyebrows and open my eyes wide, trying to make out her face in the near dark. Crewes hardly ever let a love match through, especially when it's the captain's daughter up for marriage and her husband might end up heir to the captaincy.

"How'd you fix it?" I ask.

Soli runs a hand over her belly. "I let them catch me."

"What?" My voice rings out.

"*Hsshh.*" One of the older women shushes from the bunk below us.

Soli drops her voice even lower. "I've seen girls do it before. I had already got the baby, and I knew some sure my father wouldn't drop me on a port somewhere or let me go around the ship unmarried. So the next time I was in the cleanroom, I let my mother catch sight of me and of course she went and told my father. He called us into the meet room. Then Ready, he confessed it in front of everyone, and they had us bound the next day."

"Wasn't your father angry?" I ask.

"Some sure." Soli picks at the inside of the blanket. "He wanted to push Ready out the airlock at first, but then he decided he'd rather not have a misborn grandchild, so he only had him flogged after the binding instead."

"Soli," I whisper, not sure what else to say.

"I got my way, didn't I?" She turns her head to me.

I nod. Soli strokes her belly absentmindedly.

"What about Ready?" I ask. "What if he comes calling for you tonight?"

"He won't," Soli says, eyes still closed. "Not till after the baby's born and I'm healed up."

"Does it hurt?" I ask.

"What, having a baby? I'm guessing so from all the screaming the other girls do."

"No," I say. "The other thing."

"Oh." Soli rolls heavily on her side to face me. "At first, but not so bad if he's careful. And it's much better after that. Are you worried?"

I tuck my chin into my chest and hug my arms. I nod.

"Don't." She rubs my arm. "When we heard you were coming as a bride, I figured you might be for Luck, so I told him how he'd better not hurt you or I'd break all his toes. He'll be careful. You'll see."

I smile at her, even though we can barely make out the whites of each other's teeth in the close dark. Soli rolls on her back again, and I turn to the wall. She's asleep in a few slips, her breath falling slow and regular. I lie awake, rubbing the smooth surface of my data pendant. Iri and Hannah snore lightly in the bunk below us. Some of the smallgirls whisper and break out in patters of giggles, but those peter out too, leaving only breath and the lulling hum of the air scrubbers.

I sit up. The heat coming off Soli is too much, even with cool air wafting in on us through the ventilation slits. I slide to the bottom of the bunk and sit there, my legs dangling with the extra weight of my bands. The air is wonderful fresh. It brings me awake, makes me almost giddy. I glance around at the other women in their bunks. How can anyone sleep with the air so pure? How can they expect me to sleep? My new home is beckoning me. There are rooms to explore, corridors and serviceways to memorize. And as much as it shames me to say it, I want to put some distance between myself and Soli's belly.

I drop lightly to the floor. I leave my outermost skirt, with its clacking, flashing mirrors, but tie on my plainer inner skirts and move quietly to the door. Like all the doors I've seen aboard the *Æther*, this one shows a shaded view of its other side—an empty hallway. The door doesn't have a pattern lock, but it doesn't have a manual handhold for pulling, either. I feel along its edges and on the wall where a control panel should be. Nothing. I kneel. A thin, red-lined square glows where the handhold might be. I press my palm to it experimentally. The door slides up with a silent swish of air, and I jump back, stifling a cry. The Æther crewe doesn't even lock its women in at night. Strange.

I step into the hall and touch a matching square on the other side, sending the door hushing down behind me. An empty silence cottons the corridor, and deep in my veins I feel the familiar thrill of being the only one awake. I go left, away from the ship's galley and entryway, into a section of the ship I haven't seen yet. My feet *pat-pat* along the cool floor.

I pass a run of rooms lined with tall, thin tanks for trapping gas and tabletop centrifuges, miniatures of the one I've seen from afar in our engine room. I stand with my hand pressed to the waist-high glass, taking in the sterile order of the rooms. Diagrams crammed with mysterious writing paper the walls. I tiptoe on, past more workrooms. Then comes the men's training room, with all the weight equipment sleek and new, not rust-speckled and wrapped in brittle sealing tape like aboard the *Parastrata*. I smile. Won't Soli's mother be shocked when she sends me off on some errand and I already know my way?

Beyond the training room, the floor slopes up gently. The air thickens with humidity and the smell of earth. Hydroponics. But when I reach the darkened room at the end of the corridor, I hesitate. This is nothing like Hydroponics on our ship, squeezing as much produce from as little nutrients and water as possible. I peer through the clear insulating curtain stretched across the door. Fog lies over a carpet of tender grass stretching all the way to the back of a room near large as the *Parastrata*'s outer bay. Dense shadows gather beneath the lemon trees staggered along the green. The far wall is one long window, looking out on the stars.

I kneel and lift the edge of the curtain so I can run my fingers over the grass. It tickles, but soft, the way a cat's whiskers do. The men say down groundways people grow it simply to walk on, like a living rug, but that seems almost a sacrilege. I lean close and smell. Worms and crickets, like the ones in our compost bale. The soft, rich scent of rot.

I stand and pull the curtain aside. The grass is wet, and I can't explain it, but I smell water in the air. Not the dead, boiled kind I'm used to, either, but something fresh, near live, steeped in gently pulped leaves and loam. I look up. Misters hang from a frame of girders above, alternating with darkened sun-glow lamps. I hesitate. Do the Æthers truly walk on something living? But they must, or else how could they reach those lemons? And if they don't harvest the lemons, what's the point of this room?

I put one foot over the threshold. The grass is soft, like a baby's hair. I recoil, thinking maybe it's as delicate too, maybe I've crushed it with my weight. But the shoots spring back the moment I pull my foot away. I take a hesitant step, and then another, letting the curtain fall closed behind me. I've always wondered what it would be like to walk on the old silk tapestries hanging in the *Parastrata*'s meet rooms, and now I think I know. This is luxury. This is Earth. I think I see a tiny piece of why Saeleas wept to leave it behind.

A curious tang from the lemons sweetens the air. I've heard the oldgirls say lemons are sour and only good for medicines, but my mouth waters all the same. I stop beneath a tree and lift one of the small, bright fruits. It fits perfectly in my palm. For a moment I picture myself snapping the lemon from its branch, sinking my teeth past its waxy skin, drinking the juice inside. But no. These aren't my lemons, not yet. And even if they were, it would be none proper to take a whole one for myself.

When I reach the window, I press my palms against its cool layered glass and look out on the vast spill of stars. The skyport stretches beneath me, seeming to angle down from where I stand, even though I know up and down are only tricks of the ship's gravity field. Bright repair patches stand out on the station's skin, ships cleave to its sides like sucker fish, and clusters of antennae jut from each docking station, all of it bathed in the blue-white glow of the nearby moon.

"Parastrata Ava?"

I whip around. A man sits beneath the low-hanging boughs of the lemon tree behind me. My breath stops. His hands reflect the milky light of the moon, but the rest of him is too far in shadow to see. My heart shudders. This is it, the kind of mistake Llell warned me against. But I didn't listen, and now here I am, caught and vulnerable, at the whim of a stranger who can overmatch both my strength and my word.

I dart from the window. I try to dodge past the tree, but my bridal bands drag down my steps. The man ducks out from beneath the boughs. I hobble left, but he catches me around the waist. I cry out. He claps a hand over my mouth.

"Ava, don't fight."

I struggle in his grip, try to pitch myself forward onto the ground.

"Ava. It's me, Ava."

He lets go, and I sprawl on the grass. I roll over, ready to kick him away, and finally get a good look at him. *Luck.* My head feels heavy and light all at once. Oxygen drunk. I drop back against the soft grass and laugh. It's only Luck.

He reaches down to me. "You're going to get us caught."

"Sorry." I take his hand and pull myself to my feet. "I didn't know you were you."

"What are you doing here?"

"I couldn't sleep." I look down at my naked feet and try to brush away the clips of wet grass stuck to my skirt. What was I thinking, walking out alone in a strange ship?

What if it hadn't been Luck underneath that tree? And what must this boy . . . this man, who's supposed to become my husband, think of me, walking his ship half dressed at night? Did he see me thinking on stealing his crewe's lemons?

"I'm sorry. I'll go." I try to step around him.

"Wait." Luck catches me by the arm. The warm grip of his fingers on my skin turns my whole body live, magnetized. I gasp. I stop. For the first time, I notice his feet are bare, too, and his hair rumpled.

"I couldn't sleep either," Luck says. "I go out walking sometimes when I get that way. Or swimming."

We stare at each other, linked up skin to skin.

"My father asked me to come with him to the meet room tomorrow," Luck says. "I figure you don't have to guess much to know what that's about."

"With me here as a bride, you mean." I keep my head down and finger the copper bands on my wrist, already greening my skin beneath their wires.

"Right so." He loosens his grip on my arm and stands up formal and straight. "I'm sorry for touching you before we're bound, Parastrata Ava. You were always some proper and . . ."

"I'm not." My eyes flash up to meet his and—there—

they find a place to rest safe again. It's exhilarating, this feeling of doing something dangerous and right, all wrapped up together in my chest. I step closer. "I'm not only some proper. Not always."

Luck looks down at me. He blinks into my face, as if he's trying to figure out how to mesh me with the smallgirl he knew five turns past.

I fumble for his hand and fold my fingers around his, trying to press what I feel in through his skin. "I've been practicing those fixes Soli taught me. The ones you said I could learn. You remember?"

He laughs. "What, still? After all these turns?"

I drop his hand, hurt. "I taught myself others."

"No, I mean . . . I'm only surprised, is all. That's none proper for a so girl, from what I saw on your *Parastrata*. I thought you'd be too busy with Priority. But I'm happy. I'm glad." He reaches out and squeezes my fingers lightly.

"Me too."

"Do you think . . ." He stops and glances at the entrance to the garden room. "Have you ever been swimming?"

"Swimming?" The word curls strange around my tongue. When we were smallgirls, Llell dared me to go floating in the water converter's desalination pool. We'd heard about some of the older boys sneaking down there, how the water was supposed to float you some like the Void would, but some not. *More like a giant hand holding you up*, one of them had said. But Modrie Reller caught us ankle deep in the filter reeds and made us drink from the salt pool until we vomited brine. Llell and I never went back.

I shake my head.

"Come on." Luck tugs my hand. "I'll show you."

"I don't know. . . ."

"You'll be all right," Luck says. "I swear. I know this ship backward. I know when the night Fixes come and go."

I hesitate.

"You trust me," Luck says. "Right so?"

I frown. "You swear it?"

"I swear it." Luck smiles. "Don't you want to live some before we're bound?"

I think on it. In another few months I might be weighted down with a baby like Soli and busy learning to manage the women at Luck's mother's side. But tonight, no one is looking for me. No one will notice I'm gone from my bed. It is the last night before I am fully a woman.

And so I let him lead me from the garden.

# CHAPTER .6

I follow Luck through a corridor that forks near the workrooms, and then down a laddered hatch into the hanging serviceways in the bowels of the ship. Heat rises on the wet air, reminding me of the dyerooms on the *Parastrata*. We walk single file above the humming tops of the generators, bathed in smudgy orange light.

A man's voice rings out in the echoes ahead. ". . . go and double back to get it."

Luck freezes in the middle of the gangway.

"Night Fixes?" I whisper.

Luck nods.

"I thought you said—"

"*Hsssh.*" He pulls me after him, back the way we came. We round a corner, and Luck points soundlessly to a double-doored service locker built into the wall. I nod. He pulls both doors open with a faint squeak. Heart knocking, I step over a scatter of loose fixers and dead wires and wedge myself behind a crisscross of rebar, deep in the shadow of the locker. Luck jumps in after me and pulls the door closed. We crush together against the back wall.

"Stay still," he whispers.

His shoulder presses into my nose. He smells of pulped grass and faint sweat masked by soap, some kind of indefinable Luck smell that lights me up to my heels. I let my hand rest where it's fallen on his chest and breathe slowly, trying to muffle the sound against him so the night Fixes won't hear us.

". . . point in him taking another wife, you know?" The voices grow louder.

"Talk on," a second man answers the first. "I've got some trouble what with only two."

Their steps ring close. Luck presses me against the wall. We both try to breathe shallow and slow, try not to shift our feet into the metal balanced precariously against the wall. Luck lowers his nose so it rests on top of my head. His breath is warm in my hair. I can make out every thread in his shirt, every lock of dark hair touching his neck, every pulse of blood working the veins under his skin. I should be worried about the Fixes, but all I can think on is the gentle bob of Luck's Adam's apple and the way his chest grazes mine.

"You see the bride they brought?"

"Yeh."

"She's got something odd to her, but I can't figure it."

"Dunno. To me, they're all some odd with that hair and the way . . ." The voices fade below the generators' hum.

Luck and I stand fused in the back of the service locker. This is the last place I should feel safe, but I don't want to leave.

Luck steps back slowly, carefully. "I'm sorry," he says, though I'm not sure if he means for touching me again or for what his crewemates said about me. He smiles nervously and pushes the doors open, holds out a hand to help me from the locker. "There's only the one team of night Fixes. We shouldn't see anyone else."

My heart is still skipping. I laugh, half from relief, half from giddiness. The sound fits strange in my throat, like it's coming from some other girl. Maybe the girl I could be if I was Luck's wife, without doors to lock me in at night. I grab his hand, and he pulls me into an almost-run. I feel as if the gravity's low, as if my feet are barely touching the floor as we fly around corners and down a spiraling ramp.

Luck skids us to a stop in front of a heavy, wheel-locked

door. He sets his shoulder against the wheel and pushes until it gives with a brief shriek of metal.

"Where are we?" I whisper.

He points to a lettered sign bolted to the door and grins.

I look up at the sign. I know the letters for my own name, *A-V-A*, but beyond spotting two *A*s in the loops and lines on the door sign, I can't figure it. I bite my lip and look at Luck. I shake my head.

His smile dies.

"I'm sorry." My voice wavers. "I lied."

"Don't worry on it now." He smiles at me again, gently, and tucks a loose strand of hair behind my ear. My skin tingles at his touch. "We're going swimming."

He leans against the door. It swings open on a dim, sloping room filled wall to wall with water. Light from bioluminescent fish and phosphorous deposits crusting the depths lend the water and air an uncanny glow. My mouth falls open. I know it's only the *Æther*'s desalination pool, but I feel as if I've stepped out of time, as if I've stumbled into the Mercies' private realm.

"It's beautiful," I say.

When crewes like ours come across a water-bearing planet, we mostly find salt oceans or ice. On the *Parastrata*, we leach most of our salt out in tanks, but before the water can go through the finer filters and come out potable, it rests awhile in a pond lined with scrubber fish and plants designed to nip out the extra sodium. The *Æther*'s desalination pool dwarfs ours. It looks deep as two men and far enough across to swallow up the galley. Water weeds sway in the shallows.

Luck strides down the gentle slope to the water's edge and pulls his shirt up over his head. The lines of his shoulder blades cut sharp bows in his pale back. He turns and looks up at me, something a little wicked in his eye. "Coming in?"

I shift my feet. Suddenly it comes to me how he'll see the dull foreignness of me once I shed my shirt and skirts. He'll see all of me.

"You'll like it, I promise," Luck says. "The salt'll keep you from sinking."

"I . . . I don't want you to watch me," I say.

"What if I look away till you're in?"

I rub one foot against an ankle beneath my skirts. It's some hot here below the *Æther*'s cool, civilized berth, and my skin itches with sweat. Half of me wishes Luck was only Llell or Soli so it would be easier to splash into the pool, but the part of me making my heart skip and my skin flush is glad it's Luck.

"All right," I say. My voice sounds dangerous, older.

Luck kicks off his trousers and wades into the pool. I try not to look until he's well beneath the surface, but that small seed of recklessness makes me glance up in time to see the full length of his back diving into the water.

I tug the ties of my skirts loose and try to breathe steady. "Don't look," I yell.

"I'm not," he calls back. He dives and disappears in a flash of feet.

I take a deep breath. He's going to be my husband. We'll be bound in a day or two anyway, so I might as well get over my shyness now. In one quick breath, I shed my skirts, strip off my shirt, wrap my arms across my chest, and rush into the pool, naked except for my data pendant and the copper bands. The water hits me with a warm slap, the tickle of sea plants slippery on the soles of my feet. I duck down to wet my hair and wade deeper. The water salts my lips and buoys me with each step, even under the added weight of the copper. My pendant floats, petal light, before me.

Luck surfaces. The phosphorous and fish light him from below in shifting patterns, making him look like a creature out of the tales the wives told us as smallgirls while we helped them spin wool. I glance down at his body and then my own, distorted beneath the surface of the pool. Our skin looks near the same in the half light, near enough maybe it won't make him stare.

"Your hair looks darker when it's wet," Luck says. He kicks closer to me. His eyes drift down to my nakedness, but he drags them up again. He blushes. "Sorry."

"Yours always looks dark," I say.

He lets his feet bob up to the surface in front of him. "You've really never done this before?"

I think of Llell and me coughing up unfiltered seawater by the side of the tanks. "No." I let my feet float up, too, so my toes peek out. I smile and wiggle them. "It's not something you do when you're so girl."

"Does that mean you've left off being so girl, then?" Luck teases. He gulps up a mouthful of water and spits it out again.

"Right so." I lift my smile from my toes to him. "You can't be so girl and a wife."

He smiles back. "I guess not." He drops his head back.

I do the same, letting my whole body drift to the surface now he's not watching. The boys were right. It's like a warm hand lifting you. I let myself drift on the pool's surface, like a leaf in a bowl of water.

"Ava." The water muffles Luck's voice.

I lift my head and right myself so I'm treading beside him again. "Hmm?"

"Do you want to be married to me?" Luck asks. "I mean, I know we don't have much of a say, but do you want it?"

I look at him, hair wet and eyes serious.

"You hardly know me," he says.

*But I do,* I want to say. *Or I want to.*

I swim closer. His eyes follow me, darkening as I approach.

"You know I used to daydream about being Soli's sister." I swish my hands across the surface of the water between us, making tiny waves that lap against his chest. "I used to imagine you and me and her would spend all morning talking while we milked the goats and learned fixes."

"Truly?"

I nod. I take a deep breath. "Can I tell you something?"

Luck nods in return.

"My hair really is darker," I say. "Some like yours. My modries dye it red so I'll mix better with my crewe."

"Right so?" Luck frowns and reaches out to finger a strand of my hair. "You'd never know."

"Do you think it's a sign from the Mercies?" My body

floats closer to him and my knee accidentally brushes his. "Maybe I'm meant for your crewe from the beginning. Maybe I'm meant for you."

The side of Luck's mouth lifts. "Maybe you are."

My limbs throb in time with my heart. "I don't think I mind," I say, and close the distance between us.

Blood beats loud in my ears. Luck leans in and touches his lips to mine. They're warm and laced with salt, and my own lips press back before I know what they're going to do. *I've been kissed. I'm kissing Luck.* His hand travels around my side, to the small of my back, and pulls my body flush with his. My blood becomes warm oil. We both forget to tread to keep ourselves afloat for a moment, and slide under. Luck pulls away, and we kick ourselves back to the surface. We break the water half laughing, half coughing and sputtering.

"Sorry." Luck shakes his head, spattering water everywhere, and laughs. "Maybe we should go where it's less deep?"

I push the hair out of my eyes. "Right so."

I splash after him to shallower water, where my toes just brush the bottom of the pool.

"Put your arms around me," he murmurs.

I oblige, looping my arms around his shoulders. He

brings his lips to mine, and this time, we don't nearly drown. He is salt and warmth and sweat, and I don't ever want this kiss to end. His fingers sink into my hair and fumble to unbind it. My braids fall. He sweeps them aside to kiss my neck and I shiver. Just like I imagined.

"I'm going to take care of you," he says, his lips soft on my skin, my ear. "I'll be a good husband. I'll make you happy. I swear it."

"I . . . ," I start. But then his hand brushes my breast and all my thoughts fly away, as if swept off by a solar wind, invisible and unknowable.

"I want you, Ava." Luck pulls back to look in my eyes. He swallows. "Do you . . ."

I teeter in his arms, caught between the swell of heat and an awful nagging at the back of my mind. But Luck's shoulders and arms are so strong, holding me up, and he'll care for me. He'll make me happy. He swore it. I want so much for him to love me, to be worthy of that love, and my heart is everywhere—thrumming in my neck, down my legs, in my wrists, and all in between.

"They're going to bind us tomorrow." Luck's voice is husky. He lifts my hand and interlaces our fingers, our wrists touching as they would beneath the marriage bonds.

"Thread over thread, life over life," he recites.

I let out a shaky breath. "To make one life," I finish.

Luck lays me down in the reeds with my head on the metal shore. I can barely breathe. I have that feeling again, that I'm only a passenger in my own body. Luck kneels over me. His breath is hot on my neck and face.

"Have you done this before?" My arms feel weak and my heart beats too fast.

Luck shakes his head. He gropes my back, fumbles. "I don't want to hurt you. Soli said . . ."

". . . she would break your toes," I say, and break into a nervous laugh.

Something about my laugh knocks the awkwardness from us. Luck hugs me close and laughs with me. I can feel him shaking.

He turns serious again. "Are you ready?"

I take a deep breath. "I think so." I look at him and remember the meeting at the dock, how my gaze flew to him for refuge when the rest of me was trapped still as death.

"So," I say.

Soli is right. It does hurt some, but then it doesn't so much anymore, or at least, it's a sweet kind of hurt. Luck and I move together. The fish brush our bare ankles, the water laps softly against the sides of the pool, and my sense of time, my feeling for night and day, evaporates. I lean my forehead against Luck's and breathe with him. I can already feel the fibers of my heart growing out, threading together with his where our chests meet.

When it's over, we lie tangled together in the shallows, the water covering us like a blanket.

Luck kisses my knuckles. "Ava?"

"Hmm?"

"How come your crewe never taught you reading, but they showed you figuring?"

My face goes hot. I prop myself up on one elbow. "I can write my name. And figuring, I taught myself that."

"You taught yourself?" Luck echoes.

"Mostly." I shrug.

"But reading . . . what about safety signs and directions on how to make things? Don't you need it for that?"

"Women don't read." I hear Modrie Reller's words in my mouth. "We're too busy. We have men to do it for us."

Luck rolls his eyes to the ceiling. "That's stupid. What if something happens? What if you have to try to set the distress beacon or tell if something's poisonous?"

"I'll have you tell me how to do it." I gulp a mouthful of saltwater and spit it at him.

He splashes me back. "I'm serious, Ava. After we're

bound, you have to learn how to read. It's dangerous, not knowing."

I bite the inside of my cheek. "I might be some old for it. Modrie Reller's always talking on how my father says our brains stop learning well once we're done growing, and girls are never so good to start with."

"I don't know." Luck draws me close again. "You taught yourself figuring, right so?"

I nod slowly.

"It can't be harder than that, especially with someone to show you the trick of it." He traces my collarbone with his forefinger. "You're sharp, Ava, sharper than any other woman I know. And when we're bound, you won't need to hide your hair anymore."

A lump rises in my throat. I kiss him again, harder this time.

"What in nine hells is this?" A rough, ringing voice cuts the silence.

Luck breaks away from me and staggers back to his knees. I clasp my hands over my chest and sit up.

Two men stand in the doorway, staring down at us. Night Fixes.

I reach for Luck, but he's too far away.

"Æther Luck?" One of the men cranes his neck, trying

to make out what he's seen. "That the *Parastrata* bride?"

Luck swallows. "I . . ."

"Get her out of there." The other Fix, tall and knob boned, shoves past his crewemate. He scoops up Luck's shirt and hurls it at his face. "And get yourself out."

Luck catches his shirt. He reaches down to help me up, and the Fixes glare at our joined hands as Luck leads me out of the water, shielding my body with his own. Shame swirls over me and gravity retakes my body as we slosh out of the pool. It fills my veins like lead. At the lip of the pond, the tall Fix yanks my arm up out of Luck's hand and shoves Luck at his crewemate.

Luck rights himself mid-stumble. "Where's your decency?" He looks back at me. "Let her put on some clothes."

"You're a fine one to talk on decency." The stoop-backed Fix glares at him, but he doesn't move to stop me.

I tie on my skirts and work the clasps of my shirt with shaking fingers. The fabric sticks to my damp skin. They saw us. They know what happened. They must. I want to run to Luck, cling to him, but they stand in my way. *What's happening?* I want to ask. They should be angry to find us together, yes, but this fury seems too much when we're near enough bound. Something's gone wrong. I try to catch Luck's eye as the Fixes march us up the spiraling gangway, past the service locker, to the laddered hatch, boots clanging double time.

"Where're we going?" Luck asks, finally looking up.

"Your father." The stoop-backed Fix glances at me with a look that says I'm nothing but muck and burnoff. "And hers."

My breath stops. *My father.* My legs waver underneath me. The Fixes jerk me forward, push me to the ladder. My arms and legs climb without me, automatonlike. The thought of my father's eyes on me, forming what I've done into words, makes me queasy with shame and regret. What seemed so right in the otherworldly glow of the pool seems unfailingly stupid now. We should have waited. It was only a few days. I wish I could go back, tip the balance so the me in Luck's arms some minutes past would want to lose her girlhood the proper way. But there's nothing I can do now, no going back. It's done.

# CHAPTER 7

*Maybe it won't be so bad,* I try to tell myself as they march us past the women's quarters and the darkened galley. *Soli did worse.* Æther Fortune might have flogged Ready, but he wouldn't flog his own son, would he? And Luck said he would take care of me. Everything will be raveled back right soon.

We stop before a solid door with wood carvings inlaid in the metal. The sight of it sends my heart into a canter. I know this door. The same carvings—our ancestors looking skyward, then boarding their ships, then Saeleas floating weightless with her hair fanned out like an angel—grace the entrance to the captain's quarters on the *Parastrata.* I've spent hours polishing them at Llell's side before the Day of Apogee. A scroll of words unrolls from Saeleas's mouth. I know well enough what they say without reading, the same words my mother whispered in her fever dream. *Women of the air, stay aloft and be whole!*

Then the whole verse comes back to me, and I ache with dread. I want to run, but my body isn't done playing traitor, and my limbs lock up.

*But woman, her mettle's thin,*

*Like copper sails to trap the sun's heat.*

*Cover us all, she does,*

*Tame the stars' fury and channel life.*

*In the air, she floats;*

*A perfect, iridescent thing.*

*But when her feet touch the ground,*

*Bare time till she falls crumpled and tarnished.*

*Women of the air, stay aloft and be whole!*

I feel as though the floor is falling out beneath me. The tall Fix steps forward and pounds a fist on the door. I finally catch a glimpse of Luck. His face says he's as wracked with regret as me, as tarnished as I feel, but he tries to smile at me anyway. *Don't fear.* I bow my head and let my damp hair hide my face. How can he protect me if he's as frozen by shame as I am?

A section of the door creaks open, a little hidden latchport. "What?" says the guard.

"We need to see Æther Fortune and the *Parastrata* captain." The Fix spits.

"What? Now?" says the guard. Then he catches sight of me, hair snarled with briny water, only half dressed in my shirt and underskirts, and he jumps as if someone has touched a bare wire to his skin.

The Fixes march us into the captain's quarters. Men's laughter rings through the sickly sweet smoke clouding the air. The crewemen lounge on oversize pillows of hide and silk, shouting and singing and throwing back glasses of clear rice wine. My heartbeat doubles. I've never been in men's quarters before, except for the times Modrie Reller sent me in to clean, and the rooms were empty then. My father's yellow-white hair stands out bright as a nova in a sea of dark heads. Æther Fortune sits beside him. My arms and face burn. Panic crackles beneath my skin. I try to break for the door, but they catch me and spin me around to face my father again.

My father's eyes narrow at me like a cat's. A hush spreads out around us.

He stands and shifts his gaze to the Fixes. "What are you doing with my so girl?"

"Your so girl," says one of the Fixes, sticky with sarcasm. "We caught her naked in the desalination reservoir, letting young Æther Luck put his hands to her." He shoves Luck forward.

Æther Fortune shoots to his feet. "My son?"

"We thought you'd want to talk on what they were doing there, exactly, in the full middle of night," the Fix says.

My father's eyes are metal. "And what *were* you doing with our bride, Æther Luck?"

"I thought . . ." Luck's head drops. "We . . ."

*No,* I think, despair creeping over me. *Don't act the smallboy, not now.*

"Speak up." My father looms over him. "Let us hear you."

"I . . . we were sealing our bond," Luck says. He lifts his head and tries to stare back at my father, but I can see he's shaken. The look on my father's face is enough to make me want to drop to my knees and beg mercy. "We thought it wouldn't matter so soon before the binding."

"Wouldn't matter?" Æther Fortune pushes forward. Blood flushes his cheeks and throat. "Wouldn't *matter*?"

"I know it was wrong," Luck says. "But I care some lot for Ava and once we're bound it won't—"

My father looks as though he's going to strike him, but it's Æther Fortune who does it. He hits Luck close-fisted across the eye. There is a snap, and Luck doubles over, clutching his face.

I stifle a cry.

"My own son." Æther Fortune grabs Luck by the back of the neck and pulls him up.

Luck swallows, a bruise already purpling his cheekbone. "Father . . ."

"It matters to me," he says coldly, and strikes Luck again with his ring hand.

Luck drops to the floor. His face is bleeding. He touches the cut and stares at the red smear in confusion. Æther Fortune levels a kick at his ribs. Luck collapses, all the air driven from his lungs.

"No!" I try to run to him, but the Fix holds me back.

Luck's father delivers another kick, and then another, and another. I cover my eyes, but I can't escape the sound of it—the thick blows, the grunts. Finally, an Æther creweman puts a restraining hand on his arm.

The captain steps back, breathing hard, and smoothes his hair. "It matters to me," he says again. "Ready the airlock."

"Please." I stretch out my hand and step between Luck and his father. "I let him."

A silence falls over the room, broken only by the sound

of Luck wheezing. Æther Fortune and my father turn to me slowly, and I realize what I've done. I should never have spoken, not at all. I know that; any so girl worth her salt knows that. My father and Æther Fortune stare at me as if one of the goats has opened its mouth and formed human speech.

I drop to the ground and hold up my hands in supplication. "Your mercy, so father."

"You consented?" my father hisses. His eyes are cold as the Void.

I bow my head and nod, terrified and bewildered. My father looks as though he wants to cut my throat.

"So captain." Luck staggers to his feet, clutching his ribs. "So father, punish me as you did Soli's husband. The blame is mine, not Ava's. We can still be bound, and make everything right."

"And what . . ." Æther Fortune's voice is dangerous. "What makes you think you can steal my bride, small Luck?"

Silence.

"Your bride?" Luck darts a horrified look at me.

"Yes, my bride." Æther Fortune flexes his hands into fists. His pockmarks stand out in sickly moons over his reddening face. "The ink's fresh, but the contract's signed."

Luck swallows. "I thought with it being time for me to take a wife, and you talking on how I'd need to marry before I take the captaincy . . ." His voice trails to nothing.

"So you're taking the captaincy too, then?" Æther Fortune's voice rises. "The way you've taken my bride? Is that what you are? My own son, an adulterer *and* a traitor?" He pushes Luck backward. One of the Fixes catches him before he hits the ground and pushes him back to his feet. Æther Fortune rounds on my father, breathing hard. "And you, with your some pretty lies about your virtuous daughter and her skilled hands. Now we see what they're skilled at."

"Brother Fortune," my father says. "On me and my wives, our regrets. Our deep apologies. Let me find you another girl from my crewe. A better bride, pure, more docile. I have a younger daughter by my third wife near enough come to womanhood. You could take her now and . . ."

"I want nothing of yours, Parastrata." Spit flies from Æther Fortune's mouth. "Your lies or your girls or your metals. We're done. Leave my ship."

"So brother," my father says in a soothing voice. "Only . . ."

"Leave my ship," Æther Fortune repeats, and it comes

to me he wouldn't need a knife to kill at all.

The *Parastrata* men stand tense and ready, their wine long forgotten at their feet. My father jerks his chin. His men file into two flanking columns as my father stalks from the room. He brushes past me on his way to the door, as if I'm vapor. It feels like a kick to the chest; I can't draw breath. I glance at Luck, his eye swollen and a line of blood welling over the bridge of his nose. I want to run to him, press a cool hand to his face, wipe away the blood, but his father steps between us.

"You would have been my wife, girl." His pale blue eyes are filled with hate. "Now you're nothing."

I stumble back and trip over my own skirt, coming down hard on my elbow. I scrabble to my feet. I am alone, near naked, and without my kinsmen's protection. I see my father disappearing through the small latchdoor, his men retreating after him. One of them turns. Jerej, doing me the small mercy of waiting.

I cast a last look at Luck. He stares back, his features cracked with blood and heartbreak. He cannot save himself, much less me. What will his crewe do to him? It will be worse than Æther Ready's fate, certain sure. It will be the airlock, like his father said, or worse.

I have no choice. I hurry after Jerej. The Æther men

turn away as I push through them to my brother.

"Jerej . . . ," I say when I reach the latchdoor.

He pivots and sweeps out of the captain's quarters. I follow, running as best I can.

"Jerej."

His boots clap the floor. He doesn't answer.

"Please, wait for me!" My voice pitches down the curve of the corridor, and I hate the way it sounds. All panicked and girlish high as it echoes back. Jerej steps up his pace. Tears sting my eyes like chemical burn, and dread lodges in my throat. "Please . . ."

I can feel the threads between Luck and me snapping with every step. I trip, skin my palms and knees, pick myself up again, and push myself after Jerej. He doesn't stop, even when I fall. A sharp bend in the hallway swallows him up.

"Wait!"

I round the corner and stop short.

"Jerej." My father looks at me. For a moment I think he's going to speak to me, and I would welcome it, even if his words hit me like a slap. But he speaks for my brother. "Take that back to the ship. We'll collect the women and meet you there."

"Father . . . ," I say.

He turns away and gestures for his men to follow. Jerej grips my shoulder and pushes me in the opposite direction, to the exit bay. I don't fight as he yanks me along the corridor, down the ramp. The close, once-safe walls of the *Æther* give way to the high, open bay. The weight of the station's gravity drops on me once more. The concourse stands near empty now the station is observing night. Dim blue light from the few open shops falls over the grit and dung and wasted bits of food and paper littering the broad midway floor. A thin scum of debris sticks to the soles of my feet as Jerej herds me along. I cling to him, even though his grip hurts my arm.

"Jerej," I whisper. "Please, I didn't know."

I pull back to slow him down. *Maybe if I talk, I can keep him from locking me up in the* Parastrata, I think wildly. *Maybe he'll take me back to the* Æther. *Maybe it's not too late to unpick this snarl and ravel everything back right.*

"I know I did wrong." My voice shakes. "But I would never have done it if I hadn't thought it was Luck you meant to bind me to. I swear, Jerej."

He glances at me but doesn't slow his pace.

"If you would speak to Father for me." I wipe at my eyes. Doesn't he remember us as smallones together? Watching my mother in the midst of the storm? The times he dropped his beancake at supper and I gave him my own? Shouldn't that matter now? "Please, so brother . . ."

"I'm none of your brother." Jerej stops and glares at me. "My sister Ava is dead. And you, you're naught but some bad matter left over. Don't you see what you've done?" Jerej stands close to me, too close, and his words are soft with menace. "Two decaturns of trade with the Æthers, gone to vapor because of you."

"I didn't know," I say. "How was I to know . . ."

"You weren't," Jerej says. "You were supposed to keep your legs together and do as you were told."

I drop my head and let Jerej pull me to the *Parastrata*'s dock. I don't raise my eyes again until I hear the bay door seal itself behind us, and the humid air of my home ship swallows us once more.

# CHAPTER • 8

I huddle on the floor of the utility closet where Modrie Reller and Iri dyed my hair at the beginning of the day—or was it the day before? Two days? I've lost track of time since Jerej sealed the door behind me. The old-fashioned vapor light built into the ceiling doesn't cycle on and off with the rest of the ship; it burns constantly with a *tik-tik-tik*, like a fingernail tapping the base of my skull. Dried salt crusts my arms and legs, and the copper coils at my wrists and ankles stick to my stained skin. At one point, I fall into an uneasy sleep and dream Luck has led me to the broad window in the *Æther*'s garden. We stand looking out at the stars.

"Did you know you can walk on them?" Luck says.

"Truly?" I say.

Luck climbs up into the window and steps out. He balances on the tiny pinprick of a star. "You just have to keep moving," he says, and jumps to the next one.

*We can't,* I say, but I follow him out into the Void anyway. I pull back my skirts and leap out onto the nearest star. It holds firm under my feet, solid as glass. I look up at Luck.

"You can run," he says. He grins and breaks away from me, across the starry field.

I push myself after him. The stars come closer the faster I run, until they form a shining pebbled path beneath my feet. I laugh. My skirt weighs nothing and my legs carry me like water. I'm not even winded.

*Winded.* I stop and look down at my feet. *But I'm in the Void*, I remember. *I shouldn't be able to breathe at all. My blood should be frozen in my veins, my lungs sucked empty of air and collapsed.* I look up to warn Luck, but he's gone. The Void stretches out empty around me. I open my mouth to call for him, and the emptiness rushes in and siphons all the air out of me.

I wake, gasping, on the utility room floor.

After that, I try not to sleep. Instead, I hug my knees to my chest and rock and play what's happened over and over, imagining it different. In one version, I never leave Soli's bunk. In another, I lie and tell Luck I've been swimming before, go back to bed, and marry Æther Fortune. I don't kiss Luck. I don't hold him close in the water. I never give him the chance to love me. In my wildest version, Luck and me break away from the Fixes and flee the ship, but my imagination falters once we've reached the concourse, so instead I imagine Luck talking his father down, convincing him to bind us after all.

*Maybe he will,* I think. *Maybe Soli will speak for us. Maybe Jerej . . .*

The door lock clicks. I scramble to my feet and try to stamp the numbness out of them. They haven't forgotten me. A mix of relief and dread twists in my gut. The hinges squeal as the door swings open. Modrie Reller stands on the other side. Half of me wants to shrink into the corner and half wants to run to her, to break down crying with relief at the sight of her. Modrie Reller's face is still, blank. She holds an armful of heavy green cloth close to her chest. I recognize my good mirrored skirt, the one I wore when I was so briefly a bride, the one I left behind on the *Æther*.

*Maybe,* I think, and stop myself. The best I might get is if they've talked Æther Fortune into going through with our binding, though I know that's more than I deserve. More likely they've found some nobody on the *Parastrata* willing to take me as one of his later wives, at least to smooth out the look of things. I'll end up a dyegirl all my life, like Llell's mother, but a fifth or sixth wife, lower even than her. And maybe someday when I'm old, my crewe will forget what brought me so low. *I'll take it,* I say to myself. *Anything to lift this shame off of me, anything not to be locked back in the room with the* tik-tik-tik *of the vapor light.* I open my mouth to say it, but Modrie Reller stops me.

"Not a word," she says. "Follow me."

I shuffle after her, careful to keep my head down. If I don't raise my eyes, I don't have to look into the faces of the people we pass. They all know. Out of the corner of my eye, I see our Fixes and Cleaners turn their heads to stare as I walk in Modrie Reller's wake. I know how I must look, my skin patchy with grime and my clothes stiff with sweat. An adulteress, a criminal, a whore. Their eyes light my skin on fire.

I follow the hem of Modrie Reller's skirt up from the bowels of the ship. She pauses at the back door of the cleanroom, tips up my chin with her hand, and looks at me, as if she's trying to record my face in her mind. I wrap my hand around hers, childlike. For a moment, I think she means to speak to me, but she spins on her heel and pushes the door to the cleanroom open. A broad half moon of women stands waiting for us along the tiled wall. Iri and

Hannah and my great-grandfather's other widows, Llell's mother, Lifil's mother and Eme's, and all my father's other wives. Near all the women of the ship are here.

For one bright moment, I think they've come to prepare me for a binding. Æther Fortune, one of the papermakers or Cleaners or Fixes, I don't care, so long as everyone stops hating me and the world stands solid beneath me again. But then I notice there are no children. Children always come to bindings to bless the bride and remind her of her purpose.

"What's happening?" My voice sounds high and shaky.

"Sisters." Modrie Reller's voice rings out over the silent room. She traps my shoulders beneath her hands. "We come to prepare our daughter for burial."

Lifil's mother lets out a moan, then Hannah and Iri and all the rest. Together, they lift their voices in a high, keening wail. Each voice laps over the others, one woman reaching her highest pitch as her sister pauses to draw breath. The fine hairs of my neck stand on end. They close in on me as one, arms outstretched.

"Please." I try to back away. Because suddenly it comes to me what my bridal skirt means, what Jerej's words meant. *My sister Ava is dead.* I remember Modrie Reller's kiss on my mother's cold forehead and the loose, papery feel of her skin as we washed her body, the stiffness setting into her limbs as we dressed her in her skirts and coiled bridal bands around her thin joints, the heaviness of her head as we lifted it to refasten the data pendant around her neck. The only other time a woman wears her bridal finery is at her burial. Once we've broken dock and sounded deep enough, they're going to turn me out, still breathing, into the Void.

Modrie Reller catches me by both arms and holds me hard to her breast as the other women converge on me. Pale hands unclip my soiled shirt and pull at my skirt ties. I see them undress me as if I am watching from above while this happens to another girl. My clothes disappear into the purl of hands. They pry the tarnished copper coils from my wrists and ankles, leaving only their spectral green imprints on my skin.

Iri holds a water vessel over her head, and the other women greet her with a new frenzy of wailing. Her eyes look past me as she cracks the seal and tips a stream of lukewarm water over me.

The shock of it brings me crashing back into myself. The water soaks my hair and rinses the salt from my skin in rivulets.

"No!" I twist a hand out of Modrie Reller's grasp and

lunge into the press of women. I'm not ready to be buried. I'm not ready to meet the Void. I stumble. The other women lift me to my feet and send me back into Modrie Reller's steel grip, wailing and crying all the louder as they do. I look up. For a single slip, shock freezes me in place. It's Llell. She moans, but her eyes kindle with something else, and I remember and regret all the times I've spoken hard to keep her in her place.

The women surge forward again, swallowing Llell in their ranks. I kick at them as they wash my body with water and oil, tie me into my skirts. They leave my chest bare, but weave my hair back into thick wedding braids and bind it with copper wire. They wind fresh wire from my ankles up my calves and around and around my forearms, until I can hardly bear the weight of it. Modrie Reller lowers a headdress bangled with a few cheap coins across my brow, and suddenly the wailing stops.

Modrie Reller lays her hands on my head.

"Come the last breath of stars,

Their dust fall

And make us all.

Come the last breath of man,

And dust give back again."

The women repeat her words in whispers, and each

leans in to kiss my forehead, to touch my hair one last time.

*I'm going to die.*

They lift me up on their shoulders and carry me from the cleanroom. I am floating again, not on water, but on a sea of hands as we flow out through the sleeping quarters, into the ship's central corridor. The men stop their work and stand in silence to watch our procession.

*I'll never see Luck again. I'll never be a true bride.*

We pass the kitchens and the hydroponic gardens and the canaries. The small yellow birds hop frantically in their cages, alarmed by the voices and the charge in the air.

*I'll never have smallones of my own.*

We empty out into the storage bay. The goats trot away from the gate and crowd together at the back of the paddock, bleating.

*My hands will never weave again. They'll never practice fixes.*

The women press together, two abreast, as we file into a shadowed canyon formed by stacks of copper bales, crates of sand, and reams of fiberoptic cable. They lower me to my feet. I hug my arms over my bare chest to keep myself from shivering. This way they're taking me, this is the path to the coldroom, where we store bodies until we can return to the depths of the Void to give them a proper burial among the stars. This is where my mother's body lay until the so doctor's daughter came to bury her. Anger sparks in my chest. I deserve to be punished, yes. But to die? I don't want to die.

*I won't make it easy.* I stop walking. My funeral procession shudders and jams behind me. For a moment, I think it's worked, but then they haul me up with their work-hard arms and drag me to the front. *I curse you with my death*, I think.

Modrie Reller stops by the coldroom door. It stands ajar, seeping frost smoke into the warm bay. Thin blue light from a biolume bowl built into the ceiling bathes the floor, doing more to form shadows than to illuminate the empty crates and metal-slabbed niches where bodies are meant to lie.

The women release me at the threshold. Modrie Reller rests her hand on my head. "May the Mercies carry your soul to rest, Parastrata Ava."

# CHAPTER 9

The floor sticks to my bare feet when I forget to move. I pace from one end of the coldroom to the other beneath the twilight of the biolume bowl and its circling fish. The metal slabs are empty, thank the Mercies. If I were trapped in here with a body, I might try slicing open my own neck with the sharp ends of the copper wire around my wrists. That might be the smart thing in any case. I'd prefer the burn of metal opening my veins, the slow sleep falling over me as my heart fails.

But no.

Modrie Reller and all of them, that's what they want. They hope I'll die of cold in here or else invent some way to hurry myself into death and save them the grisly task of venting me into the Void. *I curse you*, I think, and walk faster to keep my blood flowing to my fingers and toes, keep the tremors in my muscles at bay. I pull the cheap headdress from my hair and throw it. *I won't make my death easy.*

But it's cold. Layers of frost rime the marble slabs, leaving them glistening like an oil slick. No Mercies will come to save a girl like me. I'm on my own. My feet burn, my arms burn, my chest burns. Inside and out, the cold rubs me raw. I need warmth. I've heard a chill so deep can blacken a man's fingers and toes, rot them from his body. *At least my ears are warm,* I think, and laugh aloud, bitterly, my breath cloudy in the faint blue light.

*My ears.* I bury my fingers in my hair. The cold eases so slightly I wouldn't notice if I weren't holding my breath. But it eases. I rip the copper bindings from my hair and unknot the braids. My hair hangs heavy, almost to my waist. I spread it over my bare shoulders and arms like a cloak. Not as cold, but not enough.

I search the room over, looking for something useful. Anything to draw the cold away from me. Anything to create warmth. *Think, think. There has to be a fix for this.*

*At least they mean to bury you with the stars,* I tell myself. It could be worse. My crewe could choose to bury me beneath the ground. But that's only for the worst among us, the murderers and heretics whose souls might come back to haunt the ship if we let them loose in the Void. They say when a body is buried in the ground, its soul goes to dust along with its flesh.

I shiver and push the thought away. My soul isn't going anywhere. It's staying inside my body. I clink through the dioxide canisters in the corner and push aside a few frozen legs of goat swinging from hooks at the back of the room. Nothing. The broken crates are plastic and wouldn't burn, even if I had some way of making fire. And open flame on a ship is the worst kind of disaster that can happen, short of a hull breach. It burns up the oxygen in the air and shorts out vital systems. With us still docked, it might spread to the station, gobbling up oxygen and destabilizing the older ships' fission cores.

I rub my arms and spin in a slow circle. Metal door, metal walls, metal floors. I look up into the soft glow of the biolume. Small fish and krill, alight with their own body chemistry, circle in the thick nutrient bath filling the glass bowl. The mixture must protect them from the cold, insulate them somehow, or else their bodies would freeze and go out. I shove a crate underneath the bowl, climb up, and try to pry it from the ceiling. There are no screws or rivets around the biolume's metal housing, but a thin gap runs along its perimeter where it meets the ceiling. If I could pry it down somehow . . .

*Think, Ava. It's only another fix.*

My eyes fall on the heavy rings of copper circling my arm. *Maybe* . . .

I strip off the loops, pull a length of the wire straight, and wrap the rest of it tight around the straight piece so it won't bend easily. Every few moments I pause to rub my hands together and stop shivering. When my makeshift fix is ready, I shove the thin tip into the seam between the biolume housing and the ceiling. With a grunt, I thrust it in deeper and pry down until a crack sounds inside the frame. One side of the biolume sags away from the ceiling. A trickle of nutrient oil rolls down the outside of the glass.

I work the wire lever around the frame. Soft pops echo in the room every time I free a section, until only a thin metal lip cleaves to the ceiling. I stand with my left hand balancing the slippery bowl, my right straining to pull down the last strip. With a shriek, it comes loose.

I waver on top of the crate. I drop my fixer and clutch the biolume to my breast with both hands. A wave of nutrient oil spills over my chest. Instantly, my skin warms, as if someone has pressed a hand to my breastbone. I gasp. I steady the bowl, climb down from the crate, and balance the biolume on one of the empty metal slabs. I dip in my hand. Warmth floods my fingers. The fish, cool and scaly, brush my skin. I slather the oil down my arm. It leaves my skin gritty with krill, but a pleasant ache spreads over me, soaks into my muscles.

I rub the oil over my neck, my face, my shoulders. My body shakes, not from cold, but with relief as the numbness creeps from my skin and crackling fires flare up inside me as my nerve endings reignite. I reach down to scoop more from the bowl and stop. The nutrient oil has sunk below the bowl's halfway mark. The fish circle together around the bottom, their bodies twisted awkwardly to keep themselves submerged. If I take the oil I need, I'll kill the fish. And once their bodies stop processing chemicals, their lights will go out. I'll be alone in the dark.

Panic spikes in my chest, and a tiny sob breaks out of me.

"I'm sorry," I say. Stupid, girlish, crying over fish. It's not that I love them, really, the way Nan loves the bay cats, but their desperate writhings at the bottom of the bowl, the way they flop and crowd together, leave my heart ringing.

I scoop out a thin handful of oil and rub it over my right foot. Toe, arch, heel flare painfully back to life. The fish press against one another. They no longer have room to circle.

I take more and massage the feeling back into my left

foot. The fish turn themselves flat on their sides to keep their gills away from the open air. The oil's surface kisses their ventral fins.

I dip in my hand again. My skin brushes their slick bodies. I have to push them aside to draw out more oil. I close my eyes. Their tails slap and thrash against my skin.

"I'm sorry," I say again. Hot lines of tears rim my eyes as I cover my sides with oil.

The fish twitch and gasp. Some have already stopped moving. The room tips closer to darkness as the light leaves their skin.

I rip two strips of cloth from the hem of my bridal skirt and wrap them around my feet. I pull myself up into one of the niches and lean forward, clutching my knees. I don't know how long the oil will keep the cold at bay, but is seems wise to touch as little of the cold metal as possible. I watch as the light from the bowl dims and dims, until only one fish still glows underneath the bodies of the others. Shadows swallow the walls, the floor, the ceiling.

*Don't go out, don't go out.*

But then the weak blue glow falters and true black closes over me.

My mind drifts to Luck. Is he locked in some cold, dark room like me? Has his father beaten him again? Is he waiting for his own push into the Void? Or is he already dead? I imagine him holding me, his strong hands smoothing my hair. Lying beside him in the water. He can't be dead if I can still remember him so clearly. He can't be dead when I love him so. *Please,* I beg the Mercies. *Please, let him live.*

At first I think the creak of the door is part of a dream, but then light, bright and harsh, streams under my cracked eyelids. I sit up. Iri holds a flash lantern above her head. Her skin reflects the light like a bone moon.

"Stay away from me." My voice is rough and raw from the cold. I stumble numbly out of the niche and back to the nearest wall. *Iri.* That betrayal hurts worst of all. Have the others sent her with some new punishment? Or is she here to do me a mercy and see I'm not breathing when I meet the Void?

"*Hssh.*" Iri raises a hand to quiet me and squints into the dark room. Her eyes go wide when she sees the biolume dead on the table. She looks at me in an appraising way.

I peer past her. She's alone. No Modrie Reller or Hannah or any of the other women. My mind clicks over slowly, still thick with sleep and panic, as I try to piece together what it means.

"Ava." Iri holds out her hand. "Come on."

I stand locked in place. I know there's something I ought to ask her, but my mouth hangs open, and no words come.

"Hurry on, girl." A twitch of annoyance crosses Iri's face. "It's only an hour till newday."

I peel myself away from the wall. Iri turns and sweeps out of the coldroom. I follow in a fog. The air of the bay clings heavy and beautifully warm on my skin. I half wonder if I'm still asleep and this is a dream.

Iri stops to seal the door to the coldroom behind us.

"What . . . ," I whisper.

She cuts me off with a sharp motion of her hand. She presses her forefinger to her lips.

I follow her through the dark canyon of stacked cargo, out into the livestock bay. Only the steady pat of our bare feet on the floor and the rustle of our skirts disturb the silence. The goats look up as we pass, but they flap their ears and settle back into sleep on the hay. Even the chickens keep silent for once. *Thank you, Mercies.*

Iri pauses inside the outer bay door. She pulls a small square of fabric from the belt of her skirt and hands it to me. "Put this on," she whispers.

I unfold the fabric. A worn green shirt, patched and

rubbed thin in spots. She must have rescued it from the rag pile. I look up at her.

"You can't go out of the ship like that." She nods to my chest, then glances down to the torn hem of my skirt and the rags around my feet. "I would've brought shoes, but I couldn't without Firstwife Reller noticing."

I pull the shirt over my head and cinch its frayed laces so it fits me. "Why are you doing this?" I ask.

"There are some of us didn't want a hand in what's to be done with you, Ava." Iri speaks low. "There are some what say, *there but for the Mercies go I.*" She reaches up and activates the bay doors.

This close, the shriek and rumble of the doors vibrates through my whole body. My heart throws itself against my chest.

"What are you thinking?" I shout to Iri over the deafening roar of the bay doors rolling open and the pneumatic *thunk* of the ramp descending to the station floor.

"It's the only way out," she shouts back.

I glance behind us. Any second, my brother or Modrie Reller or someone is bound to come. There isn't any way no one heard the doors, even at this hour, and the Watches are sure to see the outer door's been activated. Even now, silent alarms are flashing in the watchroom.

The ramp hits the floor with a rattling thud, and the pneumatics whine in relief.

"Come on." Iri charges down the ramp, skirts swaying around her ankles with every long stride.

I rush after her, afraid to look back. We pass the gravity shift—I feel a sudden thump in my chest—and reach the latchdoor to the concourse. Iri unrolls a scrap of paper from her skirt pocket. She bends close to the pattern lock to compare the symbols she's copied to the ones on the door's lock grid.

Behind us, a single shout echoes from the open bay.

"Hurry, Iri." I glance at the symbols on the grid. There are only ten of them, but they're as foreign to me as they must be to Iri. She presses a halting finger to the first symbol in the sequence, a sharp one with two open tines on top.

More shouts.

Iri punches the second symbol, an easy one, a simple line.

The men come into view at the top of the ramp. The Watches, and among them, Jerej. He spots me. Something awful races across his face, and I know if he catches me, it won't be the coldroom I go back to.

"Iri, please."

She falters on the last symbol. Her finger hovers over the keypad. It's a tricky one, a rounded symbol with a tail, and there's another like it on the grid, only flipped. I pray to the Mercies and mash the final key for her.

The latchdoor releases. We run full tilt into the concourse. The vendors are rolling up the metal grates covering their storefronts to begin newday. I smell baking bread and the sharp twinge of ozone. The station's Cleaners have swept the corridor of all its late-night filth, and our bare feet slap the shining floor as we push through the gravity.

The latchdoor bangs open again at our backs. "Stop them!" Jerej shouts, but the vendors ignore him, and the few early morning passengers only turn their heads to stare after us in a daze. Jerej breaks into a run, the other men chasing behind. They don't strain under the gravity as we do. With every step, they gain on us.

Iri and I dart around a corner, onto a broad, open causeway, longer across than the *Parastrata* and *Æther* put together, and domed in glass. The whole Void opens up above us. I gasp. Crowds of people shuffle across the open space like bees on the face of a hive. Iri tugs my hand. We plunge into the thick of the crowd. I match her step and we lift our knees, run faster than any girls on any crewe have ever run. My lungs are tight and fighting now. My palm sweats in hers, but I grip her harder so we won't slip apart.

At the far end of the causeway, a series of black-sheened

doors leading to tiny, glowing-white rooms slide open and shut. As we close in, I see one door seal over a woman in a clinging black bodysuit with an orange robe draped over her shoulder, then open in a matter of heartbeats to reveal a man with skin as leached of color as his hair. I pull Iri's hand, slowing us.

"It's only an elevation shaft, Ava." She says it soothing, like I would talk to the goats, and her tone unknots my snarl of panic enough to keep me running.

We race to the doors. I push myself faster, air coming hard. The nearest door must sense our weight on the floor tiles and begins to slide open. Iri and I turn our bodies sideways to fit through and careen into the tiny room. I spin. Jerej and the Watches shove through the crowd and bear down on us. The doors pause, sensing their weight.

I look up. There—a grid pad beside the sliding doors. It's larger than the pattern lock on the latchport, its symbols a snarl of lines and curves all pressed against one another. And then above the grid, a panel with an orange-yellow line of light shining around its edges, some like the one inside the women's quarters aboard the *Æther*. I slap my hand against it just as Jerej reaches us. He shouts, but the door slides closed, cutting off his cry. My stomach drops as we shoot up the shaft.

# CHAPTER • 10

Our first blind trip up the shaft takes us to the repairs tier, where carracks and frigates and barques lie with their innards spilled open, solar sails tattered and rent, hulls hefted up on lifts, while sparks rain down around them. We try again, and the shaft dumps us out into a long, narrow hallway somewhere in the depths of the station, lined with greasy windows. Barracks for the station's crews, I guess, or those wanting a cheap bed between ship transfers.

We duck under lines of damp laundry strung across the corridor. A thickset girl with a metal barrel balanced on one shoulder nudges her way through the tangle. We press flat against a wall to let her pass. An older woman with lank hair and sores clustered around her mouth stares at us from one of the doorways, a grubby-faced baby toddling across the cramped room behind her. Farther on, another door swings open behind us. A pink-faced man with rotten teeth leans out.

"You ladies after some company?" He takes a wavering step toward us. The sour reek of alcohol wafts from his soiled clothes. "I got a room here if you want some company."

Iri shakes her head and presses me forward.

"One drink? We're friends, aren't we?" the man calls after us. "We can be friends."

We stride away as fast as we can without running. The hall goes on and on, smeary windows narrowing into infinity. I think the roof must be slowly sloping down on us, and any minute I'm sure another door will swing open, someone worse will block our path. The *Parastrata*'s wives are full of stories of girls who'd wandered away from their crewes being robbed or raped or cut up in tiny pieces and fed into nutrition recyclers.

Finally the hall ends in a round metal service door. Iri pulls it open and steps into the dark. I try to follow, but the moment I put my foot down, the ground shifts, as if I'm wheeling into a fall. I cry out and reach for Iri's hand.

"Here, Ava." Iri catches me.

The wheeling stops as suddenly as it started. I look

around. We're standing in a long service shaft. The lights above us fizz on, but behind us and ahead, the shaft fades into blackness. I turn to my right, to the door that brought us here. The dim corridor with its grimy windows has flipped on its side, so all the windows now lie where the floor and ceiling should be.

"What . . . ," I start to ask.

"It's the gravity," Iri whispers. "The stationmakers changed its direction to make it easier to move things between levels."

"Oh." I don't know what else to say. I never knew men could change gravity. I thought it was only something that was.

"Forward or back?" Iri asks.

"Forward," I say. The *Parastrata*'s tier hangs somewhere ahead or above us, but I don't want to think on what might be lurking in the tiers even lower than where we are now.

We walk. As we reach each new section, the lights click on before us and snuff out behind. Our footsteps echo into the dark. Each tier has its own door, with its own narrow window looking out onto the tipped level. Someone has bolted vinyl plates stamped with symbols beside each doorframe. I stare at them hopelessly, praying the trick of reading will come to me if I stare long enough. *After we're bound, I'll show you how to read. . . .*

My Luck. Have they sent him out to meet the Void? He's the captain's own son. Surely his life must be worth more than mine. Someone on his crewe will save him, as Iri saved me. Or maybe if we tell the right people, they can help us. We can save him ourselves.

How many more levels above us? How far have we come? At last we peek through a door and find a concourse stretched broad in front of us, bustling with people lugging bags and pushing hover trolleys of small crates. I crack the door to get a better look. The sweet smell of well-scrubbed air rushes in, along with the crackle of advertisements from nearby speakers and handhelds. This level is some like the *Parastrata*'s, with its vendors and food stands, but brighter. Boxed holograms of ferns and flowers extend down the center of the concourse, flanked by white benches.

"The passenger tier," Iri breathes in my ear.

"Security alert." A cool, toneless woman's voice interrupts the stream of advertisements. I shrink back. The voice echoes up the shaft. "Sixteen-year-old girl reported missing. Last seen in the company of an older female relative, believed to have abducted the girl. Both have red hair, of merchant tribe descent. Please report to the nearest security station if you see these individuals. Code five-two-nine."

Iri and I stare at each other, wide-eyed. *Nine hells.* I slam the door shut. How did they do that? How did they know? Jerej or my father must have talked someone into helping to hunt us down. They must have told them what I did. No one will help us now. I slump against the door, my heart choking me. I have to push the thought of Luck away, or I'll lie down here and never get up again. We have to keep moving.

I clear my throat. "What now?"

Iri kneels at the center of the shaft. "I thought on that." She turns out her pockets and produces rolls of homespun cloth, copper handspools, dull, greening coins from a bridal headdress, seemingly anything of value she could fit in her pockets before she fled.

"For trade," she says.

"Trade?" I echo her dumbly.

Iri nods. "I know someone what could help us groundways."

"You know someone groundways?" I gape at her, the danger of Jerej and the Watches momentarily forgotten. She might as well have said she knows some Void zephyrs.

"I do." Iri sets her mouth in a line, as if she's unsure how much to trust telling me.

I crouch down next to her and finger one of the corroded coins. "Who?"

"You remember," Iri says slowly. "You remember when your mother went on to the Void, how the so doctor's daughter came aboard to sort things with your great-grandfather Harrah?"

Her strange figure, with only her hands and face uncovered, passes before my eyes like a ghost. *Turrut and Hah. Maybe she's come to snatch you 'way.*

"I remember."

Iri stacks the coins. They *click-click-click* like dripping water. "I knew her some."

"Knew her?"

"Yes," Iri says. "If we reach her, she'll help."

"How do you know?" I ask.

Iri looks up. "Because she helped before."

Something in Iri's tone tells me not to press. Whatever the so doctor's daughter helped her do, it's something that can't be spoken aloud, even now, some ten turns later.

"Do you know where she is?" I ask instead.

"Groundways," Iri says.

"But groundways where?"

"Earth. Mum—" Iri stumbles over the word. "Mumbai."

"What's that?"

"I don't know. A city, I think."

I think on the colonies and outposts the men have come back telling us about. Little clusters of airtight buildings surrounded by fields of solar panels, nitrogen pumps, and domed dioxide converters. Even with Earth close packed as it is, could it be so hard to find a person once you've got it narrowed down to a single city?

"We send out a call to her?" I ask. "Is that what you've got in mind?"

Iri looks uneasy. She shakes her head.

"What then?"

Iri hesitates.

"You can't mean . . ." I recoil. I think I know what Iri means to do. "Oh, no."

"Only for a little bit, Ava."

"No."

"Don't you hear? They've got the whole station looking for us. They could be listening if we send out a call. The only way to reach her safe is to go there. Go groundways. I heard some of the men talking once on how you can rent out a slot on a ferry ship. You can pay to keep your name hidden, even."

"No," I say again. "Iri, what are you thinking? We

can't." As if in warning, the lights above us power down, leaving us in darkness. We've been still too long.

"Look how we are without the ship," I say. Winded and lead boned, ready to cave to the Earth's call. "Going groundways might kill us." *Or worse.*

"The so doctor's daughter bears it," Iri says quietly. She knows the Word as well as I.

But who knows what living groundways has done to the so doctor's daughter, how it's changed her? Is she still even a woman, or do you have to become something else to bear the Earth beneath your feet?

"No, Iri," I say into the dark. "Please, no."

She touches my arm. "It's the only way I can figure, Ava."

"We can sign ourselves on a work detail with one of the industrial shippers. Or hire out here for some duties, doing cleaning or what. Or beg our way onto a new crewe. I heard Jerej say one time the Nau crewe's too interbred. They need women—"

"*Aviso de seguridad,*" the woman's smooth voice interrupts, rounding into its next language cycle.

Iri huffs. "No shipper's going to hire us with that over our heads, and no crewe will take us either, not even the *Nau*. You forget, you're dead as much to them as to the

*Parastrata*. And I'm no prize as a wife either, especially on a crewe desperate for birthers."

She glances down at her flat stomach and pulls her eyes away before she thinks I see. But I do. I see. It pains her. The weight of what Iri has done in saving me falls on me. She's given up any chance of marrying again, given up any chance of trying for smallones, and all for me.

"I'll do it." I hear myself say. "I'll go."

Iri and I climb out of the service shaft and into the passenger tier. The world tips again as gravity realigns itself, but I'm ready for it this time. We slip into the crowd pushing its way along the concourse. Men and women walk freely here, and we melt into the flow of print silks and hyperbaric suits, dark skin and pale. I look for Jerej and the Watches. No sign of them, not yet at least.

"*Avis de sécurité.*"

Doors line both sides of the concourse, each with a desk or booth stationed beside it. A dark-skinned woman with a burst of gold-tipped black curls, a white shirt cut to show off her collarbone, trousers, and knee-high boots sits by the nearest one, splay-legged on a chair. Behind her, a latchport joins her short-range sloop to the station. She tracks us a few paces out of the corner of her eye, expertly cracking a nut between her palm and the flat of a long knife. She crumbles the shell to the floor and pops the meat into her mouth. A deep, puckered scar trails down the side of her nose and interrupts her red-painted mouth on one side. I press closer to Iri.

"There," Iri says. She steers us to a set of booths before the gangway to a fat passenger ferry. A ghostly image of a comet circling a planet rotates above the booths, and the woman on the other side of the glass wears the same symbol pinned to her lapel. She is all clean and smooth. Her dark hair shines, her lips shimmer an eye-aching pink-orange, and soft glitters and pigments dust all the planes of her face.

"Welcome to Hyakutake Stellar Transit." The woman leans forward with a smile. "Our service is simply stellar! Where can we fly you today?"

"M-Mumbai," says Iri.

The woman shakes her head, but her smile doesn't falter. "I'm sorry, I didn't understand. Where would you like to go?"

"Mumbai," I blurt out.

She shakes her head again. "I'm sorry, I didn't understand. Where would you like to go?"

I narrow my eyes. Something is off, the way her hair

bobs exactly the same each time she shakes her head, the same lilts and dips on the same words.

"A hologram," I say, and as I say it, I notice the faint transparency of the woman's shoulders. I step to one side, and she shrinks flat in the glass.

Iri nods as if she knows this already. "Mumbai," she repeats, clear and confident.

"Transit to Mumbai will require overland transport from landing point: Dubai International Spaceport," the hologrammed woman says. A transparent map springs up in the top corner of the glass, showing the overland path the hologram proposes in glowing blue. "Would you like to book overland passage now or when you arrive?"

"What's the cost?" Iri says.

The woman shakes her head again and smiles. "I'm sorry, I didn't understand. Please say 'now' or 'when I arrive.'"

"Now," Iri says, sharp in her hurry. She checks over her shoulder. "What's the cost, please?"

"Your ticketing options are displayed here." The projection gestures to her left, and a long pattern of columned symbols expands above her hand. Sparse Vs and As scatter through the words, but they do me no good.

"Please select your preferred pricing plan by touching the screen."

A toneless overhead voice slips itself between us, a soft warning. "*Jĭng bào . . .*"

I look at Iri, worried. Her lips press thin. "We need someone live," she says to me. She scans the crowded concourse. "Some small boat, someone we can bargain with."

"I'm sorry, I didn't understand." The hologram shakes her head again and smiles.

"Never mind. Cancel." Iri waves her hand at the hologram. "We don't . . . cancel."

The lines of symbols fade, leaving only the woman projected in the glass. "Thank you for considering Hyakutake Stellar Transit for your travel needs." She freezes with her chin slightly tilted, smiling mouth wide.

We slink away. Iri's eyes dart from ship to ship. No one manning the ticketing carrel of the midsized utilitarian carrier, only another hologram. A tall man with a shaved head glaring out at us from beside a needle-nosed transport. An older woman steeped in fuel and alcohol fumes sitting by the last ship.

Iri creeps up to the man, head bowed in respect. "Please, so, could we book passage?"

He chews something slowly, looking her over. "Can you pay?"

Iri opens a fold of her cloth bundle to display the treasures she robbed from the *Parastrata*.

The man plucks up one of the coins and rubs it with his thumb. A smudge of green wears off on his skin. He tosses it back to Iri with a look of disgust. "Credit only."

"Please, so, those are bride coins," I put in.

"Worthless is what they are," he says. "What, you think I can fuel a ship on rags and moldy coins?"

Iri shrinks as though he's slapped her. I start to speak back, but she loops her arm through mine and hurries us away. We stop in the center of the concourse. People elbow around us, dodge us as we stand like stone, Iri's treasures cradled between us.

"We can't go arguing, calling eyes on ourselves." She shakes her head over the bundle. "I thought it was worth something."

"Me too." We've never not been able to get something through trade with the other crewes or one of the colony outposts. Could the people close in to Earth really be this different from us? *How do you bargain with them?* I look up, over Iri's shoulder. The woman with the knife has her head cocked in our direction again, the scar down her face making her expression unreadable.

Iri sees me looking. She turns. "Her?" She spins back

around to me. A smile picks at the corners of her mouth. "Perfect, Ava. Good watching."

"No, wait, Iri." Something about the scarred woman makes me uneasy. Mercies know what walking on the Earth has done to her, if it's made her mind and soul as malformed as her face. In the oldgirls' stories, you can always read the map of someone's soul by her looks. I try to catch Iri, but she slips out of my grasp and strides up to the woman.

I hang back, unsure. The knife woman looks from Iri to me, back to Iri. Iri waves her free hand in circles, holds it out, pleading, and proffers the stolen bundle. The woman takes it, weighs its heft in her hand, and looks back at me.

Iri follows her gaze. "Ava, come." She waves me closer, new hope simmering in her eyes.

I hug my arms across my chest, duck my head, and walk quick to Iri's side. I scan the crowd for signs of the Watches and step light, in case I have to run again.

"This is Captain Guiteau," Iri says. She puts her arm around my shoulders and speaks to the scarred woman. "You see, we're neither of us much heavy."

The captain hands the bundle back to Iri, but she keeps her eyes on me. "I don't doubt it. But this is only a mail sloop, ladies. Now, if you've got packages, or you want me to take any of that down to the surface . . ." She nods at Iri's armful of cloth. "That I can do. Certified delivery."

When she speaks, only the right side of her mouth moves, the undamaged side. The corner sliced by the scar stays stiff, making her every word a grimace. It was some bad, whatever made this cut. I look away quick so she won't see me staring.

"Please." Iri tries again, quietly. "There's a woman we know groundways what can give you more, if you only take us to her. Just a space on the cargo floor, that's all I'm asking."

Captain Guiteau shakes her head. "I can't put live people in my cargo hold. It's not temperature regulated, much less space tight. I'm not landing with two dead bodies mixed up in my delivery."

"Please, so captain . . ."

The handheld clipped to the captain's belt crackles to life. "Security alert . . ."

Captain Guiteau flicks her eyes down to the handheld. She looks at me and deliberately switches it off. "What's down there you need so bad?" She folds her arms across her chest.

The words won't leave my mouth. I look to Iri.

"Her . . ." Iri searches for the word. "Her *modrie*. Her mother's sister."

My mother's sister. I've never heard it put together that way, what the so doctor's daughter was to my mother. My mind fumbles, trying to fit the words with my memories. *My mother's sister. My blood modrie. Maybe she come an' snatch you 'way.*

Captain Guiteau watches me. I look away and stare blindly at the crowd. Only a day or two ago, so many people pressed together made me feel near drowned, but now it's easier to watch them flowing up and down both sides of the concourse, like fish moving together. I watch their heads bobbing. Bird's-eye black and white and brown and red. I stop. Red. I try to tie my thoughts together. Red. A cluster of red hair surging along the edge of the crowd.

I clutch Iri's arm. She follows my gaze and sees what I've seen. My father and Jerej, tense with purpose, and a whole party of flame-haired men fanning out through the crowd.

"Run, Iri," I whisper. I grip her hand and tug.

"Wait!" the captain calls.

Iri hesitates.

*No. Go, we've got to go.* I pull her.

Captain Guiteau's eyes flick from me to Iri, Jerej to my father, the Watches to me. I can see her mind making its final rotation, all the pieces falling into their lines.

In that moment, my father turns. He sees me, sees Iri. He shouts at Jerej over the steady shuffle and hum of the crowd. Some of the passengers slow and stare, more and more eyes snapping on to us. Any moment they'll come shoving through the crowd and drag me and Iri back to the *Parastrata*'s coldroom, but Iri waits, her eyes locked on the captain of the mail sloop. Time slows. My father thrusts a gaping passenger aside. Jerej signals the other men with a wave of his arm.

The captain purses her mouth. Decides. "I can take one."

Iri doesn't hesitate. "Ava. Take Ava." She thrusts the bundle of cloth at me and pushes me into the captain's arms. "Run. Go now."

"But—" I stare dumbly at the bundle.

Captain Guiteau locks a hand around my wrist. "This way." She tucks her long knife inside her belt and pulls me after her to the latchdoor joining her ship to the station, wrenches it open. "Quick, now."

I turn in time to see my father tackle Iri to the ground. Her chin smacks the floor hard, a sound like an egg cracking. "Soraya Hertz," Iri shouts. Blood coats her teeth. "Your modrie, her name is Soraya Hertz. Don't forget!"

The captain pulls me through the door. It swings shut

and locks with a *fisss*, but not before I catch sight of Iri struggling on the floor beneath three men, while a crowd of open-mouthed travelers looks on.

"Iri!"

I nearly break free, but the captain is fast and stronger than me. "Come on, fi. There's nothing you can do for her."

"But . . ."

"She wanted this." Captain Gitueau spins me around so our eyes meet. "You understand? She wanted you to get away. Now we've got to *get away*. So we run." She releases my arm.

I run.

# CHAPTER • 11

The mail sloop's gravity field is low. My stomach flips and my hair stands on end as Captain Guiteau veers out of the station's orbit, toward the vast, luminous curve of blue. I hold on tight, strapped into one of the ship's two narrow seats, as the entire cabin judders under the engines' vibrations. *I'm going to be sick.* I clutch my stomach and close my eyes, trying not to think about the looming brightness below or the blood in Iri's mouth or the fact that I am leaving Luck behind.

"It's okay," Captain Guiteau says. The ship's burners whine down. "We're out of it now."

I open my eyes. Only a slim crescent of Void is visible in the viewport. The rest is bright, too bright, as if a ship's solar sails are angled face-on at me. I squint and put up my hand to block the light.

"Who are those men after you?" Captain Guiteau concentrates on pushing down one of the levers on her console by its tape-wrapped handle. "You want to tell me?"

"My father." I can't look at her, can't look out at the bright planet, can't close my eyes without seeing Iri and Luck. I turn my head to the wall. "My brother, too."

"What'd you do to rile them so? Steal something? Kiss a boy they don't like?"

The teasing's clear in her voice, but it cuts me too close. A sharp chemical burn arcs through my nose and eyes. I will not cry, not now.

"Something bad," I manage. Something so bad even she can't imagine it, this scarred, Earthborn woman who treks between Earth and sky without a man to guard her, who paints her ruined lips. So bad she's the one pitying me.

"Whatever it was, it wasn't worth what they had in mind to do to you." Her voice dips quiet again. She makes a careful study of the flickering needles and signals streaming over the console.

"How do you know what they were going to do?" For the first time I notice something sad and soft in the corners of her fierce mouth.

"That look on their faces? I've seen it before." She frowns. "It always means the same thing."

I stare at her. I can't put my mind around her brokenness and her boldness, how it can all be wrapped up in the same person.

The cabin wall behind her catches my eye. A host of flat metal figures hang from nails driven into the bulkhead—sunbursts and crowned snakes and roosters—all rattling in time with the engines.

"What are those?"

She glances up from the controls and smiles briefly. "Good-luck charms. My little girl makes them for me."

I mean to ask if they work, but Earth swells in the viewport and my mouth goes dry.

"Buckled in?" the captain asks. And then an afterthought. "You ever been planetside?"

I shake my head.

She casts a worried look at me, but it's too late. We're going in. "Hold tight," she says. "The gravity's going to hit you bad."

Vibrations pick up all along the sloop's body as we breach the atmosphere, building until the ship rocks beneath us. I cling to my crossed shoulder straps with both hands.

A flare of light explodes across the viewport, and something kicks me in the chest, hard, knocking all the wind out of me. I try to draw breath, but my lungs won't listen. They hang heavy, as if they've been dipped in lead. The ship plummets, speed pushing me into the seat. Darkness speckles my vision. I gasp. *Is this it?* Is this what the oldgirls meant when they warned us of the Earth's touch? Is this how it feels to have your soul shucked from your body? The muscles in my legs, my hands, my head, my eyelids, all of them weigh on me. My skin has turned to a shell. My heart labors against my chest, aching with every ragged beat.

"Hang in there," Captain Guiteau shouts over the clamor. "I'm taking us lower. Once we're down, we can drop speed and lose a few Gs."

I can't make sense of her words. Everything moves slow, slow, with the beat of my heart. I don't know this woman. She could do anything to me and no one would ever hear of it. Panic pierces my fog, pulls me up sharp enough to force my eyes open on the blazing white cloud tops.

"Close your eyes," the captain says. "Keep your mind on your breathing. We're almost there." As she says it, the burners whine back and the rattling steadies to a soft *chak-a-chak-a-chak*. The weight on my body eases some, enough to let me breathe shallow and clear the spots from my eyes.

Captain Guiteau snaps several switches on the console. "What was your ship's gravity rating?" she asks, not looking at me.

Gravity rating?

"I don't . . ." But then I remember the training room and how the men on groundways duty prepare themselves before they go down. They strap on weighted belts and run to keep their hearts and bodies used to the strain of the Earth's pull.

"Long-range ships mostly don't go below point six-eight Gs," the captain says, thinking aloud. "You've really never been planetside before? What were your people, traders?"

"Merchant crewe." I stop, breathe. The effort of talking is burning through all my energy.

"I know folk buck that ninety-days regulation, but I've never heard of anyone going their whole life without touching down planetside unless their ship's rated a full one G," the captain mutters. "Your people kept you on a cardiovascular conditioning regimen at least, right?"

I don't know what she's saying, but it doesn't matter. "Women of the air, stay aloft," I whisper, and smile bitterly to myself.

The captain shoots a glance at me. "You okay, fi?"

I shake my head and let my eyes close. My body feels old and crushed with pain. "I'm dead."

"Dead?" she asks carefully, as if she thinks I might be dream talking, half gone with pain and fatigue.

I nod. The sun's glare sweeps over my face as the ship ducks out from beneath a cloud, turning the world inside my eyelids red. "Dead."

# CHAPTER • 12

Heat. Clinging, humid, the kind that leaves my lungs boiled and limp. The kind I woke to each newday on the *Parastrata*. For a moment, I think I'm back, back home, with Lifil curled beside me, Iri and Luck both safe. But then I work my eyes open and the light floods in, heavy and gold, like the whole world is drowned in cooking oil. A smallgirl of maybe eight turns leans over me. Short black braids spring out below her ears. She looks at me with wide eyes a deep honey-amber, some shades lighter than her dark brown skin.

She breathes in sharp. "Manman, she opened her eyes!"

I close them again and try to remember. The world bobbing up and down, a violently blue sky. My hair soaked in sweat. Shouting and hands on my arms, lifting me. A glimpse—water all around and a . . . a . . . what's it called? A boat, painted deep purple and pink and yolk yellow, its roof stacked high with parcels and riders, cutting away through deep water. Then patchwork walls and tin roofs baking under the sun's glare. The smell of fuel smoke soaking the air, and everywhere constant, baking light and voices.

And then shade. The *tik-tik-tik* of a fan spinning lazily overhead. A man's hand, large and cool and dry, resting on my forehead. "*Li fret . . .*" His voice, rustling soft like the papery skin of his hand. "*Ki sa li genyen?*"

The captain, speaking low in the same language, folding something into his hand. The man's fingers pressed to the pulse below my jaw and something fitted over my nose, piping cool, sweet oxygen to my aching lungs. A needle prick at the inside fold of my arm, and the drop into nothingness.

Until now. I try to push myself up, but my muscles quake with the effort and I fall back on the cushioned pallet, covered in sweat. It feels as though someone is digging his thick, clumsy fingers into my muscles, pulling them apart thread by thread. All I can do is lie still and wait for my limbs to unlock.

The smallgirl stares at me in fright. "Manman!"

Captain Guiteau sticks her head into the room. She's shed her jacket and beaded belt in favor of a heavy leather mechanic's apron and welding goggles.

She kneels by my side. "Hand me one of those calcium packs, Miyole."

Captain Guiteau hangs a floppy bladder full of chalk-white liquid from a metal hook above my bed and connects it to a small plastic something sticking out of my arm.

"Give it a minute, fi." Captain Guiteau brushes the damp hair from my forehead.

The cramps pulse and fade. My muscles unlock, but my body feels shattered. I lie back, breathing hard. A streaky painting of a pink woman with a fish tail covers the wall above me. A whirring fan balances in one of the room's high windows. I look around. Captain Guiteau and Miyole crouch by my head, watching me anxiously. A wall of green-painted shelves stands behind them, bowed in the middle by the weight of food and mechanical parts stacked ceiling high.

"There now." Captain Guiteau helps me push myself up until I'm leaning against the wall. The glass in me grinds against my bones as I move, but when I look down, my skin is smooth as ever. How can the captain and this smallgirl move so quick and easy under the Earth's grip?

Another wave of nausea ripples over me. I close my eyes,

breathing hard despite the thin, flexible tubes pumping air into my nose. I finger the gummy piece of tape bound around my elbow. My own clothes are gone, replaced by a white, wash-worn shift that barely covers my knees. I clutch at my neck for the data pendant. It still hangs there, warm against my skin.

"W-Where am I?" My throat feels burned and raw; my stomach tender and empty, as if someone's been kicking my middle with a hard boot. The smell of sick lingers in the air.

"East Gyre," the captain says. She must see the look on my face, because she continues. "In the Pacific. You're Earthside, fi."

*Earthside.* I lean forward and try to push myself to my feet, but my legs give out. I slump back against the wall. "Iri . . ." It's as if my tongue has become mud. I can't make the rest of it come out.

"Don't move too much or you'll pull out the IV." The captain reaches behind her back to pull the ties on her leather apron. "You want some water? Something to eat?"

"Water."

The captain nods to the smallgirl, Miyole. She scurries off and brings back warm, bitter-tasting water in a pewter cup.

"It's the quinine," Miyole says quietly as I drink. "So you don't catch blood sickness from the mosquitos."

I sip, trying to ignore the bitterness and the cramp spreading all through my stomach. I can't remember the last time I ate, but it might have been the feast my first—and last—night aboard the *Æther*. Miyole watches me drink, serious faced, and takes the cup away when I've finished.

The captain loops her apron on a nail and wipes her hands on a rag. "I've got to make a run up to Bhutto station and then to Cuzco, but we'll talk when I'm back." She looks to the smallgirl. "Try to keep her awake, Miyole. The longer she sits up, the better."

"*Wi*, Manman."

"Come and hug me," the captain says. She kneels down and holds out her arms. The smallgirl runs into them.

"Be careful," Miyole says. "Promise, Manman."

"*Wi, ma chére.*" The captain touches her head to Miyole's. She starts for the door.

"Please," I say. There's so much I need to ask her. Where exactly I am and why I'm so weak and why I'm not dead altogether. And I should thank her. And I don't even know . . .

"It can wait," the captain says.

"But I don't even know your name." I don't recognize my own voice.

"Perpétue." She gives a funny half bow, half salute.

"Gyre Parcel Service. And my daughter, Miyole. But believe me, Ava, the rest can wait."

I close my mouth and let my head fall against the wall. I nod. With a wave, Perpétue disappears out the back door, and a few minutes later a high whine fills the air, followed by a thrumming *whum-whum*, like the giant fans deep in the *Parastrata*'s innards. The shriek and roar of the mail sloop's burners build and lift her away.

"Watch," Miyole says. She runs to the window on the other side of the room and points up to a bare patch of bleached sky.

I squint as the sloop races by, up and away into the blinding sun. Its engines judder and fade. A chorus of sharp squawks erupt from the roof.

"What's that?" I whisper.

"Manman's chickens." Miyole drops down beside me and crisscrosses her legs. "Manman said you could have soup. You want soup?"

I clear my throat. "Please so."

Miyole hops up and darts to the kitchen on the other side of the room. She sings a little song under her breath in that other language as she unfolds a portable stove, balances a heavy stew pot on top, and draws two fat fish out of the plastic cooler shoved against the wall. My eyes widen. We have our biolumes, of course. And once my father made a trade with the Nau crewe for cases on cases of tiny fish preserved in salt and oil, but I've never seen any like this. I didn't know they could grow so big. Miyole scrapes the scales from the meat. Then, with a few deft turns of her knife, she hacks off the heads, slices the fins away, and slits their bellies.

"*. . . si li pa dodo, krab la va manjé . . .*" Blue flames flare beneath the pot.

When she's done, Miyole carries a fragrant bowl of broth to me, taking tiny, careful steps to keep it from spilling. She presses a spoon into my hand. Small chunks of tender white meat float in the broth. I could near cry, it smells so good. But the spoon feels like a length of rebar, heavy and unwieldy. My hand shakes as I lift it to my mouth.

Miyole watches as I struggle with the spoon. "My manman says you were off planetside too long, and that's why you're sick and your muscles don't work right."

I clamp the spoon in my mouth. The soup is mild and thick. I thought the fish might be salty, but instead it's light. It eases my stomach.

"Were your people punishing you, keeping you off gravity like that?" Miyole asks.

I shake my head, sip another spoonful.

"Why, then?"

I hesitate. *And only men will bear its touch.* But if that's so, how can Captain Guiteau and Miyole manage? My head hurts. I'm not hungry anymore.

"I don't know." I put the soup aside and let the spoon clatter down into the near-full bowl.

Miyole hugs her knees and sticks the end of one braid in her mouth. She stares at me. "Why're you so pale?"

"Pale?" My eyes pop open. Me, pale? All my life, I've only wished to be lighter, more like the rest of my crewe. "Most of my crewe doesn't have any color to them."

"Really?" She scrunches up her face as if she doesn't believe me.

I nod. "I've got more than most on account of my mother's father."

"Was he a spaceside person like you?"

I shake my head. "He was from here, from groundways. He was a so doctor."

"Why didn't he make them keep you on gravity?"

"He died." My throat aches from talking. I close my eyes. "My mother too."

A few slips of silence tick by, and then Miyole jostles my knee. "Hey, miss. Hey, Ava."

I open my eyes.

"My manman says to keep you awake."

"I'm awake," I say. "It hurts . . ." *It hurts to talk,* I try to say, but my voice fails me.

Miyole rocks, hugging her knees and sucking on her hair. "You want me to read to you?"

"You can read?"

Miyole gives me a funny look. "Course I can." She stands.

"Please so, then."

Miyole runs to an ancient chest of drawers, pulls a metal key from beneath the neck of her shirt, and fits it into top drawer lock. She tugs it open. A moment later, she returns with a piece of clear plastic folded into a neat square. As she unfolds its leaves, they lock open and seal together into a thinner sheet. The moment they join, the sheet lights up from within, as if she's holding a little shard of sky in her hand. Pictures and symbols pulse across its surface, playing bright colors over Miyole's hands and face.

"Okay," Miyole says. "You want a true story or a made-up one?"

I stare at the light sheet, mesmerized. "A true story," I say finally.

Miyole sees me staring. "What, haven't you got tablets where you come from?"

There's no point lying. I've seen screens lit and all the men gathered round, but only from the doorway to my father's quarters. I always snuck glimpses as I arranged the cups of rice wine and then scurried out again before I could be noticed, but I'd swear we had nothing like this.

"No," I say.

Miyole shrugs. "My friend Kai doesn't have one either. My manman says we're lucky."

"It's some pretty," I agree.

Miyole gives me a long, measuring look. "You can use it if you want. But you can't touch it with sticky fingers, okay? My manman says that'll break it."

I want to smile, but I hurt too much. I can't even muster the strength to tell her I wouldn't know how to use it anyway. I nod instead.

"Okay." Miyole returns to the tablet, all business. "We haven't got a network signal here, so there's only what my manman loaded up the last time she went on a run, but there's lots to choose from. Did you already learn about the Floods in school?"

I shake my head.

"No?" She taps the tablet again. "What about the Third Library of Alexandria? The drowned city of Lanai? The subcontinental levee program?"

I shake my head.

"Ooh, no, wait. Terraforming." She looks over her tablet at me and grins as if she's found a sweet in her pocket. "I'm learning about that in the lessons Manman bought me on geosciences."

I nod and close my eyes.

Miyole clears her throat importantly. "Terraforming is a lengthy process by which planetary bodies are rendered fit for human habitation through the infusion of gases . . ." She stops and giggles, then sneaks a glance at me and puts on her serious face again.

". . . and the release of geothermal energy. Though scientists have long sought a more ex . . ." She stumbles, then rights herself. "Expedient method of terraforming potentially habitable planetary masses, the process still requires the dedication of multiple generations of colonists to achieve an atmospheric balance that will allow life to flourish where it previously did not. The lifeblood of these colonies is the fleet of government-funded and commercial trading ships whose crews volunteer years of their lives to the service of pro . . . provisioning the colonies. Each flight can take years to reach its destination at sublight speeds. . . ." She sounds some like the oldgirls, reciting their stories, reading the air, their words stiff and formal in their mouths.

And as she reads, I'm back aboard the *Parastata*, watching the silent mass of a red planet misted with green slide beneath our hull. I can almost see the stars beyond the thin stretch of the planet's newborn atmosphere.

"Ava. Hey, Ava." Miyole has stopped reading. Her voice is gentle. "Wake up."

"I'm awake," I say. I force my eyes open. "I was remembering. We had a route over the red one. Mars?"

"You've been there?" Miyole bounces up on her knees and hugs the tablet. "I want to go when I'm grown. I'm going to enroll in a flight academy so I can see Mars and Titus and all the little colonies starting up, but my manman says I have to have to keep my math up if I want to do it." She pauses for breath. "Did you really go?"

"No. Well, some. I've been above it, but women don't go down on groundways duty."

"Why?" Miyole cocks her head at me.

"We . . . we . . ." I wave my hand heavily in front of me. How can I explain? It would sully us? Leave us crippled, as I am now? "Don't. We just don't."

Miyole frowns.

"We can't," I say, but even as I say it, I know it makes no sense, when the weight of this world is nothing to her.

I give up and fold my hands over my knees. Miyole reads more, about nitrogen balances and something called the cascade effect, but the words run through me as if I'm a sieve. Am I really a husk of skin and bone, while my soul floats lost somewhere above the atmosphere? Is that why I hurt so? Can I get it back if I go up to the stars again, or is it burnt up, turned to dust in the flare of our entry? And what of all these groundways women, walking and working and having children, all under the Earth's sway? Are they soulless, too? And Luck . . .

Thinking on Luck is too hard. It makes my chest hurt.

I put my hands to my belly, suddenly remembering Soli's roundness and what Luck and I did in the pool. My own flesh slopes in slightly below my ribs. *But it's early still,* I remind myself. The thought moves my heart to pounding and fills me with a mix of dread and hope. *It could be,* I think. My head feels light. I know I didn't deserve Iri's sacrifice, but if I have Luck's smallone, that might make it worthwhile. Maybe some part of him can live on that way. Is it possible to want something and not want it at once?

When she finishes reading, Miyole serves herself some stew and sits at the table, swinging her legs. She stares at the light tablet, stopping to tap it every once in a while and swallow another mouthful of soup. When she's finished, she cleans her bowl, then neatly folds the tablet back into its square and places it carefully in its drawer. She draws out a sheet of cut metal, along with welding goggles and a little handtool. She sits cross-legged on the floor, twist-clicks the end of the tool so it buzzes to life, and leans over the metal sheet.

"What are you making?" It still hurts to talk, but it's better than thinking.

"Hmm?" Miyole looks up at me through the goggles.

"The hangings." I gesture around. "You're the one what makes them?"

"Oh. Yup." She holds the piece of metal up so I can see. "This one's going to be a fish. My manman sells them on her flights sometimes to help buy my lessons."

"They're beautiful," I say.

Miyole shrugs, but I catch a small smile at the corner of her mouth.

I lie on my cot and pretend I can feel Luck's arms around me as I watch Miyole turn the blank, jagged piece of metal into a scaled fish with lips and eyes and striated fins. The smell of burning metal curls the air. I close my eyes and picture the smallone, Luck's child, tucked in me. I see Iri again, falling. Blood on her teeth.

In the high window, the sky goes from pale, hot white

to deep, creamy blue. All the sounds below us grow louder: the lap of waves on wood, motors gunning, roosters calling, cats scrapping and yowling, people shouting. Wherever we are, it sounds bigger than I imagined. It's as if someone has settled a cook-pot lid over us, and all the noises are trapped inside. Miyole runs up to the roof to start the generator, then back down again to flick on the ceiling fans and the single tube light suspended over the kitchen table. I doze.

The *whum-whum* roar of the mail sloop vibrates overhead, waking me. Miyole dashes to the window. From my cot, I watch Perpétue's ship lights whip overhead and listen for the sigh of the burners winding down. A loud metal bang sounds, and a few seconds later Perpétue's feet beat up the outer stairs. She breezes in, humming to herself, untucks the knife from her belt and drops it on the table alongside a handful of irregular metal scraps.

"Manman, look!" Miyole holds up the fish, its scales shimmering orange in the low light.

Perpétue takes it and holds it at arm's length, careful of the pointed fins. "Lovely." She smiles at Miyole. "Sharp and lovely, like its maker."

"Did you get me more?" the girl asks.

Perpétue tilts her head to the scraps. "On the table."

Miyole skips over. She sifts through the metal while

Perpétue takes a yellowed plastic jug of water down from a shelf.

"How are you, fi? Any better?" Perpétue calls over her shoulder as wets her hands from the jug, then pumps soap into them and rubs them briskly together.

"So," I say, even though I'm not sure.

Perpétue turns to her daughter. "Did she eat?"

"Yes, Manman," Miyole says. "I read her my lessons."

Perpétue splashes water over her hands and dries them on a rag tied to her belt. "That's good, *ma chère.*" She kisses her daughter's head. "Did you eat?"

Miyole nods.

"Good. Go and wash up for bed."

Perpétue heats a bowl of soup for herself, then breaks down the portable stove and stows it beneath the table. She brings her bowl over and pulls up a chair across from my cot.

"You've been sick." She takes a bite and talks around it. "Your friend, that woman who was with you on Bhutto station, she said you have family planetside?"

I nod and swallow to clear my throat. *Iri, the blood on her teeth.* "The so doctor's daughter. She's my blood modrie. My mother's sister."

"Your *tante*?" Perpétue raises her eyebrows. "That's good. That's close family."

I shake my head. "Not really. I never met her. Or, well . . . she never met me."

Perpétue leans back in her chair. "But you know her name. What was it?"

"Soraya Hertz," I say carefully. "But I don't think she knows about me."

"You know where she lives?"

"Mumbai?" I say.

Perpétue waits. When I don't say more, she leans forward in the chair again. "That's it? Just Mumbai?"

I nod.

"No street or neighborhood or quarter?"

I shake my head.

Perpétue sighs and works her tongue around the inside of her bottom lip, eyes on the fan blades spinning in the breeze. "Anything else about her? Anything to help us track her down?"

"She's some kind of doctor," I say. "And my grandfather, her father, he was a doctor, too."

"Do you know his name?"

"He was Hertz, too," I say.

"And your *tante* never married? Never changed her name?" Perpétue rubs her hands together, deep in thought.

Panic strikes me. What if she's changed it? What if it isn't enough to track her down?

"I only saw her the once, some ten turns back," I say. "Do you think we can find her?" If Iri were here, she would know what to do.

Perpétue shakes her head. She rests her forehead on her hands. "I don't know, Ava." She looks up at me again. "Mumbai's a city of a hundred and seventy-five million. Add to that, we don't know if her name's the same, or even if she's still there."

One hundred seventy-five million. It's a number so large my mind can't grab hold of it. My crewe numbered a slip over two hundred, the Æthers somewhere near five hundred. I don't think I've seen more than one or two thousand people in all my life, counting my time at the station concourses. Any number bigger than that might as well not be real. I fix my eyes on the dark square of sky beyond Perpétue's shoulder and hug my sides, willing myself not to cry. I want to go back to sleep, to dream of Luck and the private glow that surrounded us after we sealed ourselves. Or better yet, not to dream at all.

"But we'll try, Ava." Perpétue grips my hand, bringing me back. Her fingers are strong. She presses so hard it hurts. "We'll try."

# CHAPTER 13

"Good, now once more." Perpétue holds my arm as I take another shuffling step.

I moan as I bring my foot forward and let my weight fall on it. My legs burn as though someone's poured fuel into them and set them alight. But I've made it from my cot almost all the way to the small cleanroom tucked away between the common room and the sleeping quarters Perpétue and Miyole share. Perpétue has given me my own skirts again, stiff from drying in the sun, but she burned the rag shirt. I wear one of her soft, thin-woven shirts instead. *Cotton*, she says, from over the sea.

Two weeks awake in her home and I still cannot walk alone. But I haven't bled either, at least there's that to hold on to. The chance of Luck's child. The air hangs thick with heat and waiting.

This East Gyre Perpétue brought me to is nothing like what I thought Earthside would be. My modries all told stories of dust and cold so fierce it made the Earth white, but here the air is always wet and warm, like the dyeroom when the pits are at full boil. Sometimes Perpétue's house bobs and rocks under my feet, and a moaning noise shudders up from below.

The Gyre is a floating city, Perpétue says, cobbled together from flatbed ships, buildings raised on pontoons, and abandoned research flotillas. She talks on it as I practice walking, to keep my mind off the pain. Turns on turns ago, even before the time of Candor and Saeleas, the groundways folk thought the sea would gobble up all their waste, so they fed it into the deeps. But instead, it ended up here, where the waters converge in the Gyre, and formed a vast plain of bottles and bags and milky plastic.

"Some of the first ships came to study the island the trash made, and the microbes in the water," Perpétue explains. "But then, when the Floods drowned the Earth's islands, other people fled here to make a new life, trawling the garbage. That was the start of the Gyre."

*Microbes?* I want to say, but I need all of my breath to keep walking.

Perpétue's house nestles up to the edge of the Caribbean Enclave, lashed to other craft from the lost islands of Jamaica and Cuba and Haiti, what was her ancestors' home. But there're folk from every sunken island here, the ice lands and the Philippines and the land of no serpents. She says a body can make a living scavenging and reselling the bits of plastic that make up the Gyre plain. There's so much the whole city can pick and pick at it and never run out.

"When you're well, you can go out and see for yourself," Perpétue says.

But that would mean facing all the stares and the same questions Perpétue and Miyole had for me, again and again. *What's wrong with your skin? Why can't you walk right? What'd you do to make your own people throw you out?* Just thinking on it makes me want to lie down.

"Don't forget to bend your knees," Perpétue reminds me.

Miyole clomps by in a pair of ragged-edged pants, rubber shoes a size too big, and a faded flower-print dress. She carries a danger-red kite almost as tall as she is.

"Bye, Manman!"

"Miyole?" Perpétue drops my hand. "Where are you going?"

"Kite flying with Kai."

Perpétue bites the corner of her lip. "You aren't going down to the brink, are you?"

Miyole drops her shoulders. "Manman." She draws the word in a groan.

Perpétue sighs. Even with the short time I've been here, I've already caught on they're about to have the same argument as always.

"You know how I feel about the brink, *ma chére.*"

Miyole rolls her eyes. "Nothing's going to happen to me, Manman."

"You tell that to Bjarni's mother."

"You never let me do *anything.*"

"I never let you do anything *dangerous.*"

"Manman." Miyole's voice teeters between a plead and a whine. "I'll be careful, I swear. Kai needs me. His dad's sick again, and Song and Hobb and me all promised we'd help him keep up with the picking. We're flying kites after."

Perpétue sighs again, in resignation this time. "All right. Go. But don't forget to make Kai give you a hook. I don't want you reaching down in that water with your bare hands."

Every morning I watch from the window as little packs of smallones skip the gaps between the pontoons and climb over the footbridges, on their way down to the brink, where they'll help their parents fish out a living from the plastic. Not all of them go. Miyole doesn't, except when she wants. Most mornings she either makes more metal creatures or sits with her tablet, staring and tapping into its light, stopping only to help me walk to the cleanroom or make me take calcium pills to keep my muscles from seizing.

This whole place is a mystery. Perpétue has no man in the house, so she earns her keep ferrying packages from groundways to the station, and between cities here below. Yet she washes and cooks and pushes Miyole to keep pace with her lessons each evening, and even sometimes cooks more for the sick woman with two smallones on the craft next to ours. I asked once where her husband was, but Perpétue's face went masklike. I haven't asked again.

I lie still and sweating most of the day, watching shadows track across the floor as the sun arcs overhead. Sometimes I find myself wishing they would turn the daylights out sooner, and then I remember it doesn't work that way down here. The sun keeps its own time. I close my eyes to it and think on Luck. If it's quiet, I can soothe myself into a sort of half dream—waking by Luck's side, basking in his smile; him singing to our unborn child as it grows larger inside me. I am tender all over, and I remember Modrie Reller and the other wives saying that was a sign you had got a smallone, that you ached, belly and breasts.

But then Perpétue comes and makes me move and bend and grip as long as I can bear it. She promises we can take Miyole's tablet up to the top of what was once a research ship in the neighboring Icelanders' enclave, one of the few spots in the whole Gyre where she can sometimes tap into the wireless networks broadcasting from the distant shores. There are never any storms in the Gyre, she says, but elsewhere the Earth is wracking-full of ferocious winds and sudden rainstorms and columns of white-hot fire bolting from sky to land, and a network is a delicate thing.

"Once you're strong enough," she says, a steadying arm on my elbow. "Once you're well."

I make it to the cleanroom. Perpétue has me sit while she runs a bucket of warm water down from the solar-powered boiler on the roof. She helps me wash my hair, and when it's clean, she sits me on the floor like I'm a smallgirl and combs it. I close my eyes and let myself relax into the gentle tug of the comb as Perpétue's fingers unsnarl my locks. It brings me to mind of Iri combing my hair, and me doing the same for Lifil and my other sisters. I hope the Mercies give me a boy child, but if it's a girl, at least one day I can maybe comb her hair like this.

"Why did you dye your hair?" Perpétue's voice breaks my reverie.

I put my hand up to my head. "What?"

"Your hair," Perpétue repeats. "You've been coloring it, right?"

"It's showing?" I say.

"*Wi,*" Perpétue says. She lifts a lock of hair and runs it through her fingers until they brush my forehead. "To here."

"What?" I rock away from Perpétue. My hair grows fast, but it would take weeks on weeks to grow that much. Near on a deciturn. I've been here, awake, only ten days. It's not possible, unless . . . A terrible thought hits me. How long did I sleep? I thought it was hours, days at most. It can't have been more than a few days.

"No," I say. "That's not right. It can't be."

Perpétue reaches for a hand mirror and holds it so I can see. Black hair spreads over the crown of my head, then drops to faded red at my temples. Both colors look wrong beside my face, the red unnatural, the black stark and hinting at someone I've never been so long as I can remember.

I look up from my reflection. "How long was I asleep?"

Perpétue hesitates.

"Days? A week?"

"A little over a month," Perpétue says. "You were in so much pain, we had to keep you under until the doctor said your calcium levels were high enough." She furrows her brow and presses her lips together as if there might be more.

A month. A deciturn. I push myself clumsily to my feet. Blood sings in my ears. I've been trapped here below over a full deciturn.

"Ava . . ."

I stagger away from her, into the common room.

"Where are you going?" Perpétue calls after me.

I don't answer. A deciturn lost. *A deciturn* . . . I stumble to the front of the house and grapple with the outer door. In truth, I don't know where I'm going. There are steps outside, I know, leading down to the pontoons and up to the roof with its generator and water tanks and Perpétue's chickens, but beyond that . . . I've been locked away too long, seeing the world in snatches from the window. I want—no, I *need* to see the sky.

# CHAPTER • 14

The air is sudden bright. It smells of salt, smoke, and fish. Far off, a horn sounds. The sun peaks high overhead, but the close-packed structures around me close off most of the sky.

*Up*, I tell myself. *Higher.*

I climb the first step. My knees shake and my legs burn. *I need to go up.* I anchor my other foot on the next stair, try to push myself faster. I waver. *I need to see it. . . .* I don't know why. I know I won't be able to see Luck, or the ships, or even the stars from the rooftop, but some part of me insists I try. Without warning, my legs collapse. I sag down on the third step.

"Ava, here." Perpétue appears behind me, her hands outstretched.

"No!" I say. Weeks lost to sleep, and more to Perpétue and Miyole dressing me and feeding me and helping me walk. I want no more of it. I want to haul myself back up to the sky. I want to be a woman again. I want to prove my worth so Perpétue won't throw me out when she finds I have Luck's child inside me.

I crawl up the stairs, the concrete scraping my knees through my thin underskirt. Perpétue watches from below. The heat presses on me, thick and wet. Sweat rolls down my back. The light blinds my eyes, and the sun burns. Another step. My skin feels tight. Another. At last I reach up and feel nothing. Air. I raise my head. Only the square metal walls of the generator, the water tanks, a line of clothes flapping in the breeze, and the weathered driftwood hutch housing Perpétue's chickens break my view of the sky.

I walk stiffly out onto the sun-baked roof. The sky stretches up and up, ablaze with blue. I don't know how, but it seems broader even than the Void, raked with fine, high, swaths of lambs'-wool white in its upper reaches. The sun burns through like bright, new copper. It takes my breath and dulls the pain in my legs.

*Luck*, I think. I wish he could see this with me.

I reach the wall bordering the edge of the roof and raise a hand to shield my eyes. Perpétue's house stands level with the other mismatched structures—some ships, some square houses balanced on pontoons, like Perpétue's, some a floating scavenge of metal, plastic, tarp, and heavy solar panels angled up to the sky. Crossed laundry lines and footbridges made of driftwood connect it all. The structures rise and fall ever so slightly with the sea, as if they rest on a sleeping giant's chest. The distant, muddled din of voices and puttering motors, rooster calls, and the tinny blare of handhelds carry over the rooftops.

Some ten or twelve buildings down, the enclave gives way to the brink. The floating desert of plastic spreads out to the horizon. When the wind skirts across it, it makes a sound like wings. Along its coast, dividing the trash plain from the clean, blue water, a sun-bleached city of ships unfurls as far as I can see. I spin around. To the other side of Perpétue's roof, the world gives way to unbroken blue. The sky and its darker sister, the sea.

"Ava." Perpétue stands at the top of the steps. "Come down. Your skin will burn, fi. You aren't used to the sun."

I swallow. "I don't want to stay inside anymore." I hear the pleading in my tone.

"I know." Perpétue runs her tongue inside her bottom lip. "But you really aren't well enough yet."

"I'll work at it." My voice sounds so small in the wide

open. "Please, so missus, I don't want to be useless. I don't want to lie there and have you . . ." My throat closes around the rest of my words. *I don't want to lose any more time to sleep.*

"If it takes your mind off the hurt, maybe we can give you some chores." Perpétue nods to herself. "Some small things."

"I can cook some, and clean," I say. "I was on livestock duties before. I could keep the chickens. . . ."

Perpétue waves me to a stop. "Slowly, Ava. For now, you can help Miyole with the chickens and maybe cook some. Your body's still healing, fi. Too much at once and you'll hurt yourself."

I let out the breath I've been holding. "Right so."

I feel some small bit more like the girl I was. Feeding chickens is none like minding a whole crewe of women and girls, but at least it's something to keep my hands busy and my mind awake while I wait for Luck's child and try to figure out how to find my modrie.

In the middle of the night, I wake with my innards cramped. I stumble to the cleanroom in the dark, but it's only when I've squatted over the chemical bowl that I feel the blood on my legs. I grope for the light string and pull. It clicks on, filling the room with a brown glow. I stand stock still, staring at the streaks of blood on my thighs and nightshirt until I can make myself understand. My bleeding.

*No,* I think distantly. *That's not right.*

*So I'm not . . .*

A sound halfway between a laugh and a sob breaks out of me. *There's no smallone. There's no piece of Luck left in me.*

I sink down with my back against the door and clutch my waist. I could cry, but I would be making myself. I can't feel anything but the shock of it. I've lost Luck's smallone. I've lost Luck's smallone. It's gone. He's gone. I couldn't even do the one thing I'm made to do right.

I get up and clean myself. I take a rag and soap, and scrub at the stain on my nightshirt. This, I know. Scrubbing. Cleaning. Everything raveled right. I can put away the thinking, feeling part of me and exist only in my hands.

I dress and pad barefoot to the kitchen. The moon angles bright and pale through the high windows. A tide of longing floods my chest. The sky. It will be different at night, more like home. I can glimpse the Void without the sun burning my skin. I open the door softly and struggle up the steps in the dark. The perimeter lights of the Gyre reflect in the water, but above, the sky is black and deep. The stars shimmer and wane, and closer in, the sun-touched fins of satellites and small craft burn steady as they climb and fall in an arc over the sea.

Distant lights track slowly overhead. Is one of them Bhutto station? Is the *Parastrata* still there? Usually we would have restocked our supplies and set sail by now, but what if my father and brother left some men behind to look for me? What if they put out the word of what I did among the other crewes. And what of Iri? And Luck? What's been done with them? Are they there on the station, cast off, or have the *Æther* and *Parastrata* already sounded deep and thrust them out into the Void?

The pain flares back, strong and sudden, through my muscles down to the marrow of my bones. A hard fist of panic presses against my throat. Why am I still here? Why did Iri give herself up for me? What is this body for, if not carrying my husband's children? Why have the Mercies let me live, if I have no purpose?

I am all acid and heat and truth, brimming at the mouth and eyes. My father and brother have killed Iri, certain sure. And Luck is gone, truly gone. Æther Fortune will have turned him out into the Void by now, or killed him some other way too horrible to think on.

"Ava?"

I blink the tears from my eyes.

Perpétue walks toward me. "What are you doing?"

All the softness mothering puts on her face is gone. She folds her arms across the long cotton shirt she wears to sleep. Her legs stick out bare. A deep, puckered scar runs up above her right knee and disappears beneath the shirt's hem.

I gasp. I've seen wounds aboard the *Parastrata*, but few so bad as the mangle of Perpétue's leg. "Did you . . . what happened to your leg?" I ask without thinking.

Perpétue's eyes fall. "Surgery."

"But what . . ."

"You're welcome here, Ava, but there are things I'll never question you about, and I'll ask you to do the same for me," Perpétue says.

"I'm sorry." I never meant to give offense, to her of all people.

Perpétue looks down at the rooftop.

"I'm sorry, so missus," I say again.

Perpétue shakes her head, as if waving the whole matter away. "What's wrong? You couldn't sleep?"

I nod.

"Was it the pain?"

I nod again, though it's a different pain than she means.

Perpétue nods with me, as if she understands. And she

must, with her old wound awful as it is.

I look up at the moon. "I'm bleeding." I can't look at Perpétue as I admit it.

Alarm twitches in Perpétue's face. "Where?" She starts toward me.

I lay a hand between my hip bones where the ache is the worst.

"Oh." Perpétue looks relieved. "That kind of bleeding."

Anguish and confusion twist in me. "I thought . . ."

Perpétue lays a hand on my shoulder and squeezes gently. "No, it's normal, fi. Sometimes when there's too much strain on our bodies, our courses stop. It means you're healing."

I blink. *So I wasn't ever* . . . Relief springs loose in me like a snapped coil, and then confusion mixed with guilt. *Maybe I haven't lost it. Maybe it never was.*

I laugh suddenly, from the shock of it. Perpétue looks at me odd, but I can't help it. My body feels lighter without the weight of the smallone I had imagined growing in me and all the worry that came with it. I'm shamed, thinking on it. What kind of woman am I that wouldn't want a child? But to know I won't have to go through the screaming pain I saw the older girls in? To know no one will look on me with shame for bearing a child with no father? To know my body is my own, and I am beholden to no one but myself? I know these are low reasons and all my sisters and modries would hiss to hear me say them, but I can't help the lightness I feel.

"I'm sorry." I put on a sober face for Perpétue. "I don't mean to laugh. It's only . . ."

"Laugh or cry?" Perpétue finishes for me. "Is that it?"

"Right so." I nod. "Is that so, what you said? About a woman's bleeding?"

"*Wi.*" Perpétue frowns at me. "Didn't your mother teach you these things?"

"No." If my mother had lived, she might have, but Modrie Reller didn't think it proper to talk on such things. Most of what I knew, I learned in whispers from the older girls and from watching the animals. "She died."

"Ah," Perpétue says softly. "And him?" She nods up at Bhutto station shining above us.

I've never spoken Luck's name to her, but I suppose I've said enough for her to piece together his existence.

I swallow. "He's gone, too."

"You loved him?" she asks.

I nod.

"It's not an easy thing, being widowed." Perpétue

looks out at the ocean, a light breeze ruffling her hair.

*Widowed.* I don't know if I have any right to that word, but I feel it fits in me. I wince as a fresh stab of pain shoots across my shoulders.

"You're hurting, fi." Perpétue takes my arm. "Come below. I've got some painkillers that'll help you sleep."

I lean on Perpétue, and with her help I begin the slow descent to the welcome darkness of her home.

# CHAPTER • 15

Every day the pain eases. I help Miyole with the chickens, and soon Perpétue lets me cook, though at first I have to fight their stubborn collapsible stove to come away with something that's not burnt. I'm not used to cooking with live flames.

Still, Perpétue seems glad. It gives her more time for checking Miyole's lessons in the evenings, and the two of them take turns reading to me about the Earth, its oceans and forests and molten depths, its deserts and snows, its peoples and their many wars and fragile peaces. They read reckonings of tides rising and cities turned to shoals, battles over blood-soaked strips of land, and the call to push off into the depths of the stars.

One day, when Perpétue's away on her runs, Miyole

calls at me as I come down from hanging out the wash.

"Ava! Hey, Ava!" She sits at the table, her tablet open in front of her. "Can you help me?"

I drop the laundry basket inside the door and wipe my hands on my skirts. "What do I do?" I come close and stand beside her. The soft blue light—the one Miyole said means it's casting out for a signal—pulses.

She holds up the tablet. She taps it and drags her pointer finger over its surface. Two columns of grouped symbols spring up. "All you have to do is read me the words and see if I can spell them right."

I hesitate. I haven't told Miyole and Perpétue I can't read; it's never come up. I take the tablet and sit across from her. It rests cool in my fingers, heavier than what I guessed with my eye. I scan the sheet for something, anything, I recognize. Nothing. Not even an *A*.

"Orange," I say at random, too loud.

"Orange," Miyole says evenly. "O-R-A-N-G-E."

I pretend to trail my finger down to the next word, as I've seen my father and Jerej do over shipping invoices. "Machine," I say.

Miyole frowns. "M-A-C-H-I-N-E."

"Um . . ." I bring my eyes up from the pad and search the room for inspiration. "Welding apron."

"Ava." Miyole narrows her eyes at me. "What are you doing?" She grabs the tablet from me and scans it. "None of those words are even on here."

My face goes hot. This is all wrong. I'm alone, cast down on a planet what pains me with every breath. I can barely work a flight of stairs, and a little girl is scolding me. Me, who knew every quirk of the *Parastrata*'s kitchens, who could walk her halls sunblind, who could have run all the women's work someday. Loneliness sticks in my throat. Every day, my old life is fading. I can no longer even call up Luck's ghost to wrap its arms around me. I'm beginning to forget the sound of his voice.

"I . . . ," I start, and then stop again. "I'm no good at it."

"At what?" Miyole says.

"Reading," I say. "My . . . my Luck . . ." I haven't spoken out his name before. If Perpétue were here, she would catch the break in my words, pick up another piece of my past, but Miyole only stares, kicking her legs under the table and waiting for me to continue. I clear my throat. "Luck was going to teach me."

"I could teach you," Miyole offers. "I was teaching Kai, but he said it was boring. I know the alphabet and spelling and grammar and all that."

"I don't . . ."

But she's already running for the ancient chest of drawers. She returns with a pointed stylus and kneels on a chair beside me, head bent over the tablet.

"You want the alphabet first." She taps the screen and traces the stylus over its smooth surface, then hands it back to me. A large letter A stands out in the top left corner.

I look up at her. Is she going easy on me, starting with one of the only letters I already recognize? "You won't . . ." I clear my throat. "You won't tell your mother, will you?"

Miyole chews her lip. "No. Not if you don't want."

"Good." I let out a breath. "Thank you."

"That's *A*." Miyole nudges the tablet closer. "It's the first. Try copying it."

I grip the stylus and make my mark.

Miyole nods, serious. "That's good." I hear the echo of Perpétue in her voice. She takes the tablet back from me and draws another letter. "Now try the next one. That's *B*."

By the time Miyole finishes with the alphabet, I ache from the roots of my eyes all the way to the back of my head. My letters stand up wobbly on the screen. I don't remember half of them, even with the little song Miyole sings to help keep them in order.

"This is worthless." I push myself away from the table. I need something to keep me busy, something to make me not feel so low and dull. I grab the biggest cookpot, upend a jug of desalinated water into it, slam the cookstove on the table, and start snapping its pieces together. Miyole, so smart. What does she know of how awful hard the world is, with her nice, shiny tablet and her lessons and her ship captain mother? My chest is full of bitter black, smoldering and ready to ignite. I pick up the pot and bring it down on the stove so hard the water sloshes everywhere.

Miyole sits frozen next to my empty seat. "Careful, Ava." Her voice trembles. "You'll break it."

I stop, hands gripping the cookstove's handles. A tear slips from my eye and lands in the water pot. I'm so churned up I can't tell whether I'm crying from frustration or sorrow or anger, or some awful mix of the three. I turn away and pick up a sack of beans.

When I turn around again, Miyole sits tense in her chair, hands tight around the tablet, as if she might use it to fend me off. Her mouth is set in a line I know I've seen on Perpétue's face too, something older than her years, something fierce that knows what it is to be broken and to mend.

"Don't be angry," she says.

"I'm sorry." I drop the bag on the table. "I'm sorry, I didn't . . ." But I don't know what to say, so I go about making our dinner, even though it's some early and I'll need to heat it again when Perpétue comes home. Miyole stares at her tablet without touching it, refusing to look on me.

I close the lid over the cookpot. "You want to hear a story?" I ask, gentle, for it's what I remember most of my mother, the stories she told when I was frightened.

Miyole looks up. She's only a smallgirl again. She stares at me without blinking some moments, then nods.

"What kind?" I ask.

Miyole looks away. "An adventure."

"What about the story of how Lord Candor came to be a hero?" I say.

"Who?" Miyole screws up her face at me.

"Candor," I say. "One of the fathers of the crewes. A great man."

Miyole shrugs. "Okay."

I take a breath. "Right so."

"When Lord Candor married his secondwife Mikim, she was young and fair. As the years passed, she gave him many fine sons. But Mikim grew haughty, for Candor's firstwife Saeleas had given him only girls, and Mikim knew her sons would succeed their father.

"Now, in those days the skies were wild, and men had much to fear, not only from the cold kiss of the Void and the chaos wrought by storms, but from ship strippers and corsairs. Candor fought many battles with these raiders, and guarded his sons and wives well, for it was known the corsairs took all they captured as slaves. Then one day, on the long dark trek back from the farthest outpost, three corsairs swept down on Candor's ship, blazing fire. In his wisdom, Candor fled. His ship's guns had been crippled in the fray. He hid his craft in the shadow of a moon, while above the corsairs prowled, searching for him.

"The women and smallones of Candor's ship were much afraid. Mikim gathered them together in the belly of the ship and bid everyone sing to drive away their fear. But once their voices joined, their song grew so loud, it rang through the decks and out into the black of the Void itself.

"And the corsairs pricked up their ears.

"Candor hurried below. 'Please,' he begged. 'Quiet your voices. The raiders stalk above, and only silence will save us.'

"Candor's other wives fell silent at once, but Mikim laughed. 'Husband, how little you know! Our voices will never reach their ears. The Void is vast.'

"'All the same,' Candor, ever patient, said. 'I beg you, obey me this once and keep silent, for the sake of our sons and your sister-wives.'

"But Mikim did not mind her husband. When Candor left, again she raised her voice and sang. Her song drove through the ship's hull and fell on the corsairs' ears. And before Candor could fix his craft and bring her up fighting, the raiders fell on him. They laid open his ship and snatched away all his wives and smallones, including Mikim and her sons. Candor they mocked and left for dead on the barren moon.

"Candor's heart filled with grief and rage. With what few of his men remained, he rebuilt his ship, stronger and faster, made it a machine of war. And with it, he chased down the raiders who had stolen his family, and one by one, reclaimed his wives and sons, all except Mikim. Candor harried the corsairs out into the deep, blank edges of the Void, but he never found his secondwife. The Mercies saw fit to humble her and keep her from her kin until the end of her days. So her name hangs as a banner of warning to all who harbor rebellion in their hearts.

"In memory of Mikim's fault, his other wives gathered together and agreed. From that day, though a woman might hear the sacred songs, she would no more sing them, nor lift her voice above her husband's. So the songs and scrolls of the Word were given over to men's keeping, and there they rest safe to this day.

"This pleased the Mercies well, and they blessed Candor with many sons. By faithful Saeleas, he fathered the great Neren, whose deeds are ever sung. In time, his children numbered so many they took up their own ships and spread to every reach of the Void. So Candor's name is ever spoken, and all his children bless him."

I fold my hands on the metal table and smile, lost in the sweet rhythm of the story and the memory of my mother's voice reciting it.

"That's ridiculous," Miyole says. "No one could have heard her."

I blink away my reverie. "What?'

"It wasn't her fault," Miyole says. "That isn't how sound works in space. Don't you know?"

"It's . . . it's the story," I stammer. "That's just the way it is."

"It's stupid the way it is," Miyole says. "Candor and them were out to find someone to blame, that's all. They wanted to make themselves feel better 'cause they couldn't find her in the end, so they made her the bad guy."

"No . . ."

"Ava," Miyole says in a voice that brings all my arguing to an end. "That Mikim lady was right. Sound doesn't travel in space."

My mouth hangs open. The Void is my home. Surely that's one thing I should know more about than Miyole. Still, she every day trots out words and ideas I've never run across before—*canopy* and *combustion engine* and *extinct*. I can't even hold down the letters that roll so easily from her tongue. She could be right. She's most like right.

"I don't . . . ," I begin.

A shirtless smallboy with a thick cap of straight black hair and skin like browned butter comes hurtling through the door. "Miyole!" His eyes are wide. "You got to come down and see!"

Miyole swivels in her chair. Her face comes alight. "Kai!" But then she glances at me and her smile drops. "I can't. I'm not s'posed to leave her."

Kai takes me in with a quick look. "You're that Ava girl, huh?"

"Right so," I say.

"Bring her with you," he says to Miyole. "You've got to see this."

I do my best to keep up with them. They clatter down Perpétue's steps and streak across the swinging driftwood bridges connecting each low-slung barge to the next. By the time I reach the bottom, they've disappeared. I pause. All the Gyre is quiet around me in the heat of the day. The barges creak as they bob in the water and the pontoon deck burns my bare feet.

To my right, the doors over the insulated well where Perpétue locks up her sloop at night stand closed. I edge out over them and peer down into the gap between Perpétue's barge and the next. Two meters down, the gap turns to a deep, sloshing pit of seawater. Miyole and Perpétue told me the depths are full of sharks, awful black-eyed fish with rows of jagged teeth. I shudder and back away.

"Ava!" Miyole waves to me from the top of the neighboring barge. "Hurry up!"

I pick my way over the rickety footbridge. The sea moves, blue and bottomless, beneath my feet. I try not to look down.

Miyole grabs my hand as soon as I reach the other side and pulls me into a fast walk. I wish she would slow down so I could take in more of the Gyre—there's so much more to see than I could make out from the roof—but she's anxious to catch up with Kai and reach the brink. My first real brush with the city is a blur of music blaring tinny from the upper levels of barges, faded paint peeling from the walls, a boy with a pole full of dangling fish balanced over his shoulder, and sweat-sheened men and women building new walls or lookouts on their roofs. One of the barges has a glass bottom, clear down to the sea and all the dark shapes moving in it. I pull Miyole to a halt when we step up onto it.

"What's wrong?" She frowns at me.

I look down.

She laughs. "What, this? It's solid." She jumps up and down to demonstrate. "Don't worry. We go over it all the time."

"Please." I close my eyes. "Don't do that."

Miyole sighs and stops. "You sound like my manman." She tugs at my hand again. "Come on. We're almost there."

As we near the brink, the raised pontoons give way to a broad shore of wood and plastic platforms built level with the water. Rafts and small aluminum boats with oars rest at their moorings. Beyond, the waste plain extends, flat and bleached by sun and salt, to the horizon. A clump of people has gathered by the very tip of the shore. Kai spots us from the back of the crowd and waves. We hurry to him.

"It's a monster," Kai whispers in hushed awe as we sidle to the front of the crowd. "Miko and her boys found it washed up in the middle of the plain. They say it's fresh. Maybe a shark killed it."

At the water's edge, a stout woman with short-cropped black hair and wrinkled, sun-browned skin stands over the dead beast. Its grayish, rubbery body splits into eight puckered arms, all twined around one another in death. One glazed eye looks on us.

Miyole shoves Kai's shoulder. "That's no monster, fishbrain. It's a squid."

"A giant squid," the woman—Miko, she must be—standing over it corrects. She nudges its body with the butt of a hooked spear. "Forty footer."

"Did a shark kill it?" Kai asks eagerly.

Miko shakes her head. "No. No marks on it, see?"

"Those don't come up to the surface, not on purpose." Miyole looks to Kai and me and the people standing behind us. "They're deep creatures. I read about it."

"It's a bad sign," says a red-faced woman with hair the yellow-white of the waste plain. "Means a storm's stirring up."

The man beside her laughs. "Everyone knows the Gyre doesn't get storms. It's what makes it the Gyre."

"What do you know about it, eelkin?"

"More than you, you great frozen shark-breathed bat."

The crowd breaks out in shouts.

". . . could have died of anything . . ."

"Who do you think you are, telling me how the sea is?"

". . . pure chance . . ."

". . . could have killed it, at that . . ."

Miko slams the butt of her spear against the dock—three short raps. Everyone falls silent.

"My sons and I scavenged it, so I'll say what it means." Her voice arcs over the crowd. She grins. "And I say it means a feast."

A shout of agreement goes up, and men and women with their fishing knives and hooked spears close in to help butcher the beast, their quarrels forgotten.

That night, a thousand small cookfires spring up at the lip of the brink. Some of the smallones fetch their kites, and we watch them flutter against the sunset. Miyole and I sit with Kai's family around their raised fire trough while chunks of squid steam and crackle over the flames. When I bite into my share and its hot juices run down my chin, it's enough to make me forget the hard lines of pain in my legs and back. Miyole tells a story she read, about a fish-tailed girl who falls in love with a prince and trades her voice for a pair of legs. Only when she gets them, it ends up the prince doesn't love her and every step she takes is like walking on knives. The sadness of it hangs on to me even when Miyole is done. Then Kai's brothers and sisters push a little stringed instrument into their father's hands.

"Sing with us, Ava," Miyole begs when Kai's father starts to hum a song they all know.

I shake my head. I couldn't sing, even if I knew the words. I sit listening to the strum of music and popping fire and the gentle lap of water, and I wonder if there really might be such a place as doesn't have storms.

# CHAPTER • 16

Miyole kneels beside Kai and his older brothers and sisters on his family skiff as his mother paddles them into the Gyre plain. The sun hasn't broken above the water yet, but the sky is lavender and warming. The waste plain radiates a soft, eerie glow, as if it's lit from within, rather than above. Some of the other scavengers have already rowed so far out into it, they're nothing more than dark shapes on the horizon.

"Be back before the sun's high," I shout to Miyole. "Your mother said."

"I will," she yells back. "Don't forget to practice your reading."

"Right so!"

I wave again and turn away. Miyole's tablet keeps

stories inside it. Now I've got my alphabet, she wants me to try out the sounds of words by reading stories what try to trick with their words that sound near the same. There are so many words to remember, new kinds of animals and things to do with the sky and the movement of the Earth. Some what I thought were empty words—*fog* and *wane* and *flock*—make more sense now than ever they did closed up in the *Parastrata*.

But oh, the numbers. Much simpler. Clean, elegant marks, one for each of my fingers. Miyole helps me draw them on my knuckles in ink, and I match the symbols to my counting as I cook and wash, scatter grain for the chickens on the rooftop, and draw my mind away from my little lingering pains. Perpétue still offers me her pills, but they give me drowning dreams. The worst is the one where Modrie Reller feeds me stones and leads me to the dark water gap between the pontoons, then pushes my head below the waves. All the while, Lifil and Miyole splash together on the sunlit surface.

I wander back over the Gyre's bridges. This is my favorite time of day, the hush straight before sunrise. Most of the scavengers have already gathered on the shore and everyone else is still indoors, cooking breakfast, or waking children, or hanging out clothes to dry. I can drift among the houses and ships alone, my own ghost.

"Luck," I whisper. "Are you there?"

And I know it's only fancy, but I listen anyway.

"I miss you," I tell the air, and I wait for some sign, a gull blown off course or a sudden shift in the wind.

Perpétue's house comes into view, and my emptiness slips away. There is no room for ghosts here. I pad across the deck and mount the stairs. I have chickens to feed and laundry to hang, and then reading to practice. Twice now, Perpétue has offered to take me up the Icelanders' tower to search the network for my modrie, but I've put her off. The more I learn about reading, the more I see what a fool I'd seem if she found out how little I know. Sometimes I take out Miyole's tablet and sit looking into its bright, blank screen, trying to work up the will to bring it to life, practice tapping my own words into it. But the most I can ever do is stare at its pulsing blue network light and the word fading in and out beside it, the one I know best now. *Searching . . . Searching . . .*

"Ava?" Perpétue's voice rings up from the sloop's docking well. "Is that you?"

I pause on the stairs, hurry to the side of the well, and poke my head over its lip.

Perpétue stands ankle deep in salt-clouded water,

working a hand pump. The ship rises on its struts behind her.

She shades her eyes and looks up at me. "We've got a leak. Give me a hand?"

"Right so." I lower myself down the ladder and splash in beside her. The cold water seeps into my skirt hem, making it leaden.

"Keep pumping." Perpétue turns the handle over to me and kneels in the water to feel along the seam where the docking well's floor meets the wall. She doesn't seem to mind the cold water soaking her up to her knees, but all I can think on is how fast the docking well would fill if the leak got worse, how my heavy clothes might drag me to the bottom as the water rose around my head. I wouldn't even need a bellyful of stones. I pump faster.

"Ah, *wi*. Here it is." Perpétue sloshes to her feet and fetches an L-shaped piece of metal and a cold fuser, like the kind I saw Jerej use. She kneels again. The cold fuser fills the water with blue light and a muffled hum, and the surface boils in sudden, choppy ripples. But then there's a choking sound, and the light cuts out sudden.

"Damn." Perpétue pulls the fuser out of the water and smacks its side with the heel of her hand. "Always shorting."

I hesitate. If this machine's anything like the piston seal or the coaxer Soli showed me how to fix, I might could do it. Couldn't I? Do I dare ask her? Before I let myself think on it too hard, I push the words out. "Could I look at it, so missus?"

"You?" Perpétue's face is all surprise.

"Right so." I try not to mind how the water's creeping up along my leg and hold out my hand. "I could try."

Perpétue shrugs and hands it over. "You can't make it any worse."

I turn the fuser over in my hands, careful to avoid its burning cold mouth. It looks well raveled, all except a hairline crack in the groove above its trigger. I carry the cold fuser over to the wall where Perpétue keeps her fixers mounted and choose one I know will make the machine's casing open easy as a hand unfolding. Perpétue drops a worktable down from the wall and snaps on a light for me. The water laps at my calves, but I clamp my teeth together and ignore it. Perpétue doesn't seem to mind, but then again, she's wearing boots up to her knees. I lay the cold fuser open and lean in close to inspect it. Tiny beads of moisture dot the workings and the metal around the power cell.

"The seal's cracked," I say. "It's the water what's shorting it out."

I reach for a drying fix and hold it over the fuser long enough to steam off the water, then check the connections and snap the machine back together. It closes seamlessly around itself. All the while, Perpétue watches me.

"D'you have any of that gummy stuff what's sticky on one side and metal on the other?" I ask. The water touches the back of my knees.

Perpétue raises her eyebrows. "Steel adhesive?" She presses the catch on a drawer built into the wall and rummages through its depths. She comes up with a tight-coiled spool of exactly the stuff I need. "This?"

"Right so." I nod my thanks. I pull off a strip and press it over the crack above the trigger. *Quick, quick*, I tell it. I wish Perpétue would go back to pumping, but I don't dare say so, and she seems content to watch me work, even as the water inches up around us. As soon as the steel tape finishes sealing itself, I mash the fuser's bright red button. It powers up with a healthy whine and all its indicator lights blink on, one by one.

"Try it now." I hand the fuser over to Perpétue.

She gives me a long, appraising look.

But I'm thigh deep in saltwater and my chest is a panic. I hurry to the pump and begin bailing seawater back out of the docking well while Perpétue finishes working on the leak. I don't look up again until the fuser goes quiet and the water drops below my knees.

I find Perpétue watching me. "You want to go on a run, fi?" she asks.

"I . . . I don't . . . a run?"

"I've been needing a first mate to help me. Load cargo. Maybe learn a thing or two about flying." Perpétue turns the cold fuser in her hands. "I always thought maybe Miyole would want to fly with me when she was older, but really, I could use the help now. Runs are safer that way. And you." Perpétue carefully hangs the cold fuser on the wall, next to all her other fixers. "You've got more in you than feeding chickens, fi."

I blink at her. Me, flying? My father's words rattle around the back of my head. *You can't nurse a baby and run a navigation program.*

"I don't know." I look from Perpétue to the sloop to the square of cloud-patched sky above our heads.

Perpétue follows my gaze. "They threw you out," she says. "That doesn't mean you're worthless. It only means they didn't see your worth."

I look back at her in the shadow of the docking well.

Her jaw is set and her eyes alight. "You can show them," she says. "You can make your own way."

In that moment, something ignites in me, as if all the pain and sorrow of these past months was fuel soaking the rags of my heart, and Perpétue's words a torch held to it.

I am angry. There's power in that. I can taste it in my mouth, giving me heat, giving me something to live for.

"Right so," I say.

We spend the night at home, check to make sure Miyole has everything she needs for the day, and set out before the sun breaks. I'm dressed in Perpétue's old clothes: a faded red shirt speckled with white dots and cinched to my waist with a thick brown belt, calf-high boots, and a pair of heavy work trousers. The feel of fabric hugging my legs is some odd, and the boots more so. It feels some like armor, the kind Lord Candor was said to wear.

Perpétue laughs when she sees me squirming in my new clothes. "Get used to it, fi." She smiles roughly. "It's time to see what you can do."

Perpétue's hands dance over the controls as we lift off. The Gyre shrinks beneath us, and for the first time, I see how truly vast the waste plain is. A body could row for days and not reach West Gyre on the other side.

"Where are we going?" I ask as a long strand of green islands skips by beneath us.

"West." Perpétue doesn't look away from the viewport. "And north. I've got a hull full of scavenge to sell in Mirny. Then we take those profits to a rice broker down in New Bangkok and cart the rice and probably some desalination pills back to the suppliers in the Gyre. I want you to watch me, Ava. Follow what I do."

Perpétue talks me through some small tricks to running the sloop. Here is the throttle, for pushing fuel and pressing us faster. Here, the altitude readout, always pulsing with numbers. I test myself to see if I can sort them out and name them before they blink away. Some three hundred kilometers out, the long-range coms finally pick up a network signal and flicker to life.

We break over a rocky coast and a green stretch of grasslands. Perpétue guides the sloop north. Ice forms on the craft's wings and the land rolls up into hills, and then mountains, carpeted thick with spiking green trees. *Pines,* Perpétue names them. Every now and then a city or a town scabs up out of the forest, as if the Earth has cracked and buildings and lights and roads are what leaked out. Farther north, a fine white dust cakes the land. *Snow.* The Earth flattens to a dull, white-gray swath.

"There." Perpétue points.

I squint. "I don't see . . ." But then I do. A giant hole

lies open in the Earth north and west of us, whorled around the edges with thin lines spiraling down into its depths, as if some enormous creature has bored down into the bedrock. Tiny, snow-covered buildings scatter out around it like pebbles.

Perpétue takes us lower. "Mirny used to mine diamonds, before people figured out how to manufacture them." As we slow and dip down, the thin lines around the hole's mouth become roads leading down into the mine. "You've got to be careful to keep away from the cut. The air currents suck ships down in there all the time."

Perpétue kicks the engines down to quarter power and slows us over a fenced-in landing field covered in a dirty slush of ice melt. A handful of ships sit in dock. Groundcrawlers cart pallets of scavenge from the ships—metals, plastics, foams, paper and cardboard, even what looks like a rotting mash of plants wrapped tight in translucent packing sheets.

We settle down in an empty corner of the docking yard. I follow Perpétue below, where she pulls two thick coats from a storage locker in the berth and hands one to me. She unseals the door and leads us out into the gray. The cold bites my lungs. The smell of cooking oil soaks the air as one of the groundcrawlers rumbles by. *Corn diesel*, I remember. One of those things Miyole read to me about. I rub my hands together and look around. Bare white trees spindle up beyond the fence. The air rattles with groundcrawler engines and the shriek of their forked limbs as they lift stacks of pallets. Men and women, so bundled up in hats and coats I can't tell them apart, shout over the roar. My breath comes out smoke.

We don't stay long at the docking yard. Perpétue speaks to a woman with chapped cheeks in a thick, rolling language I don't understand—*"Kak dela! Skol'ko let, skol'ko zim!"*—while the groundcrawlers empty stacks of scavenged plastic from our sloop's berth. Perpétue and the woman grip arms and slap each other on the back, and the woman hands over five small squares of pay plastic all threaded through with copper circuits. Then we're off again.

Mountains scrape by beneath us, then a pale, stony desert, and shiny rivers gold under the sun. At last we drop lower and skim a vast plain, divided into a patchwork of flooded fields. Men and women bend, ankle deep in mud, then shield their eyes and look up as the shadow of our ship passes over them. In the distance, a city rises out of the haze.

We set down in one of the mud-washed docking yards, next to a high cinder-block wall. Perpétue leaves me to guard the sloop while she goes off in search of the rice broker. She keeps gone a long while. At midday, I open my lunch tin and find Miyole has packed it full of tatty reading books, the paper kind, what she and Kai must have stolen from a kindling pile somewhere. They're all stories for smallones about talking dogs and magical creatures like zebras. I try to read them as I wait. I do. But my brain stumbles and sticks. I toss them into the empty berth, knowing I've sounded out the words like Miyole's showed me, but I haven't gotten the trick of how to piece them together into sense. I cradle my head in my hands. Give me numbers any day.

Perpétue finally comes back with the rice broker, a short man with slick hair and a silver jacket, followed by a line of thin, bare-chested men with sacks balanced on their shoulders. No loading machines here. The rice broker tries to have the men stow the rice straight away, but Perpétue stops them and slashes open the top of one bag with her knife.

She half smiles at the rice broker. "No sand this time, I see."

"No, lady." He rubs one hand nervously across his neck. "No sand."

She drops two pay squares into his hands. "Good. Let's keep it that way."

Perpétue whistles up at the children watching our trade from along the wall and tosses a handful of candies in their direction. They yelp and spring after them.

"*Kob kun kaa,* lady!" shouts one girl missing both her front teeth.

By the time we make it back to the Gyre, hull full of rice, the sun is a pink ribbon slipping down over the horizon. We land the sloop at the supply docks some clicks down from home, sign our cargo in with the suppliers, and join the other captains who run supplies around a fire one of them lit in a metal drum.

Perpétue presses a sweating bottle into my hand and takes another for herself. She pops the top from mine with the dull side of her knife and clinks our bottles together. "To first mates."

I tilt the bottle back. The liquid hits my tongue, sour and full and cold. I make a face.

"Ah, young one here," a round woman in a bright purple dress teases. "You never had a beer before, kid?"

I shake my head.

Everyone laughs, but it's all smiles and good nature, even from the men, as if I'm one of them.

"Where'd you find this one, Perpétue?" the round woman asks.

"This is Ava. She's got the makings of a natural mechanic," Perpétue says proudly, and she tells them all about the cold fuser and my first run. No one notices she never answers the question, and soon enough, talk turns to other things, the price of fuel cells and the monster Miko found and what it means.

"I'm going up spaceside again soon," Perpétue says as we stand by the fire. "I want you to join me, fi."

"Oh," I say. It comes on me how the Gyre has become my life, how the constant pull of work has smoothed away the bits of glass still in my flesh, and here I am, washed ashore and laughing, one of a crewe. And now to face the Void again . . . I look up at the sky, with its stars hidden by the fat yellow moon. To see the place where I lost Luck and Iri and everything I knew. Sadness tugs at me, but it doesn't push me under. I wonder if that means my soul is growing back.

"How do you feel, going up there again?" Perpétue asks.

"I don't know." I grip the bottle tighter. My crewe will be long off on a new run, but I can't shake the prickles of fear what crawl over my skin when I think on my father's face, on Jerej and Æther Fortune. What if they aren't gone? What if they're hanging in port, waiting for me to surface? What if they're still looking for me?

I hug my arms close. I'm worrying too much. They surely aren't there anymore. And to see the stars again in all their unblinking span, to see that one piece of home . . .

"I wouldn't ask if I thought you weren't ready," Perpétue says.

I draw a deep breath and nod. I'm going back to Bhutto station.

# CHAPTER • 17

I button my red shirt, fasten the work trousers over my hips, and buckle the belt around my waist. At first I felt naked without my skirts, but now my legs swing free and light. I tie my data pendant snug against my neck. Only one thing left to do before we go. I comb my hair forward with my fingers and stare into Perpétue's cleanroom mirror. My hair tumbles past my waist, straight and black to my ears, then wisping in faded, brittle red the rest of the way. I hold out a hank of it, raise Perpétue's kitchen shears, and saw away until the long red locks fall to the floor. I lift another handful and cut. Lift, cut, fall, lift, cut, fall, until my hair hangs ragged around my ears.

I stare at my face. I am a different girl. Older, cheeks sharp-planed from my months recovering and working aboard the sloop. I'm stronger, too, I can tell, although my body still feels heavy and ungainly under this Earth's weight. But my skin has warmed from pale gray to a honey hue now that I'm more accustomed to the sun.

I gather the hair from the floor for composting, snap off the light, wave good-bye to Miyole, and jog down the stairs to where Perpétue awaits me in the docking well. She's been teaching me fixes. New fixes, better, more intricate than ever the ones I learned off Soli, but the same at their core. I can reroute power to the secondary fuel drive, unjam the landing gear, swap out the glow panels in the cockpit, operate the emergency cooling sluice, and more besides. And now, Perpétue says, I'm good enough with numbers I can try my hand at flying.

I pull myself up into the cockpit. Perpétue glances sidelong at my hair from the copilot's seat but doesn't say anything. I settle myself into the captain's chair, look down at the array of instruments spread out under my hands, and try to recall how to breathe.

"Remember, how I showed you," Perpétue says.

I force a breath and tick down my checklist. Check my safeties, engine warm-up and temperature readings a go, hull pressurized, coolant levels good, no smallones or animals lingering under the thrust burners.

We kick up in a cloud of salt and grit. The engine reaches a healthy rumble-roar as we shoot up over the Gyre. My heart goes weightless. I push the ship faster, riding the thrill of commanding something so powerful.

"Steady, fi." Perpétue winks at me, and I realize I'm grinning.

I ease off the thrusters. The Gyre shrinks to an uneven gray line between the blue and the waste plain, and then we rise higher still, until the Earth lies curved below us. The atmosphere thins and darkens. High winds rock the cabin.

"Are you ready?" Perpétue checks her shoulder straps.

"Right so." I push us forward, and the ship surges under my touch.

We break through the atmosphere with a small shudder. My stomach lurches as the ship's artificial gravity takes over. My lungs blossom full of air, and the small lingering pains I carry with me vanish. I am featherlight and strong.

"You feel that?" Perpétue asks.

I turn to her slowly, eyes wide. The hairs on my scalp prickle. I nod.

"Every time," Perpétue says, and lets out a giddy laugh. "Every single time it's like that."

I smile with her and breathe deep, drunk with the

sudden luxury of not fighting my body for movement and air. Our ship rotates as we pierce the Void, so the stars spin out against the black, like a fan opening. Perpétue has me guide the sloop around the Earth's curve until the lights of Bhutto station come in to view, blinking in high rotation above the planet. I grip the controls. Is the *Parastrata* docked there? The *Æther*?

"Easy, Ava." Perpétue's voice nudges me gently. "Check our vectors."

I drop my eyes to the instrument readouts. The numbers trickle up and down. It still takes all my concentration to translate them into sense.

"We need to bear up," I say, eyes locked to the vector display. "Thirty-four degrees portside."

"Good." Perpétue watches as I guide the ship smoothly into our assigned entry bay. We touch down with a muffled *thunk*. "Pretty soon I can kick back while you fly this thing on all our runs."

I laugh, but nervously. I'm already scanning the bay. We power down and unload our cargo of smelted plastic and cold-packed fish onto a trolley. Six other small ships share the dock with us, and the floor is thick with men. Some of them drag their cargo across the floor on carts like ours, while others sit with their legs dangling from their ships' open berths, spitting tobacco on the grimy floor and swilling coffee. I try to keep my head down, but I start every time someone brushes by me, or when the men break out in riotous laughter. I can't help looking up, searching faces for a sign of someone I know.

One of the men catches me looking. A rangy, bearded man in a knit cap. "Hey, girlie!" He whistles, as if to call a stray dog. "Girlie. Hey."

I catch Perpétue's look telling me to act like I don't hear, but it's too late. My eyes meet his.

"I got a nice slot on my crewe for you." He slaps his knee in invitation. "If you don't mind working up a sweat."

I stare at him, fish mouthed, till his meaning sinks in, then flush hot and duck into the sloop's hold with my face on fire.

"Eyes on your own crewe, *hákarl* sucker," Perpétue spits back. She sticks her head in the hold. "Ava—"

"I'm sorry." I pick up another bundle of plastic and drop it on the hand truck with a clatter. "I don't know how to do this right, Perpétue."

"You're doing well," she says. "I should have warned you. Around these crewes, you can't be a girl. You've got to be hard, be one of them. Here." She grabs my hands and molds them into fists, then pries the center finger up.

"That'll speak wonders for you."

We try it out on the bearded crewman as we climb out of the hold. He goes red. His mates laugh and hoot and prod him until he shakes his head and goes back to his work. But we're left in peace to unload the rest of our cargo and truck it to the distribution deck for our pay.

Perpétue presses a slip of pay plastic into my hand. "There's information ports you can rent outside the commissary on tier five. See if you can dig up something about that *tante* of yours."

"Alone?" I ask, suddenly uncertain. I've got only the barest idea how to use an information port, and that from watching Perpétue do it on our runs. "What about you?"

"I'm going to pick up some fission cakes, and then I'll be down on tier thirteen, taking in packages," Perpétue calls as she wheels our empty trolley to the service lift. "I'll find you when we've got enough of a load to head back."

I stand on the deck, surrounded by pallets of fruit and steel sheeting, clutching the thin square of plastic. I make for the personnel lifts, head ducked low, but I can't keep my eyes from fluttering up to the face of every man who passes me.

I close myself in the lift. A strange, dizzy familiarity tugs at me. If I shut my eyes, all I see is Jerej running, the door closing, the look on his face, and then blood on Iri's teeth. My father, holding her down. *Soraya Hertz, don't forget. . . .* I open my eyes. I'm alone in the lift. The keypad stares back at me. Only this time, I recognize the etched numbers: TIERS 1 TO 42. A thrill zips through me. One to forty-two. What perfect lines the world falls into with this small scrap of knowledge. I'm a different girl than I was the last time I was here. I don't have anything to be afraid of.

I push the button for tier five. The lift drops, and when the doors roll open for me, I feel even in my skin, balanced and right as I haven't felt since the moment I stepped off the *Parastrata* for the first time.

Steam billows up to the commissary ceiling from a row of cookpots and woks. The cooks shuffle their pans over red electric coils and shout back and forth with the people waiting in line. Thick support pillars jut up throughout the room, each spoked by a circle of metal carrels housing the information ports. I slide into an empty one and sit staring blankly at it. A series of silent advertisements rotates on the screen, showing people standing by the seashore, laughing into their handhelds, and others pushing a tiny dog in a screened-in stroller down a tree-lined street. The words flit by too fast for me to make out.

I touch the screen. An orange light pulses to my right,

above a slot in the machine. Someone has stuck a piece of adhesive paper to the side of the light, with block letters printed there.

*Pa . . .* PAY HER. *What? No. Here.* PAY HERE.

I slide the pay plastic into the slot. The machine sucks it in and spits it back out at me again, but the screen blinks to life, opening up one of the searcher programs I've seen Perpétue use. I hunch over the screen and peck in the name I had Miyole spell out for me.

S-O-R-A-Y-A H-E-R-T-Z

Columns of words and pictures spring up and crowd the screen. I sigh. This is going to take some while.

I tick through the links one by one. I hate how slow I am. By the time I figure one link is talking on a dead woman long gone, and another on a girl my age who's known for her skill at racing a huge beast called a horse, I've already chewed up precious minutes. But then, far down at the bottom of the page, I spot a word in the tangled mess of letters. *Mumbai.* Mumbai! I open the link.

A small, grainy image of a woman standing before a seated crowd spools across the screen. A lavender scarf drapes neatly over her head and around the shoulders of her tailored shirt. A small, dark triangle of hair shows where her scarf pulls back from her brow. I raise my hand unconsciously and touch the ragged tufts of my own hair.

Is it her? Letters float beneath the woman as she speaks.

*Dr. Soraya Hertz.* My heart leaps. That *D-R*, that's what Miyole says I should look for, what groundways folk use to show a person's a so doctor.

There's more. The first word is easy. Mumbai. But the next? *Un–Univer—Univer-sit—y. University.* Mumbai University. I take a deep breath and push on. *At*, that's an easy one, but I trip over the next. *Kal . . . Kalina.* Kalina, it's no word I know. My heart knocks in my chest. A place, maybe?

"Mumbai University at Kalina," I whisper aloud. "Dep . . . Depart . . . men—"

"Hey, kid."

I spin around. Someone thickset—a man, I think at first—stands behind me, thumb hooked under the strap of a traveling bag. Bristly red hair sticks out beneath his short-brimmed hat.

*Parastrata. Run.*

No. His skin is chapped with windburn. He's groundways. And then I look again. It's not a man, but a woman hidden beneath the rough traveling clothes. I'm leaping at shadows. I grip the back of the chair.

"What?" I say.

"You can't be here 'less you've bought something." She points to the line of people waiting near the commissary kitchens. "That's the rules, don't you know?"

"Oh." I glance at the frozen image of Soraya Hertz. I still have twenty minutes left on the port. "Sorry, so. Thank you. I'll be straight back." I stand, pocket my pay plastic, and hurry to the line. I pick out a cup of something that ends up being sweet, spiced tea, too hot to drink just yet, and slide my plastic through a reader, mimicking the people in front of me. But when I get back to my carrel, the red-haired woman has planted herself in my chair. She sits with one leg sprawled out in the aisle, tapping her thumbs against the keyboard.

"Pardon, so missus?" I say quiet.

She doesn't look up.

"So missus?" I touch her shoulder.

She whirls on me. "What?"

"Can I have my seat back?"

"What, this?" She pulls an innocent face.

The balanced feeling hisses out of me, like air from a pneumatic lift. My first thought is to slink away, but I try to think what Perpétue would do.

"Right so," I say. "I was looking at something. I claimed that port."

"Did you now?" She makes a show of looking the terminal up and down. "Now how do you figure that?"

"You're using the time I paid for." Precious money what could go to cooking oil or replacement parts for Perpétue's ship, burning away under this woman's fingers, and me childish fool enough to fall for her petty trick.

"You accusing me of stealing?"

*She's used to getting away with this,* I realize. I wet my lips. "Right so I am, missus."

Anger ripples over her face, but then she swallows it and smirks. She turns back to the screen. "I guess we'll see what you can do about it, then."

I wish to the Mercies I had a knife like Perpétue's. Then no one would cheat me or step on me or push me aside as though I were windblown trash. No one would grab my face or drag my body where I've no want to go. My insides wouldn't go to jelly when someone yelled at me. I press my nails into the teacup's soft cardboard sides. *Not again. Never again.* I dash the cup forward. Its steaming contents splash over the back of the woman's neck. She screams. The galley goes silent around us.

"Bitch!" she shouts. "I'll have your guts, you little psychopath!"

I stand still as carved wood. The empty cup hangs from

my hand, dripping steaming liquid over my fingers. *What have I . . .* And then I bolt. Away, dodging tables and pillars, stumbling over chairs, down the corridor to the lifts. It's only when the door is sliding closed and I'm jamming my finger against the button for tier thirteen that I realize no one has come after me.

I race back to Perpétue's ship, head down, ignoring the crewemen calling at me. I activate the ship's cargo doors and crawl up into her dark berth. *What have I done?* I press my palms over my eyes and sink down against the wall. The woman's scream still echoes in my head. She wasn't my father or Jerej or even Modrie Reller. She was a stranger, happy to cheat me the same as that rice broker tried to cheat Perpétue. Only Perpétue never tried to burn his skin off, so far as I knew. Maybe I was wrong to think some bud of my soul was left, that it might be growing back. Else, how could I do something like that?

"Ava?" Perpétue squints into the dark. "I've been looking everywhere, fi."

I can't stop the awful, animal sound that falls out of my mouth. I turn away from her.

"What's wrong?" She hurries to kneel by me. "Did someone hurt you?"

"No," I say, choking on a sob that won't come. If

only that were all it was.

"Tell me, fi, tell me." She pulls me close and rubs my arms, as if it's cold I'm suffering from.

I shake my head. "No. You'll hate me." I can't let her see what kind of girl I really am.

"Did you steal something?"

"No." I wipe the wet blur away from my eyes. "I think I found my modrie. She's at a place called Mumbai University at Kalina. There was more. I almost had it, but this woman tried to chase me off, and I threw hot tea and burned her."

Perpétue stares into my face as if she's waiting to hear more. She blinks. "Is that all?"

I nod, miserable. Thank the Mercies I didn't have a knife.

Perpétue laughs, then quickly stifles it. "Guess we know you're no angel, then."

"It was bad, Perpétue. What with . . ." I stumble. "The way . . . If I know what it is to hurt, doesn't that mean I should know better than to bring that back around on someone else?"

"No."

"No?"

"All this suffering." Perpétue looks deep and

unblinking at me. "It doesn't make us saints, fi. It only makes us human. You understand?"

I shake my head. I don't know if I believe her. "You would never have done that."

"You think I'm a good person?"

"Right so," I say.

"Why?"

I look up into the dark recesses of the berth, thinking. "You're kind to me and to Miyole. You never cheat anybody out of their share when we ship in supplies to the Gyre. You're . . ." One of Miyole's words comes to me. "You're *civil* to people."

Perpétue draws her knife. She turns its blade over in her hands. "You know why I carry this?"

I shake my head. "Protection?"

"That part's show." She flips the knife and catches it. "Mostly it's so I remember."

"Remember?"

She holds the blade up to her face, beside the deep scar running ruin through her lips. "This knife gave me that. There was a man. . . ." Perpétue looks away. When she speaks again, her voice has the bite of metal. "Miyole's father. He meant to kill me, but I did for him instead."

I want to say something, but the air around us has gone so still, I don't dare disturb it.

Perpétue looks at me. "Would it have been *good*, Ava, would it have been *civil*, if I'd let him kill me?"

"No," I whisper. "But you don't go around cutting people up either. Or burning anyone."

"There's a balance," Perpétue says. "There's what you're forced to do, there's what you choose, and everything else—most things—are a mix. At best, you'll spend your life trying not to get hurt, but trying not to do the hurting, either. You won't always come through, but it's the best anyone can do. It's the trying I'd call good."

Perpétue turns the knife around so its pommel faces me. "Here."

I look from it to her, confused.

"You're the one who needs it now."

"I can't," I say. "It's yours." I can't imagine me with her knife any more than I can imagine her without it.

"You can," she says, and presses it into my hand.

My fingers close over the grip.

Perpétue smiles and slaps my shoulder. "Come on, we've got enough cargo to head back planetside. Miyole's waiting."

# CHAPTER • 18

Perpétue lets me break dock and fly us back through the atmosphere. The sky looks sick as we approach the Gyre. Over the open water, clouds mass and muddy themselves to an ashen yellow-gray. Lightning branches above the waves.

"I thought it never stormed here." I risk a quick look away from the instruments.

"It doesn't." Perpétue frowns at the thunderheads looming like monstrous prows over the waste plain. Rain begins to fall, mixing with the salt spray clouding our front viewport. "Here, hand over the controls."

I surrender the captain's seat to her. High swells rock the whole of the Gyre by the time we fight our way through the winds to the Caribbean enclave. Sea and sky churn.

Perpétue's face is gray. Neither of us has to speak what the other is thinking. *Miyole.*

We bring the ship to a hover over Perpétue's barge. Waves foam over the deck, and the whole structure rocks to and fro. Something red flashes on the roof. Miyole's kite, snarled in the clothesline. As I watch, it snaps taut, and then the wind snatches it up, out to the roiling gray. The water heaves the docking well up with each crest, then slams it down again into the trough. Impossible to land.

*The monster,* I remember. *They were right.* . . .

Perpétue smacks the controls and curses the sloop. "Come on." She brings us in lower, lower, until the waves slap its tile-armored belly.

"Perpétue . . . ," I say, nervous.

An awful crack breaks through the howling roar. A three-story structure on a barge several roofs down comes loose from its pontoons with a metallic shriek. It tips to the crashing sea, slow, so slow, and then it hits, sending up a flume of dark water and foam. A great wave rolls toward us, snapping the makeshift bridges.

"Perpétue!" I scream, and reach over to pull up on the thrusters. The sloop heaves up just in time to keep the wave from dragging us under.

Perpétue unbelts herself and climbs out of the captain's seat. "Take the controls."

"What are you . . ."

"Take them," she snaps.

I clamber in, snap the shoulder straps over my chest, and grab the thruster handles. Perpétue already has the engines at three-quarters power, trying to fight the wind.

"Bring us low." Perpétue clips a short-range radio to her collar.

I struggle to keep the sloop righted above the water. It shudders and jags in the wind, but I bring it to hover some twelve meters above the landing pad on Perpétue's barge.

"Open the hatch."

I don't have to ask what she means to do. I pull the hatch release. In a matter of breaths, I see Perpétue out in the gale, clinging to the end of the steel ladder. The wind lifts the ladder sideways, even with her weight added to it. I bring the ship lower. The walls of Perpétue's house loom dangerously close, windows dark gray as the sea.

The short-range coms crackle. "Ava?"

I flip the coms to hands-free. "Here!"

"Magnetize the ladder. The switch by the hatch release."

I see the one she means. "Got it!" I snap the switch. The ladder drops to the metal-plated deck.

Crackling silence.

Then, "I'm down." I can barely make out Perpétue's voice over the whipping of the wind and the roaring waves. "Try not to go higher or the ladder'll pull free. I'll be quick."

Wind batters the ship, and all around, the water moves in great, rolling, gray-green hills. Debris from the waste plain washes over the decks and swamps Perpétue's docking well. The far edge of the barge lists to the side, partially swallowed by the waves.

Perpétue's panting fills the coms channel. "She's not here!"

"Where else—" But then I see, through the sheets of falling water and crashing waves. Miyole, and Kai beside her, waving from the widow's walk of a ramshackle construction two roofs down.

"Perpétue!" I shout. The wind shoves the sloop lower, and for a slip, all I see is terrible, deep water with no end, but I bring it up again. I can't see Miyole anymore, but I know which building it is. "I saw her!"

"Coming!" Perpétue dashes from the house to the ladder, slipping and scrabbling in the wet. She doesn't bother to climb beyond the bottom rungs. "Up, Ava, quick."

I pull the ship up, away from Perpétue's house, and swing wide to come around to the widow's walk. I hold the sloop steady as Perpétue dangles from the end of the ladder. I squint through the lashing rain. The only metal to latch on to is the thin railing itself.

*She'll never get down*, I think, but then a sudden break in the wind drops us almost on top of the neighboring house.

"I see them." Her voice squawks through the coms. A beat. Then, "I'm down. Sending Miyole up."

"Right so." Sweat slicks my palms, but I don't dare let go to wipe them dry.

At that moment, darkness falls over the viewport. The whole of the Gyre sucks down, away from the sloop.

"Oh, God," Perpétue's voice is suddenly clear. Lightning flashes, illuminating a vast wall of water, higher even than the sloop, rolling straight at us. It sweeps up the debris and the structures of the Gyre and hovers above us. It turns white as it begins to curve over.

"Fly, Ava!" Perpétue shouts. "We've got the ladder. Fly!"

I jam the thruster controls up, fighting the wind and the blinding rain, engines hot. Pieces of plastic sheeting and plasterboard rush by, and then the wave is there, racing to meet us.

"Up!" Perpétue screams.

But it's too late.

The wave's crest slams us sideways, and we spin over the water. The viewport is sky and water, sky and water. *I'm going to die,* I think, but my body acts without me, fighting for even keel and height. We roar up into the sky, engines at full power. The clouds revolve and thicken, and everywhere is darkness.

Then suddenly bright, cold sun and blue sky. Below, a vast pinwheeled storm sweeps its arms over the water.

"Perpétue! Miyole! Kai!"

The open coms line fisses with static.

I program the ship's autopilot to keep us in a holding pattern, unstrap myself, and climb below. Waterlogged packages spill across the floor, what's left of Perpétue's delivery. The wind whistles from the open mouth of the berth. I crawl to the edge of the sunlit square.

"Please," I whisper to the Mercies, but then I reach the bolts holding the ladder to the sloop. My hands brush frayed bristles of metal rope. The ladder is gone. I push myself up on my knees, away from the edge. "No."

A whimper cuts the darkness behind me. I turn.

"Miyole?"

She hugs her knees with bloodied hands and presses her back hard to the berth's wall. "They were behind me," she says. "My manman and Kai. They were behind me."

○ ○ ○

There is nothing we can do but wait while the storm slowly churns its way north and west, away from the Gyre. Or what once was the Gyre. Some hours later we duck back below the tails of the clouds to find the sea below us picked clean and glittering. I check our coordinates. They're right. I bring us lower and skim back and forth over the water, praying to the Mercies I'll spot the remains of a pontoon or a piece of driftwood, anything Perpétue and Kai could have caught hold of. But there's nothing. The Gyre is simply gone. No boats, no pontoons, not a scrap of the waste plain what gathered there over the generations.

A hollow space opens in me, like my chest is filled with Void. It sucks all the air from my lungs. I was not ready for this, this total, spinning loss. Was it even a day ago Perpétue was joking I should fly all our runs? And now her gone. And Miyole . . .

"Miyole." My voice sounds unsteady, and I feel cold, as if I'm watching everything from somewhere deep inside.

She lifts her head and stares at me from the copilot's chair. We've washed her bleeding hands with saltwater and wrapped them in strips of silk from one of Perpétue's parcels. I cut open all the packages with Perpétue's knife while we waited out the storm. Mostly, they were full of oddments and luxuries, gold-painted eggs, cold-sealed vials full of something what might be quicksilver, cloth so thin you could make it flutter with a breath. Nothing useful.

"We've got to find someplace to land," I say.

Miyole nods.

"We can look for your manman and Kai from there," I say, even though I know they're empty words. We can look, but they're sunk to the endless bottom with the monsters and mermaids and all else the Gyre folk liked to talk on around their fires.

Miyole looks out the window into the soft dusk falling over the ocean. She's aged a million turns since we left her safe on the Gyre before the storm.

"My manman's dead," she says. "Her and Kai."

"Do you have any other family?" I ask, even though I think I already know the answer.

Miyole shakes her head. She turns from the window. "We should go to that place you always talk about. Mumbai," she says. "We can find your *tante*."

Dr. Soraya Hertz, Mumbai University at Kalina. It isn't much, but it's more than nothing. One of the sloop's aft engines has taken on a gutter and whine. I haven't been able to check the ship's armored tile plates, but I suspect some of them are damaged or else ripped off altogether in the storm. We need to set down, and soon.

"Right so," I say. "Mumbai."

I scroll through the navigation log and select the location of the nearest city east of us—the one with the slippery rice dealer. Once we're nearer to land, we can pick up the network and find Mumbai's coordinates. And then we're gone, skimming unsteadily over the water with the engines at quarter lift. The sun goes down before us. We are alone in the air. I can't afford to look away from the sloop's jittering instrument panels, but I reach out my hand and take Miyole's as the night swallows us whole.

# PART II

# CHAPTER • 19

When we first see Mumbai, I think I've fallen asleep at the controls. Only I could never dream something like this. A towering seawall surrounds the city. Clusters of squat, round buildings cling to the top of it, like the barnacles that grew on the sides of the Gyre's ships. Inside, massive crystalline structures rise from the earth and disappear into the low-lying clouds. *Skyscrapers*, that's the word Perpétue would have used. To the north, the land rises in a patchwork of roofs and trees, divided by gray trainways and the gossamer threads of rivers.

"Miyole," I say.

She stirs awake. We both stare at it, the city growing before us. The sloop's controls lie forgotten underneath my hands, until the coms channel crackles and a clipped voice directs us to somewhere called Navi Flightport on the outskirts of the city. I guide us lower and eastward, where the houses become concrete, and then crooked roofs and blue tarp, swaths of shanties blossoming along the edges of a swamp. At last the flightport comes into view. The sloop rocks as we descend through the air currents and finally touch down with a clumsy bang on the landing pad.

The ship's as bad as I feared. There are gaps in its skin where the wind tore shield tiles free. The whining aft engine is a snarl of bent, blackened metal. We can limp along without it, but there'll be no more runs up to Bhutto station or even across the sea until we find a way to fix it. I still have the square of pay plastic Perpétue gave me for the information port, but it takes near half what's on it to dock the sloop at Navi Flightport for a day, and the rest to buy our own entry into the city without "papers," as the uniformed woman corralling us through the entry gates calls them, though she really means a palm-sized smart card what tracks our comings and goings.

The hallway outside the gates funnels us past advertisements playing on the station's walls, past shops selling food and hats and tiny motorized fans. The crowd from an arriving passenger flight swallows us up and pulls us along, down into a narrow room lined with seats. It isn't until a soft chime sounds and the doors seal themselves shut that I realize we've boarded a train car. I wish I could feel the thrill of it—my first time aboard a train—but I cannot. It whisks us through a dark tunnel, and then out into the dazzling sunshine, along the side of a landing yard crowded with thousands of craft glinting in the sun.

The car slows. The chime rings again, followed by a woman's voice speaking a bubbling, melodic language I don't understand, and then, "Navi Flightport Authority welcomes you to Mumbai, located on one of the world's oldest surviving peninsulas. Please enjoy your stay in our beautiful historic city. *Svaagatam!*"

I want to ask Miyole if she knows what a peninsula is, but she looks the way I feel—wrung out and hollow, as if any words might echo through her.

"All we have to do is find my modrie." I squeeze her hand. "We're close. Don't worry."

We stand on the lip of a crowded platform outside the spaceport. Everything is too bright and loud. Hulking passenger trains roar by, stirring up gusts of hot wind. The smell of burnt ozone, simmering spices from the pushcart at the far end of the platform, and the oily stink of hot pavement stews in the air. On the palm-lined street below, crowds of people press by, some on foot, some high on creatures I think are called horses.

I should be awed, but I only feel numb. The world should be silent and gray now Perpétue is no longer in it, not teeming with voices and light.

"There's got to be a map someplace," I say. And then I spot it through a break in the crowd, a freestanding smartboard in the middle of the platform.

We make our way over. "How do we . . . ," I start to ask, but stop when I glance down at Miyole's face. It's utterly blank, as if whatever makes Miyole Miyole has evaporated from her body.

She steps up to the smartboard. "Map," she tells it, and an aerial view of the city springs up in front of us. To me, it looks like a knot of letters and lines and shapes, but Miyole focuses it easily with one bandaged hand.

"We're here." Miyole points to a flat, beetlelike shape to the far right of the tallest buildings. "Mumbai University, please," she says.

A column of rectangular boxes springs up, each connected to a spot on the map by a thin white line. There must be a dozen of them.

Miyole frowns at me. "Which one is it?"

For one brief, panicked moment, I can't remember. I haven't slept in over a day. My head feels thick and grainy.

"Ka . . . Kalina." The name comes to me in a rush of relief. "Mumbai University at Kalina."

Miyole taps the map. It zooms in and focuses on an image of a weathered gray building flanked by palm trees. A light breeze stirs their fronds, and blurs of people pass by on the pavement.

I step closer. "How do we get there?"

Miyole touches a series of yellow dots, which link together and form a line from our place on the map to the university. A train schedule slides into view at the corner of the board. I can piece out the words now, the number and times. *Train fifty-nine, estimated arrival 10:48 a.m. Train twenty-four, estimated arrival 10:52 a.m.* Iri might be alive now, we might both be safe with my modrie Soraya already, if only one of us could have read what the hologram was trying to tell us. I would never have met Perpétue and Miyole and brought all this trouble on them. Perpétue might not have been gone that day if she hadn't been teaching me to fly. She might be alive, and Kai and his family, too. . . .

*Stop.* I hear Perpétue's voice, as if her ghost is speaking in my ear.

"It says we can take train twenty-four to cross the river and then switch to number one-oh-five." Miyole looks up at me.

"Right so." Together we walk to the edge of the platform, away from the other travelers.

"When we find your *tante*," Miyole says, looking down at the track. "Will she let me stay?"

"Course she will," I say, even though I'm not sure if she'll let *me* stay.

"Why should she?" Miyole kicks at the line of glow paint by the edge of the platform. "I'm not her blood."

"I wasn't your blood when your mother took me in. But now . . . you're my blood, now." I squeeze her hand so she'll know I mean it. "I won't stay without you. We'll go back up in the ship and find work at Bhutto station if we need to. Your mother—"

I choke to a stop. A soft hum rises from the magnets below us, and far down the track, a sleek white vessel turns toward us. TWENTY-FOUR glows on the smartboard across its face.

"The train," says Miyole.

We step back as it blows past us into the station, glass doors and windows tripping by. It brakes to a smooth, sudden halt. The doors open, and we climb in, wary of the dark gap between the car and the platform. It reminds me of the shark-filled gaps between the Gyre's pontoons. Miyole sits with her back to the window, the sun setting the tiny curls that have escaped from her braids alight and casting her face in shadow.

Bodies pack in around us. Men in dark suits and collarless white shirts buttoned at the neck, chins shaved and hair oiled and tucked behind their ears; women dressed the same, with diamonds or gold rings studding their ears and noses; others in pretty printed dresses and scarves, or wide-cut, flowing pants. The ones standing alongside me in middle of the car grab hold of a rail above our heads, so I do the same. The sharp odor of so many sweating bodies packed together nearly suffocates me.

The city whips by, the closer buildings a blur of metal, glass, and gray stone, with only the faraway towers and treetops moving slow enough for our eyes. Suddenly, the train's windows darken. Thick, white letters glide over the glass, BAY MOUTH STATION, and at the same time, a calm voice rings out from the ceiling, repeating the name aloud in English and that same bubbling language I don't know. We come to a stop. Our train empties half its passengers out one side of the car, then opens the other side to let more pour in. A young man calling, "Chai! Chai!" edges through the car with steaming drinks balanced on a tray hung around his neck.

We pull out again. The train is building into its steady,

silent glide, slipping under the midday sun, when a rushing sound swells up beneath our feet and the floor jerks under us. The car fills with screams as we crush together, too close packed to fall to the floor. *The gravity's malfunctioned*, I think for a half a breath, but then I remember we're groundways. Something's wrong—bad wrong. The train screeches and shudders to a halt.

A stunned silence holds us all for a moment. Then a baby breaks into a frightened cry, and the car fills with shouts.

"*De!* Watch it!"

". . . every time I'm running late."

"*Hawa aane de!*"

"Dammit. What, again?"

"Miyole?" I shout.

"I'm here." She clutches the bar beside her seat. Her eyes are wide, but she looks unhurt.

I breathe a sigh of relief and right myself. "Sorry, so. Sorry," I mutter to the man in front of me, whose back I slammed into.

"Ava?" Miyole slips her hand into mine. "What's happening?"

"I don't know." I go up on tiptoe to look. My back prickles with sweat.

"It's a washout," the man I fell into says. He points up to the ceiling. "Any minute now, they'll call it. Listen."

The speakers sound a soft *bong*, and a woman's soothing voice fills the car. "Attention, we are currently experiencing flooding in the line—"

A collective groan goes up among the passengers.

"Remain calm and stay in your seats until a transit authority officer comes to escort you to the nearest station."

Near the front of the car, someone has forced open a door and people are jumping, one by one, across the small gap between the track and a walkway. The crowd nudges forward, pushing us along with it.

"Aren't we supposed to wait?" I ask the man in front of us.

He shrugs. "You wait if you want. I have to make it downtown by three."

I glance back at Miyole, worry building in the pit of my stomach. If we leave this train, how will we find our way to the other one that's supposed to take us to my modrie?

But we don't truly have a choice. I try to press myself against the row of seats, stay out of the way, but everyone is pushing. There's nowhere to go but out the door, into the steaming afternoon heat. The man in front of us jumps, lands with a heavy clang on the metal walkway, and then turns and holds out a hand to help us across. Miyole takes it and springs over the gap. He reaches back for me. I know I should take his hand, know he's only doing me a kindness, but his hands are so large, with soft skin and perfectly rounded fingernails. I can't let him touch me. I leap across on my own and land with an awkward wobble.

All up and down the tracks, people pile out of the train cars, into the burning sun. Most of them choose the walkway, but a few climb up onto the lev train's back and skirt the shuffling crowd altogether. Below us, a muddy trickle starts to fill the bottom of the magnetized pit.

"Do you think . . ." I look down at Miyole and stop. Even though her hand is in mine, she isn't with me. Her eyes stare unfixed at something I can't see, and her mouth turns down in a way I've come to know means she's sunk deep in her own thoughts.

By the time we make it back to the nearest station, the sun is past its peak and my shirt is plastered to my skin. The backs of my eyes burn. Everything comes to me muffled, the way the world sounded with my ears beneath the water in the desalination pool. This silvery city seamed with green, the constant roar of ships passing overhead, the bright colors and burning sun . . . none of it seems real. My head swims.

I drag us to the nearest smartboard and wait behind the other passengers lined up to use it. When my turn comes, I squint at the lines twisted around one another like wires. One of them flashes blue. OUT OF SERVICE. What was the one we were aiming for again? One-oh-five? I scan the board, but there are so many different numbers and words and lines. I finally find one-oh-five, but now twenty-four won't take us to it, and I could maybe figure out if another might, but I don't know the name of the tiny station we've wound up at or which of the trains will be coming through.

"Miyole?" I say hesitantly.

"*Jaldi karo!*" The woman behind me huffs. "Hurry up, please."

"Sorry, so." I can see the way everyone is looking at me. It's the same look I'm sure I had when the kitchen girls forgot to add protein powder to the bread meal or something dull headed like that.

I pull Miyole back through the crowd and sink down on a bench beneath a tree in the middle of the platform. I'll check again when they've all cleared away, when I have more time to trace the lines. I try to swallow, but my throat is dry.

"Are you thirsty?" I ask Miyole. If I am, she must be

too. Maybe more so, since she probably swallowed saltwater in the storm.

She nods.

I push myself to my feet again and scan the platform. Most of the other passengers have their own bottles of water clipped to their belts or the bags they wear over their shoulders.

"Please, so." I stop a woman wearing darkened glasses and carrying a slick black bag. "Do you know where we could get water?"

"There's a store inside." She waves over her shoulder at the small building behind us selling tickets and cold juice. "You can buy some there."

"Buy?" I frown. In the Gyre, everyone shared their water. If we were on our way back from the market and got thirsty, all we had to do was ask, and one of Perpétue's neighbors would give us a drink. It was always warm and flat from boiling, but it was never something we worried over.

"We don't need it cold or special or anything," I tell the woman. "Just regular water."

She raises her eyebrows and pulls off her glasses to give me a withering stare. "No such thing as free water, kid," she says, and stalks away.

Her words hit me like a cold slap, and anger flares in

my chest, sudden and ice hot. I grip the haft of Perpétue's knife. I'm going to swing at her. I'm going to run her down and shove her face in the trickle of dirty water skimming the bottom of the trainway. I'm going to cut the strap of that shiny bag of hers and run off with the full bottle hanging from it.

Then the memory of the red-haired woman and the tea washes back over me. Perpétue comforting me in the ship's hold. Perpétue on the ship's ladder. Perpétue lost in the storm. All the fight goes out of me.

I let go of the knife. The sun is high overhead and there are no shadows. Sweat rolls down my back. The crowd still mills around the smartboard maps, but a few people have taken a raised footbridge over to a different platform, where a train waits with wide-open doors.

I grab Miyole's hand. "Come on."

I expect her to ask where we're going, but she follows me mutely across the bridge. I don't even glance up at the name of the next station gliding above our heads as we wedge in next to the window. It doesn't matter where it's going, as long as it's away from here, away from that horrible woman and all that water held out of our reach. Besides, it's cooler in the train cars than out on the platforms. We won't notice our thirst as much.

The city closes in around us as we pick up speed. The buildings creep nearer to the trainway and then rise and rise so we can't see their tops from inside the car. Hand-painted signs on the sides of buildings give way to smartboards and windows playing enormous images of smooth-skinned women with teeth as tall as Miyole. Every now and again, a break in the buildings lets in a blinding flash of sunlight.

We slow to pass through a crowded section of the city. People pack the broad avenue outside the window, most of them on foot, but some on horses. And then in the flow of bobbing heads, I spot a broad, gray animal face with great flapping ears. My mother started to see things when the virus took her. She would reach out, even when there was nothing there. Am I getting sick the same way? I close my eyes tight and open them again. The animal is still there. Its back rises level with our train car, and it holds its long, armlike nose in an elegant curl.

"Miyole." I pick at her shoulder. "Do you see that?"

Miyole looks at it and shrugs. "It's an elephant."

*An elephant.* I remember a picture in one of Miyole's tablet stories. I had thought it was imaginary, like the Void zephyrs or zebras. A canopied platform rests on its back. A woman sits behind the animal's ears, and a man, three children, and a silver-haired woman ride behind her.

The old woman beside Miyole glares at me and clears her throat. I'm stepping on the hem of her dress. I back away with an apologetic glance.

The train stops at another station. I know I should step off, look for water again, try to figure out where we are, but there are so many people, all of them packed in tight like fish. My legs feel too heavy to move. I can't call up the energy it would take to edge my way through the crowd, much less pull Miyole after me, so I watch the unfamiliar station names glide along the windows. The world is getting bigger and bigger and I am shrinking in it.

Finally the buildings drop back from the trainway and the crowd thins. Clusters of man-tall pipes run alongside our window for a time, and then veer off into a different part of the city. Light still fills the sky, but it has a tarnished look to it, like old metal. The day is nearly spent. A hill rises into view. Houses and naked pipes crawl up all of its sides but one, a sheer face that drops down to rooftops below.

The train glides to a stop.

"End of transit line," the overhead voice tells us.

All of the remaining passengers file to the exits. I look down at Miyole, who has fallen asleep in her seat, her head slumped against my shoulder. I wish I could do that. Lie down and drop out of the world for a space. I glance around. The train is completely empty now, the doors standing open.

My eyes ache. My body is so heavy I would swear Mumbai has its own, more powerful gravity. I want Perpétue. I want her to tell me, "Don't worry, fi," and find my modrie for me so this can be over. I want Iri or, better, my own long-gone mother to pull me against the warmth of her chest. I want Luck to stroke my hair and tell me he'll fix everything.

But he won't. None of them will.

"Miyole," I whisper. "Time to keep moving."

We walk out onto the train platform. The train sighs behind us, waves of heat rolling off its metal skin. Across the street, shops selling tea and long bolts of lightweight cloth pack in close to the road. Reddish stains color the bottom of the white plaster walls, as if the foundations have been dipped in a dye bath. Men and women shuffle along, or else thread their way carefully through the crowd atop jingling two-wheeled machines and the occasional horse. Maybe here we'll have more luck with water.

I spot a smartboard near a cluster of benches and a stunted tree in a concrete pot. I squint at the board. Scratches cloud its face, and the low angle of the sun washes out the letters and lines on its display.

A man in a light blue uniform makes his way down the platform toward us, stopping every few strides to check inside the empty train cars.

He takes in our clothes before he speaks. "You girls are waiting for the next train?" His voice is buoyant and rolling.

I nod.

"We'll not be leaving for another two hours." He waves a hand at the train. "Maintenance stop."

I stare at him dully. *Maintenance stop?* I know what those two words mean, but my mind won't put them together. All I can do is stare at the badge on his shirt, glinting in the late sun.

"Why don't you go find some dinner?" He smiles. "Come back in a few hours when the line is running again."

My despair must be showing on my face, because his smile dissolves. "Are you lost? How long have you been traveling?"

"Since the morning," Miyole pipes up, her voice a soft rasp.

He sighs. "You didn't bring extra money for water, did you?" He shakes his head and fumbles at the water bottle clipped to his belt, holds it out to us, annoyed. "Here."

I snatch it up and hand it to Miyole. She drinks long and

deep, a little trickle running down the side of her chin. At last she pulls back with a gasp for air and hands the bottle over to me. The water is cool—perfect—almost sweet. I drink and drink until the last drop is gone.

The look of annoyance is gone from the train man's face, replaced by a furrow of concern between his brows.

I hold the empty bottle out to him. "Thank you, so."

He shakes his head. "Keep it." He looks from me to Miyole as if he wants to say something. He shakes his head. "You girls take care of yourselves, okay?"

I don't know what to say. What other choice do we have? He backs away and resumes his inspection of the train cars.

I hand the plastic bottle to Miyole, and she crinkles it in her hands, *click-pop*, like a heartbeat. Across the street, a gaggle of smallones races along a cinderblock wall, laughing, and cart pushers shout promises of juice and fried things and tea, switching between English and the other language.

My stomach growls. The water has woken it back up and cleared my head some.

"Are you hungry?" I ask Miyole. Maybe I can work out some trade with one of the vendors. I can carry and clean for them, or practice my fixes.

Miyole shakes her head. *Click-pop, click-pop.*

"Still thirsty?" I say.

She nods.

I close my eyes and call up my memory of the city from above. There were streams and rivers, weren't there? If we can find one of those, we can fill the bottle back up. We can look for water while we're stuck here, and then we can figure out where we are and get back on the train. We'll find my modrie and everything will be all right.

I tug on Miyole's hand. "Come on. We'll find some water."

She shakes her head and looks up at me. "I'm tired, Ava."

Her eyes are wide and bloodshot with grief and exhaustion. They're her mother's eyes.

"I know." I kneel down beside her. "Here. Climb up."

Miyole loops her arms around my neck, and I lift her up onto my back.

We join the crowd moving along the street. Lights flicker on in the shop windows and flash along the edges of one of the gigantic pipes rising above the rooftops. People stand on the second tier balconies above the stores, laughing and calling out to one another, or scolding dogs and calling children in from the streets. Small green machines scuffle along the road, scraping horse droppings and bits of trash off the pavement and tilting it into their mouths. Dust muddies the air.

A girl in an elaborately wrapped orange dress and gold and blue bangles leans beneath an awning, intent on her handheld.

"Pardon," I say. "Do you know where we can find water?"

She looks up at us and frowns, shakes her head as if she's confused.

*She doesn't understand,* I realize, and wish for the hundredth time that Perpétue was with us. She always seemed to know at least some scraps of language wherever we landed.

I point to the water bottle and hold up a hand in a helpless gesture.

She twists her mouth as if she's thinking, then shakes her head again and drops her gaze back to her handheld.

We keep walking. I smell salt in the air, but I can't see the ocean. A muffled hum and a rushing noise grow in my ears as we pass beneath the elevated pipe. The flashing red lights illuminate a puddle on the muddy ground. *Water.* I almost drop Miyole. As we stand watching, a drop falls from the pipe into the puddle.

"Look!" I let Miyole down.

I hold out my tongue to catch the next falling drop, but when it hits, it tastes of salt and iron.

I spit it out. "Seawater."

Miyole stares at the puddle.

"Don't worry." I try to smile. "We'll find some."

I lift Miyole and keep walking. We pass a series of small landing fields crammed with ships of all sizes. Lean, patchy animals throw themselves at the mesh fences as we pass. It takes me a moment to place the right name to them. *Dogs.* In Miyole's picture books, they were always helpful creatures, playing with sticks and chasing away strangers. Only now we're the strangers, I s'pose. Miyole tightens her grip on my neck.

"Maybe we should go back," I say. The sky isn't black, exactly, like it was in the Gyre at night, but it has taken on an odd purple glow. Ships scud overhead, lights blinking against the velvet darkness.

We turn around. The street is empty except for a lone sweeping machine trundling along in the distance. We pass the dogs and landing fields, and the massive pipe dripping seawater. My legs shake with weariness. Only a bit longer and we should see the trainway and the platform with its smartboard that can tell us where to go. If nothing else, we can get out of the heat, which hasn't let up despite the darkness.

I walk and walk, Miyole growing heavier on my back. I should have seen the station by now, I'm sure of it. I stop and turn in a circle. The streets all look the same in the dark, and I don't see as many people out, except for two women with tight-cut dresses and eyes ringed in glittering paint loitering beneath a streetlamp. Most of the shop windows are dark. I push on past another row of buildings, and another, as fast as I can go. Any breath now, I'll see the station. It has to be there.

Shouts and laughter ring out ahead. A group of men saunter down the other side of the street, heading in our direction. The hair on my arms rises. *Run,* my body says. But that would only catch their eyes. I don't think they've seen us yet. I whirl around. A few paces back, an alley opens between two buildings. I make for it.

"Ava, what—"

"*Hsshh.*" I crouch behind a pile of garbage, Miyole still clinging to my back, and wait until they've passed.

I creep out again and walk faster, running on fear now. The road curves and another raised pipe appears against the sky. Its winking signal lights blink on and off, showing and swallowing a symbol painted across its underside—

two sets of jagged lines intersecting, forming diamond shapes.

I stop. I know I haven't seen this before. I double back the other way. Still no station. Nothing I recognize. I try to swallow the panic creeping up the back of my throat, but there's no stopping it. We're lost.

# CHAPTER .20

The morning sun hits the water, near blinding me. I can't remember which word I'm supposed to use. Creek? River? Stream? It's the bigger kind, but not the very biggest. Miyole would know, but she's asleep under a lean-to of shipping pallets in the alley where we spent the night, and I don't want to rouse her. Let her stay away from this world as long as possible. And when she wakes, at least I'll have water.

I roll up the legs of my pants, pull off my boots, and tie their laces together so I can sling them over my shoulder. Then I slip down the muddy bank and slosh into the shallows. The water is cool. On the opposite shore, a group of people wade into the slow-moving current to bathe. Farther down, a group of gangly boys in shorts stand on a concrete slab jutting out over the water. As I watch, one of them pushes another over the side, and then they're all shrieking and jumping in. *Swimming*, I think. I clamp my mind closed on the memories that try to rush me.

A ship passes low overhead, sending a thrum through my body I can feel as much as hear. It follows the water's path upstream, then pivots right and sinks between the rooftops. I lower our bottle beneath the current. We were so close to this place last night. If only we had walked a few streets over.

I lift the bottle from the water and tilt it back to drink.

"Wait!" The bottle flies from my hand and splashes down into the mud.

"Nine hells!" I wheel around, my body singing for a fight, and come face-to-face with a boy maybe a turn or two older than me. Sweat plasters his black, short-cropped hair to his neck and temples. He wears thick, squarish glasses with black plastic rims. Tattoos scroll down his bare brown arms and up his neck.

"Sorry." He steps back and holds up his hands. His nose has been broken and mended, and his eyebrows angle down, as if he's thinking. "You don't want to drink that. Unless you're into gastroenteritis or something."

I make a face. "Gastroenteritis?"

He bends down and scoops my bottle out of the mud. "Yeah. You know . . ." He pretends to gag and vomit into the river.

I stare at him.

He gives me an embarrassed smile. "Sorry. I guess maybe that wasn't the best way—" He stops himself, takes a breath, and holds out a hand. "Let me start over. Hi, I'm Rushil. You don't want to drink the canal water. It'll make you sick."

I take his hand. "Ava." I glance over at the people swimming. "What about them?"

"It's all right for swimming and washing and all that," Rushil says. "But for drinking, you really want the filtered stuff from the stores."

I drop down onto a rock jutting out from the bank and stare at my muddy feet. "That's what everyone says."

Rushil peers at me as if he's taking me in for the first time. "You okay? You don't look so good."

I think about lying, but I'm too tired. I shake my head.

"You just get here?"

I raise my eyebrows. "It's that clear?"

"Well, you're not dressed like a Mumbaikar." He looks pointedly at Perpétue's leather jacket tied around my waist. "Most people around here don't go in for the whole dead cow thing."

I look down. Any leather we had aboard the *Parastrata* was goat hide, and I'd thought this was the same. "How do you know it's . . ." What did he say again? "Cow?"

"Point taken," he says. "If anyone asks, I'd just say it's synthetic."

I cover my eyes with a hand. "Look, as much as I'd like to sit around talking about cows . . ."

"Of course. I'm sorry." He holds out a hand to help me up. "Come on, I'll show you where you can get water."

I shake my head. "We don't have any money. We used the last of it to dock our ship."

Rushil raises his eyebrows. "Your ship?" I can't tell if the look on his face is surprise or alarm. "Where is it?"

"Navi Flightport?" Why does everything I say turn into a question?

"Navi?" Rushil grimaces and sucks air past his teeth as if he's stubbed a toe. "You'd better get it out of there before they make you start paying in blood."

My skin goes cold, despite the sun. "Blood?"

He catches the look on my face. "Oh . . . no." He laughs. "It's just a . . . you know, an expression."

"Oh," I say.

"But you really should take your ship out of there," Rushil says. "Especially if you're staying awhile."

He looks out over the water at the boys jumping into the canal and then down at his feet. "I've got a shipyard. You can dock with me for much less."

Ah. So that's it. I couldn't figure why some strange boy would want to help me for nothing, but this makes more sense.

"I told you." I sigh. "We're out of money." *So piss off,* I want to add, but I hold my tongue.

"Wait." Rushil looks up, unfazed by my tone. "We?"

"Me and Miyole."

"Miyole?"

"She . . ." I falter. How much do I want him to know about us? "She lost her mother. I'm looking after her."

"A kid?" He blinks. "Where is she?"

I nod to the buildings at the top of the bank. "She's asleep back there in the alley."

"*In the alley?*" His face darkens, and suddenly he changes from a boy hanging out by the canal to a young man full of purpose. "Come on. Get up."

My hand creeps down to Perpétue's knife. "Why?"

"Because you can't leave a kid asleep in an alley." He rolls his eyes. "That's why."

I lead him quickly back up onto the street. I can't help staring at the ink scrolled around his arms. A horse and its rider. A tiger savaging a soldier. A formless, blossoming design some like the intricate ironwork on the doors and balconies we've passed. A name around his wrist. His arms are strong beneath the tattoos. Not bulky, but muscled in a way that makes me think he works with them.

"No offense, but what are you doing in the Salt?" Rushil interrupts my thoughts.

My face flames. I look down, away from his arms. "The Salt?"

Rushil waves his hand at the streets around us. "The Salt. Well, Old Dharavi on the maps, but no one calls it that except the transit authority."

"We got lost," I say. "We were looking for my modrie, and—"

"Your what?"

"My . . . my . . ." I sift through my memory, trying to think of the word Perpétue used for Soraya. "My *tante*?"

Rushil shakes his head.

"My mother's sister," I say.

"Your auntie?" he says. "Shouldn't she have met you at the flightport?"

"She didn't know we were coming." I swallow. "In fact, I'm not even sure she knows I exist."

That makes Rushil shut his mouth. We walk the rest of the way to the alley in silence.

I kneel down beside Miyole and shake her shoulder. "Mi?"

She starts awake. "Manman?" She blinks the sleep from her eyes, and I watch her face contort as the memory of the last days falls back over her.

My throat tightens. "It's me, Miyole." I look behind me. "And that's Rushil."

Something tender and stricken plays across Rushil's face, and I realize it's pity. A shudder of anger passes through me. I don't want his pity. I don't want anyone's.

"Listen, my house is only a few blocks away." He stuffs his hands in his pockets and tilts his head back in the direction of the canal. "You lot look like you could do with sitting down. Maybe get some food in you."

The part of me still shaking wants to refuse, give him that sign with the finger Perpétue taught me and stalk off on my own. That's what I would do if it was just me, but it's not. There's Miyole. I've got to keep her alive, keep her fed, find water.

"Right so," I agree. "Lead the way."

We pass back along the same dusty streets Miyole and I walked the night before. Now that the sun is out, men and women squat on squares of bright-colored cloth in the small space between the shops and the road, hawking jewelry, painted shells, bolts of cloth, scuffed handhelds, and other trinkets. More of the little green street sweepers whirr around the crowd's feet. I have to jump over one that darts in front of me. The pipe hovers overhead, its dripping-paint shapes scrawled on the underside. Juice vendors have set up shop in its shade, propping up colorful umbrellas to protect them from the constant dripping.

When we reach the landing fields, the dogs come back, barking and snarling as we pass the fences.

"Yeah, yeah, we know," Rushil says to them. "You're terrifying. You're the most vicious creatures on Earth." He grins over his shoulder at me and rolls his eyes.

We stop beside a wire-link fence with a keypad lock. Razor wire curls along the top. Rushil taps in the access code and holds the gate open for us.

"*Mademoiselles*, welcome to my humble estate."

We duck through to the other side. A dirt-and-concrete lot covered in a jumble of ships and spare parts stretches back as far as I can see. Sun-reflecting tarps cover some of them, but others are clearly junkers.

"Come on in. I'll see if Pala has the tea ready." He tilts his head at a low-slung metal trailer propped up on cinderblocks in the corner of the lot. Broadcast needles and receiving dishes cover its roof. A stringy cat uncurls itself from a dish on the roof, hops down, and darts into a hole in some latticework. Two folding chairs sit in front of the trailer, one of them holding the narrow door ajar.

"Got some customers there, Vaish?" A lanky boy lolls atop a sleek, two-engine daytripper in the next lot over.

Rushil stops. "What do you care, Shruti?"

Shruti grins and dangles his legs over the ship's side. "Just watching out for these ladies." He eyes me. "You looking for a place to dock, *chikni*?"

I look at Rushil and shrug.

Shruti shakes his head. "Don't dock with Rushil Vaish. He'll chop up your ship and sell its bits."

Rushil closes his eyes. His jaw tightens. "Shruti, I swear . . ."

Shruti slides down the side of the daytripper and hooks his fingers through the fence. "Dock with me. I'll make you a much better deal."

"So?" I spare a quick glance at Rushil.

"Yeah." Shruti locks eyes with me and gives me a sideways smile. "You can dock with me for nothing."

"Nothing?"

"That's right," he says. "But if we're doing each other

favors . . ." He drops his eyes to my breasts and cocks his head, grinning with all his perfect teeth.

"*Satak le,* Shruti." Rushil smacks the fence between them. "Gross. No one's going to fall for that."

"She would." Shruti raises his eyebrows at me. "How about it, *chikni*?"

"N . . . no," I stammer. "*No.*" My skin crawls.

Shruti winks as he backs away. "Open offer. You know where I am if you change your mind."

"Sorry about him." Rushil pulls the chair propping open the trailer door out of the way. "Whoever put Shruti together only gave him one setting."

Inside, every spare surface is crammed with junk. A dozen fans bolted to the ceiling and walls stir the air. At the back of the trailer, a sheet barely covers an alcove with a raised bunk and a window. In the front, I see a cramped kitchen with a portable stove some like the one Perpétue kept, only streaked with grease all over its sides. It looks like no one ever takes it apart to clean it.

"Where's—" I start to ask, but Rushil pulls back the sheet, waking an enormous white dog with pointed ears. It blinks sleepily at us and thumps its tail on the bed.

"There you are, Pala." Rushil kneels down beside the dog and ruffles its ears. "Did you make tea for us? No?"

Rushil shakes his head. "He's a terrible housekeeper."

"Oh," I say. I'm stretched too thin to laugh. Miyole doesn't say anything.

The dog stands and jumps down to the floor, and it's only then that I realize it's missing one of its back legs. It hobbles after Rushil, wagging its tail, as he scoops a stack of warped paper repair manuals and a battered tablet from the trailer's one sagging chair, drops them on the bunk, and then pulls the curtain closed to hide the mess.

"I'll get the tea brewing." He edges around us. "I think I've got some roti in here, too. I can heat it up."

I circle slowly in middle of the cramped trailer. "You live here alone?"

"Yeah." Rushil grabs an armful of dirty mugs and cups from a small table by the wall, then hurries into the tiny kitchen. "Well, me and Pala. This place was my uncle's before he died."

"Oh," I say again.

"Sorry about the mess." Rushil scoops the rest of the junk from the table—connecter lines, coins, a multitool, bits of paper covered with numbers, tacks, an old leather-stitched ball—and dumps everything into a plastic bin half full of snarled cables."I keep this stuff to reuse, but sometimes I forget."

He waves a hand at the chair. "Go on, sit down. Tea's almost on."

I sit. Miyole crowds into the chair beside me. She leans her head against my shoulder and picks at her bandages.

"Don't scratch," I say. Another thing we need. Medicine. Proper bandages for her hands.

Pala limps up to us and snuffles Miyole, then props his head on her knees, giving her a hopeful look.

"Pala, don't beg!" Rushil comes back with a teapot, some plates of flat, round bread, and three glass cups. "He's not much of a guard dog, either."

Rushil hands me a sloshing-full glass of tea. I take a sip. The tea is hot and milky, sweet, but with a bite of something, clove maybe, and something else we never had on the *Parastrata*. We drink in silence. The tea is perfect, and the bread a little stale, but I swear it's the best thing I've ever eaten. I try to eat slowly, but I can't keep myself from pushing more and more into my mouth. Miyole is eating, too, thank the Mercies.

Rushil watches us in wonder. "What happened to you two?"

I stop with a scrap of bread halfway to my mouth and lay it down on the plate again. "We were up on a run. Her mother . . ." I look at Miyole. She sits frozen, her eyes glazed over, but I can tell she's listening to every word.

Nausea fingers the back of my throat. *I can't talk on it now*, I want to say. *If I start talking on what's passed, it will turn me inside out.* "I'm sorry, I can't—"

I'm going to be sick. I push myself out of the chair and run outside. I double over behind a pile of rusted metal corrugate beside the trailer. My stomach buckles and heaves, and all the bread I've eaten comes up. I spit into the dirt. I wipe my mouth and look out on the roofs of the Salt. Solar panels glare back at me, and laundry hangs stiff on runners. A breeze kicks up a puff of dust, sends it curling.

Rushil stands in the door, looking worried. "You okay?"

"I think I ate too fast."

Rushil kicks the dirt. "That can happen."

"Right so." I catch his eye and a strange, soft feeling passes through me. I want to thank him for acting as if everything is even keel, but I also want to slink under the house with his cat and pretend I'm dead for a little while.

"You need water," he says. "Come back inside. I'll get some for you."

"What about . . . ?" I grimace at the stacks of corrugate.

"Oh, don't worry. Pala will get that sorted."

It takes me a moment to realize what he means. "Ew."

He cracks a smile. "He's not such a bad housekeeper after all."

I laugh. A small, brittle thing, but I can't help myself. I think of Perpétue on the roof. *Laugh or cry, is that it, fi?*

I drink the water slowly, taking little sips so I'm sure it will stay down. Miyole rubs Pala's ears absentmindedly, humming to herself.

"Your aunt," Rushil says. "She lives here in Mumbai?"

"I think so. She works at a university. She's a so doc—I mean a doctor." I shrug. "At least, that's what the feeds say."

"Maybe . . ." Rushil studies his knuckles. They're knobby and thick with old scar tissue at the joints. They've been broken, I realize.

"I don't mean this the way Shruti did," Rushil says, still looking down. "But maybe we could work something out. Maybe you could keep your ship here and pay me back when you find your aunt." He looks up at me.

I tighten my jaw, wary. The thing that Shruti boy said comes back at me. What if this is some kind of trap?

"You won't come after us for more later?" I say. *You won't come looking for favors? You won't chop up our ship and sell its bits?*

"Of course not." Rushil rolls his eyes. "Don't listen to

anything Shruti says. They had a break-in over there last month. Lost two craft to ship strippers, and now they can't keep their clients, so he's trying to pick off mine."

I look from Miyole to Pala, and back to Rushil. Maybe this is the perfect fix.

*Too fast, too raveled*, a small voice says in the back of my head, a faint echo of what I felt before. But I ignore it. What choice do I have?

"Done," I say.

# CHAPTER 21

"Miyole." I try to shake her awake. Morning-blue light filters in through the sloop's open hatch.

She rolls over and blinks at me. "What?"

"Time to get up." After we flew the sloop to Rushil's lot yesterday afternoon, he spent some time on his grimy old tablet, showing me how to get to Kalina. We're going to find my modrie.

Miyole buries her head in her mother's jacket. "I don't want to."

I rock back on my heels. She doesn't want to?

"Mi." I try again. "Come on. All we have to do is ride down to—"

"I said I don't want to!" Miyole shouts. She shoots me an acid look and wraps her arms over her face, as if that will hide her.

I stand. "Fine. Stay." If she wants to be a brat, she can be a brat alone. "I'll be back in a few hours. Don't go anywhere, right so? If you need something, tell Rushil."

On the way to Sion station, two men in white linen clip by on horseback, swishes of gold thread braided into their animals' tails. I step aside, into the gutter. The more I see horses, the more they unnerve me. So far, I've seen no oil-fed groundcrawlers in Mumbai like there were in Mirny. It seems anyone halfway wealthy rides a horse or, more rarely, an elephant. Rushil told me they're trained not to run over people on the street, but I can't make myself trust them.

As I ride the floating trains through south Mumbai, the annoyance trickles out of me, and guilt grows in its place. I shouldn't have snapped at Miyole. She's just lost her mother, her home, everything she knows. I should have spoken kinder. I should have given her more time.

I peer out and up at the skyline at our next stop. The buildings shoot up in spiraling confections of reinforced glass and sheer, stately reflective metals, so tall the streets would stand in twilight every hour but midday if it weren't for the glow of smartboards. Glittering words and pictures span the sides of the higher buildings, and past them, the sky crawls with ships.

A man sitting on one of the concrete stairs between

buildings catches my eye. Stringy gray hair falls over his ears, and his feet are bare and covered in sores. He holds a sign: HUNGRY. HELP PLEAS. DHANYAVAD. Even I can read it. But everyone on the street walks by all the same, as if he's a ghost.

The man sees me staring and springs up. He dodges through the morning traffic and approaches my window, hand outheld. I start back. I have nothing to give him. Can't he see that? Shame boils in me—for him, asking, and for me, with nothing. I shake my head. His face falls. He raises a fist and starts yelling something in that language I can't understand, muffled by the window. He smacks the glass, and then, mercifully, a soft *bong*, and the train pulls forward again. He melts into the crowd as we pick up speed.

I sit down in one of the empty seats, shaken.

"You can't let them know you see them, dear," says a plump, middle-aged woman next to me. She looks me up and down. "Especially when you're dressed like a tourist."

I nod, too confused to argue. The train starts to fill with a younger crowd as we come closer to the Kalina campus. Young men and women sit quietly thumbing through their handhelds, or else laugh together. I shrink in my seat and stare out the window, willing myself invisible. I know they're only a turn or so older than me, but somehow that feels like a gulf what can't be bridged. Any breath now, one of them is sure to point me out for the fraud I am. *She isn't one of us. She doesn't belong here.*

But no one says a word. No one even seems to notice me as we pile off the train together at the university stop. I hestitate on the platform, unsure of where to go. The crowd of students flows around me, down the broad, shady paths to the buildings visible through the trees. Behind me, the train pulls away in a gust of hot air.

"Room two-oh-three, Wadla Building for Linguistic Sciences." I recite the address Rushil found to myself. I take a few steps and stop. *What if* . . . What if this doesn't work? What if Soraya won't help us?

*Come, Ava, courage.* Perpétue is in my ear again. *What choice do you have?*

None, I know that. But what good will it do to arrive at Soraya's door so nervous I can't keep my tongue from stumbling? I should walk a bit, calm my head. Perpétue left Miyole alone for longer than this most days; she'll be safe inside the sloop. I can steal a few minutes to give the ground time to firm up under me.

I follow the path under the trees. Students sit together on benches, or read on blankets spread out in the shade. A whole herd of young men and women jog along in a pack.

The sun has barely cleared the treetops, but the heat is already closing in. I follow a trickle of students to a weathered stone building with an immense, jeweled window set in its face. Ornamental spires rise from its roof. I can't help staring up at the tinted glass until I pass beneath the stone arch, into the cool darkness.

A sudden hush descends inside the building. The only illumination comes from a series of lighted glass boxes along the walls. The nearest box holds what looks like a tablet, only larger, and encased in a bulky shell. It even has movable keys for clicking—a pretty thing, but not very sensible. Next to it, a book lies open on a red velvet stand. At least, I think it's a book. It looks nothing like the thin scraps of bound paper Miyole scrounged from the kindling piles for me. It dwarfs the tablet beside it, and I can almost feel the weight of it through the glass. A deep ocher hide stretches over the book's cover boards, and even the paper looks heavy—almost clothlike, with rough edges.

To my left, someone sneezes. I look up and see a stone arch leading to high-vaulted room dusted with sunlight. Long, dark wood tables run in two neat rows on both sides of a central aisle, and on the far side, someone mans a high, crescent-shaped desk. Two identical stairways curve up, leading to another level, this one lit by high windows. And all around, rows on rows of ancient, bound books paper the walls. The silence is so complete, I can hear a page turn, a muffled cough.

"Can I help you?" A quiet voice reaches out of the darkness to me.

I gasp and turn. A woman with dark hair and a gold-rimmed round of glass hung around her neck sits at a small desk behind me.

"N-no. Thank you, so . . ." But she's already standing and walking around the desk to me. Her shoes make a sharp *clack-clack* on the stone floor.

"Are you looking for anything in particular?" She smiles at me, but her words have a point to them.

"The . . ." I grope for something to say. "The Wadla Building. So doctor . . . I mean, Dr. Hertz . . ."

"Ah." Her face softens into a genuine smile. "Are you a potential student? Considering Mumbai University?"

"Right so . . . yes." It seems a safe thing to say, since she's smiling.

She makes for her desk. "I can contact one of our student ambassadors, have them give you a guided tour, if you like."

"No!" The word comes out louder than I mean. I lower

my voice. "I mean, thank you, so, I'm fine on my own."

"All right, but if you change your mind . . ." She waves a hand at her desk. "If you go out the back entrance, through the rose gardens, and then turn right past the new biophysics labs, you'll find the Wadla Building. It's the yellow one, three floors."

"Thank you, so missus." I hurry away before she can salt me with more questions and offers to help.

The back entrance opens up on blinding sunlight and a smell so sweet I can near taste the air. I've seen flowers before—beans have them, and squash, some of the crops we grew in hydroponics aboard the *Parastrata*—but they were always delicate things that withered away in service of their fruits. The ones overflowing their beds before me are lush, layers and layers of thick, velvety petals bursting from their stems in showy reds and soft pinks and yellow. Fat bees buzz around them.

I put out a hand to the warm stone wall to keep myself from sinking down to the thick carpet of grass. To have such beauty around you all the time—and to have the luxury to waste soil and light and water on something meant only to please. It fills me with awe and anger. How do some people live this way when their neighbors go without food or water? Do they not care? Or do the flowers simply help them forget what they can't change?

I pace the garden slowly. This is Soraya's world—flowers and books and decorative glass. Why should she care about anything outside it? Would she even understand what it has taken to come this far, to find her? Why should she help me?

I hurry from the garden. Better to finish this, once and for all. Better to get it over with and go back to Miyole. I walk fast, head down, avoiding the gazes of students passing me on the path. I look up only to check for the yellow building the woman in the book room told me about.

As I round a corner, I nearly collide with a pale-skinned, sandy-haired boy.

He darts out of the way just in time. "Oh. Sorry."

I think nothing of it, forge ahead with my head down, but then he calls to me from behind.

"Hey, um . . . miss? Excuse me?"

I turn.

He holds something cradled in his palm. "I think you dropped this."

My pendant? But no, it's still fast around my throat.

"I don't think—"

But he's already walking to me. My hand opens without me, and he drops two round metal coins into it.

I look down at them in confusion. "I don't think these are mi—"

"Hey, a rupaye's a rupaye, right?" He winks at me and shrugs. "Bad luck to leave them lying around."

"You don't want them?"

He laughs. "What am I going to do with that? Buy a cheap curry?" He shakes his head and turns to walk away.

I stand frozen in the middle of the path, not understanding. Is this enough to buy a meal? Who would sniff at that? But I know, don't I? The same kind of people who would use their precious ground for roses.

The Wadla Building sits solid and plain faced at the end of the path, its only decoration the shimmering solar panels on its roof. I skirt the cluster of students in the foyer and duck down the nearest hallway. Blue glass doors look in on rooms full of tables with tablets built into them. I check the plaques beside the doors. Room 124, 126, 128 . . . the hall ends in a stair.

*Room 203*, I remind myself, and climb.

Quiet reigns on the second floor. I try to walk softly, but the soles of my shoes beat out a heavy rhythm. Room 226, 224, 222. My breath comes shallow.

What if she doesn't believe me about who I am? What if she doesn't want me?

*Why should she care for you? Even if she does believe you, she'll know what a nothing you are. She'll know your own crewe cast you off. She'll know you must have done something terrible to deserve such a fate.*

I try to push Modrie Reller's voice to the back of my mind, but it follows me down the hallway. My heart beats faster with every step.

Room 216, Room 214, Room 212.

*You're nothing. You're muck. You're dead to us.*

Room 210, Room 208, Room 206.

*You don't deserve grace. You don't deserve mercy. You're worthless.*

Room 204. I stop. Room 203 stands across the hall, its door open. A woman wearing a blue headscarf sits at a desk with her back to me, staring into a wide, bright screen. My breath comes loud and harsh. I try to swallow it, but that only fills my lungs with fire.

Room 203, Wadla Building for Linguistic Sciences. This is it. All I have to do is reach out and knock on the doorframe, speak her name.

So why can't I raise my hand?

Soraya pushes back her chair and stands. Any breath now she'll turn around. She'll see me. My modrie Soraya, she'll see me, and then I'll have to explain. I'll have to spill everything out to her—my crimes, my shame, my failure. I can't do it. I spin on my heel and flee, down the hall and the stairs, through the foyer, past the buildings new and ancient, and the beautiful, useless roses.

# CHAPTER .22

The sky has gone purple by the time I make it back to the Salt. Soft orange lights buzz on above me, one by one, as I thread my way through the patches of people drinking on street corners and leaning against storefronts, tinny music blaring from the bright, wide-open doors. My stomach growls. I haven't eaten since sunrise. I've spent most of the day riding the trains, too shamed to go back to the shipyard and face Miyole, too fearful to return to Kalina and try again with my modrie. But now the sun is setting, and I have no room for shame. Miyole will be hungry and worried, waiting for me. I dodge a man riding a bicycle one-handed while talking on his handheld, and duck into the nearest doorway that smells of food.

A line of people wait by the serving counter. The rest

of the small room is crammed with families and workers squashed together around tables, all shouting to be heard over the din. I take my place in the line and close my hand tight around the coins the boy at Kalina gave me.

The glow board above the serving counter crawls with cramped letters and prices, but everyone seems to be asking for the same thing, anyway.

"A curry, please," I say when I reach the counter, parroting what I've heard from the people ahead of me.

The woman behind the counter drops my coins in a jar and fills the bottom of a container with rice, then slops in a delicious-smelling mixture of meat, vegetables, and yellow-gold broth after it. She folds the box closed and pushes it across to me.

"Next!" she shouts.

As I step out of the shop, a boy shoots by, nearly knocking into me and dodging around a crushed ice vendor. I flatten myself against the building.

"Stop him! Thief!" a woman shouts as she puffs after him. "*Rukho! Chor!*"

The entire street pauses as she barrels after the boy, skirt hiked up around her knees, dust flying in her wake. They both disappear around a corner, and the street jostles into motion again.

I walk the rest of the way to the shipyard with the food held tight. If someone snatched it from me, I don't think I'd have enough fight in me to chase him. I might just sink down in the dirt and stay there. As I push the gate closed behind me, I spot Rushil up on his roof doing something with one of the receiver dishes. He waves, and then goes back to whatever fix he's trying to make. Pala gallops up to me, sniffs at the curry, and licks his chops.

"Sorry," I tell him. "Not today."

He drops down on his haunches and whines.

"Pala!" Rushil whistles for him. "Leave Ava be."

I make my way to the sloop and mash the hatch controls with my elbow. They start up with a healthy hum, but then a rattle clicks loose somewhere inside. The pneumatics shudder and shriek to a halt. A burnt chemical smell wafts from the half-open hatch.

"Miyole?" I call up into the dark interior.

She doesn't answer.

"Miyole?"

Still nothing. I settle the curry box carefully on the ground and spin the hand crank to open the hatch manually. The door ratchets down with a noisy, metallic *ca-chunk-ca-chunk-ca-chunk*.

"Miyole?"

I'm getting ready to boost myself up into the darkened berth when she appears, ghostlike, in the open hatch. Her hair and clothes are rumpled from sleep, and her eyes look feverish.

"There you are." I try to smile for her. "Are you hungry? I got some curry for us on my way home."

"You eat it." Miyole stares blankly at the dirt behind me. "I'm not hungry." And then she turns and disappears into the dark.

"Miyole, wait. Come back!" I call after her. I need to tell her I'm sorry. I need her to be herself again. But she's gone, swallowed up in the dark again.

I stalk out from underneath the ship and kick a pile of scrap rubber as hard as I can. "Nine hells!"

"Bad time?"

I look up. Rushil stands a few wary feet away. His glasses reflect the streetlamps' orange glow.

"No." I clutch my arms to myself, suddenly embarrassed. "It's just . . ." I gesture back at the ship. "She won't eat."

"She's been through a lot, huh?" Rushil says, but it isn't so much a question.

"So," I agree.

"She's kept herself locked up inside all day." Rushil frowns. "It's got to be hot in there without the ship's environmentals running. I thought maybe you were trying to bake her." There's reproach under his teasing, not too harsh, but it's there.

"I know." I rub my eyes, exhausted. "I didn't mean to be so long."

"Did you find her?" Rushil asks. "Your aunt?"

I have my lie at the ready. "No." I sigh. And then a truth, of a sort. "I don't know if I can afford to keep looking. We have to eat." I think about that man I saw at the train stop earlier, and the boy at Kalina pushing the coins into my hand. That's not who I want to be, living off other people's scraps.

"I can help with that, you know." Rushil looks down and shuffles a foot in the dirt.

"No," I say quickly. He's already helping enough, waiting for our payment.

Rushil flinches, and I realize the word came out harder than I meant.

"All I mean is, I don't want to be in anyone's debt," I explain.

Rushil nods. "I get that." He looks out over the yard. "You have no idea how much I get that."

A snuffle and scuff come from behind me. I turn and find Pala sniffing the curry container.

"Pala!" Rushil and I both shout at the same time.

The dog hops back and gives us a guilty, pleading look.

"No way." Rushil shakes his head and points at the trailer. "You have your own food."

Pala's tail droops, and he slinks off into the dusk.

I pick up the container. "Do you . . . I mean, would you like some curry?"

"Yeah?" He raises his eyebrows.

"Right so." I can feel the heat rising in my face, and I'm glad of the darkness. I don't want Rushil to think I mean anything more than to return the kindness he's done me. "I mean, Miyole doesn't want any, and there's too much for me alone."

"I never turn down free food." He glances over his shoulder at his trailer. "Let me go get some spoons."

I watch him jog back to his house, and then I climb inside the sloop. Miyole huddles in a corner, on top of several of the snow jackets Perpétue kept in storage. I kneel next to her and brush the sweat-soaked hair from her face. I've never seen her look so small.

"Miyole?" I whisper. "Are you sick?"

She burrows deeper into the coat.

"Miyole . . ."

"No." She opens her eyes and rolls over to glare at me.

"I'm not sick. Leave me alone."

I sit back, stung. "I'm sorry," I say, and then I notice the fresh white bandages wrapped around her hands. "Who did this?"

"Rushil." She closes her eyes. "Can I lie back down now?"

"Course," I say. Rushil. First feeding us, then waiting on our payments, now this. How am I ever supposed to repay him when he keeps doing so many kindnesses for us?

When I drop back out of the hatch, Rushil has dragged over his two folding chairs and positioned them next to each other beneath one of the sloop's wings.

"She okay?" he asks.

I hand him the curry box and collapse into a chair. "I don't know."

Rushil sits in the other chair. "You said her mum died?"

I look at him, and my face must show how I feel.

"I'm sorry," he says. "It's none of my business."

He opens the curry. "This smells amazing. Where did you get it?"

"One of those little places across from the station."

"Chander's? Grand Tasty?" He takes a bite and his eyes go wide. "Mmm. Not Durga's, is it?"

"I don't think it had a name." I turn the spoon over in

my hands. "I don't mind, you know . . . if we talk about Miyole."

Rushil goes quiet for a moment, digging around in the curry.

"My mum ran off when I was around her age," he finally says. He takes a huge bite and hands the box back to me. "That's when I came here to live with my uncle."

"The one who died?" I ask.

Rushil swallows and nods.

"I'm sorry." I take a bite and hand the box back to him. "You don't have much family, then?"

Rushil shrugs and takes another bite of curry. "I do okay." He holds the box out to me. "What about you?"

I nearly drop my spoon, startled. "What about me?"

"D'you have any family other than that aunt of yours?"

My eyes stray to the sky, but the city is so bright, I can't see the stars. Anger streaks through me. "Do you think I'd be here if I did?"

Rushil lowers the box. "Point taken."

"Sorry. I just . . ." I look up at the ship. "All I have is Miyole."

Rushil lays a hand on the arm of my chair, more serious than I've ever seen him. "I meant what I said. Any way I can help, I'm in."

I stare at his hand a beat too long, those scarred knuckles, and then look up and clear my throat. "What I need is work. If the ship weren't so bust, I could do runs. . . ." I shake my head and sigh.

"Maybe I could help you patch it up." He cranes his neck back at the wing above us, adjusts his glasses, and grimaces.

I laugh. "Does it look that bad?"

"What? No! I didn't mean it like that."

I raise my eyebrows.

"Okay, it's a little rough," he says. "But I'm sure it's got good bones."

"The best." I smile.

His eyes meet mine. They are wide and black-brown, the rich color of the soil where the *Æther*'s lemon trees grew. Something passes between us for half a breath—a flicker of energy. And then it's gone, leaving me uneasy. What was that? We stare at each other awkwardly under the shipyard's perimeter lights. I can't quite grasp the rules here. What is safe? What is proper? Back in the Gyre, I thought I was learning the way this world worked, but things are so different in Mumbai. I have to start all over.

I remember myself, remember his offer. "No. I can do it on my own. Thanks."

"Oh, come on." He nudges me, all teasing again. "Don't be like that. It'd be fun."

"No, truly. I can't let you."

He cocks his head to the side, as if he can't figure whether I'm joking.

"I mean it," I say.

"Okay, how about this?" He leans forward in his chair. "I show you where to find a job and you bring home some more of this curry for us to share. Because—*chaila*—it is the best I've had in a long time."

I bite my lip and look up at the sloop's wing, thinking. The sooner I find work, the sooner I can pay our own way. And the sooner I fix the ship, the sooner I can make a life for us, Soraya or no Soraya. I guess food would keep us even in the meantime. Besides, tonight marks the first time I've smiled since we spotted the storm over the Gyre. It feels good to talk to someone. It feels good to talk to *Rushil.* I wish it didn't, but it does.

"Ugh, that was a terrible idea," Rushil says. "Never mind. You shouldn't listen to me."

"No. I mean, I'd like that."

"Yeah?" A lopsided smile breaks out over his face. It's an odd thing, that smile. It changes the whole look of him.

"Right so," I agree.

Rushil drops his spoon in the empty curry container and leans back in his chair. "What kind of work do you want?"

"I don't know." I look at the ship again. "Flying, maybe?"

"Sure, as long as you can show your license."

"License?" I say.

"Your piloting license."

I shake my head.

"You don't have a piloting license." He leans forward in his chair and sighs. "Okay. What else can you do? Bookeeping? Data entry?"

"I can fix things," I say, uneasy. "And I was on Livestock duty."

Rushil looks at me blankly.

"Chickens and goats," I explain.

He looks pained. "Anything else?"

"I s'pose . . . I can clean." I make a face. Who would want to go back to that drudgery after the thrill of flying a ship? "And cook a little."

"Maybe . . ." Rushil perks up. "There's a labor placement office near Sion station. All you have to do is show them your ID and . . ." He stops. "You don't have an ID tag either, huh?"

"Is that the same thing as papers?" I say, thinking back

on how expensive it was to get past the flightport without them.

Rushil nods.

"Nine hells." I want to kick the empty curry container across the shipyard.

"I'll take it that's a no."

"Isn't there any way to work without a tag?" I pick at the hem of my shirt. It would be better that way. No records of me, no danger of my father and Jerej finding the smallest thread leading here.

Rushil looks at me, all traces of humor gone. "You don't want that kind of work. Believe me."

And I do. The chill that passes his face tells me everything I need to know.

Rushil stands and paces to the nearby fence, and then back again. He frowns, sits down, stands again, and stares out at the street for so long I think he's forgotten me.

"Rushil?"

He doesn't answer at first, but when he does, he forces a smile. Not the easy one I saw some minutes ago. This one doesn't reach his eyes.

"Don't worry," he says, but there's something in his voice that makes me think I should do exactly that. "I know someone who can fix that for you."

# CHAPTER .23

"We'll just go in and out." Rushil's eyes dart across the rooftops. Nothing moves up there except laundry baking dry in the midday sun. The buildings in this part of the Salt form a windowless corridor of rusted metal corrugate, splashed with painted words and symbols. The streets are eerily quiet. At a time of day when the rest of the Salt is full of foot traffic and vendors shouting and smallgirls selling flowers at the train station, this neighborhood feels empty.

"In and out," Rushil repeats. "Simple business."

I double my pace to keep up with him, sidestepping a gutted street sweeper. A drainage ditch, glassy with sewage, runs along the road beside us. A dozen times now, I've started to tell Rushil not to bother, that I don't want any record of me floating out there, that I'll find another way to make money and pay him back. But then I think about my choices—the begging man with the sores, the women beneath the streetlamp, the thief—and I clench my jaw shut again.

"How do you know this . . . what's his name? Panaj?" I ask instead.

"Pankaj," Rushil says. "I knew him a long time ago. Before . . ." He trails off.

"Before what?"

Rushil doesn't answer.

I sigh. "You're being weird again." A word I picked up from him.

"I know. If I promise to stop being weird as soon as we get out of here, will you stop telling me that?"

"Maybe," I say.

We stop in front of a gate painted with an interlocking diamond pattern.

Rushil looks up at one of the black spheres mounted on top of the wall. "Pankaj!" He waves. "It's Rushil Vaish."

Nothing happens.

"Maybe he's out working?" I look over my shoulder.

"More like he's still asleep. Pankaj!" He waves at the spheres again. "Come on, man, I know you can hear me. Open up. I've got some business for you."

A buzzer sounds, then a metallic shriek, and the gate slides open enough for us to pass through single file.

Pankaj's yard makes Rushil's look like a neat-raveled piece of work. Tiny plastic bags and other bits of trash litter the tract of mud separating the cinderblock house from the fence. Weeds sprout here and there, partially hiding broken glass bottles and scraps of cellophane. The windows have been boarded shut, and a two-wheeled groundcrawler leans against the side of the house, bulging with fuel tanks and a chrome-plated engine. I haven't seen anything like it since Mirny. I didn't think they had them here.

Rushil cuts his eyes to the groundcrawler as we pass it. "We didn't see that."

"Right so," I agree.

The door swings open. "Rushil Vaish." A wiry man a few turns older than Rushil slouches against the doorway. "I thought we were never going to see you again."

"Pankaj," Rushil says.

"What's this?" Pankaj looks me over. "A peace offering?"

Rushil's jaw tightens. "A *customer*."

Pankaj holds up his hands. "All right, all right. Can't blame a man for asking. What do you need, *chikni*?"

I glance at Rushil, suddenly nervous. "An ID tag. For work."

Pankaj looks to Rushil, too. "Why doesn't she just work off the books?"

"She's not doing that."

"I hope you've got full pockets, then, *chikni*." Pankaj turns back to me. "Seventy-five for the basic tag, two-fifty for the works—database trail, ghost records, the lot."

"Two hundred and fifty?" I feel ill. How deep am I going to fall in debt? Waiting for my ship docking payment is one thing, but this is real money.

Rushil touches my arm. I jerk away before I realize he only means to calm me, the way I used to calm Lifil or the goats by laying a hand on their backs.

"Just the basic tag," he says. "Enough to get her past the employment screeners."

"Rushil—" I protest. He has to know I don't have the money.

Pankaj shrugs. "Let's see some plastic."

Rushil reaches inside his shoe and pulls out a square of pay plastic. Pankaj takes it, taps it against the screen of his handheld, and eyes Rushil. "The straight and narrow's been good to you, huh?"

Rushil shifts uncomfortably. "I get by."

A crooked grin breaks out over Pankaj's face. "Where are my manners?" He steps back into the shadowed entrance and holds the door for us. "Step into my laboratory."

The room is cold, so cold I almost think my breath will smoke. Cables hang low from the ceiling, and a jumble of machines covering two rows of tables cast a chilly blue-green light into the darkness.

Pankaj snaps on a light aimed at a blank blue wall. "Over here."

I stand where he points. The glare half blinds me, but I make out the image of Pankaj raising his handheld.

"You know, I could make you a deal for the full treatment," Pankaj says over his shoulder to Rushil. "If you were up for a barter arrangement."

The strain in Rushil's voice is clear from across the room. "What kind?"

"Nothing much. Just some courier work." Pankaj looks back at me. "Stand still, *chikni*." His handheld gives a polite beep.

Rushil stays quiet for a moment. "No," he finally says. "Not interested."

Pankaj sighs and shakes his head. "Your loss." He switches off the light, and for a moment, ghosts of the bulb linger in front of my eyes. "You're done, *chikni*."

I step away from the wall, closer to Rushil, so my shoulder lines up with his. I glance at the door, and we exchange a look.

"What now?" I say.

Pankaj cracks his knuckles. "Now you wait while I do my magic."

Rushil and I wait outside in the trash-strewn yard.

"You didn't have to do this for me," I say. "That's a lot of money, Rushil."

Rushil shrugs. "It's not like I got you *the works*."

"Still . . . ," I say.

"I know you'll pay me back." He flashes a smile at me, quick and tight. "You're good for it."

I raise my eyebrows. "How do you know?"

"I just do," he says.

"How?"

He kicks a plastic bottle into the weeds. "Miyole."

"Miyole?" I blink. "What does she have to do with it?"

"You watch out for her." He stuffs his hands in his pockets and looks away. "You don't give up on her. So I know you'll follow through."

I laugh, but there's no mirth in it. "Of course I watch out for her. What else am I supposed to do? Drop her all alone in some place like this?" I fall silent, realizing what I've said.

Rushil stares at me as if I've hit him with an electric

current. For a time, we don't say anything. He paces the yard, kicking Pankaj's trash back and forth.

*Stupid, stupid, Ava.* Poking my finger in the wounds of the one person trying to help me. I stare straight ahead at Pankaj's fence. The jagged diamond shapes have been painted there, too, flanked by two tigers rearing up on their hind legs.

"What is that anyway?" I say without thinking.

Rushil stops. "What?"

"Those lines." I point. "The diamonds. I see them everywhere."

"It's an M and a W." He traces the letters. "See, they're laid on top of each other."

I cock my head. Now that he's pointed them out, I see each one, but I don't know how I could have figured it otherwise.

"What does it mean?" I ask.

"Marathi Wailers." Rushil glares at Pankaj's closed door. "He's one of them."

"And that's bad?" I guess.

Pankaj's door swings open, cutting off his answer.

"Hot, hot indentity fraud." Pankaj tosses the tag to me. "There you go, *chikni*. As long as your screener's a little sloppy, that should work. Come back anytime."

I pocket the card without looking at it. *Never, ever,* I think, and make for the gate, Rushil a few steps ahead of me.

"Hey, Rushil," Pankaj calls.

Rushil stops with his hand on the latch.

"You ever change your mind, you know where to find me." He smiles and closes himself in his house.

Rushil and I don't speak until we're back in the bustle of the main road near Scion station.

"Okay." Rushil takes a deep breath. "I'm ready to stop acting weird now."

I laugh. "I think you were the least weird part of any of that."

"I try. And on the plus side, we didn't even get mugged."

"Probably because you're so fearsome looking."

"Actually, I think it's you the muggers were afraid of," Rushil says. "You're terrifying."

"I try," I say, copying his voice.

"Speaking of. What do you think of Pankaj's handiwork?"

"I don't know." I pull out the tag. A tired-looking girl stares back at me. Her eyes are bruised hollows and her hair is a ragged mess.

I scowl. "Is that how I look?"

Rushil leans over my shoulder and studies the picture. "Not at all."

I squint at the card, examining the tiny gold lines that appear when I tilt it toward the light. I hope this thing is worth the risk. "Shouldn't it, though?"

"Nah, it's perfect," Rushil says. "Your ID tag is supposed to make you look like a tar addict. That's how you know it's real."

"Ha, ha," I say drily. I don't know exactly what a tar addict is, but the way Rushil says it tells me it's nothing good.

"No, really." Rushil reaches into his pocket and pulls out his own ID. "See?"

I take his tag. "Whoa."

The Rushil in the picture looks like he wouldn't hesitate to break my kneecaps. His hair is shorter—nearly shaved—and without his smile, his eyebrows give him a hooded look.

"Told you." Rushil snatches the tag back. "We're an unsavory pair."

I hide my grin. "We should get back. Or I should. I need to check on Miyole."

"Don't you want to try out your new tag?" Rushil asks.

"Now?"

"Why not?" He hooks his thumb over his shoulder at a plain, low-slung building. "You can bring home some good news to Miyole."

I frown at the sign above the doors. OLD DHARAVI LABOR PLACEMENT AGENCY.

My mouth goes dry. "Pankaj said it would only work if the screener was sloppy. . . ."

"I wouldn't worry." Rushil digs in his pocket again. He pulls out three coins and presses them into my hand. "If the screeners aren't sloppy, you can always make them sloppy."

"You mean . . ." I frown down at the coins and then take in a sharp breath when I grasp what he means. "Oh. Right so."

"I'll wait out here for you."

"You don't need to." I clutch the coins. He's done enough. More than enough.

Rushil arches an eyebrow. "Maybe I want to."

My face goes hot. "I'll . . . I'll be back soon," I stammer, and hurry into the office without looking back.

"Identification?" The middle-aged woman behind the desk at the labor placement office taps at her trackboard without looking up. Her black hair sweeps up from her forehead into a gravity-defying pouf.

I slide my new tag across the metal counter. It comes up to my shoulders, even though I'm standing.

"Any documentation of work history?" the woman asks without looking away from her screen.

I look down at the countertop, smudged with fingerprints from all the people who've stood in this same spot before me. "No, so missus."

She holds my card out at arm's length, then narrows her eyes and looks from it to me. *Nine hells.* Of course I would get the one screener who isn't sloppy.

"Please, so missus." I keep my voice low and lean close as I can. My heart picks up a sickly, too-quick beat. "I've got a smallgirl to watch out for."

She frowns at me. I can tell she's trying to figure my age, pick out my life story from my face and clothes, and she doesn't like what she sees. Is this the time? I turn over the coins in my palm. What if it isn't enough? Or what if she thinks it's dirty what I'm doing and starts yelling like that woman chasing the thief? She has my tag. I'll have to run out of here and leave it behind, and then I'll be stuck without work and even more in debt to Rushil.

I place the coins on the counter and slide them across to her.

"There's got to be something," I say.

She looks at me sharply, the swipes up the coins and pockets them. I let myself breathe.

"Very well." She looks back at her machine. "Entry level, low-skill jobs. I have a laundry aide at a state end-of-life facility. Sorter at an electronics recycling plant. Powell-Gupta Dynamic needs a chai wallah, and there's a synthetic diamond manufacturer on the east side that wants a chemical stripping assistant."

"Which one pays the best?" I ask.

"Chemical stripping assistant." She looks level at me and some of the formality drops out of her voice. "But those fumes will strip your lungs, too. That job will age you twenty years in a month. I wouldn't take it if I were you, not if you have a little one to look after."

"Which one would you take?" I ask cautiously.

"Chai wallah," she says without missing a beat. "It's not the best pay, but it's down in a good part of the south city and you'll be safe. It'll help you build up a work history." She gives me a meaningful look.

"Right so," I say, even though I don't have a clue what a chai wallah does. "I can do it."

Her machine clicks and spits out a thin plastic card. "You start the day after tomorrow. Scan this with your crow, and it'll direct you to Powell-Gupta. Feed it into the exterior lock system, and the building will show you where to go from there."

"Crow?" I repeat. None too much of what she said makes sense, but that part I didn't understand at all.

The woman holds up her handheld, a shiny, berry-red machine the size of her palm. "Your crow," she repeats, as if I'm slow. She looks me over. "And see if you can't pull together some more professional clothes. You look like you stumbled off a waste freighter."

"Right so." I take the card.

"Welcome to the workforce, Miss Parastrata."

"Thank you." I clutch my ID tag and the employment card to my chest as I hurry past the line of people waiting for jobs and out into the afternoon sun.

I spot Rushil sitting in the shade of a tree, thumbing through his handheld—I mean crow—and I can't help but smile. Because the tag worked. Because I'm going to pay him back. Because finally, finally, something is going right.

# CHAPTER .24

A chai wallah turns out to be a type of servant who runs tea to everyone too important to leave his or her post, some like the man with the tray I saw on the train when Miyole and I first got here. I'm not the only one at Powell-Gupta, which has an entire black-glass tower to itself on the outskirts of south Mumbai. Each floor gets its own chai wallah, dressed in white pants, an acid-green shirt, and a saffron neckerchief, the company's banner colors. At least the woman at the employment office ended up being wrong about needing to buy new clothes. I tuck my data pendant beneath the scarf and leave my street clothes in the narrow hall where we workers can store our things during the day.

"You make the tea, you set up the cart, you bring the tea." Ajit, the senior chai wallah, leads me though the kitchens in the basement. He can't be too many turns older than me, but all his teeth have gone brown. "You see if they want anything else, and if they do, you get it for them quick as you can."

Dayo, an older woman with dark skin and a lilting touch to her words, looks up from her cart. "What Ajit means is, you do whatever anyone says and you don't foul up."

Ajit glares at her. "Do you want to do the training?"

"I'm only telling her how it is." Dayo raises her hands in mock surrender.

"How about you get up to fourteen and do your job instead of trying to do mine?" Ajit says.

Dayo shakes her head and continues setting out the thick glass cups on her cart.

Ajit gives me a cart of my own, complete with a silvery urn of tea, cups, a warming compartment full of damp towels so the people I serve can clean their hands, and a data pad where I can take down any requests.

"I'm giving you twenty-seven," Ajit calls over his shoulder as I trundle after him to the service lifts. "That's an easy start. When you're done we'll check your times and see if you're ready for something more challenging."

"You're timing me?" I pause midstep. The cart squeaks a meek protest.

"Of course." Ajit turns. "Pay scale's based on your efficiency rating. Didn't I say that?"

I stare at him warily. "No."

Ajit shrugs. "Chop chop, then. Clock's running."

My cart and I ride the service lift up to the twenty-seventh level. The tiny block of numbers at the bottom of my data pad climb higher and higher with the seconds. How long is too long? I hate leaving Miyole alone, even though she's some used to it. This city feels different from the Gyre, as if it might eat her up when I'm not looking. But we need money. We can't keep living off Rushil. I can't afford to be slow.

The lift doors open on a glare of light and a waft of cool air. A wide room with an expanse of floor-to-ceiling windows spreads out in front of me, crammed with a maze of desks and man-high frosted-glass partitions. A man or woman sits at each post, poised above a data entry screen, fingers flying, or talking into the onscreen feed receiver bolted upright at each station.

"Finally." One of the women spins around in her chair and eyes my cart. She waves me closer. "Miss! Miss?"

I wheel my cart over to her. "Tea, missus?"

"Of course I want tea. Why do you think you're here?" She narrows her perfectly painted eyes.

"Right so, missus." I fill a cup from the urn and hold it out to her.

She stares at me as if I'm offering a handful of goat-fouled hay. "Aren't you forgetting something?"

I cut my eyes sideways to the cart.

"The towel." She huffs. "Don't they teach you people basic etiquette?"

"Oh." I put the cup down on her desk and slide open the lid of my cart's warming compartment to fish out a moist, neatly folded linen square. "Right so."

She wipes her long fingers delicately and tosses the towel back at me. I catch it against my chest.

"Will there be anything else, missus?"

"Now I'll have my tea," she says.

"Right so—I mean, of course, missus." I gesture to the cup I've already poured for her, waiting on her desk.

"No." Her voice is sharp. "That one's gone cold. I'll take a new cup."

I pick up the cup I've just poured. There's no place to stow it except on the top of the cart, so I cram it beside the clean glasses, slopping sticky milk tea down in the process. My stomach knots up and my hands shake with the strange mix of fear and anger. I pour a fresh cup and try again. "Will there be anything else, missus?"

"No." She flicks her hand at me, and for a moment I see Modrie Reller. All she needs is a fan. "That's all for now."

I push the cart around the room, stopping at each post. Not all of them are so awful, but they all want something.

"Take these cups downstairs, would you?"

"Could you see about getting me a mango lassi from that *tapri* around the corner?"

"You're going by accounting on your way down, right? Would you drop this scanner back with Dipak and tell him thanks for me?"

"Do you have any caffeine pills on you?'

"And what about some *pakoras* if you can round them up?"

I try to scratch out everyone's orders as best I can on the data pad, but by the time I round the last desk, my cart is littered with dirty cups, wrappers, a used finger bandage, and the uneaten edges of some fried, crusty bread, all swimming in a shallow layer of tepid tea.

"You know, you shouldn't have started with Nandita," the last man I serve says as I fill his cup. "She's only been here seven months. You should start with the senior employees first."

"I'll try to remember, so," I say politely, though by this time I feel close to screaming.

I truck the cart back to the lift and ride down to the kitchens, where Ajit is waiting for me.

"There you are." He's in the middle of inspecting two newly returned carts. "Try to pick it up a little next time. Your rating's not too bad for the first day, but still. Try to pick it up."

Then he sees my cart. "What's this?"

"I . . ."

He snatches up a dirty glass, dripping with tea. "Why didn't you stow this in the used glassware bin?" He picks up the crusty bread between two fingers. "And why didn't you use the compost container?"

"I . . . I didn't . . ." I feel myself shrinking again, all the strength the Gyre gave me gone. I'm back with my crewe, bowing my head and scraping and terrified. I can't bring myself to look Ajit in the face. "I didn't know they were there."

Ajit laughs. "You're kidding, right?" He presses a seam in the cart's side. It swings open to reveal a sliding compartment perfect for dirty glasses. He pushes a button on the cart's handle, and a compost chute slides out from the back of the cart. "Now you know."

I wish the floor were water so I could sink down into it.

He turns to my data pad. "At least you took some orders

while you were up there." He squints at the pad, and then holds it out for me. "What does that say? M-A-G-O-L-A-S-I. Magolasi?"

"Mango lassi?"

"Not exactly the top of your class, were you?"

I stalk away. My eyes blur as I burst through the kitchen doors, into the hallway where I've stowed my things among the other chai wallahs' crows and lunch bins. I sit down on the narrow metal bench bolted to the wall and drop my face into my hands.

A few moments pass, and then the door squeaks. Someone crosses the floor and sits next to me. "You okay, love?"

I look up. Doya smiles back at me.

"I mucked it all up," I say.

"Don't worry." Doya pats my back. "It's only your first day. No one's first day is perfect."

"I served everything all out of order, and one of the upstairs women yelled at me, and I used the cart wrong, and Ajit couldn't even read my writing." My voice breaks. For some reason that hurts worst, that my hard-won writing isn't good enough.

"I'll tell you something." Doya leans back against the wall. "You know why they have us?"

"No," I say into my hands.

"All those people upstairs, the ones you fetch things for, they aren't allowed to leave their desks for more than a few minutes. They've got efficiency ratings to keep up with, too. Their bosses have us around so they can't leave off working and run down the street for a nice beer or some tea. You understand?"

I nod.

"So every time one of them screams at me, I think, *You're stuck here with yourself all day, but in a minute or so, I can walk on.*"

I nod again. "Right so."

We sit in silence for a moment.

"Where are you from?" Doya asks.

I hesitate. "Come how?"

"That funny way of talking you have," Doya says. "I know I've heard it someplace before, but I can't place it."

"I was born on a crewe ship." The words are out before I can think on them too much.

"Ah." Doya's eyes light up. "The ones that run supplies out to the colonies and outposts?"

"So," I agree.

"I knew it." She frowns. "But you don't look like most of the crewe folk I've seen. And I've only ever seen the boys."

"The boys?" I repeat.

She nods. "My daughter, she's an instructor at a state boarding school. They've got a whole wing of boys from crewe ships who've been dumped off on Bhutto station or left behind down here. Strange things. Pale." She looks me over. "You sure you're one of them?"

"Right so," I say. "But . . . they got left behind?"

"Mmm-hmm. My daughter says their old men marry up all the girls, and there isn't anyone left for the boys, especially the ones from less powerful families. So they dump them off here. Awful." She looks at me. "No offense."

I shake my head. Some boys I knew died on their first journeys groundways, but Earth and its outposts could be dangerous places, like Modrie Reller and my father always said. And once Soli told me about a boy who had been banished from the *Æther* after some bad matter came over him and made him stab his friend. But nothing like that ever happened on the *Parastrata*. Surely that was never something we did. Was it?

A sick feeling creeps over me. "Do any of them . . ." I swallow. "None of them have red hair, do they?"

"Oh, sure." Doya shrugs. "All colors. Red, brown, white, yellow, black."

My head reels. I lean back against the wall. For a

heartbeat, I'm back aboard the *Parastrata*, ten turns old and watching Llell's mother sink to her knees before Modrie Reller. *My Niecein. Couldn't they bring back his body?* That night I had laid awake, thinking of Niecein's soul gone to dust and thanking the Mercies the men were the ones to brave the Earth instead of me. But now . . . Have all those dead boys been here the whole time?

And there was something else Doya said, something prickling at the back of my mind. *Red, brown, white, yellow, black.*

Black. The hairs on the back of my neck rise.

I sit up straight. "Are any of them my age?"

She frowns and leans back as if she can see me better from farther away. "Maybe," she says uncertainly. "They're mostly younger. Twelve to fifteen, maybe?"

"But *mostly*, right so? You said *mostly*."

Doya tilts her head. "I guess. I mean, I only visit once a year for Holi."

"So there could be some older?" My skin is electric.

Doya frowns. "I've never seen any, but—"

"But maybe since you visited last, they found more boys."

Doya purses her lips, and then nods. "My daughter says they're always finding new boys, so I guess it's possible. Maybe."

"Where is this place?" I lean forward. "The one where your daughter works."

"It's up in Khajjiar, in Himachal Pradesh."

*Khajjiar, Himachal Pradesh. Khajjiar, Himachal Pradesh.* I try to write it in my memory. "Is that far?"

"Why?" Doya raises an eyebrow. "You're not thinking of going there, are you?"

"No," I say quickly. As kind as Doya is, I'm not spilling all my sadness and shame for her. "I mean . . . I don't . . . I was just wondering. I thought maybe one day I might. To see if I knew any of them."

"Ah." Doya shrugs. "It takes most of a day on the bullet train. Not too bad if you're going to stay awhile, I guess."

"Thank you, Doya." I squeeze her hand and then stand.

"You ready to go back to work?" she asks.

I'm not. I want to run out of here right now and climb aboard the bullet train, but I can't. I have to stay here, be faster, do better. Ajit and the upstairs folk can shout at me all they want, because as soon as I'm paid up with Rushil and see that Miyole has what she needs, I'm taking that train to Khajjiar to see if Luck is one of the boys who was left behind.

# CHAPTER .25

Rushil crouches at my side below the sloop's underbelly, box of fixers at the ready. "Is it that one?" He points to one of the blackened shield tiles and pushes his glasses up his nose.

"I think so." I slide past him and run my fingers over the tile's rivets. My attempts to keep him away while I fix the ship have completely failed. "Do you have something that will get these off?"

Rushil rummages in his box and pulls out a multitool with a flat-headed rod on one end and a power socket on the other. "Here." He rolls it to me.

I unbolt the tile, fit the flat end of the multitool into the thin crack between the ship's scales, and pry it down. All at once, a sticky gush of coolant pours out, spattering the pavement, and a burnt-plastic smell chokes the air.

Rushil hops back in time, but my legs ends up soaked in goop.

"Ugh." I push a slick of it off me.

Rushil pulls a rag from his back pocket, utterly failing to hide the fact he's trying not to laugh. "At least now you know what knocked out the door motors."

I send a mock glare his way and reach up to wipe a glop of coolant from the sloop's connectors with the rag. He's right. The coolant leak has shorted out almost all the connections between the secondary power cell and the door's motorized functions. The connectors are all bust, blackened and giving off the acrid smell of burnt electronics. I cover my nose with my arm and finish cleaning them off as best I can. Rushil watches as I pop out the connectors what haven't fused themselves to the backing panel, then chip out the ones that have. When I'm done, all that's left are the ash outlines of the connectors, and frayed sets of wires pigtailing out of their reinforcement tubes.

I slide back the panel leading to the coolant conduits. More of the viscous goop slops out. *Maybe a break in the line,* I think. I flip a switch on the multitool so it beams a blue-white circle of light and wriggle the top half of my body into the ship's innards.

"What's wrong? Can you see?" Rushil's voice comes muffled from the other side of the hull.

I slide the beam along the conduits. Long splits and fissures glisten with leaking coolant all up and down the length of the lines. I let out an involuntary gasp, and then a groan.

"What is it?" Rushil asks again.

I run the light over the lines again, only half believing what I see. I've never seen anything so bust. Stress fractures split them like gashes down a man's back. It must be from the ship's inner workings changing temperature too quickly, too many times. I half remember Perpétue saying something about having to lay down a good sum to replace them again soon.

"The coolant conduits are ragged," I call out.

"Here, let me see," he says.

I duck out and hand over the light to him. His torso disappears into the ship. At last he speaks. "This is bad, Ava."

"I know." I give a short, hysterical laugh.

Rushil ducks out of the ship and crouches beneath it. "You're lucky it didn't choke and send you into a death spiral on the way over from the flightport." He flicks his light up. "Can you fix it?"

I bite my lip, weighing everything. "I maybe could, but it would take forever. And the money for parts . . ."

I stare at Miyole, sitting in the shadow of Rushil's trailer. She pokes at the dirt with a stick, Pala asleep beside her. I've managed to keep up my end of our curry bargain and even pay Rushil back some, but one ticket for the bullet train to Khajjiar costs more than my fake ID. And I've realized I don't need just one ticket, I need two. It's bad enough leaving Miyole alone while I work. It near kills me how much longer it means I have to wait, but I can't leave her for two full days while I go chasing Luck's ghost.

"You know, I might have some extra tubing," Rushil says.

I close my eyes. "Stop. You know I can't take anything more from you."

"It's really nothing, Ava." Rushil gestures at the jumble of ship parts piled nearby. "Half my business is stripping old ships for resale parts. And I know a girl, my friend Zarine—she sells new components. She'd give us a deal on anything we couldn't scrounge up here."

I stare at him, wary. I want my ship fixed. Of course I do. Because then, forget the train, I could fly to Khajjiar. I could be there in an afternoon, and Luck would see my ship's shadow on the grass and come running. Then I wouldn't ever have to go begging to my modrie, because Luck and me, we could take care of Miyole ourselves. And then I might stop feeling like my heart is choking me.

"I don't get much for scrap tubing. You'd be doing me a favor." Rushil breaks my reverie. He examines his hands as he squats in the shadow of Perpétue's ship, and then squints up at me. "I want you to have it."

I smooth my data pendant with my thumb. The thought of Luck running to me makes my body ache, I want it so much. But then I count my debts—docking and the ID, coins for the screener and a hand with repairs, plus a thousand other small kindnesses, tea and blankets and bandages. I run a hand over the ship's tiles. "Let me think on it."

Rushil's smile drops. "Sure." He ducks out from beneath the sloop and glances at the time on his crow. "Sure. You know, I've got . . . stuff to do. Repairs. Anyway . . ."

"Rushil, wait."

He stops and turns back to me. We stare at each other, the awkwardness growing. I don't know how to say what I mean—that his kindness is making me uneasy, even if it's well meant.

"Can I show you something?"

I climb into the sloop's hold and mount the ladder to the cockpit. Rushil follows me silently.

Dust has settled on the controls, and the air has gone stuffy and still. I move aside so Rushil can see the cockpit walls, covered floor to ceiling in Miyole's metal art. The fish-tailed women and roosters and boats ripple in the afternoon sun, muted colors surfacing in the brown and gray metal, like the rainbow in an oil slick.

Rushil comes to a stop in the door, mouth open. I recognize the look that crosses his face—surprise, confusion, slow-dawning delight. It's how I felt the first time I saw all of her creatures gathered together this way.

"What are they?" he asks.

"Miyole makes them." I swallow a lump in my throat. "Made them. Before."

Rushil touches one of them, a flaming heart, gingerly. "They're beautiful. She could sell these down by the station."

I shake my head. "She made them for her mother."

"Oh." Rushil winces. "Sorry. Foot in mouth."

"When we lost her . . ." I stop and clear my throat. "They said it never stormed there, but there was a storm. And Miyole's mother, she had me fly the ship while she went down to the rooftop. . . ."

I stare straight ahead at a sun radiating wavy lines. "Sometimes I think, *It should have been me.* I should have gone down to get her, and then Perpétue would be alive, and Miyole wouldn't be like this. They would both be alive."

"But you wouldn't be," Rushil says quietly.

I shrug. "What difference would that make?" If I weren't in the world, who would even know? Wouldn't Perpétue have been of more use alive than me?

"Don't talk like that." Rushil's voice is low, but there's a tremor to it. "You don't know . . . you don't know how it would have been different."

"I'm sorry." I sink down in the captain's chair. "I just . . . I don't want her to be like this anymore. I want her back to herself."

"I know." He takes the other seat, putting us knee to knee. "It's only . . . you never know who's going to need you. Or want you here." He reaches out and squeezes my hand.

I freeze at his touch—he's a boy, a man, a strange man—and then the gentle pressure on my palm sends a tender warmth through me, from my heart to my fingertips. I near shiver with it. How often has someone touched me kindly?

I meet his eyes. I never thought a boy—a man—would be the one to understand me, or even want to try. Rushil leans forward, as if to say something.

*But Luck*. I close my eyes. How can I forget Luck, even for a breath? I pull my hand from Rushil's.

He clears his throat. "So how does she make these?" He twists around to look over Miyole's collection.

"Scrap," I say. "And a metal burner."

"Maybe she could make some new ones." He turns back to me. "Give her something to do, instead of lying in the dark all day."

I shake my head. "We lost her burner."

"*Psssh.*" Rushil waves my words away. "You can get a cheap one from any of the junk dealers down by the station."

I start to protest, but Rushil holds up his hands. "I'm not trying to buy anything else for you. I'm just telling you where you can get one if you want it."

I smile. "Thank you."

"But if you want some scrap metal . . ."

I groan. "Rushil!"

"What?" He grins.

"Stop being so nice to me!" I'm only half joking.

"Okay." Rushil lays a hand over his heart. "I solemnly

swear to be a total *gandu* from now on."

I can't help it. I laugh, and playfully punch him in the arm. "Come on. I owe you a curry for this afternoon. You can be a . . . a *gandu* while we eat."

# CHAPTER 26

I step off the train at Sion station in the early evening, coins from my day at Powell-Gupta jingling in my pocket. I'm getting better at being a chai wallah. I can make the tea nearly as fast as Doya can, and I've learned everyone's name on the twenty-seventh floor—floor, not tier—as well as their particular tastes. Sweet pickles for Mr. Darzi, cigarette gum for Miss Sharma, who Rushil has taken to calling Miss Shirty on account of her being so impatient, and caffine pills for Ms. Chaudhri, who has two smallones at home. I'm even starting not to care when Ajit shouts at me. And best of all, now I have enough to buy Miyole a metal burner.

Dozens of street vendors sit outside the row of shops and *tapris* across from the station, their wares spread out around them on blankets. I pass booths selling glasses some like Rushil's, what seem to be the fashion in parts of Mumbai, jewelry in cheap, candy-bright plastic, printed fabric rolled up in bolts, and finally, what I've come for, tubs full of used crows, power cells, and other parts.

"Looking for anything in particular?" The vendor, a girl a few turns older than me with neon bangles clacking up and down her arms, wanders over to inspect the bin with me. "Those are all fifteen rupaye apiece. You won't find a better price."

I push a clump of stick-on LED lights aside and spot what I'm looking for. It's mostly bust and sports a bigger, clunkier grip than Miyole's old burner, but Miyole's hand will grow into it, and I'm certain I can find whatever fix it needs. It will set me back a small bit in the way of repaying Rushil, but more than I need even ground with him, I need Miyole well.

A voice catches my ear. "On me and my wives, our thanks."

The words pierce the friendly market buzz and strike me still. *It can't be.* I make myself look up from the bins.

A group of bleached-pale men stands a half dozen strides down the street, talking to a Mumbaikar in a gray suit with an orange pocket handkercheif. On first glance, they all look like the same man—the same long, straight white hair under their broad-brimmed sunshield hats, the same rubber-padded white suits standing out stark against the street's gingery dirt, the same chalk-pale gloves hiding their hands. The protective shadow cast by their headgear hides their faces, but I know them. The Nau. Here, in Mumbai, in the Salt. What are the Nau doing here?

"You like it?" The girl nods at the burner I hold clutched to my chest. "It's a good one. Only needs a little shine and it'll work again."

"R-right." I glance at the burner and then back to the crewe. I should be answering the vendor, haggling down the price, but they're so near. I can't breathe. Will they know me on sight? If they do, they'll tell my father and brother where I am, certain sure, and then I'll have to run again. Except how far will we get without the sloop?

The head Nau—the captain, most like—delivers a curt bow to the gray-suited man and motions the others to follow him up the street. They're coming my way. I duck my head and pretend to examine the bin's contents again.

"*Kumaari?*" The vendor touches my arm. "Are you all right?"

I come aware of my own breathing—loud, harsh gasps—and try to swallow it down.

"Fine." I wave her concern away. *They won't know me.* I look some different than I did when I left my crewe. They'd be looking for an ash-faced, red-haired girl. But my heart won't listen to reason. The Nau move closer, strolling, examining the vendors' wares. Every few feet they stop, point, and mutter to themselves.

My head goes light and gray spots fizzle through my vision.

They stop at the blanket next to me, the nearest man's feet a handsbreadth from where I kneel alongside the parts bin. They whisper among themselves. Then one, a tall, skinny Nau with his voice barely breaking into manhood, steps forward.

"My father asks, how much?" He points to the bolts of cloth propped up against the wall behind the vendors.

"Which one?" The man tending the cloth reaches a hand back and pats the bolts. "Different weights, different prices."

"The gold one." The boy points to a thick roll of fabric embroidered with flying cranes.

*For a bridal gown,* I realize. My modries all said the Nau dress their daughters in the color of the sun when they marry. What will the girl who wears it think of the birds? Will she know what they are, or will she trace their stitched wings in wonder? Does she yearn for something of the vastness beyond her ship's hull?

I grip the metal burner. That girl's fate is no longer mine. I may be cast off, but I am also free. I am my own, and I mean to stay that way.

The Nau boy turns my way. My limbs lock, ready to fight, ready to flee. For a brief moment, his eyes meet mine.

*Run,* my body screams.

But then his eyes slide away and come to rest on something behind me. I follow his gaze—a horse tethered outside a hair cutter's shop. I am no one to them. I am merely another repeating shape in the tapestry's pattern—a soiled groundways girl, like all the others in the market. And I am glad of it. I watch the Nau pay for their fabric and continue down the street.

I shove fifteen rupaye into the vendor's hand, too shaken to bargain with her, and hurry for home, stopping only to pick up a bag of rice for Rushil along the way. The late afternoon sun catches the dust stirred up by passing feet and trains, dissolving the sky in an orange fog. When did it turn so late?

Inside the shipyard, the lights burn in Rushil's trailer windows, but our own sloop is dark. I peer into the berth.

"Miyole?"

I climb up into the ship and blink until my eyes adjust. There. She's still curled beside the wall, as usual.

I crouch beside her. "Miyole?" Impatience and helplessness rise in the back of my throat. "Miyole, wake up. You can't sleep all the time."

She stirs and blinks up at me.

I make myself smile. "I've got something for you. A surprise."

Miyole stares at the burner, dead eyed.

"It's not working right now, but I'm sure I've got the fix for it." I hold it out to her, smile still firmly in place. "You could start making your creatures again."

She takes the burner from me, turns it over in her hands, and then rolls over to the wall again.

"Miyole!" I shake her shoulder. "Don't you want to take a look at that metal Rushil said you could have?"

She shoots me a tired glare, then pushes herself to her feet and walks mechanically from the ship.

"Miyole . . ." I follow her to the lip of the hold.

She doesn't look back, only walks deeper into the lot in the falling dusk.

*I'm only trying to help,* I want to say. But she's too far gone to hear. I watch her disappear into the maze of docked ships and shadows.

I sink down on the loading ramp. I was so certain it would work. I was so certain I would see some spark of her old self again once she caught sight of the burner. I heave up the bag of rice and balance it across my shoulder. Most like it'll come back to us cooked and served up in round pewter dishes, but I'm too tired to fight Rushil about debts tonight. I knock on the thin trailer door. The lights are still on, but he doesn't answer.

Streetlights tick on along the side of the lot facing the street. I should find Miyole, make sure she's okay. I should try to talk to her again, explain I didn't mean to yell, that I was only worried. I drop the bag of rice on the steps and turn to go.

"Shoulda gone with me, *chikni*," Shruti calls down from a ship top in the neighboring lot. The red-gold ember of a cigarette lights his face. It's a bigger ship he's perched on this time. Eight engines stacked in rows, with gleaming white shield tiles. He sucks in, then lets out a breath of smoke into the sky.

"Let me alone, Shruti."

"Just saying, I would've put you up for favors alone." Shruti taps the cigarette ash over the side of the ship. "I wouldn't have tried to squeeze rice out of you, too."

"It's not like that." I cross my arms over my chest. "He isn't—"

"Maybe not yet," Shruti interrupts. "But you can bet it's coming anytime. He's a hard one, Rushil Vaish. You seen his ink? The tiger? That's for the Marathi Wailers. They make their new blood cut a man before they give that mark."

All the breath goes out of me. "Come how?"

"The Wailers." Shruti points to Rushil's trailer. "He's one of them. Didn't you figure that out yet?"

Pankaj. That's how Rushil knew about him. What he said about the straight and narrow . . . And the tiger. I knew I had seen it somewhere besides Pankaj's gate. It's one of the marks on Rushil's arm. An ache throbs to life behind my eyes. Rushil's been wearing his sleeves rolled down ever since we went to get my tag, hiding his arms. He didn't want me to see. He didn't want me to put it all together.

"I hear they're always on the lookout for girls to fill their brothel beds," Shruti goes on. "Maybe that's why he hasn't made his move yet. He wants to recruit you. Maybe Miyole, too, for later."

"Stop," I say, but my voice shakes. Not Miyole. Never Miyole. The world has gone dark around the edges. How could I have missed all the signs? How could I have been so stupid, so blind?

"Whatever." Shruti tosses the butt of his cigarette over the fence into Rushil's lot. "Don't say I didn't warn you."

"I—"

The trailer door swings open, and Rushil leans out. He smiles at me. "Hey, sorry. Were you knocking?" Then he sees the look on my face and shoots a dark glare up at Shruti. "Is he bothering you again?"

Shruti makes his eyes wide and innocent as he shakes another cigarette out of its pack and fits it between his lips. Could he be right? The debt, the favors, the kindness—is it all to draw me into trusting Rushil? Is it all some kind of trap?

"No. No, he's . . . he's not."

Rushil sends Shruti a warning look. He starts to step out of the trailer but notices the cloth bag slumped against the bottom step. "Is that rice?"

"Right so." The darkness only grows, as if I'm watching everything through a bloodstained veil.

"Excellent. Thanks." He scoops it up and holds the door open for me. "You want to come in?"

"I . . ." I try to think past the roaring in my ears, the anger and fear spiking my blood—*run, fight, run, fight.*

Rushil smiles on with his funny, lopsided mouth. Is Shruti lying about him? When Rushil looks at me like that,

I can't fathom him doing any harm. *But the tiger.* And he knew Pankaj. And he knew about the Wailers. But if he's one of them, why hasn't he sprung his trap yet? Why didn't he give me over to Pankaj when we were inside his gate?

I don't know, but if I run, I'll never find out.

"Course." I send a deliberate glare Shruti's way and step up into the trailer.

"I, um . . ." Rushil starts to say, but then I see what he's been doing, why he didn't answer the door straightaway.

The trailer is clean. Or not clean, but ordered some. The bed is made, cups washed and hung on hooks above the stove, and all the scraps of paper and metal junk stacked in bins. He's even wiped the table of all its sticky spots. I frown. How this figures into a plot to turn me and Miyole over to the Wailers, I don't see.

"I didn't have people in here much before." He looks down at the thin carpet. Crumbs and grit still dust it, but now I can make out a pattern of faded blue elephants linked nose to tail around its border.

"It's . . . it's nice," I say, turning in place.

Rushil lets out a sigh of relief. "You like it?"

"Right so." I walk into the kitchen. Grease still gums the stove, but he's cleared off the counters enough so he can use them.

"You hungry?" Rushil holds up the bag of rice. "I was going to make dinner."

"So." I fold my arms across my chest.

"Excellent." Rushil pulls down a jug, dumps water into a pot, and snaps on the stove, oblivious to the chill in my tone. "Where's Miyole? Did you find her a burner?"

I tense, and then nod. What does it mean, this talking on Miyole? More playing nice? More feigned concern? Lulling me into feeling safe? I wish I had never shown him her metalwork.

"I wish I could make things like she can," Rushil says, stirring rice into the pot. "I can only put things other people've made back together again."

I watch Rushil's muscles flex beneath his wash-worn plaid shirt. The tiger's tail curves around the back of his arm, peeking out beneath his sleeve as he stirs the pot. It's there, clear as empty. Maybe Shruti is right. Isn't all of this—the cooking, his help with the ship, the work permit—isn't it too good to be true? I grip the counter behind me. No one would do this for me, not for nothing.

"You think she would make one for me?" Rushil asks. "I mean, I could pay, of course. . . ."

"Why're you being so kind?" The words burst out of me. "Why're you doing all this for me and Miyole?"

Rushil looks up. "I . . ." He rubs a hand over the back of his neck. "What do you mean?"

"You must want something. Shruti said you did."

"Shruti." He clangs the top down over the pot.

"Is he right?"

"Ava . . ."

"Is he?"

He stands only a step from me in the small kitchen. "I don't want some*thing*," he says. "I want you."

My heart picks up again. *Run, fight, run, fight.* Shruti was right. All that kindness and understanding, that was all for show.

He sees the look on my face. "But it's not . . . I mean, only . . . *Chaila* . . ." He looks away and hits the counter so hard the cups rattle on their hooks.

"What about that?" I nod to his right arm. "The mark you're trying to hide from me. Shruti told me what it means."

Rushil's hand flies to cover the tattoo. "This?"

"Right so." I fold my arms. "Did you think I couldn't figure it out? Did you think you could hide it from me forever?"

His face has gone gray. "It was a long time ago, Ava."

"So you're not denying it anymore?"

"I wasn't denying it," Rushil protests. "You never asked!"

"I asked how you knew Pankaj!" I shoot back.

Rushil doesn't answer. He stares at the floor between us.

I shake my head. "You lied to me, Rushil."

"Because I knew you'd hate me if you found out." His voice rises until it breaks. He clears his throat and starts again, softer. "I thought if you had some time to get to know me first . . . I haven't been with them for years."

I soften, if only a slip. "If you'd told me from the start . . ."

He runs a hand over his face and looks away. "I'm sorry." His throat works as if he wants to say more, but he doesn't. Instead, he braces his arms against the counter and bows his head.

The pot begins to simmer.

"I understand if you want to go." He speaks to the small bottles of cooking oil and spices lined up beside the stove. "You don't owe me anything. You probably have enough to dock somewhere nicer now, anyway."

I watch him, wary. If I were him, would I have tried to keep it secret? I haven't told him about Luck, about my own shame. And if he's canceling my debt, easy as that, then Shruti's wrong about his plans for me. Are we always our mistakes? Does anything we do heal them? I reach out, hand trembling, and lay it over his shoulder.

"Rushil . . ."

He turns. Before I have time to draw breath, his mouth is on mine, and the counter edge digs into my back as he presses his body against me. For a moment, my mouth works without me, giving to his kiss as I would have given to Luck's. His rough hand brushes my cheek. And then I remember where I am, who I'm with, what he is.

"Rushil," I try to say. Our teeth scrape together.

"Rushil." I twist my head away. "Rushil, stop."

He backs away. We face each other, breathing hard.

"Ava, I'm sorry. I thought . . ."

But I don't give him time to finish. I stumble out of the trailer into the hot, dark night. *Stupid. Girlish and stupid. Trusting Rushil, thinking he didn't want anything from me* . . . I storm past the sloop, kicking dust, and disappear between the silent ships and piles of salvage. *That's all any of them want.* A thought comes to me. *What about Luck? Was that all he was after, too? Am I so simple and easy to fool? Did he ever even love me?*

I run. Past yachts docked for the day and gutted ferries leaning in the shadows. The perimeter lights disappear behind me. I dodge a pallet of shield tiles and a small pyramid of barrels. Faster. I narrowly miss a jumble of rebar and jog left to jump a pile of rubber scraps. I come down uneasy. My foot catches on a stray pneumatic arm. I pitch forward and go down. The packed dirt knocks the air out of me.

I lie sprawled in the dust until my breath comes back. After a moment, I sit up. A wet, dark scrape covers my knee, but otherwise, I'm unhurt. The perimeter fence shows its stark pattern under a buzzing orange light. A steady trickle of running water gushes under its electric hum. I must be near the western end of the lot, where one of the city's many rivers cuts through the Salt.

I limp to the fence. The river creeps by below, black water rippled with light from the streetlamps and neighboring buildings. On the far side, the city glows, turning the sky to a swath of chalky lavender, and the earth to a dense, starry field of electric lights.

An orange flicker bobs into view. I look down. A small stub of candle in a paper boat sails into view on the river below. I forget to breathe as I watch it riding lonely and sure along the slow-moving current. And then another small flame rounds the river's gentle bend, and another, and another, until the river is aglow with a fleet of delicate boats ferrying their flames over the water.

"It's to remember the dead." Rushil's voice comes from the darkness behind me.

I close my hand over the hilt of Perpétue's knife and loosen it in my belt. I won't let him put his hands on me again.

He steps to my side and looks down at the lights. "People go upriver and light them. One for everyone someone's lost."

The lines around his mouth cut deeper in the candlelight. He shows no sign of moving closer. What does he want from me? He says he doesn't want anything, but then he kisses me, and that can only mean he expects more. Right? I wish Perpétue was here so I could ask her what he meant, what all of this means. I finger the knife's worn hilt. I didn't want him to kiss me, did I?

"I'm sorry, Ava. I never . . ." He rakes a hand through his hair. "*Chaila.*"

Miyole's bandaged hands flicker in my memory. Rushil listening to my stories about the tea drinkers at work. Sitting with me outside Pankaj's house. Squeezing my hand in the cockpit. I loosen my grip on the knife and look at him.

"Really, Ava. When you touched me, I . . . I thought maybe you wanted to, or I would never . . ."

I want to believe him, but something hard sticks in my chest. I need the truth. I will be tough, like Perpétue showed me, not some soft girl. "What do you want from me, Rushil? Let's be true about it."

His mouth hangs open. "Nothing, I—"

"Come on." I step toward him. I feel heavy, thick and toxic with all that's happened to me, happened to Miyole. "I'm not some innocent. If you want what Shruti says, at least say it to my face."

"No, I don't, I—"

"Then why are you acting so kind all the time? Making food? Fixing our ship?" I move close. My head only comes up to his chin, but he steps back. "What's a Marathi Wailer doing acting the good heart?"

"I told you, I'm not a part of them anymore."

I fold my arms across my chest. "And that's supposed to make it all better?"

He looks to the river. "No, it doesn't. Only it means I'd never hurt you, Ava." He drops his hands to his side. "I want you to believe me. I haven't run with them in five years. Not since I was a stupid kid. Not since I've had this place instead. But it's always coming back on me."

"Why'd you kiss me, then?"

"I . . ." He closes his eyes. "I like you, Ava."

I lean against the fence. The lights on the river are almost gone. "Oh."

"I thought you maybe liked me, too," he says. "I'm sorry. I wasn't trying to make you . . ."

"Oh." I look at my dirty, cracked fingernails under the perimeter lights. Something wet rolls down my cheek, and I reach up to swipe it away.

I clear my throat and concentrate on scraping away the dirt beneath my nails. "When I was growing up, my modries told me you only ever kiss the man you're given to marry."

*And now I've kissed two men, and married neither.*

Rushil's eyes go wide. "I never meant . . . Here it's only something you do to say you like someone."

I close my hand so my nails dig into my palm. "I believe you."

Rushil sits beside me in the dirt. "Do you think you could like me back, Ava?" The wanting on his face is so plain it hurts.

"I don't know." I reach out and hook my finger around a broken link at the bottom of the fence. *Luck, Luck,* my heart twinges with every beat. How can I ever love someone who isn't Luck? It feels like betrayal, even if I know I might not find him in Khajjiar after all, even if he might well be dead.

"M-maybe, but . . ." But it's too much. I can't finish. I can't even think about it. I turn away and bury my face in my hands. I can't let Rushil see me dissolve into tears, can't let him see me weak. I bite my tongue so I won't make any noise.

"Ava." He scuffs closer to me. His hand brushes the hair above my ear, and it's all I can do not to lean into his touch. "I'm sorry. Whatever happened, whatever people've done to you before, it's not what I mean to do. I swear. Can you let me prove it to you?"

I sit with my face in my palms.

"Let me make you dinner tonight. You don't even have to eat with me. You don't have to give me anything or do anything you don't want to. Just please, let me be your friend again. I want things back the way they were, that's all."

I sit up and rub hard at my eyes with my wrists. "Right so," I say.

# CHAPTER .27

I come back from a twelve-hour shift at Powell-Gupta to find the sloop empty. Panic hits me. I hurry to Rushil's trailer and bang on the door.

"Miyole?" I bang again. "Rushil?"

Pala barks from somewhere behind the trailer.

"Ava?" Rushil calls back, his voice muffled. "We're over here."

I walk around the back of the trailer and find Miyole and Rushil in the midst of a small wedge of garden I've never noticed before, huddled around an old wooden baling spool turned on its side like a table. Cucumber vines wind up a makeshift lattice behind the table. A pile of scrap metal sits between them, and Miyole holds the burner I fixed for her.

"You have to do it slowly." She holds up a metal shard

for Rushil to see, and drags the burner's white-hot point over its surface. "Like this."

"Huh. I see." Rushil catches sight of me and sits up straight. "Hey, Ava." He smiles. "Miyole's been showing me how to use a metal burner."

Pala limps over and smacks his tail against my leg. I pat his side absentmindedly.

"I'm making a dragonfly." Miyole bites the inside of her lip, thinking, and for a slip, she's the picture of her mother. She looks at me. "Do you want to learn, too?"

Relief floods me. She's out of the sloop. She's making her creatures again. *Mercies, thank you.*

"I'll watch." I lean against the side of the trailer so I can look over her shoulder. She's already outlined the basic shape of the creature and is beginning to slice out a delicate cutwork inside its wings. The metal itself shimmers with undertones of turquoise and rose.

"Oh," I breathe. "Miyole, that's some lovely."

She cranes her neck up at me and narrows her eyes, as if she isn't sure she believes me.

"I mean it." I squeeze her shoulder and blink back a tear. I don't want to spook her by crying.

Rushil clears his throat and stands. "Anybody want tea? Miyole?"

"Yes, tea," she agrees.

He pushes his chair in. "Ava?"

"Please so."

He opens a small door in the back of the trailer I've never noticed before and steps into the kitchen. Miyole picks up her burner again.

I lean in the doorway as Rushil balances the kettle on the stovetop. "You got her talking."

"Yeah." Rushil spoons dry tea leaves into an old brass teapot.

"Thank you."

Rushil darts a look at me and shrugs. "It was nothing."

"I couldn't do it." I look over my shoulder. Miyole frowns in concentration as she rounds out the creature's eyes. Pala has settled beneath her chair, and Miyole rubs the dog's back with her feet as she works.

"Well, I have to know how to talk to kids if I'm going to be a counselor."

I raise my eyebrows. "A counselor?"

Rushil's face darkens. He speaks down at the cups he's holding. "Yeah. For kids who are . . . like me. Like I was. Who want out of the Wailers and gangs like that."

I step up into the kitchen. "Right so?" I'm not sure exactly what a counselor does, and I don't know what else to add.

He touches the tiger. "I was thirteen when I got this. A few months later, I got caught running white tar to a dealer near the hotels, and they sent me down south to a juvenile detention camp." He shrugs. "I spent three years there before they sent me back to my uncle."

I look away. "I'm sorry."

The kettle puffs and builds to a low keen. "Don't be." Rushil pulls it from the burner. "I met a counselor there who was with Kere Haavu before he went straight. He got me to study, finish school while I was locked up. I want to try and do the same."

We lapse into silence. I think on how tense and sick he looked when we went to visit Pankaj, and how it all lifted the moment we were away. He didn't want to be there, but he took me anyway. He didn't want to be there, but it was the only way to find me work on the books, work that would keep me away from men like Pankaj and boys like he used to be.

I watch him pour tea and carry the tray out to Miyole. He pretends he's going to dump the whole contents of the sugar bowl into her cup, only to pull back at the last minute. She giggles and reaches as he holds the bowl over his head. I watch them, watch Miyole smiling true for the first time since we broke the cloud caps over the Gyre.

Rushil looks up at me. In that moment, I realize I'm smiling, too, and cover my mouth with my hand.

Rushil knocks softly on the sloop's hull. I put down one of the old paper books I've been practicing my reading on and climb out of the berth as quiet as I can.

"She's sleeping," I whisper.

"Sorry," Rushil says. He pauses as if he's not sure what to say next.

I lead him away from the ship so we don't have to go on in whispers. "What is it?"

"I was going down to the TaTa Talkies tonight," he says, looking more at his feet than me. "I thought maybe . . . do you want to come with me?"

"What's the talkies?"

"It's this old theater down by the levees. From back when Mumbai was the movie capital of the world. They keep this room on the second floor set up like an antique cinema, with a light projector and everything. The midnight show is always packed. Hold on." He pulls his crow from his pocket. "It's Musical Marathon night. You want to go?"

"I, uh . . ." I hesitate. I don't want to admit to Rushil I have no idea what a marathon is, or a musical, exactly. "I don't have the money." That's true enough. Why would I spend what precious little I have on music?

"My friend Ankur works there," Rushil says. "He can get us in for free."

"But Miyole . . ." I look back at the sloop.

"She'll be safe," Rushil says. "You can lock up the ship and I'll set the gate alarms."

I press my lips together, thinking. I've seen smallgirls and boys some younger than Miyole out running the streets alone all day, and here she'll be locked up safe. Even if ship strippers did break in, ours is the last they'd go for, with its burnt-out engine and missing tiles. I wish I could be as light as Rushil looks now, even for one evening.

"Come on." Rushil smiles and punches me playfully on the arm. "You deserve it. She'll be fine. Besides, musicals are no fun alone."

I bite my lip and look back at the sloop again. "How long will we be gone?"

"Two hours," he says. "Maybe three."

I'm off some longer for work each day, and besides, Miyole's asleep. She won't even know I'm gone. "Right so." I smile tentatively. "I s'pose I'll go."

I scrawl out a note saying I'll be back soon, in case Miyole wakes up, and then grab Perpétue's jacket. It's too hot to wear it, but I feel better having it with me, even if it's only draped over my arm.

We walk down to Sion station and take the train past the center city. As we glide closer to the massive levees on the west side, a sprawling white building with a dome and spire roof shines out among its neighbors. A sign glittering with millions of tiny lights projects above its top floor—TATA TALKIES—backed by the immense blankness of the levee wall. I stare past it, up at the round houses perched atop the walls like glittering lanterns floating in the night sky.

"Come on, this is our stop." Rushil pulls at my sleeve.

We walk to the front steps of the building. I pause before the wash of light streaming from the theater and watch the people filing in. Their sleek, armless shirts, loose-cut pants, and gossamer scarves reflect the foyer lights. They take the steps gracefully, their thin-soled slippers and sandals bending with the curve of their feet. They leave me feeling shabby and heavy in my boots, my faded cotton button-down and patched trousers from the Gyre. Except for my work uniform, I only have one set of clothes, and I haven't washed them in three days.

I turn back. "Maybe this was a mistake."

"What's wrong?" Rushil asks.

"I don't . . . I don't know. It's . . . I don't think I belong here." I wave my hands at myself, my clothes, my snarled, uneven hair.

"No one cares. Besides, we're not going in that way." Rushil nods at the brightly lit grand entrance.

"No?" I frown.

"Nope." Rushil grins. "Ankur's giving us his employee discount."

We skirt the crowd and head down an alley to the left of the building. A metal fire stair zigzags up its side.

I hang back. "Up there?"

But Rushil is already banging up the steps. The whole staircase sways slightly under his feet, as if it isn't entirely anchored to the building anymore.

"Rushil!" I call as quietly as I can. I climb the first few steps, and feel them bob under my weight. "Rushil!"

"Come on," Rushil calls down from the top tier. "Don't worry. I've climbed this thing a million times."

I swallow and step lightly up the staircase. It wobbles and sways, but I make it to the top.

"See?" Rushil says. "It's nothing."

I peek through the cracked door into a hallway lit with dozens of glass-beaded chandeliers. A crowd shuffles in from a grand staircase, filling the close space with mumbling and excited whispers.

"Maybe we should go back," I say.

"It's dark in there." Rushil leans over my shoulder to check on the crowd. "No one's going to notice us."

I put my eye to the slit in the door and look on the crowd again. Maybe he's right. Maybe I won't seem so out of place in the dim light, with everyone's minds on the musical.

"Right so," I say, then catch myself. "I mean, okay."

I move to pull the door open, but Rushil stops me with a tug on my hand. "Why do you do that?"

"Do what?"

"Make yourself say things our way. There's nothing wrong with the way you say it. It's *atranji*."

"What?"

He frowns and stares up at the levee, searching for words. The glare from the glittering sign and all the lights of Mumbai mute the sky to gunmetal gray. "It's like . . . well, strange, but that's not how I mean it."

"Thanks?"

"No, I mean . . ." He sighs in frustration. "Extraordinary, that's it."

I smile a little. *Extraordinary*. "Right so?"

"Right so," he says, and I have to laugh at how funny

my crewe's words sound coming from his mouth.

We slip through the door and join the line inching down a hallway. Chai wallahs and vendors selling dark beer and juice edge through the crowd, handing over glasses from the trays around their necks and scanning in payments from people's crows.

At last, we break through into narrow room built on a slope, with a vaulted ceiling and rows on rows of cushioned chairs climbing up to the back wall.

"Up there." Rushil points to a black door behind the last row of seats.

I barely watch my feet as we climb. An immense chandelier, the mother of all the little ones from the hallway, dangles above us. At the top, I turn to find myself facing a white square taking up the whole of the room's front wall. A smartscreen? But no, those go a kind of gray when they're off, and this is bright, bright white without any kind of glow, somehow. All the seats face it. The crowd filters in, murmuring in a way that sends pleasant shivers through me.

The door swings open. "Hey, man."

I start and look up. A handsome, dark-skinned boy with perfect teeth and hair in tight ringlets stands in the doorway.

"Come in, come in." The boy waves us up.

We follow. A low-ceilinged room jammed with machines and racks of small metal cylinders stretches away into the gloom.

Rushil grins, slap-shakes with the boy, then fakes a jab at his ribs. "Hey, Ankur. Thanks for letting us in."

"No problem. Bai's here too." He waves down into the crowd. "We're going over to Zarine's later, if you want to catch up."

Rushil glances back at me. "Maybe. I don't know."

Ankur notices me. "Oh, hey. You're Rushil's girl?"

"I'm not—" I start to say.

Rushil speaks up at the same time. "No. Just friends."

"Okay," Ankur holds up his hands in mock surrender. "*Chaila.*"

Rushil shoots a worried look at me and winces. *Sorry.* "Ava's new to the city. I'm showing her around."

"Ankur," Ankur says, holding his hand out to me. When I take it, he raises my knuckles to his lips. "Tell Rushil not to keep you hidden, huh? He always tries to keep the good ones to himself."

My skin goes roasting hot. I duck my head so I can hide behind my hair.

"Quit your *bhankas*, man." Rushil rolls his eyes at me.

"Don't mind him. He's contractually obligated to flirt."

Ankur slaps Rushil's shoulder again. "I've got to get the show started. Grab a seat anywhere."

We find seats in the last row. I glance around, still nervous, but no one spares a second glance for me.

"How did you hear about this place?" I whisper to Rushil.

"Ankur and me, we used to work here selling drinks, after I, um . . . after I got out. He runs the whole night shift now."

Just then, the chandelier dims. A shaft of light beams down from the back wall, and the empty square before us bursts into a flurry of colors and swirling lights. Music booms down from the ceiling, sudden and brassy, full of drums and horns, and one long word in the script I've seen used for Hindi jumps onto the screen. A woman's voice joins the music, and at the same moment, she dances into view, spinning over the letters—*bapabapabapabapa*—in time with the tempo. When she reaches the end of the word, a man steps in and catches her hand. Then they're dancing together, leaping over the letters and out into a restaurant, where they land on a table. The cooks and waiters and everyone sitting around them all leap up and join the dance, too.

It's too much. I've seen feeds and grainy clips on ship-to-ship transmitters, plus the glittery moving ads on the sides of buildings, but there's something different about this. The colors bleed too thick and rich, as if the figures in a tapestry have sprung to life. I cover my eyes and lean forward, dizzy.

"Are you okay?" Rushil whispers.

I nod and sit up.

"You want to go?" Rushil asks.

I shake my head. I lean as far back in my chair as I can and look at the screen again. Now the woman sits alone by her window, plucking petals from a violently orange flower, the kind I've seen sold in the Sion station market. Kohl rings her eyes, and a single tear tracks its way over her cheek without leaving a smudge. She starts singing again, and even though I can't understand the words, I can tell her song is about heartbreak. But she's not content to sit around destroying flowers. She flings open the doors of her family's house and draws her sisters, and then her mother, and then the family's servants out into the courtyard to sing to her father about how cruel he is to keep her away from her love.

"I'm okay," I whisper. "It's only . . . I didn't know what to expect."

But now I see. It's like my mother's stories, only with live people saying the words. I can follow it some. Half the time the people talk in Hindi, half the time in English, but I can tell something about the two lovers' families is keeping them apart. The man flies a passenger ship for a living—there's another song and dance in the narrow aisles of the craft that has something to do with some of the passengers wanting coffee and others wanting tea—but she's heir to her family's electronics business, and they don't want her leaving home. There's a lot of hiding in closets and singing, but in the end they get married and she runs the company from the ship, and everyone—the man and woman, their families, and the passengers all end up happily dancing together on the craft's wings.

I find myself humming the tune to the coffee-and-tea song as we sneak out the back of the theater and rattle down the fire stairs. Rushil joins in, bobbing his head from side to side and batting his eyes like the woman in the show, and soon I'm laughing too hard to keep singing.

We trip around the front of the building as the crowd disperses into the night. We race across the promenade and stop, out of breath, beside a marble wall overlooking one of the city's artificial bays. It laps below us, closed off from the sea by the levee. A set of *gaats* leads down to the water, where twinkling pleasure boats ferry their riders out into the bay. Voices and laughter echo to us across the water.

"That's the Gateway of India." Rushil points to a massive stone arch lit up like the moon on the far side of the bay, and then to an even grander building behind it. This one has red domed towers capping its top and corner rooms, and lighted windows setting it aglow from within. "And that's the Taj."

"Is it a palace?" Another word I learned from Miyole's books.

Rushil laughs. "Close enough. It's a hotel."

"It's beautiful," I say.

Mumbai shines along the curve of the levee. I feel lighter, more than I have since . . . maybe ever. I hoist myself up onto the wall and let the ocean breeze play with my hair. Rushil leans beside me. I look down. VEER + JIHAN 4EVR. I trace my fingers over the letters scratched into the stone.

I look up and catch Rushil watching me.

"Did you have someone?" he asks. "Back where you're from?"

I nod. I should tell him about Luck and what we did, about the whole mess of it, but the words stick in my throat.

I swallow. "What about you? Did you ever . . . I mean . . ." My face goes hot, thinking of that afternoon in the cramped kitchen, his lips on mine.

Rushil shrugs. "Once. Before I got sent away, there was this girl Shama. We were only kids, but . . ." He looks over at me and smiles sadly. "She was the first girl I kissed. Anyway, when I got back, she'd found someone else. She has a kid now. . . ." He trails off and stares out over the city.

"I'm sorry," I say.

"What can you do, you know?" He drops his eyes to the water, and then looks over and gives me a half smile. "At least we're here."

"We are," I agree.

A silence follows. I trace the names in the stone again.

"Thank you," I say without looking up. "For tonight."

"I'm just glad I got you to do something other than work," Rushil teases.

I shrug. "It's what I've got to do. For Miyole."

"I get that." Rushil nods. "But you've got to take care of yourself, too."

I look up at him, trying to draw the sense from what he's said.

"What?" A self-conscious smile picks at the corner of his mouth.

"Nothing," I say, and smile back. "I'm happy, is all. I'm glad I came tonight."

"Me too." Rushil hops down onto the sidewalk and holds out his hand to help me down from the wall. "Let's go home."

# CHAPTER .28

Two blocks away from the shipyard, a crowd of boys shoves past us, running full tilt. One of them lets out a whoop as he knocks Rushil into the chain-link fence along the side of the road.

Rushil picks himself up. "Pankaj?"

The older boy wheels around, eyes lit up with glee. He gives us the same sign with his fingers that Perpétue taught me on Bhutto station and dashes off into the night. Rushil stands frozen, staring after him.

I clutch Rushil's arm. "What's he doing here?"

Rushil doesn't answer. He grabs my hand instead and pulls me into a run. "Come on."

The moment the shipyard comes into view, I know something is wrong. All the floodlights are on, washing the perimeter in something brighter and colder than daylight, and smoke clouds the air. An alarm blares up in a long, winding howl, then trips off and winds up again. The sound rings through to the marrow of my bones. Rushil and I exchange a look.

*Miyole.*

I let go of his hand and dash for the fence. The section near the entry gate is blown apart. The razor wire still curls along the top bar, but below, the mesh bows inward and splits into two blackened sections, leaving a hole wide enough to drive a small vehicle through. I stop at the opening. The sharp bite of ozone hangs in the air, and beneath it something sickly sweet.

"Miyole?" I try to shout above the alarm.

A metal barrel lies on its side against Rushil's trailer. Small puddles of liquid burn around it, licking at the siding and sending up a thick, ugly cloud of smoke.

"*Chaila,*" Rushil curses and runs for the flames, ripping off his jacket.

I duck through after him. The sick-sweet burning smell grows stronger. *Mercies, please let her be in the sloop. Please let her be safe.* I pull my shirt up over my nose and run.

Our vessel looms out of the smoke, lit by the flashing perimeter lights and then plunged into night again. I sprint for the hatch.

"Miyole!" The alarm blares on, deafening. I bang on the sloop's side and scream again. "Miyole, it's me. It's Ava!" The door stays sealed. I spin around, searching for Rushil, but I can't see anything through the smoke clouding the passage to his trailer. I should never have left her alone, not even for a few hours. Not with what I knew about Wailers and thieves. *Mercies, please, let her be smarter than me. Let her be safe in the ship.*

"Miyole!" I try again, thumping my fist against the sloop's hatch. "It's—"

Suddenly, the lights stop their flashing and the alarm cuts off. My voice rings out in the silence. "—Ava. Are you in there?"

A muffled thunk echoes from inside the sloop, and then the hatch rattles open. Miyole crouches by the opening mechanism, eyes wide, one arm tight around Pala's neck.

"Mercies." I run to her side.

She clings to me, utterly silent and shaking. Relief floods me, and then guilt. I never should have left her alone to go do something so foolish. A musical. What was I thinking?

*You weren't. You're the same selfish girl you always were.*

"I couldn't find you, Ava," Miyole says into my shoulder. "There were men outside trying to get in the gate, and I couldn't find you, so I got Pala and sealed the door and stayed quiet."

"You did the right thing." I hug her tighter. "I'm so sorry. I'm just glad you're safe."

"What happened?" She lets go of my neck and looks at me.

"I don't know. But I think Rushil does."

I tramp through the smoke and harsh lights, carrying Miyole. Pala runs ahead. We come upon Rushil kicking dirt over the small pools of flame beside his trailer to stop the fire from spreading. I put Miyole down. A small knot of people have gathered near the hole in the fence. I spot Shruti among them, laughing about something with the woman who owns the shipyard across the way. Bad fortune for their competition means good fortune for them, I guess.

Rushil lifts the drum upright with a grunt and steps back to inspect it. "Looks like they used thermite on the gate, but this is only gasoline. A lot of smoke and fire, but no real damage done." He looks up and catches sight of me and Miyole, her face smudged with ash where she's been rubbing at her eyes.

"Oh, God." He takes a step toward us. "They didn't hurt her, did they?"

I don't stop. My limbs hum with rage and fear. "What happened?" I shove him in the chest. "You said you were done with them! Why were they here?"

I catch him off guard, and he goes down in the puddle of gasoline. Confusion flits across his face, then a flash of anger. For a slip, I think he's going to stand and swing at me.

"I *am* done with them." He picks himself up. "If I was still with them, why would they try to set my house on fire and blow up my gate?" He swings an arm wildly at the twisted fence.

"Why would they do it either way?" I'm shouting now. I know I'm not making much sense, but I can't seem to stop.

"Because they want me back!" Rushil turns away and kicks the drum so hard it falls over in the dirt with a hollow thunk. "They're trying to scare me into it, show me what they can do if I don't. *Chaila*."

"And you didn't say anything?" My body ticks with anger. "You knew they were after you and you let me leave Miyole here alone?"

Rushil runs his hands through his sooty hair. "They're always threatening me, okay? Anytime I run across them and they remember I exist, they start up again."

We fall silent. We both know I'm the reason they remembered him this time, me and my work tag.

Rushil looks at Miyole. His jaw and fists clench tight. "Are you okay? They didn't hurt you, did they?"

"No." I answer for her. "She's frightened, is all. She locked herself inside the ship with Pala when she heard them coming."

"Smart kid."

I sit down hard on Rushil's front step and bury my head in my hands. Being smart will only take Miyole so far. It's too dangerous here. She could have been killed when the gate blew. She could have been taken by Wailers, and all because I let Rushil distract me. I let him talk some nonsense about having fun, taking care of myself, and I nearly lost Miyole again.

"It's not good enough." I shake my head. Perpétue was wrong. It's not enough to try to do good. What comes out in the end matters, too.

"What isn't?" Rushil says.

"This." I wave my hand at the smoke-filled shipyard. "It isn't good enough. Not for her."

"Ava . . ." Rushil's voice is soft, pleading.

I stand. "This is your fault." My words are sharp as razor wire.

Rushil's face crumples, but I don't care. I grab Miyole's hand and stalk back through the clearing smoke to the sloop. No more weakness. No more waiting. No more dodging. I've got to do what's best for Miyole. It's time to confront my modrie.

# CHAPTER .29

The second time I see Soraya Hertz, she's sitting on a low cinderblock wall in the small park across the street from the university, eating her lunch. I've been lurking around the green, shady Kalina grounds all afternoon, trying to find the right time to talk to her. Earlier, Miyole and me snuck into the shadowy berth of the lecture hall while she stood under a wash of light on the far end, talking on about English and Hindi, and how they're threaded into each other now. She wore a lemon yellow scarf loose wrapped over her dark hair. We stayed until a man in a security uniform started walking our way.

She's even more real now, dusting crumbs from her hands for the pigeons trilling softly around her feet. She wears midnight-blue pants cut loose in the Mumbai style, with white slippers and a white silk shirt clasped tight at the wrists with glass buttons. Her scarf has fallen back from her head. She's some how I remember, but not quite. I had thought she would stand out clear, as she did on the *Parastrata*, but here among these groundways women with their parrot-colored skirts and scarves and saris shot with gold thread, she could disappear as surely as the tree branches overhead weave into one dense, leafy roof.

Miyole and I sit on a stone bench, partially hidden by a juice vendor. Between us and Soraya, old men and couples and mothers with babies rest under the long arms of the trees. A tangle of skinny boys scuffle together, kicking a ball against the cinderblock wall.

Soraya snaps the top over her lunch tin, checks her water bottle to be sure the lid is screwed tight, and stows them both in her bag. She stands and brushes the wrinkles from her pant legs.

"Wait here," I whisper to Miyole.

I feel as though I'm trailing along behind my body as I take one step and then another, around the juice vendor, past an ancient, knobby rain tree, barely breathing. Nearer now, five meters, then two, then an arm's breadth. I stop. There's some of my mother in Soraya's face. Only my mother never had strands of silvery gray laced in her hair. She never lived that long.

Soraya looks up. "Can I help you?" She frowns. "Aren't you in my morning lecture session? Don't tell me. Is it Pakshi?"

*She doesn't recognize me.*

I stop short. But of course she doesn't. She never even saw me aboard the *Parastrata*; Modrie Reller made sure of that. And even if she had seen me, she'd be expecting a pale, amber-haired girl in skirts, not me with my darker groundways looks and my boots.

"No, missus." My voice sticks in my throat. "You're . . . you're Soraya Hertz?"

"Yes." She eyes me warily and secures her bag across her shoulder.

"The so doctor?" I want to be absolutely sure.

Shock twists her face. "What did you say?"

"I asked . . ." I look over my shoulder at Miyole, suddenly unsure of myself. "You're Soraya Hertz, right so? The so doctor?" I shake my head. "Dr. Soraya Hertz?"

"Who are you?" Her voice climbs high and tight. Her eyes flick to Perpétue's knife at my belt, then over to the juice vendor and the smallones at the water fountain.

"I . . . I'm Parastrata Ava, so missus. My mother, Ete, was your sister. You're my blood modrie."

For a moment, the afternoon hangs still around us.

Horses and foot traffic trundle away on the nearby street. A crack and distant cheering rise far behind the trees, on the other side of the park.

"No." Soraya turns away. "My sister's dead. She never had any children." She stands, grips her bag tight, and walks away from me at a brisk clip.

"Please, missus." I follow her. "I don't have anyone else to go to. I . . ."

She rounds on me. "I don't know who you are or who put you up to this, but it's sick, do you hear me? Despicable."

I stop in the middle of the path. She doesn't believe me. Her slippers slap the paving stones as she hurries away. If only I had some proof, some way to make her know . . . I reach for my throat. The data pendant, my ancestry charted back generations on generations. The disk rests warm on my skin, still threaded on its leather cord.

"Please, so missus." I pull the cord up over my head and run after her. The disk gleams as it twists in the afternoon sun.

"I'm calling the police. Do you hear?" She holds up her crow. "I mean it."

"Missus, please." I hold the pendant out to her. "Look at this. It's all I'm asking."

She pauses mid-dial and looks up. Catches sight of

the disk. My throat closes tight.

"Is that . . ." Soraya lets the hand holding her crow fall to her side. She reaches out and cups the pendant in her hand. Its delicate whorl of circuitry glints in the sun. She lets out a breath and slowly, heavily, raises her eyes to mine.

Children run by us as they barrel around the trees in a game of chase.

"If you look on it, so missus, you'll see," I say. "You only have to look. That's all I ask."

"No," she says, hoarse. She tugs at the scarf wrapped around her neck and shoulders. "I don't have to." The satiny cloth parts, and there it hangs, strung on a silver chain at the hollow of her throat, a data pendant twin to mine.

The *tapri* is loud, brimming full of people, but Soraya finds us a quiet spot at a table wedged between a wall and a window.

"I think I saw you," she says, studying my face. "When I came aboard to bury your mother, I saw a little dark-haired girl. You were running with the other children, but I didn't think anything of it. They told me Ete never had any children, that she was cursed."

*Cursed.* I swallow. "I saw you too. But these boys, they

were teasing me and saying you were a giant come to take me away, so I hid."

Miyole looks up from her yogurt drink and eyes us curiously.

Soraya shakes her head. "But I don't understand why they lied to me about you."

*I do*, I think, but I don't say it aloud. What good would it do to tell her my crewe thought her corrupt, an outsider muddying our pure world with traces of the Earth? They must have wanted her gone, wanted all our ties severed.

She holds her pendant up to the light. "This was your mother's. Iri and your great-grandmother Laral gave it to me when we buried her." Her face changes suddenly; she looks stricken. "If I had known she had a daughter, I never would have taken it."

*Iri.* I push my tea away, suddenly queasy. "It's no matter."

Soraya frowns and leans forward over her own cup of tea. "Are you married, then?" She says it quietly, as though speaking to someone who's fallen ill.

I close my hand over the pendant. "No."

"No?" Soraya frowns.

"No." I say it firm. I can't talk on this, not now, not with her, not ever.

Soraya straightens herself in her chair. "So you flew here?"

"Right so," I say.

"By yourselves?" She glances at Miyole and pulls a handkerchief out of her pocket to mop up the yogurt Miyole has dripped all over her shirt. "Here, dear."

I nod. "Miyole's mother showed me." I stir my tea. It seems wrong to say Perpétue's name now, as if the sound of it is still too loud for human ears.

"You poor girl," Soraya says, still dabbing at Miyole's collar. And then to me. "You should have come to me sooner. Straightaway."

"I couldn't." I talk down into my tea. "I mean, I wasn't sure . . ."

"Of course." Soraya lays her hand awkwardly over my own, then pulls away again quickly.

"Iri said something, before they . . . before she . . . when I left," I fumble. "She said you helped her with something, something worse than . . . I mean, something secret."

Soraya purses her lips. "Yes, Iri. And Laral, too. They're the ones who showed me your mother's body. They told me she was my sister."

My great-grandmother Laral? I see her body again, waiting peaceful for the Void to accept her. Her bone-white hair in marriage braids, her skin thin and yellow like aged rice paper. "But what did you help them do?"

"Bury your mother," Soraya says. "You know that. But it's not the way you think. Your great-grandfather Harrah didn't want her buried *ad astra*. He wanted me to bring her body back here and bury it beneath the earth or burn it, the way we do—"

A small sound escapes my throat. Even with all the crimes on my head, my crewe still meant to give me over to the Void. They never would have done me the shame of burying me beneath the earth.

"But Iri and Laral couldn't let that happen," Soraya continues. "They found me and brought me to her body. They told me what it meant, and together we buried her with the stars."

I work my mouth. "But . . . why?" I finally push out. "Why would my great-grandfather do that to her?"

Soraya picks a piece of lint from her lap and flicks it away. "Harrah said she was cursed. Her looks made her hard to marry off, and then she had trouble getting pregnant. He said her ghost would tail your ship and bring everyone bad luck."

Her words hit me full in the chest. I touch my hair. *Some bad matter.* Everything comes together. Modrie Reller dying my hair. My father and brother trying to marry me off-ship. My kinswomen so eager to send me into the Void. *They were trying to sever the ties to me, too. First my grandfather, and then all the rest of them. Did no one want us?*

"The important thing is, you're here now. You don't have to worry anymore."

That brings my head up. "You'll help us?"

Soraya nods. She taps her spoon against the lip of her teacup—*clink clink clink*. "You'll have to come and live with me. Both of you."

"You mean it?" I sit stunned, my tea forgotten. *After all this time, so easy . . .*

"Of course." She leans back in her chair. "We can enroll you both at Revati Academy. The headmistress is a friend of mine. I'm sure we can work something out so you won't have to wait until the next semester begins."

"Thank you, so missus. That's some kind, but I couldn't go. I've got my job to keep up with." Miyole would love that, but me?

"Your job?" She blinks. "How old are you?'

"Sixt—no." I was only some few months shy of my birth date when Modrie Reller told me I was to be a bride. "Seventeen."

Soraya huffs. "You don't need to work at seventeen.

You need to be in school." She checks the time on her crow. "You can give them your notice tomorrow."

"But how will I pay back Rushil?" My voice sounds panicked. "And what about the ship?"

"The ship?"

"The sloop," I say. "What we came here in. We've got it docked nearby, and I still owe Rushil some weeks' rent."

"How much do you owe?" Soraya asks.

"One hundred and fifty," I say. "Plus another two hundred if we're going to keep it there another month."

"Oh, that's nothing." Soraya waves her hand. "Don't worry, I'll cover the docking fees until we figure out what to do with the ship. Is it in salable condition?"

"Salable?"

"Is it ready to sell, or will it need repairs?"

Sell the sloop? Maybe I've made an awful mistake coming to Soraya after all. She doesn't even know me. How can she ask me to stop working, sell the sloop, and go to school? What if things don't work out with her, or something happens to her? I'd have nothing.

"It . . . it needs repairs," I say cautiously.

"Well, we can have someone take a look at it later." Soraya smiles over at Miyole. "Did you get enough to eat?"

Miyole slurps the last of her drink and grins. "Yup."

*Miyole.* I'm not doing this for me. If I have to sell the sloop to keep her safe, so be it.

The sun has sunk below the rooftops by the time we leave the *tapri.* Even though I'm still some angry with Rushil, I mean to tell him what's happened, where we're going. But he and Pala aren't in his trailer when we go to collect our things. Even the shipyard cats are hiding. A patchwork of plastic and metal cover the gaping hole in the fence. Soraya stands awkwardly inside the gate, clutching her shoulder bag and darting her eyes at every dog barking or shout from the street while I stuff our few possessions in a rice sack and seal up the ship.

"Aren't we going to say bye to Rushil?" Miyole asks as I turn the hand crank to close the loading ramp. Rushil and I haven't finished replacing the burnt-out power couplings to the door motor yet. We had planned to fix the coolant conduits first, but now I don't know if that will ever happen. I had gotten used to spending my off days and evenings with him, tearing out the old lines and scraping crusty coolant residue from the ship's inner hull, but the Wailers put an end to all that.

"No," I say, glancing at Soraya. "We can't wait."

"But I was making a present for him," Miyole says. She clanks through the rice sack and pulls out the dragonfly she was making the first day I found her up and about. "He won't know where we went."

"You can leave it for him," I say. "We'll write him a note so he won't worry."

I scribble out a few lines on a scrap of cardboard—*found my mowdri. leaving. will send pament for ship dokking. miyole wants you to hav this*—and leave it and the creature on his doorstep. My eyes prickle as I stand. If it hadn't been for him, Miyole might still be curled up in the dark, wasting away. I didn't want it to come to this. I want nights singing the coffee and tea song by the bay and Miyole playing with Pala and the dignity of earning my own keep. I want to bring Perpétue's ship back to life. I want Rushil to make me laugh. But I make myself walk away anyhow.

*This is all his fault*, I remind myself, wiping furiously at my eyes. *If he hadn't lured me away from the shipyard, if he hadn't convinced me to leave Miyole alone, if he hadn't ever taken up with the Wailers. . . .*

The train that carries us up to Soraya's house is smaller and less crowded than the ones I ride most days, all clean white steel and unscratched windows. We pass quiet houses, some with deep-shaded porches and an old look to them, others new and round, with gardens on their roofs. My modrie must be rich someways, I figure, living on higher ground in the north city. I doubt the lines ever flood here.

Miyole holds my hand tight as we leave the train and walk to Soraya's place. Her house is one of the older-looking ones, narrow and long, made of brick and wood. A covered porch full of potted ferns peeks out from the second story. A single rosewood tree stands in the narrow strip of dirt between her house and the road.

The lights quietly turn themselves on as Soraya lets us through the front door. The air wafts cool on my skin, and the walls swallow all the city's sound. We walk through a low-sunk sitting room with cushioned chairs, gleaming wood floors, and shelves for paper books built into the wall. The back end of the room is all glass, looking out on a brick-walled garden. A tree with star-shaped leaves, so purple they're near black, shades the corner of the yard.

"You'll want to wash, maybe." Soraya twists her hands. "Unless . . . are you still hungry?"

I am, but Miyole's eyes are heavy and she's swaying on her feet. "Thank you, missus," I say. "But maybe, if you had a place she could sleep . . ."

"Of course," Soraya says.

I pick up Miyole, and she lays her head on my shoulder. Soraya leads the way up a flight of waxed wood stairs to a hallway splitting off into five rooms, each with its own sliding door, rugs cushioning the floors, and thick windows of double-paned glass.

Soraya stops at the last room on the right. A quilt in soft rose, green, and blue covers the bed, and a long desk rests against the near wall. A brass telescope on a stand stares blindly up at the shuttered window, and an empty birdcage peeks out from one corner.

"This was my room when I was a girl," Soraya says, swiping a thin coat of dust from the desk. "This is my family's house. I mean *our*. Our family's. I really should hire someone to dust in here."

The room smells musty but clean. I settle Miyole on the bed and fold the blankets over her, then follow Soraya out into the hall.

"The bathroom's there." She points to the door across from Miyole's. "Take as long as you want. You can sleep in the next room down. It was my mother's study when we all lived here. It's the guest room now."

She says it sad, and I can't think but Soraya's mother must be gone now, too.

Soraya smiles tightly. "Make yourself at home. I'll be downstairs if you need me. My room is on the bottom floor. First on the right."

And then I'm alone in the quiet, cavernous house. Soraya's cleanroom has its own tile compartment where the water spigot lives, closed off by heavy glass doors. When I step inside to investigate, hot water shoots down from overhead and I scramble back to the tiled corner, clothes dripping. Rushil didn't have running water on his lot, so whenever we wanted to bathe, we went down to the river.

I work at the spigot's handles until I think I have the trick of it, and a stream of water patters down around my feet like warm rain. I undress and stand under the flow. I thought I understood luxury before, but this is beyond anything I could have imagined. Sweet-smelling soaps and creams in pump bottles rest on a ledge inside the tiled room. I lift each of them to my nose and smell, letting the warm water slough the dust and sweat from my hair and skin. I feel some sick thinking what the expense of all this water must be, what precious stuff is swirling around the drain at my feet. I turn off the water, lather soap over myself, then turn the spigot again and quickly rinse off.

Afterward, I wrap myself in a thick, downy towel and pad across the hall to the room Soraya said could be mine. The porch I saw from the street extends from this room, and through its open glass wall, the harsh orange and purple of the Mumbai sunset breaks in. A wide, pillowed bed heaped with midnight-blue blankets soft as fluffy rice takes up most of the room. A sleeping gown and a matching robe wait folded at the food of the bed. Soraya must have left them. The faint scent of her perfume hovers in the cloth.

I change and sit on the bed, sunk deep in the silence of the house. Soraya must have some sort of shield against the noise, for even in this plush place, we're still in the city, more or less. I stand. The glass wall to the porch slides open for me, and I push out into the warmer air. The brilliant lights of south Mumbai shine beyond the rooftops. I can just see the trains crawling in a curve where the towering seawall meets the water. The luminous buildings reflect one another, until the city hazes over with its own brilliance. Rushil is out there somewhere. Did he find the note? Is he wondering what happened to us?

I shake my head. I don't need to worry over Rushil anymore. Soraya will take care of the ship docking fees and everything else to do with him. And maybe, since the fees are so little to her, she might help me buy a ticket to Khajjiar. I can let myself think on finding Luck again. I can let myself hope.

# CHAPTER .30

I wake to the full brightness of the midmorning sun and make my way downstairs. Miyole sits on the back steps, facing the purple tree. She wears one of Soraya's button-down blouses like a dress, and someone has combed out her hair and smoothed it into four springy braids. A book rests open on her lap. She doesn't hear me through the thick glass doors.

The kitchen is empty and quiet, except for a machine on the counter making a burbling noise.

"Hello?" I call. "Sor—so missus?"

Only silence. I look back along the hallway where Soraya said her room would be. At the end stands a dark wood door.

"So missus?" I say again, softer this time. My bare feet

sink into the carpet as I edge down the hall. Is that the door to her room? I can't remember half of what she told me last night. Most of the other doors in Soraya's house slide sideways into neat pockets when they open, but this one is heavy wood with an aged brass doorknob and a tiny glass eye fitted into the wood at head height. I turn the handle.

"Ava?"

I spin around. Soraya stands at the open end of the hallway, staring at me.

"I—" My face goes hot. *The door on the right,* I suddenly remember. She said the door on the right.

"There's nothing in there," she says sharply. She pulls the door shut. And then, softer, "Are you hungry? I have breakfast ready."

I follow her, shamefaced, to the dining table. What was in that room? Something private, I s'pose. Something you don't show to a girl you've known for less than a full day, even if she is your half-sister's daughter.

Soraya hands me a plate of golden potatoes mixed with rice and a small bowl of papaya. She sits across from me at the table and sips her tea as I eat.

"Did you sleep well?"

"Right s—I mean, yes, thank you." I've never slept so soundly in my whole life. It was like falling asleep on a cloud.

“Would you like some tea?” She gestures to the carafe in the center of the table. “Miyole and I already drank a whole pot earlier.”

“Thank you.” I reach for the tea, but Soraya waves me away.

“You sit. Eat. Let me pour.”

I watch her fill my cup. Should I ask her about Khajjiar? Last night everything seemed so simple—I thought it would be nothing to ask, but now I don’t know. I’m a stranger here, living at her expense. I can’t afford to ask for too much, especially since the roof over Miyole’s head depends on it, too. And what if I press to go to Khajjiar and he isn’t there?

Soraya finishes pouring my tea and settles herself back in her seat. “Whenever you’re done eating, we can go. We have plenty to do to make sure you’re ready for Revati Academy and your residency papers are in order.”

“Right so, missus,” I say and smile. Whatever she wants us to do, I’ll do, so long as it keeps Miyole safe.

“Please,” my modrie says. “Soraya.”

I nod. “Soraya.”

Miyole comes in from the garden, places her book on the table, and leans her head against my shoulder. Her hair is soft and clean, and it comes to me what a poor job I’ve done of caring for her. When was the last time I made sure her hair was washed or her clothes properly scrubbed? I lean my head against hers.

Soraya pushes back her chair and carries the dishes to the kitchen. "I need to stop in with my lawyer to start my custody registration for you and Miyole," she calls over her shoulder. "And after that I thought maybe we could go pick out handhelds for both of you, since neither of you seem to have one."

"Really?" Miyole perks up.

Soraya comes back around the corner. "Yes, really." She smiles at Miyole, and I can read her pleasure in sorting these things clearer than any words. "You'll need one if you're going to be at school all day."

"Crow-crow-crow. My very own crow," Miyole sings to herself. "My very own, very own crow."

Soraya laughs. "You are such a goose!" But then she looks over at me and frowns. "Ava? What's wrong?"

"Nothing." I put my smile back in place. "Nothing at all."

The first place Soraya takes us is a woman doctor, who makes us dress in paper gowns and fills our arms full of shots. The doctor asks me all sorts of questions about how I lived in the Gyre and on the *Parastrata*, and again if I was married and if any men ever touched me or hurt me. I'm glad I never asked Soraya about Khajjiar. I don't want to have to explain to her or this strange woman about Luck, about what passed between us. That shame is mine alone. As for Khajjiar, I'll find another way. So I lie and lie until at last the doctor frowns and says she believes me.

After, Soraya takes us into the heart of Mumbai to buy clothes.

"I don't need anything more, so missus," I try to tell her.

"You can't wear that to Revati, Ava." She shakes her head at my faded Gyre shirt, my secondhand boots, and Perpétue's knife looped through my belt. "Maybe it didn't stand out in the Salt with all the foreigners passing through, but you're in the city proper now. You have to dress like it. And I told you, you don't have to call me missus."

We take the floating trains into the terminus nestled in the heart of the center city and step out into one of the crowd-choked canyons cut between skyscrapers. Powell-Gupta is in an older district, so I've only ever seen the city center in passing. The streets run thick with people and cows, bicycles, horses, elephants, and solar-powered rickshaws, all weaving around one another with quick precision. The rich waft of spice and oil-fried dough from the food carts swirls together with the smell of animal dung and the faint metal tang the trains leave in their wake. Herds of street sweepers roll along behind the cows and horses, chirping and banging to a halt when the animals stop.

We fall into the flow of traffic. Miyole gapes at the towers as we follow Soraya up from the ground level, onto a walkway arching gracefully over the train trough in the center of the street. A tier of smooth-planed pathways connect the buildings on opposite sides and covered gangways link to the shops. Above us, still more walkways climb to higher and higher walking tiers, with hanging vines and flowers trailing from their undersides. Glass pods full of passengers slide up building faces and stop gently, poised above the street as the people inside empty into the buildings.

Soraya leads the way up to the third tier, to a high-ceilinged shop on the top floor of an older building.

"Conditioner's broken. Sorry," the woman behind the counter calls out as we come in, fanning her face with a heavy piece of foil. The shop's barely hotter than outside, but I'm beginning to learn the rich folk of Mumbai pride themselves on not letting on they sweat.

Soraya waves and smiles, a kind of no-worries gesture, and weaves her way between the racks of embroidered tunics and raw silk saris in flame blue and persimmon. The back room is stuffed end to end with identical shirts and pants and skirts in a streak of colors.

"Here, try these." Soraya pulls out a pair of knee-length saffron skirts and scoop-necked black shirts that button up the back. A gold-picked crest with some kind of horned bird and a circle stands out above the breast. REVATI ACADEMY is stitched below the bird's feet.

Miyole makes a face. The clothes look some stiff to me, too, but if this is what we have to wear to earn Soraya's help, I'll swallow it. I take the clothes and let Soraya herd me to the dressing room at the back of the shop. Miyole pulls her tongue back in her mouth and follows.

I put on the shirt in the humid dressing room, and instantly my skin goes cool. I rub the fabric between my fingers. How did they weave cool air into cloth? My crewe would trade all their copper for that secret, and I bet the Gyre folk would have done, too.

I step out of the dressing room, still staring at my new uniform.

"Do you like it?" Soraya asks.

I look up. "It's *cool.*"

Soraya laughs. "Of course it is. Haven't you worn smartfiber before?"

I shake my head.

"The wonders of civilization," Soraya says. "Go on, get changed. We'll buy some street clothes for you, too. You can't go around sweating like a horse all day."

As we stack our new clothes on the counter, Miyole circles a slowly spinning carousel of jewel-colored saris at the front of the store.

"Can I get one?" she asks Soraya shyly.

Soraya melts. "Of course." She holds a lavender one dotted with silver-thread arrows next to Miyole's face. "What do you think, Ava? Doesn't this suit her?"

I freeze, mortified. "Oh, but missus, you don't need to—"

Soraya sighs. "Really, Ava, I wish you wouldn't call me that. There's no need to be so formal."

We head home with an armload of saris. Miyole even wears one on the train, sky blue with gold horses parading along the borders. The blue is lovely against her skin. She looks like a different girl. Younger, rich, the kind of girl who would never have cause to sleep in an alley or cut her hands climbing a ladder in the midst of a hurricane. Soraya bought a sari for me, too, in midnight blue rippling with undertones of honey rose. I tried to shake her off, but that started to make her cross. How can I ever ask her about Khajjiar if I'm already in debt to her over a stack of pretty clothes?

*I should be down fixing the ship*, I think as Mumbai skips by outside the train windows. *I should be working, shoring up extra money against what's to come. Not trying on clothes.* I finger the pommel of my knife. I need to be ready, in case something goes wrong here, like it did aboard the *Æther*, like it did in the Gyre. Nothing this good can last.

# CHAPTER .31

Revati Academy turns out to be an old stone building in south Mumbai, near the college where Soraya teaches. Miyole and I stand hand in hand before the sliding doors of its main entrance. I'm sweating despite the smartfabric. The knowledge that the satchel slung over my shoulder hides a glistening new crow Soraya insisted on buying makes me sick some. She bought us tablets of our own, too, but they were too nice. I couldn't bring myself to carry mine with me and left it at the bottom of the chest of drawers in the guest room—*your room*, Soraya says.

A crush of other girls in matching uniforms pushes past us. They're beautiful, all of them, the way I'm beginning to see being rich gives everyone a gloss of beauty—fine clothes, straight white teeth, shiny hair, subtle paints for lips and eyes, and soft, unblemished skin in browns and peaches and pearls. No one here is missing eyes or teeth or has hair bleached and brittled by malnutrition. I smooth my own blunt-cut hair and grip Miyole's hand. I wish I had my knife. I tried to tuck it in my belt this morning, but Soraya caught me and made me leave it behind.

Miyole, though, she's caught up in the swirl and luster of it. She tries to drag us both up the building's front steps. I hold back. Despite Soraya's talks on board-certified instructors and advanced classes and individual progress assessments, I only have the muddiest idea what waits for me inside. Will the girls teach each other, like Miyole taught me my letters and figuring, or are we left to sort things out on our own? Do they have books? Or tablets? Or both? What happens inside these walls that couldn't happen in the solitude of Soraya's house, where I could grind out my ignorance in private?

Finally I let Miyole drag me through the front doors. A woman in a pale blue suit with her black hair pulled back in a loose bun catches us as we step inside. "Miyole? Ava?"

"Yes." My voice squeaks.

"We've been expecting you. I'm Dr. Lata, dean of new students at Revati Academy. If you'll come this way, please?"

We follow her through the broad front hall, then alongside a small courtyard full of ferns and a trickling fountain. Girls sit in clusters on the fountain wall. One of them, tall and dark haired, with a gemstone stud in her sharp nose and gold bands crisscrossing her long hair, cuts her eyes sideways at us and leans close to her friends to whisper something. A stab passes through me. *Soli. Llell.* I used to have friends like that. Where are they now? Soli will have had her baby. And Llell, I hope she found the husband she wanted. Even if she wanted me dead along with the rest of my crewe, she was my friend, once.

Dr. Lata leads us to a lamp-lit, windowless room on the third floor, filled almost to its walls by a table. Two rows of bronze-framed tablets, thinner and more transparent even than the ones Soraya bought us, are anchored in the wood.

"Please, sit," Dr. Lata says.

We take seats side by side at the wide table, across from her.

"Dr. Hertz has informed us of your . . . ah . . . unusual situation," Dr. Lata says. "I assure you, one of the benefits at Revati is the individualized tutoring you'll receive to bring you up to speed. The young ladies who graduate from our institution have a ninety-eight percent placement rate in the world's top postsecondary learning establishments."

I look at Miyole. She has her eyes on Dr. Lata, nodding as though she's understood, so I nod along with her. A sinking feeling sucks at the center of my chest.

"But first we need to assess your learning needs." Dr. Lata gestures to the pristine tablets before us. They blink on, already brimming with text blocks and equations. "If you'll each complete the entrance exam, the headmistress and I will review the results and inform you of your class placement at the end of the day. In the meantime, Ava, we'll put you with the junior class, and Miyole, you may join the third-grade girls."

"But I want to stay with Ava," Miyole says.

"You may see each other at lunch, and during free study," Dr. Lata says.

"Please, so missus, it would be better if we could stay together," I say quietly.

Dr. Lata pauses before she speaks and folds her hands together patiently. "We like our students to interact as much as possible with their own age group. We feel it puts everyone at ease in the learning environment and enhances social development. Now, if we were to put you two together in the same grade, we would hardly be serving your potential for emotional acclimation and cognitive growth, would we?"

It seems best to nod.

Dr. Lata smiles warmly at us. "I'm glad you understand." She stands. "I'll be down the hall if you need me. Ava, I trust you'll leave Miyole to do her own work and not give her any hints, hmm?"

I stare after her as she closes the door softly. Miyole giggles and rolls her eyes. As if she would be the one in need of hints.

The tablets ding softly, reminding us to start.

"Good luck," I whisper as I pick up the slender stylus clipped to my tablet's side.

"You too," Miyole says.

I stare down at the screen in front of me. Miyole's been teaching me figuring since Rushil coaxed her into talking again, explaining about words like *integer* and the language of symbols. It comes more natural to me than the reading, but still, we haven't gotten very far. Equations some like the ones Miyole had me practice file down the left side of the screen.

$6^2 + b^2 = 144$

$a|-1| + 12(3 \cdot 4a)/5 = 1{,}729$

$z(144/2^{2+3}-24) = 45$

I push through them, then others asking the percentage of elements in a serum and the likely increase of a population given a two percent death rate per year. But too soon the questions throw up words like *matrices* and *sine* and *cosine*. They ask me to change an equation to a sloping line on a graph, and I'm utterly lost.

I switch to the other column, the questions about reading and words.

*Its var-variegated coat provides cam-camo-camouflage from the . . .*

I'm even worse off here, though I didn't think that was possible. I rub my pendant's smooth surface with my thumb as I try to read.

*. . . was the first to con-conduct Deep Sound ex-explor-explorations with the as-assist-assistance of neo-neoaccel-neoaccelerant tech-technologies . . .*

The words I do know bleed together or lose their sense next to the ones I've never heard. Their meanings go soft and slippery in my head, so all I can do is jab half blind at the answers Dr. Lata must want. I lay down the stylus, close my eyes, and lean my head in my hands.

I glance up through my fingers. Miyole leans over her tablet, mouth parted, eyes jumping back and forth across the screen. Every minute or so, she pauses to record a mark on the tablet, then goes back to reading, the stylus pressed against her lower lip.

I pick up the stylus again and stare at the questions.

*India's progress has provided a cat-catal-catalyst for eco-economic growth and improved standards of living in neighbor—* no—*neighboring countries . . .*

I scroll down. I've only finished a third of the figuring questions, and hardly any of the ones that take reading. What do they expect from me? And why can't I do this? Why don't they let me show them all I can do with my hands instead? I can weave and practice fixes and fly a ship all on my own. Doesn't that count for anything?

Miyole clips her stylus neatly to the tablet's side. "Done." She grins at me.

I taste something caustic on my tongue, as if my heart is leaking bitter bile. *How can she be done when she's a smallgirl, and I'm near a woman? What's wrong with me?* I swallow my desire to say something sharp and put Miyole in her place. I force a smile back at her instead.

"You should go tell Dr. Lata," I say. "I'm close on finishing. I'll be after you in a slip."

She slides out of her chair and disappears through the door. I flip through the questions again, striking answers, scribbling clusters of words I know, random numbers, anything to be done with these questions.

Miyole returns, Dr. Lata following close behind her.

"Done?" Dr. Lata asks brightly.

I nod, feeling more sick than I did on first sitting down at the table.

"Excellent," she says. "Go down and find your classes. Miyole, I think your group is in Civilizations on the first floor, and Ava, I believe you have Equestrian Studies out near the stables. I'll call you back to my office once we've looked over the results."

"Right so," I say, but the nervous-sick feeling creeps up into my throat. I've never heard of anything like Equestrian Studies, so it must be some complicated. Though if that's the case, why would they hold it in the stables? Maybe it's some like animal husbandry, but more of why animals work the way they do. I want to ask, but something about Dr. Lata makes my voice shrivel back under my tongue.

I walk Miyole down to her classroom. She peers through the glass door at the other third-grade girls and chews her lip. They look like something out of the advertisements on the buildings—clean cheeks, neat braids, pressed shirts. I would bet all the rupayes I earned at Powell-Gupta none of them have ever gone hungry. Miyole looks up at me, eyebrows knitted.

My petty jealousy turns to vapor. "Don't worry. You're quicker than any of them, Mi."

She smiles nervously at me.

"Go on." I give her a brief sideways hug. "I'll meet you in the courtyard when they let us out."

"Okay." She straightens her shoulders, adjusts the bag on her back, and pushes open the door.

My steps echo down the empty hall. I follow the signs for the stables to the back of the school, and then out a set of sliding doors. A flagstone path cuts around a glass greenhouse, its windows fogged even in the heat of the day, past a field where girls play some kind of game with flat bats, to a fenced ring of well-trodden dirt beside a brick building. The tang of manure in the air tells me I've reached the stables. I step up to the fence and breathe deep. The thick smell of the barnyard eases my nerves some, tells my body I'm home.

Suddenly a huge beast thunders out of the barn and swings toward me. Its eyes glisten black in its long face. Its metal-ringed hooves kick up a spray of dirt as it bears down on me, a girl clinging to its back. *A horse*, I have time to think as I trip back from the fence. *I told Rushil* . . . I hit the ground and scramble backward on my elbows as the beast charges past me in a rush of wind.

A line of girls and an older woman in a pea-green sari come running from the barn to my side. Some of them help pull me up, while others brush the dirt from my back and arms.

"Are you okay?"

"Is she hurt?"

"Advani-madam, come quick!"

"What was she doing next to the fence like that?"

"I'm fine, I'm fine." I rub my elbow, face burning. Horses. Of course. It had to be horses.

The girl atop the horse guides the animal back to the fence at a slower pace, her pale face flushed. "I'm sorry, I didn't see her there. I thought everyone was inside."

The older woman claps her hands. "Enough excitement, everyone. Back to the stables. Miss Labhsha, I believe you're next to ride." She looks at me. "Parastrata, is it?"

"So." I clench my teeth. If I had known Soraya was going to have them put down my name as Parastrata, I would have begged her to let me use her name instead. The last thing I need is to leave a trail for my father and brother.

"Dr. Lata said you were coming. I'm Shushri Advani, the equestrian instructor."

"Pleased to meet you." Soraya made sure I knew that phrase before she let me out of the house this morning.

"You've never handled a horse before?" Shushri Advani asks.

"No." I shake my head. "I've milked goats." I realize how stupid I sound as soon as the words are out.

"I don't believe the horses will require that particular skill." She cranes her neck to look past me. "Chennapragada?"

Two matching skinny girls with black hair cut straight at their shoulders break from the crowd by the fence. Twins, maybe? We never had twins on the *Parastrata*, but the Makkaram crewe was supposed to be full of them.

"Prita, Pia, show Miss Parastrata the ropes, if you please," the instructor says.

"All right, Advani-madam," one of the girls says.

Her sister nods to the barn. "This way. Come on."

I follow after them, flicking dust out of my skirt and trying to ignore the stares latched on to the back of my head. I'm going to have some nasty bruise on my tailbone tomorrow.

One of the girls turns and walks backward. "I'm Prita." She nods at the girl beside her. "That's Pia."

"Hi." Pia throws me a smile over her shoulder.

"Are you twins?" I ask.

"No," Prita says, dead serious.

"What gave you that idea?" Pia asks.

"Truly?" I frown.

The two girls turn their heads to look at each other as one, then burst out laughing.

I scowl at the dirt.

"Sorry." Prita giggles. "Everyone asks us that."

"Oh." I can't think what else to say. "Sorry."

"So what's your name?" Pia asks. "Or should we call you . . . Parastrata?" She draws my family name out in an imitation of Shushri Advani.

"Ava," I say. "Just Ava."

"So you really never rode a horse before?" Prita asks.

"No."

Pia spins around so she's walking backward with her sister as we pass through the close brick walls of the stables. "Not even your family's?"

The horses stare at me from their shadowy alcoves. Their glassy black eyes make my skin prickle.

"We, um . . . we didn't . . . we had goats," I say lamely.

Prita scrunches up her face. "Goats?"

Pia rolls her eyes. "God, Prita. Advani-madam said she's not from here, remember? They probably tied them all to a cart or something." She looks at me. "Is that what you did? Tied them to a cart?"

"I, uh . . ."

Pia doesn't wait for me to answer. "Want us to show you how to brush one down? Or would you rather start with the stalls?"

"Stalls," I say quickly. Maybe I can talk Soraya or Dr. Lata into letting me study something else. After all, I'm never going to be rich enough to ride one of these monsters around the city anyway. Not even Soraya has one, and she gets around fine.

Prita looks disappointed but leads the way to an empty stall in dire need of mucking. Pia passes around pitchforks and brooms, and the two of them groan and giggle and make faces at each other as we start scraping the floor clean. I try to breathe through my mouth until my nose adjusts to the horse smell and my heart stops racketing around in my chest. At least this part is something I can do.

"So where'd you move from?" Prita asks, slopping a messy heap of straw into a wheelbarrow parked in the corner of the stall.

"I lived some lot of places," I say.

"Like where?" Prita leans on her pitchfork.

"I was down in the Salt a while when we first got here."

"The Salt!" Prita latches onto that. "*Chaila*, girl, you should have said earlier. We have to go down there together sometime. All the best clubs are in the Salt. Oh, and our brother's renovating an old warehouse on the hill. He's going to make it into apartments."

"Oh, Pri-ta," Pia sings. She staggers at her sister, pitchfork weighed down by dirty straw. "I've got a present for you."

Prita shrieks and drops her own pitchfork with a clang. The horse in the stall next to us lays its ears flat against its head, snorts and stamps, and rolls its eye down at us. I cringe.

*They're smallgirls,* I think. *The same height as me, the same age, but even Miyole's older than them inside.*

A chirp pulses from Prita's pocket.

"Did you bring your crow?" Pia asks.

Prita pulls out a slick blue crow and gives her sister a withering look. "Like I wouldn't." She pauses, deep in reading the screen. "Lali's going to ride. She wants me to catch it for her page."

"God, that girl's obsessed."

Prita shoves her crow in her pocket and makes for the door. "Ava? You coming?"

The stall's only half done. I look from the twins to the muck-smeared floor. If Modrie Reller saw this, she'd take a wire to the back of my legs, or else make me clean the rest of it with my bare hands. "Won't we get in trouble?"

"Trouble?" Prita laughs. "Why?"

"We didn't finish. . . ."

"Oh, the machines'll get the rest of it." Prita waves her hand. "All Advani-madam cares about is that we practice so we 'appreciate the historical aspects of equestrian care.'"

"Come on, Ava." Pia grabs my arm and links hers through mine. "Lali likes a crowd."

I walk with them back out to the paddock. The girl I saw earlier, the one with the diamond in her nose, sits high in the horse's saddle, back straight. One of the other girls checks the horse's straps and stirrups while the instructor looks on, smiling.

Prita climbs up on the fence, pulls out her crow, and aims it at the girl on horseback. "Okay, Lali. I've got you!"

Lali kicks the horse into a run. Its hooves beat the soft ground as it circles the paddock and rounds past us again in a spray of dirt. Lali leans forward over the horse's neck, moving with it as it builds to a full gallop.

I sit on the fence beside Prita and Pia. All around me, the girls laugh and cheer Lali as she brings the horse to a high-stepping trot. I'm surrounded by girls who've had horses their whole lives, who've had nothing to do but perfect their riding, who don't fear leaving something half done.

*I want to feel that,* I think as Pia throws back her head and wrinkles her nose in laughter at something one of the other girls says. *How does she do it? How does she let go?*

I scowl at the fence. Maybe girls like me aren't made to be petal light and carefree. I'm the girl who cleans up after goats, who makes her own tea, who fixes machines these Revati girls will never touch. Or I was. Now I'm . . . what? Pretending to be one of them? Pretending the rest of my life never happened? For them, this whole world of horses and fine clothes and slick machines will never end. It's all they've ever known, ever will know. But for me, one wrong tug and everything could come unraveled in my hands.

## CHAPTER .32

Dr. Lata sits me down in a plush chair facing her desk. She stands on the other side, fingers resting on its glass top. "I'm concerned, Ava."

I keep quiet, waiting for her to continue.

She draws her hand across the touchpad on her desk, and the tablet screen beside her springs to life, full of what can only be my botched entry exam. She seats herself, stares at it, and sighs. "Your reading scores . . . well, I find them troubling for a girl of your age."

I don't disagree.

"And your mathematics scores are erratic." She looks up. "I understand you leaving the trigonometry questions blank, but how is it you've mastered intermediate algebra, yet you've never learned geometry?"

"I . . ." I swallow, feeling sick. "I didn't know. . . ."

Dr. Lata waves her hand in dismissal, mistaking my answer for sullen childishness. "Who was responsible for your education?"

"Miyole," I say. "And me."

"Miyole?" She glances over at my records on the screen. "Your aunt says you lived on a transport ship most of your life?"

I nod.

"Surely there was a certified instructor aboard?"

I shake my head.

"An instructor in training?"

I shake my head again.

"How did you learn even the basics, then? Addition? Multiplication? Someone must have taught you those."

I open my mouth, then close it again, afraid if I begin to talk about my life on the *Parastrata*, I'll have to talk about what ended it, too.

"Ava?"

"I don't know," I say. But I see the frustration building on her face and I hurry on. "I taught myself at first. And then Miyole showed me the symbols and gave me puzzles like the ones there." I point to the screen.

"Ava, we want what's best for you. You know that, right?"

"Yes, so missus."

"For that reason, we'll be keeping you with your social peers as much as possible, but assigning remedial academic coursework until you catch up." Dr. Lata taps the touchpad, and my exam disappears.

*Remedial.* I don't know what it means, but the way it drops from Dr. Lata's mouth tells me it's something bad. Trash. Burnoff. Me.

"Can't you put me in a class with Miyole?" I say. "I can catch up there."

"Ah." Dr. Lata wipes an invisible dust mote from her desktop. She won't look up at me. "Well, Miyole. That's another matter."

"What matter?"

"Miyole is . . ." She looks past me, out the window into the streaming Mumbai sunshine and the ships passing calmly over the city. She smiles. "We don't have many students like Miyole." Her smile drops. "I'm afraid it won't be possible to place you in the same class."

"But why not? I'm her . . . her . . ." I falter. Her what? Sister? Family? "Friend," I finish lamely.

"Exactly," Dr. Lata says. "Miyole's education is a matter for her guardian—your aunt Soraya—and for me. You need to take some time to put yourself in order, Ava.

Concentrate on your own education. Don't worry so much about Miyole. She'll be fine. More than fine."

I leave Dr. Lata's office, storm into the nearest bathroom, and kick open the stall doors to make sure they're empty. I bury my face in my hands and scream. *She'll be fine,* they say, when they know nothing about her except her skill in reading and figuring, nothing about the girl who used to fly her kite above the Gyre, who survived a hurricane with bloodied hands, who had to hide from the Marathi Wailers.

Suddenly, my crow chirps. I gasp and near drop it. I've forgotten it was on me, hidden in a clever, slim pocket sewn into my skirt at the hip.

I finally wrestle it open. "What?"

"Ava?" It's Soraya. Her voice sounds wary, unsure. I can't help thinking how Perpétue never would have sounded so. She understood me. She never would have sent me here to be humiliated.

"I wanted to tell you not to worry about waiting after school for Miyole," Soraya says. "Dr. Lata called. They want her to stay after to take advanced placement tests, so I'm coming to meet with her instructors. I'll take her home afterward." Her voice glows with pleasure.

"Is that what Miyole wants?" My words come out near a growl.

"I'm sure it is. You can talk to her yourself if it makes you feel better."

"Maybe I will." I snap the crow shut before she can say anything more.

I stomp down to Miyole's classroom, where I pace outside the door until the session ends, and a pack of smallgirls comes streaming out into the hall. Miyole catches sight of me.

"Ava!" Excitement bubbles in her voice.

"Miyole." My anger melts a little.

"I'm learning Mandarin," Miyole announces. "And Ms. Sarangapani says we're going on a field trip to the bioelectronics labs at Bangalore later this year."

"That's great." I smile and fix one of her braids what's gone askew. "Soraya says they want to test you more after school. Is that what you want?"

"Oh, yes." She's practically hopping. "Dr. Lata said if my scores were good, I could take biochemical engineering with the older girls."

"That's wonderful. You want me to wait for you after?"

Miyole frowns, thinking. "Isn't Soraya coming to get me?"

"Right so," I say.

"You don't need to wait, then. Soraya can take care of me."

I step back. "Are you sure?"

Miyole nods. "I talked to her already. She says we can stop and I can try kulfi on the way back. I asked Vishva about it, and she says it's this sweet thing, but it's cold." She's so excited she near forgets to blink. "I've got to go. Vishva and Aziza said we get to build our own bird glider in biomimetics."

I leave Revati Academy alone. The rail, with its mash of people and suffocating heat, feels less foreign and luxurious now. I've stopped looking out the window. Instead of riding it all the way up to Soraya's house, I step off early at the Salt.

The fence around Rushil's shipyard is whole again, a section of it patched over with metal sheets. His trailer sits quiet in the corner of the lot, flanked by ships docked for repair or salvage. I picture his garden with its cucumber vines, and him and Miyole sitting together, trying out the metal burner. I close my eyes and lean against the gate. It wasn't his fault the Wailers came that night, not any more than it was mine for needing a work tag.

"Hello?" I call.

Pala barks somewhere deep in the lot. I hear the uneven scuffle of his paws before he rounds a skiff and hobbles up to the fence to sniff me. I wait, eyes on the line of ships, but Rushil is nowhere in sight. I should slink away, go back to Soraya's house, but now that I'm so close to the ship, I want nothing but to crawl up into its cockpit and sit in silence. Maybe Rushil will have found some tubing for me. I can apologize for blaming him and for the way I disappeared with Miyole, and we can start fixing the ship together again.

"Hello?" I call a second time.

But no one answers, not even Shruti. The heat warps the air above the shipyard's white concrete and dirt. Some few lots down, a pack of dogs set one another off in a fit of baying.

*Like I was never here.*

I don't know why I do it, but before I can think too hard, my hands are unknotting the leather cord holding my data pendant around my neck. I slip off the disk and stow it in my pocket, then loop the cord around the gatepost and tie it in a bow.

*I was here*, I think. *Maybe he'll see this and remember. Maybe he'll know I came back. Maybe he'll know I'm sorry.*

I'm walking back to Sion station when the plan hits me. *Khajjiar.* I stop in my tracks. There's a sleek new tablet at the bottom of my dresser what should more than cover the price of a ticket once I've hawked it to a street vendor.

Would anyone even notice I'm gone? Miyole doesn't need me now, much less Soraya or Rushil. I'm worthless—*remedial*—at Revati. I can't wait any longer. If there's even the smallest chance Luck is out there, I need to find him.

# CHAPTER .33

My crow has been chirping nonstop for the last two hours. I pull it from my pocket and check the screen. SORAYA. Outside the train window, trees and small villages flash by in the last light of day. The man across the aisle looks up from his tablet and glares at my crow as if he wants to shove it down my throat.

I take a deep breath and flip it open. "Hello?" I was going to have to answer sooner or later, anyway.

"Ava? Thank God. Miyole and I have been worried. Where are you?"

"On a train."

"A train?" Soraya sounds confused. "Are you on your way home? When will you be here?"

"I don't know." I glance across the aisle. The man is

staring at his tablet, pretending not to listen in. "There's something I need to do, something important. I'm sorry I didn't say anything before I left, but I promise I'll tell you when I get back."

"And when will that be?"

I wince. "Tomorrow."

"Tomorrow . . . where are you going, Ava? What's so important you have to disappear without any warning?"

"Khajjiar," I say.

"Khajjiar," she repeats. "That's all the way up in Himachal Pradesh. What are you doing? Did you even bring a coat?"

A coat? I look out the window. The land is flat, sandy scrub. I doubt I'll need Perpétue's old jacket, much less a coat. "I'll be fine. I'll explain everything when I get back. I promise."

"Ava—"

"Tell Miyole not to worry," I say, and snap the crow closed before she can answer.

The cabin lights come on as the sky darkens, replacing my view of the countryside with a wan reflection of the train car's interior. The man with the tablet, an old woman asleep with noise-dampening pads over her ears, my ragged haircut and hollow eyes. I look like a ghost of myself.

If only Rushil were here with me. He would make up a terrible, ridiculous nickname for the eavesdropper across the row, help me keep from worrying over Luck with talk of the ship and how we're going to repair it. I switch off the overhead lamp, wrap myself in my jacket, and curl up with my head against the window. The night rolls out dense and black, broken only by a scattering of distant lights, as the train carries us to Khajjiar.

I blink awake to hills, misted and blue in the early morning light. My forehead aches with cold where it rests against the glass. I sit up. Jagged white mountains range across the horizon, so high they pierce the clouds. The trees and valleys are green but dusted with frost. My breath clouds the window.

We pass clusters of houses, their rooftop solar panels glinting bright with the sunrise, and then elegant white wind turbines staggered across the hilltops. The light melts over the snow-capped mountains like buttery ghee.

"Tea, miss?" A woman pushing a cart stops beside my seat and leans in close so as not to wake the other passengers.

"Thank you." I hand her a square of pay plastic and sit sipping my tea as the train slows through the mountain passes. We pull up to a station. Past the terminal, a town rises on the gentle slope of a hill, closed in on the back and sides by a dense green forest. Most of the other passengers are busy gathering their bags and stowing away their tablets. I wrap Perpétue's jacket tight around me and step out onto the platform.

The wind bites, but the sun burns off the morning chill some as I make my way into town. I stop at a store that sells *pakoras* and sit down to eat them at the counter.

"Have you heard of a home for boys around here?" I ask the white-haired woman who owns the shop. "A state boarding school?"

The woman frowns at me. "Eh?"

"A home for boys without families." I point up. "From spaceside?"

The woman says something in a language I've never heard before. Not Hindi or Marathi or any of the other dialects I've heard in the Salt. I squint and lean forward, as if that will help me suddenly understand.

"*Kyaa aap hindi boltii hein?*" I ask in halting Hindi. *Do you speak Hindi?*

"Wait," she says in English and holds up a knobby finger. I stand beside the counter feeling foolish as she hobbles away, and then returns with a girl some few turns older than me wiping her hands with a dish towel.

"You speak English?" the young woman asks. She wears a long-sleeved plaid shirt rolled up to the elbows and a scarf loose wrapped around her neck.

"Right so." I nod.

She nods with me. "Go ahead. I know it."

I clear my throat. "I heard there was a state home here for boys from spaceside who got left behind. I was wanting to know if either of you knew where it was, exactly."

"Oh, the pale boys." The girl's eyes go wide. "At the seed bank farm. It's about an hour's walk on the trail leading west from here."

The shopkeeper interrupts her with a pat on the arm and adds something.

"It's the only building out that way this side of the lake," the girl says. "You can't miss it."

"Thank you," I say to her, and then again to the shopkeeper. "*Dhanyavad.*"

I follow the trail out of town with my jacket buttoned up to my neck and my boots crunching the gravel. Cool, damp air soaks under my collar, but I know I'll warm up as I go. Only an hour of walking and I might see Luck again. Only an hour and I might touch him, hold him. Late-morning mist clings to the path. When I see him, will I run to him, or will I stand watching him, ticking down the seconds until he sees me? Will he know me, changed as I am? A bird calls from somewhere in the trees, a small, sad sound. What if he's not there? What if Doya was right and all the boys are younger? What if he was never there, and all I have left is his ghost? Will Soraya take me back after all the trouble and burden I've been, especially if I return empty-handed? I try to jog, but the air is thin and leaves me winded after a few strides. I settle for walking as fast as I can.

At last I crest a hill and look down on a farmhouse in a rolling green pasture. A stable some like the one at Revati stands across from the house, beside a small pond. Behind the house, a sprawling complex of greenhouses and gleaming white windowless buildings forms a hexagon in the center of the valley. As I watch, a figure walks from the stables to one of the greenhouses, carrying something.

I half walk, half stumble down the hill. *Oh, Mercies, please* . . . The person—a man, I can tell for certain now—shifts his burden to one arm and reaches for the door.

"Wait!" I'm out of breath and clammy with sweat.

He turns and I see his face. And he's tall. And he's pale.

But he isn't Luck.

His eyes are brown, his skin a freckled tea-with-cream

color, and his face makes him some turns older than Luck. Twenty-something, maybe even thirty. I stop midstride, as if I've run into a wall. "Oh."

"Can I help you?" He takes a step closer to me. "Are you lost?"

"This is the state boarding school, right so? The one for boys what got left by their crewes?"

"It is." He shifts the box from one arm to another, wary. "What do you want with us?"

I take a deep breath. I have nothing to lose. "I'm looking for someone. Someone from the Æther crewe."

"The Æther crewe." He frowns. "How did you say you heard about us, again?"

"This lady I used to work with told me." Even as I'm saying it, I hear how cagey I sound.

"A lady you used to work with," he repeats. "Uh-huh."

A drip of cold sweat runs down my back. "Please so, if I could only come inside—"

His eyes go wide, and his whole expression changes from guarded suspicion to full-out shock. "Who are you?"

"I . . ." I hesitate. "I was only looking—"

"Are you . . ." He shakes his head. "But they don't leave the girls behind. And you don't look . . ."

I draw myself up. "I'm Parastrata Ava." The name

sounds strange on my tongue. How long since I've said it? Half a turn? More?

"Parastrata?" He squints at me. "Aren't they the ones with the red hair?"

"My grandfather was from groundways," I say. "From here. That's why . . ." I guesture at my hair and skin.

He chews his bottom lip in thought.

"Please so," I say again. "I won't bother you long. I only need to know if someone's here and then I'll be on my way."

"Hold on." He unhooks an old crow from his pocket and holds it up to his mouth. "Hena?"

"Go ahead," a woman's voice comes back.

"I have a visitor here who says she's looking for an Æther boy. Is Vina in?"

A pause on the line. Then, "A visitor? Very funny, Howe."

Howe looks at me sidelong. "We don't usually see anyone who isn't a social worker or a government inspector." He raises the crow again. "I'm not kidding, Hena. We have a real live visitor. Can Vina see her?"

"You know she doesn't like to be disturbed," the woman replies.

Howe eyes me. "I think she's going to want to talk to this one."

The woman sighs. "I'm down in the southwest biome. I'll run up to the farmhouse and see."

"Cheers, Hena. Out." He clips the crow to his pocket again and pulls open the greenhouse door. "Come with me. Hena's gone to check if the director will see you."

"Thank you." I follow him inside.

The air shifts instantly from damp cold to muggy. Waist-high tables covered with rows of delicate green shoots fill the room. Cucumbers, tomatoes, yellow squash, okra, and young carrots reach up for the clouded glass roof. I unbutton my jacket and turn in place, taking in the sea of green around me. And this is only one of the greenhouses I saw from the top of the hill.

"What do you do here? Why do you have so many plants?"

Howe stows his box on a shelf and brushes the dirt from his shirtsleeves. "We're a self-sustaining outpost. Some of it we eat. But we also run a seed bank here, the oldest one in Himachal Pradesh." He opens the door to a white-tiled hallway and holds it for me. "This way."

I step through. "A seed bank?" The woman back in town called it the same thing.

"We grow different plants and harvest their seeds to distribute to farmers." He closes the door and waves for me to follow him. "You know, so the whole tomato crop doesn't get wiped out by disease. If one kind gets blight or something, we make sure farmers have other varieties to fall back on."

"Oh," I say, even though I'm not sure I understand completely. The right side of the hallway looks out on a garden, boxed in by more greenhouses on the far side. A blank wall, broken only by identical white doors and reinforced windows, runs along the left. We walk in silence past a sterile-looking dormitory, another greenhouse, and then a training room full of the same sort of equipment the men used to keep up their strength aboard the *Parastrata*. It strikes me how much this place looks like a crewe ship, and I wonder if it's on purpose to make the boys here feel more at home.

"I have to say, I've never heard of a crewe abandoning a girl before," Howe says.

I look out on the garden, where pear trees are beginning to fruit. "It happens."

"I've worked here seven years and I've never seen a crewe girl. Vina will want to hear all about you."

We stop at a set of steps leading up to a green door with an old-fashioned knob, like the one in Soraya's house.

Howe pulls out his crow again. "Hena?"

“Vina’s there. She says to go in whenever you’re ready.”

“Thanks, Hena.”

She snorts. “It’s your funeral.”

The green door opens on a kitchen. Shelves run along every wall and above the counters, every surface crammed with seed packets, clothespins, books, and cheery jars of jam, chutney, and pickles. Sacks of potatoes and pears slump against the bottommost shelves. A stack of plates dries by the sink.

“Vina?” Howe calls.

“In here,” a woman answers from the next room.

We follow the sound of her voice into a small office. She sits at an enormous desk. Wires, used mugs, and scraps of paper litter her workspace, along with a crook-necked lamp, a tablet, and a scanning machine. Behind her, yellowing log books climb the shelves all the way to the ceiling. I crane my neck to read the print on one of the spines. PSYCH EVALS A–B.

Vina doesn’t look up from the tablet she’s been scribbling on. “This had better be good, Howe.”

“Vina, this is Parastrata Ava,” Howe says. “She’s here about some records.”

Vina looks up and narrows her eyes at me.

“My grandfather was from groundways,” I explain

again. "That's why . . ." I wave a hand at my appearance.

Vina nods and steeples her fingers beneath her chin, but still doesn't say anything.

"I'm looking for someone from another crewe. A boy named Æther Luck."

"I thought you'd want to talk to her," Howe says. "Seeing as—"

"Thank you, Howe." Vina nods. "I can take it from here."

Howe breathes a sigh of relief, and then he's gone and I'm alone with Vina.

"Well." Vina leans back in her chair and raises her eyebrows at me. "Would you like to have a seat?" She waves at a tatty blue chair in the corner.

"Thank you, so missus." I sit, nervous. My eyes flit over the books behind her. GRAIN INTAKE MAY-DECEMBER. WORK SPONSOR RELEASE FORMS. RESIDENT INDEX.

Vina clears her throat. "So you're looking for someone?"

"Right so." I shift in my chair. "Æther Luck."

"How old?" She stares at me, not moving.

"Now?" I try to stop fidgeting and make myself sit up straight. "Um, nineteen or twenty turns—years—I think."

"That old?" Vina frowns. "And when would he have come here?"

I count back in my head. “Some time in the last eight deci—I mean, months.”

Vina grimaces and clicks her tongue. “I don’t remember anyone that old in the last year. Most of the boys we get are much younger. Thirteen, fifteen. But I’ll check my records.” She spins her chair around and reaches for the log labeled RESIDENT INDEX. “You know, you could have submitted an information request through the feeds. You didn’t need to come all the way out here.”

My body goes hot, and then cold. Why didn’t I think of that? I could have known all this time. I could have found Luck months ago.

“I . . . I didn’t know that.”

“Here we are.” Vina drops the thick log book on her desk. She pages through. “Æther, Æther. Yes, okay.”

My heart lifts.

She continues. “Æther Talent, Æther Mercy, Æther Far.” She flips the page. “Æther Till. Æther Keep.”

She looks up at me. Her mouth twists in professional sympathy. “I’m sorry, those are all the boys we’ve found from the Æther crewe over the last year.”

I sit stunned for a moment. “Can . . . can I see that book, please?”

“Certainly.” Vina hands it over.

I flip through the pages, reading the same names she recited, each with his own page of data. Intake date. Height. Weight. Approximate age.

"But . . ." My mind skitters, trying to find a way for her words not to be true. "Are there other places—homes, like this one—where he could be?"

"Not really." Vina lifts the book from my hands. "We get all the boys left in-country and on Bhutto station, but most states don't want to spend money on rehabilitating a bunch of vagrant boys."

I open my mouth to protest.

"That's how they see them," Vina says quickly. "In most of the backwaters out there they end up stealing to eat, getting in fights, begging. A lot of them wind up in detention facilities. It's the fortunate ones who are picked up and sent here. And we're only open because we're nearly self-sufficient, really. We don't take much government funding."

"I see." I stare blankly at the stack of papers on her desk.

Vina closes the log and replaces it on the shelf. "I'm sorry. I hate to be blunt, but if he didn't come through here, your chances of finding him are slim to none." She swivels back to me. "Are you absolutely sure his crewe left him behind?"

I bite my lip. *Luck's face bleeding from his father's ring. The metal look in Æther Fortune's eyes.* "No," I say. The word tastes like copper.

"That's good, then." Vina smiles, but she looks tired. "That's the best we can hope for, really, that his crewe didn't abandon him after all."

"Right so," I say quietly. But she doesn't understand. If Luck's crewe didn't leave him, that can only mean he's dead.

"Now, I've answered your questions. I hope you'll be so good as to answer mine." Vina reaches over to her tablet and taps.

"Recording started," a mechanical voice says.

Vina leans forward at her desk and laces her fingers together. "We've never had a girl from one of the crewes turn up here before. You're quite the find."

"Thank you, so missus, but I have to walk back and catch the train. I have people waiting for me."

She frowns. "You've clearly adapted much better than most of our boys. Your experience could be invaluable in improving our socialization techniques."

I bite my tongue. She sounds like Dr. Lata, trying to overrun me with words. Why should she expect me to tell her things I've never even told Rushil or Soraya?

“Thank you, so missus,” I repeat, sharper this time. “No.”

“Well, at least let me offer you some tea before you go.” Vina forces a smile and pushes back her chair. “It’s a long way back to town.”

“Thank you,” I say dully.

Vina bustles around the kitchen, running water into a kettle and crinkling open a wax paper pouch of loose tea. “You know, we have so much to learn from each other,” she calls over the running water. “You could give us such insight into the crewe system. And we can always use a pretty face to help convince parliament to increase our funding.”

A spark of anger flares in my chest. She’s asking me for help? Me? She’s just told me in so many words that Luck is dead, and now she’s grasping at me.

Vina returns with a tea tray, all smiles. “Think about it, Ava. Imagine all the good we could do together.”

I rub the spot between my eyebrows. “I don’t know.” I look toward the green door. An idea strikes me. “Could I talk to the boys?”

It’s a risk but a small one. None of them should be able to figure out who I am by my looks, and if they piece it together, who would they tell?

"The boys?" Vina's smile fades. She places a cup on the edge of the desk before me and fills it with amber tea. "Why would you want to speak to them?"

"Maybe one of them knows something." I pick up the cup. "About what happened to Luck."

"Perhaps." She pauses, filling her own cup, and her smile creeps back. "Yes, I think that could be managed. In fact, why don't you stay here tonight?"

I stiffen. "I have to get back. The train—"

"The next train leaves in . . ." Vina checks her crow. "Ninety minutes. I thought you wanted time to speak with the boys?"

"I do, but—"

"Well, then, stay the night." Vina gives an elegant little shrug that says *simple.* "Howe will drive you back to the station tomorrow. And who knows, maybe after you've rested, you'll feel more like talking."

I grit my teeth. "Right so." I put my teacup back on her desk, untouched. "I think I'd like to see them now."

Vina arches an eyebrow. "I have to warn you. They don't fancy talking to women much."

I almost laugh. "I think I can handle it."

"Of course." Vina nods and picks up her crow. "Howe?"

"Yes, ma'am."

"Will you escort Miss Parastrata down to the vocational workshop? She'd like to interview some of our charges."

"Yes, ma'am," he says. "On my way."

"See?" Vina says. "I told you we could help each other."

# CHAPTER .34

Howe opens the door to the vocational workshop—a long, windowless room, bright with artificial lights. Sallow-skinned boys with hair of black and red and white-blond sit at tables spread across the room, each intent on a different task. Two scrawny boys hunch over welding pens, fixing electronics, while others peer into tablet screens or sit in small groups, talking. It takes me a slip or two to figure what's wrong with the scene. I can't hear anything. Not the whine of the welding pen or the soft tapping of fingers on a trackboard, or the murmur of voices. The room must have a sort of sound shield, some like the one what protects Soraya's house from the city noise.

"What crewe was your guy again?" Howe asks.

I walk forward. "Æther," I say, craning my neck to

check the faces of the boys at the tablets. As we draw nearer, the sound shield fades and I can hear their fingers clicking. "His name is Æther Luck."

"I think we have a few Æther kids over in the socialization workshop." Howe nods at the group slouched around a table in the corner. Another man with a neat-trimmed black beard, maybe a teacher of some kind, sits at the head of the table, gesturing and talking to them.

The teacher looks up and smiles at us as we approach. "Ah, look everyone. We have visitors. You all know Instructor Howe." He turns his smile to me. "And what a perfect opportunity to practice our conversation skills. Who would like to ask this young lady her name?"

The boys cut looks at me, but none of them answer.

"Keep? Darrad?" The instructor looks from a skinny, dark-haired boy to a slightly older boy with close-cropped hair the color of a persimmon.

*Darrad.* For half a breath, I'm sure he'll recognize me. He belonged to one of the dyegirls. Four turns ago they said he was dead—killed in an accident on his first trip groundways. All the wives held his mother's hands while she wept.

The boys stay silent, arms folded, eyes on the table. None of them so much as look at me.

The instructor sighs. "Amon?" He looks to the frail,

white-haired boy beside him, who is chewing on a nail. He's young, younger than all the others around him.

Amon glances nervously from the instructor to the other boys. He looks in my direction, but his gaze floats somewhere over my head. "Pleasetomeetyoumiss."

"Very good," the instructor says. "And now, what's next?"

"I'mAmonNauwhat'syourgoodnameplease?"

"Ava," I say.

Darrad's head snaps up, his face a mix of confusion and suspicion, but he doesn't say anything.

"How can we help you, Ava?" the instructor prompts. He smiles too wide.

"I'm looking for someone." I turn from one boy to another, but they all keep their eyes down, even Amon now. "His name is Æther Luck. He'd be about nineteen turns now. Black hair, blue eyes."

None of them answers me, although I can tell from the way the dark-haired boys shift in their seats and dart furtive looks at me they know exactly who I mean. Luck was their captain's firstborn son, after all. And who am I? A stranger. A girl.

The instructor scratches his chin. "We don't have anyone that old here right now." He looks at Howe. "Have you taken her to look at the records up Vina's?"

"First thing. She—"

"Please," I break in, addressing the boys. My search can't end here. This can't be it. "If any of you know anything . . . if you've ever heard anything of Luck . . . I'm begging you, please tell me."

The boys exchange looks and go back to staring at their hands or the tabletop. None of them says anything.

I stare at the Æther boys, my eyes burning. "Please."

One of them shakes his head ever so slightly.

"Come on." Howe touches my shoulder. "They're not feeling talkative today."

I back away.

"See you in biome five this afternoon, guys," he calls as he leads me toward the door.

The sound shield closes behind us. Some months earlier, I might have left steaming with anger that the boys clung so hard to their crewe ways, that they wouldn't deign to talk to me. But now, looking at them, I only feel sad. How will they ever make their way in this world if they can't bring themselves to talk to anyone but men? And how alone they are. At least I have Miyole and Soraya, and maybe Rushil.

I lie awake in the seed bank's guest quarters, worrying the edge of the scratchy blanket. Some hours ago, Howe's voice came over the coms. *Ten o'clock. Lights out.*

Was there something the Æther boys weren't telling me? Was there something I missed?

*Blue eyes, dark hair,* I tell myself. But I can't make Luck come alive in my memory the way I used to. I can't make myself believe he's lying beside me.

I roll out of bed and pace the small room. Maybe there's something more in Vina's files. Maybe she overlooked something. Or chose not to tell me. Maybe she wants something out of me first, some trade. My face, the story of my life, for news of Luck? But if so, why wouldn't she come out and say it?

I chew on my lip. Perpétue would have tried to get Vina talking with a flash of her knife and an arched eyebrow. Rushil would bribe her. Soraya would appeal to her reason or, failing that, call in her lawyer. But what can I do? I don't have Soraya's lawyer or her way with words, I don't think the knife would work this time, and the one thing Vina seems to want from me is the last thing I want to give.

I pull on my boots and go to the door. It whisks aside for me, revealing the darkened hallway. No locks for me here. Moonlight slants up the walls and silvers the pear trees on the other side of the glass.

I creep along the corridor toward Vina's office, pausing to listen at every doorway. Nothing but silence. The boys and all the staff are long asleep. At least, I think they are. This place mimics a crewe ship in other ways; it might have its own Watches and night Fixes patrolling the grounds as well.

Before long, I come to the green door. I kneel and press my ear against the wood. No voices, no music, no clinking of cups and plates, not even the soft beeps and trills of a tablet or a crow. I reach up and try the knob. Locked.

*Nine hells.*

There has to be another way inside. There were other rooms in Vina's house, but I only saw the kitchen and her office, both looking out on the garden and the greenhouses. . . .

*The garden.*

I creep back along the hallway, past the guest quarters, past the training rooms and the boys sleeping in their bunks, to where one of the greenhouses joins up with the rest of the complex. Inside, stark white lights hang over the rows of plants. I keep to the walls, out of the glare.

I am nearly to the door on the other side of the greenhouse when it bursts open and Hena and Howe tumble in. I duck below the nearest table, out of sight.

"I couldn't wait to see you." Howe's voice. And then—kissing? "I've been thinking about you all day."

Hena laughs. "Me too. I was worried you weren't going to come back from Vina's alive."

They stumble against one of the tables, and Hena stifles a shriek. "Careful."

"No, *you* be careful," Howe says. And then he gives a playful growl.

I twist around, searching for a way out. And then I see it. A long, low window built into the side of the greenhouse at the floor level. I push against the latch.

"What was that?" Hena says as I roll out into the night air.

I push the window closed behind me with a soft click.

"Probably just one of the cats." The glass muffles Howe's voice.

I pick myself up and shiver. Night creatures chirp and chitter in the grass. The moon is full, bringing out the harshness in everything's shadow. I move from tree to tree.

A light shines in Vina's window—buttery, low, not at all like the greenhouse lamps. I drag one of the wooden chairs beneath the window and climb up. Vina sits at her desk, poring over her tablet. Every now and then, she makes a mark in the book. As I watch, she pauses and rubs her hands over her eyes.

I jump back down and crouch against the side of the house, hugging my knees. After a time, the light goes out.

I count to one thousand and then climb back up. The window beside Vina's desk comes up easily, thank the Mercies. I boost myself up into the opening and pause, listening. Silence.

I slide in headfirst and manage to make only a muffled thump as I land. I hold still, hidden by Vina's desk, and count to five hundred. Still nothing. I peer out of her office into a sitting room at the front of the house. To one side, a staircase climbs up to a second floor. To another, a latch door leads out onto a covered porch, and then the moonlit wild.

Right so. First, Vina's tablet. I find it on her desk, half covered by a file marked SUPPLEMENTARY FUNDING. At my touch, the machine springs to life with a faint chime. I stiffen and glance toward the sitting room. Nothing moves.

I turn back to the screen. A small box flashes in its center—PASSKEY CODE.

*Outh.* I look up. What would Vina keep as her code? I know nothing of her, except the work she does.

*Khajjiar,* I try.

INCORRECT.

I look for the right symbol for *Æther*, but I can't find it. *Parastrata*, I type instead.

INCORRECT.

*Nau. Makkaram.*

INCORRECT. INCORRECT.

*Seed bank*, I try, desperate.

INCORRECT. ACCOUNT LOCKED DUE TO MULTIPLE FAILED LOGINS.

I stifle a groan. There has to be something here. Some clue. Something, anything. If I can't get into Vina's tablet, at least I can go through the files filling the shelves behind her desk.

I pull down RESIDENT INDEX and hold it in the moonlight by the open window. I start from the beginning, scanning each page for any mention of the Æthers. Their crewe has left plenty of boys behind, but none in this past turn. I linger over the last boy's name. Æther Keep, age thirteen, left a little over a turn ago. Did Luck know him? Did he wonder where the younger boy had gone? Was he on the landing party that left Keep, or was he back on the ship?

If he was on the landing party, did that mean he knew about leaving the boys behind?

No. Not Luck. He would never have stood for it if he'd known.

*But even if he did know, what could he have done about it?* another part of me asks. *He couldn't even stop his own father from leaving him behind, or worse. . . .*

I don't let myself finish the thought. I can't think on Luck being dead, not when there could be a trace of him here in Vina's papers. I leave the log open on her desk and pull another bundle of files from the shelf. BHUTTO TRANSFERS. SOCIALIZATION PARAMETERS. WORK-STUDY RELEASE. VOCATIONAL WORKSHOPS.

Nothing in any of them, nothing about Luck, anyway.

I pull more. REFERRALS. BEHAVIORAL THERAPY. PHYSIOLOGICAL REHABILITATION CHARTS.

Nothing, nothing, nothing.

Vina's desk overflows with folders. In desperation, I pull down GRAIN INTAKE, even though I already know what I'll find. Nothing but columns of numbers. I let the last file fall on her desk. But then I spot a thin book near buried beneath the mess. Hardly a book, even. A tiny paper thing, even smaller than the ones Miyole would pick out of the refuse piles for me to practice reading on. I fish it out. *On the Cultural I . . . dio . . . syncra . . . sies of Trans-Celestial Merchant Tribes*, by Dr. Vikram Hertz.

*Vikram Hertz.* That's my grandfather's name.

A stack of papers unsettled by my rifling begins to slip

over the side of the desk. I lunge for them, but they slither to the floor with a *thwap*, *thwap*, *thwap*, like fish hitting a deck.

A light flicks on at the top of the stairs. "Hello?"

Vina. I freeze, and then bolt for the front door. I throw back the lock and plunge out into the darkness, out into the cold, the fear in my blood pushing me fast, faster. Past the greenhouses, past the pond, up the hill, into the utter darkness of the forest. It isn't until I'm well down the footpath to town that I stop running and realize I still hold my grandfather's book in my hand.

Soraya meets me on the train platform. The sky is hazy black beyond the station lights, and she wears a sober brown-and-blue striped scarf.

"Khajjiar," she says. Her lips have all but disappeared in the firm line of her mouth. "They have a state home there for boys who've lost their crewes?"

"Right so," I say.

Soraya nods. Her eyes flicker to the trains behind me, lost for a moment, and then find me again. "Don't ever do that again."

"I won't." All I want to do is sleep and sleep. Luck is gone. I don't have any fight left in me.

"You had us worried sick." She grips her scarf to keep the light wind from pulling it away.

"I know. I'm sorry, and true."

Her face looks raw, vulnerable. "If you don't want to live with me, Ava . . ."

"I do," I say. "I only . . . I had to find out . . ." I stumble to a halt, on the verge of spilling everything to Soraya—Luck and the coldroom and Iri with blood on her teeth.

Her face softens. "Was he there? The one you were looking for?"

She can't know who Luck was, but she knows the shape of things—my being here, the data pendant, and what there is in Khajjiar.

"No," I say. "He wasn't."

She holds out an arm, and I let her gather me under it. Then we turn and make our way home.

# CHAPTER .35

"Who can name for me two of the unintended consequences of Partition?" Our Historical-Literary Connections instructor, Mr. Pallavi, gestures to the smartscreen at the front of the classroom, where his projected drawing of a triangular blob labeled INDIA is separated from PAKISTAN by a zigzag line.

No one answers. I pretend to mark down a note on my tablet, which Soraya replaced after the Khajjiar incident. I had to agree to come to Revati every day, and then be home to Soraya's before dark.

I'm only supposed to be able to write on the tablet's note screen, but Miyole showed me how to trick it so I can draw, too. I've been thinking more and more on fixing the sloop again. It makes more sense than my lessons, so I spend my time in class sketching out schematics for rerouting the cooling conduits. I can't make it so they won't ever leak again, but maybe if I isolate them, a leak won't short out the other components. . .

Mr. Pallavi sighs. "Let's back up. Ava . . ."

I look up, heart pounding. Dr. Lata had a talk with all my teachers on not calling me out in class until my reading is better, but Mr. Pallavi sometimes forgets.

"What year did Partition take place?" he asks.

"I . . . uh . . ." I stare down into my tablet, throat tight. Miyole and I read this last night. I remember what Partition is, when India and Pakistan split off from each other, and I remember about all the bloodshed that happened before and after it, so why can't I remember the year?

Prita jumps in. "1947."

*I knew that. Why couldn't I get it out?* I clench my teeth together.

"Good," Mr. Pallavi says. "Chennapragada to the rescue, once again."

The class laughs, and I sink behind my tablet. I'm not made for this place. Dr. Lata and Soraya and all of my instructors talk about sculpting my mind and cultivating me, as if I'm some piece of clay or a spot of ground ripe with seeds, when really I'm more like plastic that's already cooled and hardened into its mold.

I put my head down and wait for geometry. Geometry is the only part of my day what doesn't make me feel like screaming. I have it in a sunny room on the school's top floor with Miyole and a handful of other girls midway between her and my ages. It's figuring, but put to things that matter in the real world. Height and volume, buildings and fuel, how many meters of tubing I'll need to thread all the way around a circular tank. Our instructor lets me and Miyole sit together and help each other with the puzzles she sets us.

But come the end of the day, Miyole stays behind for special studies with Dr. Lata and Biomimesis Club, while I'm cast out into the city alone. I've been past the shipyard a few times on my way home, but I haven't seen Rushil. I haven't gotten up the courage to go in and apologize.

That night at dinner, Soraya sets down her glass and eyes Miyole across the table. "Dr. Lata's been telling me things about you, little one." Her hair is down, spilling in black crescents over the shoulders of her yellow blouse.

Miyole stops midchew and stares at us with her cheeks full of potato. I duck my head to hide a smile.

"She says you placed into the accelerated program. You'll be done with Revati and have a few college credits under your belt by the time you're fifteen." Soraya raises her eyebrows and points her fork at Miyole in mock seriousness. "I hope you've thought about what you want to do for college, young lady."

"I have," Miyole says.

"Oh?" Soraya sneaks a look at me, winks, and sips her tea to hide it.

"Yes," Miyole says, all seriousness. "I want to be a Deep Sound bioengineer."

Soraya nearly chokes on her tea. "Really?" Deep Sound is what the people at Revati call long-range voyages into the Void, like the ones my crewe made. "Oh, Miyole. Are you sure?"

"Yes," Miyole says. "I was reading about it, and Shushri Veer said they need people like me out Deep. Did you know bees go into stasis the minute they're out in the air on Titan? And, oh, did you know you can engineer a spider to spin self-sealing thread for Deep suits and ship hulls? We hatched a whole bunch of them in our class."

Soraya shudders.

"Besides, the Deep's not dangerous anymore." Miyole looks to me. "Right, Ava?"

I pause with a glass of sugared lime juice halfway to my mouth. What do I say? The Void is dangerous. Full of solar storms and rock belts and the odd stripper ship waiting to latch on to unsuspecting traders and sell the crewe and cargo piecemeal. But then again, groundways is dangerous, too. It has its storms and its wars and its droughts. Besides, if Miyole goes as some kind of engineer, they'll most likely stick her on one of those mile-long research vessels what dwarfed our *Parastrata* when we passed under their shadows. She'll have a good hull and maybe even soldiers or trained guards to keep her safe.

"Depends," I say.

Dismay creeps into Miyole's face.

"But it's not too dangerous if you're smart." I reach out and pinch her arm playfully. "You've got no problem being smart, do you?"

She grins and shakes her head.

"Well, you have plenty of time to think it over, anyway." Soraya raises her glass. "To our scholar."

Miyole and I clink our glasses with hers.

"I wish I didn't have class tonight." Soraya sighs and reaches out to straighten a stray piece of hair over Miyole's eyes, then pretends to steal her nose.

Miyole giggles and bats at her.

Suddenly, the sight of the two of them, how close they've come, it hits me bittersweet. How fond of Miyole

Soraya is. How Miyole uncoils whenever Soraya's near. But it's undercut with sadness at what Miyole lost to bring her here and at the lonely stretch of years Soraya must have come through to meet us in this place. And me, what would my life have been if my own mother had lived, or if my grandfather had stayed with us? What would it have been if Luck and I hadn't been caught? Or if Iri had gotten away with me? The pull of all that sadness is too much. It sucks me away from our happy table, into the realm of ghosts.

I push away and carry my dishes to the kitchen. Soraya follows me a few minutes later, shrugging into a jacket. "Are you okay putting her to bed?"

I nod and concentrate on carefully feeding my dishes into the cleaner.

"Ava," Soraya says in a way that makes me look up. "Are you okay?"

I nod again. For some reason, it feels better to be alone with my ghosts, like if I told someone about them, they might vanish, and then I might forget. "I'm fine." I slip my hand into my pocket and worry my data pendant with my thumb. "Just tired."

Soraya gives me an awkward one-armed hug. It's quick and hard, as if she's afraid I might catch her on fire if she touches me too long.

"I'll be back at ten." She steps back and tries to smile.

"Right so."

I put Miyole to bed and practice reading to her from my tablet. I'm getting better. I hardly ever get so stuck I have to ask her to look at a word for me anymore. After we've done an article about storms at an Arctic research station, I wave my hand to dim the light and switch on the air-cleaning machine Soraya brought up to scrub out the musty smell. It fills her room with a steady hum.

"Ava?" Miyole says.

I turn. My eyes haven't adjusted yet, and I can't find her in the dark.

"Will you be upstairs or down?" Miyole asks this every night.

"Down," I say. "Till Soraya gets home, at least. I'm going to practice reading a little more."

"Okay." Her voice relaxes, and the dim outline of her head drops against the pillow.

I slip out of the room. The distant whirr of air pumping through the vents and all the house's tiny clicks and beeps leave me jumping in my skin. This house is so big. Whenever I'm alone, I start to imagine someone creeping around after me, pale-skinned crewemen peeking through the windows and men waiting in the shadows with knives.

I walk soft to my own room, reach under the mattress, and pull out my grandfather's book. A shiver of guilt passes through me. I've been waiting for a night like tonight, when Soraya is gone and Miyole fast asleep, to try and read it.

I drop my crow on the kitchen charger and stand at the back window, listening to the dish cleaner gurgle and looking out at the dark leaves of Soraya's tree lifting in the breeze. Miyole took a picture with her crow and had it tell us what kind of tree it was. Japanese maple. Saved from one of the drowned islands west of here before they went under.

I mean to switch on the lights and curl my feet up under me on one of the plush couches, but as I pass the downstairs hallway, the heavy oak door at the far end catches my eye. We don't talk about the door, not even Miyole and me. Soraya pretends it isn't there, and so we do, too.

I pad toward it, one arm out before me, the other clutching my grandfather's book. The eyehole glints down at me dully, and the brass handle is cold under my palm.

I crack the door open. Dank and must hangs in the air. I edge into the dark. I don't know what I expect. A sealed room of rare books, or cold, humming machines like the ones in Pankaj's house. But as my eyes adjust, all I make out is a broad, dark wood desk in a sea of white carpet.

The picture window on the right side of the room looks out on the garden and the maple. Empty bookshelves line the walls.

I shut the door, walk around the desk, and pull out the leather chair. Its skin crackles softly as I sit. The house keeps quiet here. None of its little life noises reach past the heavy door. I snap on a lamp. Buttery light floods the room. Across from me, a red-and-gold-spotted chair waits, empty. I run my hands over the desk's wood top, feeling the grains and pits and places where the veneer has worn off after years of use.

Whose desk was this? Not Soraya's. She never comes in here. But I can read the desk's battered top like the back of a tapestry. Someone sat here, wrote here, read here every day. My grandfather Vikram, whose book I hold even now? I rub my finger against one spot on the desk's edge where it's worn down to yellow wood. The worn place fits the width of my finger perfectly. Did my grandfather rub that spot unconsciously as he fell lost in reading every day? Did he drink tea here? Did he think on my mother here? My grandmother?

I tug open one of the desk's drawers. A deep smell, something rich and smoky sweet, floods out, but the drawer itself is empty. It smells indefinably old, as if whatever made the scent has been trapped there for years. I try the next drawer below it. Nothing. Then the two drawers on the other side. Still nothing.

*Soraya was right,* I think. *There's nothing here.* Only one left, the thin center drawer above my lap. It sticks, but I tug and jiggle it, and finally, with a tooth-rending screech, it opens.

A smooth, palm-size device, dark as stone, sits alone on the right side. I pick it up. It's cold, heavy in a pleasing way, as if it's meant to rest in a hand or the bottom of a pocket. I smooth my thumb over its surface, and it flickers to life. Light and color resolve themselves into an image. A youngish man with delicate lines of gray threading his beard leans down to put an arm around a lovely, dark-haired woman with warm brown skin, wearing a pink checkered scarf much like one of Soraya's. A smallgirl in a yellow dress perches on her lap, all big dark eyes and black curls. Behind them, the purple-black leaves of Soraya's maple reach down into the frame. I lean closer to the screen. *Who . . . ?* But then it comes to me. My grandfather. Him and his firstwife and . . . Soraya. Soraya is the smallgirl.

I brush a finger over her cheek. At my touch, the picture jumps and dissolves into a different image. A girl near my own age, hair a pale flame and shell-white cheeks cracked with burst capillaries, lies propped in a birthing bed, a rose-skinned baby in the crook of her arm. I recognize the room and the arched doorway beyond her bed. It's the *Parastrata*'s birthing room. And I recognize the baby's dark hair. It's the same hair as little Soraya's, the same as mine. The mother-girl smiles out at me, so drunk with love it pierces the screen and all the time in between that moment and this.

*Maram, my grandmother. And my mother, Ete, the baby.*

I lower the picture to my lap. Gingerly, I untuck my grandfather's book from beneath my arm and lay it flat on the scored desktop. The paper crackles as I open it.

FOREWORD

In the course of my study on the trans-celestial merchant tribe Parastrata, or crewe as they prefer to be called, I was required to take extraordinary measures to gain their trust and complicity. Some contend I have strayed beyond the line of proper scientific inquiry. To them I say, what is propriety compared to the pursuit of knowledge? In modern sociological research, one must, at times, set aside one's own societal norms in order to collect the most accurate data. Without my transgression of our scientific community's rather provincial taboos, the fascinating culture of the Parastrata would remain a mystery to this day.

I frown. The most accurate data? Fascinating culture? I read on, glad for the practice I've been getting at Revati. I don't know all of the words on sight, but my grandfather's meaning is clear. Maybe school isn't completely wasted on me.

During my time aboard this vessel, it was requested of me by the captain, Parastata Harrah, that I marry his youngest daughter, Maram. Had I refused, the entire course of my research would have been thrown into jeopardy, as I would have been required to disembark at one of the terrestrial outposts or orbital stations along our route, rather than completing the crewe's traditional two-and-a-half-year circuit with them. Thus, I entered into merchant crewe society not as a mere observer, but as a participant in its unusual and vibrant cultural life. From this vantage point, I was able to document the peculiarities and superstitions that make up the everyday interactions of merchant crewes, as well as their most sacred rituals, which would normally remain closed to outsiders. Through my marriage to Harrah's daughter, the birth of a child, and my young wife's unfortunate demise shortly thereafter, I witnessed the unique customs surrounding the ceremonies of betrothal, birth, and death. Lest my critics accuse me of heartlessness, note that, although I have completed my period of observation aboard the Parastrata, I continue to maintain a relationship with the crewe and support the issue of my short-lived marriage through the regular provision of gifts.

*The issue of my short-lived . . . ?* My eyes widen. My mother. He means my mother. It's no more than I already knew, but the way he puts it is so cold.

I have elected to allow my daughter by Maram to remain with her crewe. Though I myself may be willing to alter my own cultural framework in the interests of scienctific inquiry, I have no desire to disrupt the pattern of life among the objects of my study. Thus, I have seamlessly inserted and removed myself from the course of crewe life with a minimum of disruption. My tactics may prove unorthodox, but I have not acted without moral consideration for my subjects' welfare, and thus I remain confident in my methodology. Everything I have done, I have done with the pursuit of knowledge foremost in my mind.

I lower the book, my grandfather's words ringing behind my ears. *Objects of my study? Seamlessly . . . with the pursuit of knowledge foremost in my mind.* Seamlessly? What about my mother? What about me? And Soraya, all alone in this house until we came? His choices are still echoing through us, even so many generations later. Shouldn't we have mattered more than knowlege? Everything I knew of my grandfather—the gifts for my mother and how good and kind he was to my grandmother, how he supported our crewe from afar, how he wasn't a meddler—shatters. I pick up the book again, heat flooding my cheeks. I flip through and stop on a random page.

. . . found gender roles to be strictly divided aboard crewe ships. The Parastrata is typical in this regard. Women shoulder the brunt of the most basic functional work, putting in long hours dyeing cloth, cooking, cleaning, washing clothes, and caring for animals and children. Their hands are never idle. Even in their spare moments, they are always weaving cloth or mending ripped seams. Virginity is highly prized, and thus, girls are married off as early as thirteen to ensure paternity and maximize each woman's effective childbearing years.

I should stop reading, but I can't. I slip my hand inside my pocket and grip my data pendant without looking away from the page.

Meanwhile, the work of navigation and repairing the electronic and mechanical components of the ship is reserved for men, as are trade negotiations. These often must be conducted planetside. As a result, it is necessary for men to maintain the physical capability to withstand the increased gravitational pull exerted by large planetary bodies. To counteract the painful and potentially damaging effects of transferring from the crewe ship's relatively low gravity field to a high-gravity environment, the men and boys engage in daily strength training and periodically spend time in compression chambers that simulate the effects of one full G of force, equal to the gravitational pull of Earth. From examination of early crewe records reviewed in preparation for my field research, it became apparent that, early in their history, crewes required gravitational acclimation training (GAT) for both male and female members. Captain Harrah and the other senior men aboard the Parastrata insist this is not so, and that part of the reason the crewes originally left Earth was to spare their women contact with "the impure world." One must presume the practice of allowing women to participate in GAT changed gradually over time and became incorporated into the crewes' shared origin mythology. The long-term effects on crewewomen's health are unclear, but warrant further research.

I draw in a sharp breath. *He knew.* I lower the book and blink into the yellow light. He knew what staying on the creweship would do to my mother and to me. He knew we would spend our days weaving and baking and cleaning until our fingers blistered, that we would be married off to produce baby after baby. He knew what would happen to our bodies if we ever tried to leave. And he left us there.

"I thought you'd come here sooner or later."

I jump and reach for my knife.

Soraya stands in the door. She lowers herself into the chair across the desk and holds out her hand for the book.

I let go of the knife and push the book across to her. A red crescent moon marks my palm where my data pendant dug into my skin.

"Where did you find it?"

"Khajjiar," I say.

She sighs, a heavy sound. "To be honest, I'm surprised you haven't run across this before now."

"Is it . . ." I'm not sure how to say what I mean. "Have a lot of people read it?"

Soraya nods. "My father, your grandfather, built his reputation on this book, this research." She rests it carefully on the edge of the desk. "He was a controversial man. What he did, that's not how research is done. There was the scandal over his marriage to Maram—my mother left him over it—and so of course everyone wanted to read it."

"Is that what I am?" I look down at the book. "Is that all we were to him—my mother and grandmother and me? Research?"

I think on Modrie Reller talking up how the so doctor once sent us a pair of cats, a queen and a tom, so we could breed them and sell their offspring to other ships or outposts overrun by rats. *So generous,* all the oldgirls agreed. We could make good money that way. Now I look around at the wealth of this place—water so plentiful we can use it to bathe, and machines to do the cooking and washing—and it's clear that was nothing to him. Those cats were likely strays plucked off the street or bought for the cost of a cup of tea, an afterthought.

*You should be grateful he thought of you at all,* Modrie Reller's voice scolds at the back of my head. But he didn't. He didn't care to think on what would become of my mother and me. I always believed he did, that he cherished us from afar. But we were worth no more to him than those cats. He wasn't alive when my mother died, still so young, or when my father tried to trade me off to Æther Fortune, but he knew what our lives would be when he left us behind, and he didn't lift a finger to stop it. It's all there in black and white.

I push the chair back and turn to the window. I didn't understand before how mere marks on a page or screen could cut and ricochet. I didn't understand the power they could have. Suddenly it seems too dangerous to be cooped up here, neatly folded inside when I could burst into flames any minute and bring this whole house, this whole world, down around me.

"I need to go," I choke out.

"Ava." Soraya stands, steps between me and the door.

"Please. I can't be in here right now."

"But it's late." Soraya wavers. "It's dangerous, a girl out alone at night."

"Soraya, please." I hear the desperate, wavering whine in my voice, but there's nothing I can do to stop it. No one has ever cared what happened to me, and right now, I don't either. I only know I need to be away, out of this house, alone. I bolt for the door. Soraya steps aside at the last slip, before I knock into her. I grab my crow from the kitchen charger and stuff it in the pocket of Perpétue's jacket, wrap the leather tight around me, and throw open the front door.

"Ava, wait!" Soraya calls as I duck past the rosewood trees.

But I ignore her. I shut myself down, double my steps, and barrel forward into the humid Mumbai night.

# CHAPTER 36

I tramp down from the quiet residential paths, house lights winking behind thick shrubbery, to the lev train stop. I ride until I reach the edge of the city and hop off at a random station. The streets teem with people and a whirl of neon and colored signs—JUICY POW! GET SOME NOW!—RAM'S DREAM—HOT, HOT HOT! I thread through narrow streets, dodging a pack of kids staging a water-gun battle and a group of women parading one of their number, a twenty-something girl with hennaed hands and a T-shirt reading KISS THE BRIDE, ahead of them. They sing at the top of their lungs. The close buildings and the haze of streetlamps muzzle up the sky and cast everything in a perpetual half day.

Then the buildings part on a footbridge and it rises into

view, the Salt, with its water pipes and its light-studded hill looming above me like a great circled hive of lamps and people and buildings. I didn't know where I was going until I was here.

I step quick, half to keep away from the men smoking in alleys and drunks stumbling down the side ways, and half because I can't bear to stand still. All that anger and fear and hate packed tight in me radiates as it burns. The drunks step out of my path and the smokers slip their eyes past me, looking for other girls giving off less heat.

I rattle up against the fence of Rushil's lot. Perpétue's—my—ship curves sleek under several layers of protective sheeting on the other side. I hang against the fence. Now all I feel is empty and old, full up with yearning for something familiar. I key in the number-lock code, slip inside, and race across the darkened lot to the cool, familiar hulk of the sloop.

One sharp tug and the protective sheeting falls around my feet. *My ship. My home.* I punch in half of the code to open the hatch before I remember Rushil and me never finished wiring in the new couplings or the refabricated power cell we gutted from an old fission-powered two-seater. I could open the door manually, but not without enough metal shrieking to wake the entire block.

"*Outh.*" I bang the sloop's side with my fist and scan the yard. There, beside a black clipper, a simple steel ladder. I drag it over, lean it against the sloop, and climb the rungs to the top.

Scorch marks from past atmospheric entries streak the tiles, and they still hold the day's heat. I push myself up onto the sloop and sit. From here, I can see all of the Salt and the taller spikes of the city proper beyond, wreathed in a mist of saltwater and light. I wish Perpétue were here to see it. And Luck, him too. The city goes blurry before me. I was wrong. It's not true that no one ever cared for me. It's only that anyone who ever did is gone.

A faint *tap-tap-tap* rings on the ship's ventral side. "Ava?" A muffled voice reaches up to me. Rushil.

I hurry to wipe my eyes and lean over the ship's side. "Here," I say. "It's me."

Rushil steps from under the ship, nervously gripping a cricket bat and a hooded lamp.

"What are you . . . Are you okay?" He leans the bat against the sloop's side and starts up the ladder with the lantern still in one hand.

I wait until he reaches the top to answer. "I . . . I don't know." I don't even know where to begin. There's too much.

Rushil slides back the lantern's hood and balances it on the ship. The light reflects in his glasses. "I saw someone up here. I hoped it was you."

"Is that why you brought your bat?" I know Rushil only means he hoped it was me and not a shipjacker, but a strange, small thrill trips through me all the same.

He grins. "Yeah. I thought you might have been one of those superintelligent rats that are supposed to live in the drainage pipes. Ankur's convinced they're real."

I laugh. "Sorry. I didn't mean to frighten you. It's only . . . I wanted to be alone some. I didn't know where else to go."

Rushil holds the ladder's top rung. "Do you still want to be? Alone, I mean?"

"What? No." My words come out half laugh, half cry. I wipe at my eyes again. "No, not anymore."

Rushil climbs up and sits beside me. "Wow, it's nice up here. I can see why Shruti spends so much time up top."

I laugh again, and the sadness in me breaks some.

Rushil moves his foot next to mine. At first I think it's an accident, but then he taps a little rhythm against the side of my boot. I still feel turned out and empty, but I smile and tap back. Rushil lays his hand over mine, and something soft brushes my skin. I look down. A worn strip of leather doubles around his wrist. *My cord.* I raise my eyes to his, lips parted. *He knew I came looking for him. He knew I was sorry.*

He doesn't say anything, but the rough warmth of his palm brings tears to my eyes again.

"I'm not from the Gyre," I blurt out.

"You're not?" Rushil blinks. "But Miyole . . . you said . . ."

"She is. Her mother took me in before she died. She's the one what taught me to fly this ship. But I came from up there." I let my eyes drift up. Even the brightest stars can't pierce the city's haze.

"From . . . from spaceside, you mean?" He squints through his glasses at me as if I must be mistaken.

I nod.

"But your aunt, you said she was from here—"

"It's complicated." I take a breath. I have to let him know. "Rushil, you don't want me."

He raises his eyebrows. "Don't I?"

"No. You think you do, but I'm not . . ." The words stick in my throat. "I'm some bad matter. Everyone around me only gets hurt. And I . . . I did something . . . something so bad my crewe—my people—didn't want me anymore. That's why I'm here."

"Ava." Rushil rolls his eyes. "What could you possibly have done?"

"There was . . . there was Luck." When I say his name, something gives in me, and everything comes pouring out, all the parts of my past I've hidden away so careful. About Soli and Iri and the way of wives. How I gave myself to Luck, and how we were caught, and how I left him bloodied and shamed. And finally the sentence laid on me, and how Iri saved me, sent me down to the Earth instead of out into the breathless Void.

A tense silence settles between us. "They . . . they tried to put you out alive?" Rushil says at last.

I nod. I let my hair fall over my face.

"Oh, Ava . . ." Rushil tightens his hand over mine.

"I'm sorry," I say. "But you understand now?"

"I do," Rushil says.

I sigh. "Good."

Rushil hooks his thumb around my own. "I don't care if you've been with someone else."

I pause, shocked. "You don't?"

"No," Rushil says. "You're still you, Ava, either way."

A slow warmth spreads through my body. In the ashes where my heart was, a small green shoot nudges up through the black.

Without thinking, I lean across the short distance between us and find Rushil's mouth with mine. He tenses, but then his lips give soft, his hand reaches up to touch my face, and he leans in to me. It's nothing like kissing Luck. This is different, a slower burn what builds and builds, as if our lips are amplifying the charge between us the longer we stay linked. I never thought anyone would touch me this way again, never thought my heart could carry the charge. I give deeper to the kiss, lost in the unexpected heat of it.

When we finally break away, a nervous laugh bubbles out of me.

Rushil stares at me wide-eyed, out of breath. "Ava, I don't—"

But I cut him off with another kiss.

We lean back on the ship's warm tiles. Rushil's breath is sweet with cloves and cardamom, but a pleasant air of fresh sweat clings to his body in the muggy night, too. His palm is rough as he brushes the hair from the back of my neck, but his touch is gentle. I want nothing but to drown myself in kissing him.

After a time, we roll away from each other and lie shoulder to shoulder, staring up at the sky.

"It's late," Rushil says. "Do you have to go home?"

"No."

"You want to head over to Zarine's with me?" Rushil tips his head toward me. "She said she scrounged some extra tubing I could have for the sloop."

I sit up. "My sloop?"

Rushil pushes himself upright. "No, I hear the superintelligent rats are starting their own Deep Sound Institute." He smiles and pokes me in the ribs. "Of course yours. Who else's?"

A tingling, awake feeling tickles under my skin. I feel strong. Young. Whole. I don't want to go back, not yet. I want to be out, a part of this night with Rushil. "Okay. Let's go."

Rushil's street is near empty, but the closer we come to the hill, the more the streets tick with people. Packs of girls lean together, laughing, high heels clacking on the pavement as they walk. Boys Rushil's age stand in circles under the streetlights, drinking and feigning jabs at each other. Couples stroll by, arm in arm. Rushil reaches back to grab my hand.

"You know this used to be a slum?" he says. "And then they built the railyards and it turned into mostly warehouses. But now—"

Even from far off, the buildings on the hill hum with voices and muffled music and the buzz of solar generators.

We trek deeper into the Salt. It isn't like the south end of the city, all jammed with hot, bright signs trying to draw you in. Here, you have to know where you want to go. Each building is a little boxed glance into another world. A *tapri* full of clinking cups and waiters edging around the crowded tables. A blue-lit room packed with dancing bodies writhing together under a constant beat. A man glancing up from a wrought-iron basin brimming full with dark water. Dozens of shadows milling behind the gauzy curtains of an upstairs loft.

The street sweepers here have all been scooped up and modded at some point. One trundles by carapaced in a fake turtle shell. Another looks as though it's been hennaed. Another blares out tinny music as it charges across the street. We ring up and up, closer to the top of the Salt. Every now and then we catch narrow glimpses of the city and its tight-woven carpet of lights between the buildings on the hill's outer rim.

Two-thirds of the way up, Rushil stops. "Here." He points up at an old warehouse some three stories above us, hanging halfway out over the hill and the lev train tracks below. Thick metal struts anchor the dangling edge to the raw earth of the hill below. A murmur of distant voices and music filters down to us from the lighted windows.

"Here?" I say.

Rushil cups his hands to his mouth and shouts up. "Hey, Zarine! Zarine!"

Someone—a man, not Zarine—leans his head out the window.

"Hey!" Rushil waves his arm. "Let us up."

A low *clank-clank-clank* starts above us, and slowly, a platform lowers into view, suspended by metal cables. It touches down in a puff of dust beside us. Rushil hops on, and I follow.

"How do we . . . ," I start to ask, but Rushil grabs a hand crank built into the side of the platform and turns it in a slow, smooth circle. The platform shudders and lifts from the ground.

"Zarine and some friends put in drywall and plumbing and all. It's apartments now," Rushil says, looking up at the base of the warehouse as he rotates the winch. We rise level with the building, and the noise builds to a steady hum of voices and music. As Rushil locks the platform in place and secures us to the side of the building, the door flies open, letting out a wave of lamplight and high, twanging music.

"Rushil, you made it!" A tall, curvy woman with a wild toss of hair leans across the gap between the platform and the doorframe to hug Rushil. A black dress hugs her waist, and round brass earrings as big as fists dangle from her ears. Everything about her seems scaled for giants, her hair, her eyes, her legs. Behind her, a kitchen separates us from a warmer room where a small crowd lounges on floor pillows, couches, and round, shell-like chairs, talking and sipping beer or tea in glasses. A handsome, dark-skinned young man with a sitar balances on the back of the nearest couch, cradling the neck of his instrument and picking its strings absentmindedly as he talks to the couple across from him. *Ankur*, I realize.

"Hey, Zarine." Rushil hugs her back.

"You must be the one Rushil was talking about." She takes my arm and helps me across the gap. "Ava, right? Who rescued that little girl?"

Her words knock me shy and off-balance. Does she mean Miyole? But that wasn't rescuing. "Oh, no, I . . . I'm not . . . ," I try to say, but the rush of voices in the neighboring room drowns me out. *Is that who I am?* I look at Rushil. *Is that how he sees me?*

"You want a beer?" Zarine shouts. "Or some tea?"

"Tea," I say.

"Go on, help yourself to a cutting." Zarine waves a bangled arm at a clutter of cups and pitchers covering the blocky table in the center of the kitchen. "Rushil?"

"I'm good, thanks." He throws a look at me. "I was telling Ava you had some tubing for us. . . ."

Zarine sighs and feigns hurt. "I swear, you only want me for my spare parts. You have to promise to stay and at least have some tea after."

Rushil grins. "I promise."

Zarine flashes her teeth in another smile. "Come on, I've got that tubing downstairs in the utility room."

Rushil leans close. "You want to come with us?"

A burst of laughter breaks out from the sitting room behind me. I look over my shoulder. Young men and women, all my age or a little older, sit mingled together, easy with one another. I've never been in a place like this.

I turn back to Rushil. "I think I'll stay here."

"I'll be back in a minute." He squeezes my arm briefly and follows Zarine around the crowd of people and out another door. The room suddenly feels dimmer without her, as if a lamp has gone out.

I pour myself a glass of tea and sit cross-legged on the outskirts of the sitting room crowd. Everyone around me is dropped deep in conversation, talking on music and who's setting up a gallery show and who's been off planetside and how long, only none of it's anyone I know.

"Hey, Ava." Ankur drops down next to me, sitar in hand.

"Fancy meeting you here. How do you know Zarine?"

"I don't." I take a sip of tea. "Rushil brought me."

Ankur gestures to the doorway Rushil and Zarine disappeared through. "I lost my muse. You want to sing with me?"

I nearly choke.

"I don't know." I swallow, buying time. "I'm not from here. I don't think I know any of your songs."

"Not even 'Melt It Down'?"

I shake my head.

"Or 'Burn, Sita, Burn'?"

I shake my head again.

"'Droughtsick'? Everyone knows 'Droughtsick.'"

I shake my head a third time.

Ankur picks at the sitar's strings. "Well, why don't you sing something from where you come from, and I'll try to play along?"

A nervous current zings through me. Panic. "I can't."

"Come on." Ankur smiles his perfect smile. "Nobody here's going to bite. I'll tell them not to trap it for their pages, huh?"

"It isn't that." I rest my empty teacup on the floor.

"You one of those shy girls never does anything but listen in on other people talking?" Ankur teases.

"No," I say, even though he's probably right. "It's . . . I'm not supposed to."

"Not supposed to?" Ankur says.

"Sing." It feels strange to say, especially here, now.

Ankur stares at me as though I've said I'm not supposed to breathe or grow fingernails. "What, is it going to send us hurling ourselves into the trainway? Is it that bad?"

I open my mouth to answer, but then I realize I don't really know what will happen if I sing. Something bad, something to catch the ears of bad spirits, or so the story of Mikim and the corsairs would have it. But now, I don't know. Miyole was right. Now that I know more of how the universe works, Mikim's story makes some little sense. And besides, all the verses in the Word about what befalls a woman in the Earth's grip, those were only part true. I may be tarnished, but I'm still whole. So maybe nothing will happen if I sing. Maybe no harm will grow from it at all.

"Right so." My voice croaks. I clear my throat and say it stronger. "Right so."

"Okay then." Ankur adjusts his strings. A few of the people around us hush, then others turn their heads our way. "When you're ready."

Ankur picks out a single, soft, vibrating note. Another cluster of people go quiet. At that moment, I spot Rushil standing in the doorway, a bundle of plastic tubing under his arm. I close my eyes to block out all the faces looking my way, sink anchor deep in myself, and let out one of the songs I've heard through the walls, one I've sung inside my head at night in my bunk with my sisters warm at my sides. Saeleas's song of mourning, the song she sang through her tears as the Earth slipped away, those thousand-some turns ago.

"Farewell to rock and tree and vale,

Farewell to birds high-flying,

For duty calls me far away,

So sing my heart through sighing."

Ankur strums to match my voice, soft at first, then louder as he catches the scheme. The whole room has gone quiet.

"Pick up, pick up this heavy thread,

Quiet, child, your laughter,

For we must leave this world we know,

And wander e'er hereafter."

I open my eyes. Rushil stands still past the sea of heads, looking at me as though my song has run him through. I raise my voice and sing Candor's answering verse to his wife. Ankur doubles the tempo to meet my urgency, his strumming fast. It molds together into something new, something both of this world and not.

"Think not on rock and tree and spring,

Think not on birds high-flying,

Our freedom calls us high away,

For here were our hearts dying."

My voice breaks and the room blurs, but I blink away the salt from my eyes and fix them on Rushil.

"Mourn not for what you've lost, my love,

Think not on what you're leaving,

Let all your heart and mind hold fast,

This new life you are breathing."

As the last line rings out of my chest, I let go. Let go Luck, let go my crewe, let go what might have been. Rushil holds my eyes, and I stand empty and clear, ready to be filled with what my life might yet be.

# CHAPTER .37

I creep back to Soraya's in the dull gray of morning. The house welcomes me with a low beep and a click as the door seals itself shut behind me. I pull off my boots and tiptoe to the stairs, thinking of nothing but soft pillows and the dark comfort of my bed. But then I turn the corner to mount the stairs, and run headlong into Soraya. She loses her grip on the full metal ewer she has balanced in her arms. I stagger forward and manage to catch it before it clangs across the floor, but not before it sloshes cold water down the front of my shirt.

I freeze, soaked through. "Sorry," I gasp.

Soraya stares down at me, lips parted in surprise. She's draped a pale blue scarf over her head in preparation for her morning prayers. She looks like some kind of holy woman, clean pressed and fresh from sleep. I'm all too aware of the dust and dried sweat stiffening my clothes and the sour taste of a night without sleep in my mouth. My face goes hot as I remember how I left. Shouting like a spoiled smallgirl.

I shift the ewer in my arms. "You want me to carry this for you?"

Soraya's breathes out. "Yes, please."

I haven't seen her use it before, but I know the water is so Soraya can wash her hands and face and feet before her morning prayers. I've seen the ewer newly emptied by the gray-water sink and sitting by her bedside in the evenings. I carry it to the corner of the common room where Soraya keeps her prayer mat rolled and pour the water into a basin.

"Thank you." She casts an eye at my wet shirt. "Why don't you go and change, and then we'll talk?"

I nod and slink away to the stairs, but something makes me look back as I reach them. The sun tips pink light through the glass doors on the east side of the house. Soraya unfurls her prayer mat and eases herself to her knees. She holds her hands together before her and murmurs into the early morning light. I duck my head and disappear up the stairs. If I were her, I'd want to be left alone to my praying.

I look in on Miyole, fast asleep in the rosy darkness of

her room. Her breath comes even and her face is peaceful, free of the little furrow that appears between her brows when she's been worrying. I change my shirt in the close quiet of my room. I spend a long moment contemplating the bed, but I shake myself awake. I owe a talk to Soraya, and better sooner than later.

By the time I shuffle down, the ewer and basin stand empty at the sink again. Soraya has tea going. She sits by a collection of cups, spoons, and saucers laid across the table, waiting for me. She waves a hand at the chair opposite her. I sit.

Soraya pours a cup of tea for me. "I was worried about you." She speaks quietly to match the early hour. "Where did you go?"

"Walking." The word comes out scratchy and raw. I sip my tea and try again. "I went down to the ship."

"The ship?" Soraya sets her own teacup down, surprised. "Miyole's mother's ship? How did you get in?"

"I have the keycode," I say. "From back when me and Miyole were living there."

Soraya frowns as if she'd rather not remember where she found us and drops a sugar cube in her cup. "That ship is important to you, isn't it?"

"It is," I agree.

Soraya heaves a sigh. "You know how I feel. The Salt isn't a safe place to go wandering around at night."

"You don't need to worry, I was with Rushil the whole time," I say, and wish at once I'd kept my mouth shut. *Stupid, stupid.*

"Rushil?" Soraya says.

"Rushil Vaish," I say. "He owns the lot where we have the ship docked."

Soraya looks sharp at me. "That young man? The one with the glasses and all the tattoos?"

"Right so." My voice goes small. "That's him."

Silence grows around us. Soraya pours herself another cup of tea. "And what did you two do all night?" There's another question buried in there. Her eyes shift past me to the antique books behind my head.

"Talk." I look down. Even if I'm not lying outright, I can't look at her when I'm not saying the whole truth. "And we went over to his friend's house." I don't want to tell her about the singing, or the electric burn of his lips. I want those memories to myself.

Soraya sighs and pulls the scarf from her hair. It lies in rumpled swaths around her neck. "You know, I can send you back to the doctor, if that's what you want." She closes her eyes and rubs the bridge of her nose. "There's a shot they can give to keep you from conceiving."

I sit straight in my chair. Heat rushes to the tips of my ears. "But I'm not . . . We didn't!"

Soraya raises her eyebrows at me. *Truly?*

"We didn't," I say again.

Soraya taps her fingernails softly against her teacup and nods to herself. "I believe you." She fixes me with her big, dark eyes. "But if you ever think you're going to, promise me you'll come talk to me first. Promise you'll take care of yourself."

I nod, face raging hot.

"Children are so much . . ." She trails off and smiles sadly. "I only want you to be able to be a girl for once. I want you to have that chance."

"But I'm not a girl," I say. I haven't been for turns.

"A young woman, then," Soraya says. "All I mean is, your life doesn't have to be so heavy. There's so much out there for you, so much you can do."

"I know. I'm sorry, and true. I didn't mean to worry you."

Soraya sighs. She looks tired, face thin. "I only want to protect you. I know I'm not your mother, Ava, and you're nearly an adult. But if anything happened to you . . ." She jostles the teacups as she reaches out and clasps my hand.

Her fingers are cold, all tendons and bones.

"I don't think the way my father did, Ava. You aren't research. You're my only living blood. If something happened to you, I . . ." She stops, lets out a sharp breath, and composes herself. "You can't know what it's like to have a family again after all this time."

"You'd have Miyole," I say.

"Yes," Soraya says. "But I wouldn't have you." She leans back in her chair and holds a hand over her eyes. "Please, Ava. You have to stop running."

She's crying, I realize. *But why?* Only the barest thread of blood connects me and Soraya. *But all the blood in the world didn't stop your crewe from plotting to rid themselves of you from the moment your mother died. It didn't stop them from trying to discard your mother's soul along with her body.* I think on Soraya and Miyole giggling at each other over dinner, Perpétue holding my arm as I took my first knifing steps on the Earth.

I squeeze Soraya's hand in mine. "I won't run off again," I say. "I swear. I'm sorry, Soraya."

"I am, too," Soraya says. "If only I'd found you earlier. If only I'd looked harder when I came aboard to bury your mother . . ."

But I can't regret it. It's no good wishing to change

what was. If Soraya had spirited me away to Earth when I was younger, I might never have suffered the shame I did after what happened with Luck, and I would have grown up well schooled and groomed and mannered. But then I never would have loved Luck, either. I never would have learned to fly a ship or been there to take the controls while Perpétue climbed down to rescue Miyole. I might not have seen the wonder in this world if it hadn't been hidden from me so long. I'm not glad of the way it happened, but I can't be sorry either.

"It's none of your fault," I say. She's not Perpétue. She won't always understand me or be everything I wish she could be, but she loves me. Not all the people who care for me are gone, after all.

"All that's past," I tell her. "This is my life now."

"Did I get you in trouble?" Rushil turns his head from the tubing brace he's finished fusing to the sloop's inner wall and flips up the hood of his welding mask.

I pull my welding goggles down around my neck and let my torch go out. The handlamps hooked above our heads shine dim inside the ship. I blink, half blind. "Some."

"A lot?"

I shake my head. "I have to tell her where I'm going if

I'm out past dark. And I'm supposed to keep the crow on me all the time, so she can call if she needs me." I make a face at the crow clipped to my belt. "And she wants you coming by for tea someday soon."

"Tea?" He sucks air past his teeth, as if someone's kicked him in the shin. "*Chaila.* I'm in for it, aren't I?"

I think on what would have happened if it were Modrie Reller meting out punishments, not Soraya. My eyes drift up the darkened conduit to the ceiling.

Rushil follows my gaze. "Do you miss it?"

I drop my head. "What?"

"Being up there," Rushil says. "Spaceside."

I bite my bottom lip and lean back against the hull. "Some small bit." I flip the toggle on my welding torch so it hisses and dies, hisses and dies. "I don't miss the dyeworks or always worrying on being caught and spied on. But circling the dark side of a planet, hanging up there with all those stars like you're one of them? I do miss that."

Rushil nods. "I bet it's beautiful. Everyone says it changes you, seeing the Earth from above."

My jaw drops. "You've never seen it?" I push myself from the wall.

Rushil shakes his head. "I've been planetside my whole life." He laughs shortly. "I've never even been outside Mumbai, except for the detention camp."

Street-smart, clever Rushil, who could thread his way through the Salt blind, has seen less of the universe than me? I fake a cough to cover my shock and scrape around for something to say. I nudge his foot with mine—*tap*, *tap*, *tap*. Our secret code. "You will."

"You think?" Rushil gives me a pained smile what says he doesn't believe me.

"Right so." I bump his arm and smile sideways at him. "You think I want to take this thing up all by myself?"

"You'd take me?" Rushil's voice breaks with excitement as he says it, and I see a piece of the smallboy he once was.

"Course." I take his bulky, gloved hand gentle in mine. "It can be our first flight."

Our eyes meet under the yellow glow of the hand lamps. If I leaned forward a mere slip, I could touch the warm, flat plane of his chest, let the electromagnetic pull take over and meet his lips with mine.

Rushil tucks a strand of sweat-damp hair behind my ear. "You're beautiful like this, you know?"

I laugh. "What, covered in grease?"

"No," he says. "Happy."

We meet chest to chest, and his lips find mine. I don't know what's better, the warm press of his mouth or holding him, being held. There are no expectations here, no hurry. Our time is our own. My muscles and bones melt, and the world narrows to this cocoon of yellow light. Even when our lips break apart, his arms stay around me. I rest my head on his shoulder. He leans his temple against mine and we stay there, wrapped in each other.

"Guess we'd better get back to it if we ever want this thing flying, huh?" Rushil finally says.

"Right so."

He steps back and squeezes my hand, then smiles and pulls the welding mask down over his face. I position my own goggles and fire up my torch. White-hot flame sparks from its tip as it touches the metal. Rushil and I stand back-to-back as we weld neatly spaced rows of tubing braces along the ship's inner hull and wall. The heat of his body is warmer even than the reach of the flame through my fireproof gloves.

When we've fused the last clamp in place, Rushil kills his torch and makes for the hatch. "I need some air."

I follow after him. The bright daylight clears out my head after the cramped, stuffy confines of the conduit shaft. Rushil and I sit on the lip of the loading hatch and breathe in the fresh afternoon. The sun glints on the fuselage of the ships parked around us.

"So what are you going to name her?" Rushil says.

"Name her?"

"Yeah." Rushil pats the ship's hull. "When you register her with the Subcontinental Flight Bureau, you've got to give a name for her."

"I . . . I don't know." I never thought to name Perpétue's ship, since she hadn't. I stare down at the pavement and swing my legs back and forth. It's got to be something Miyole would like, something what tells all we've been though, me and Miyole and the sloop. Something strong, something . . . I smile.

"*Perpétue,*" I say. "We'll call her the *Perpétue.*"

# CHAPTER .38

On the morning after we finish refitting the sloop, I rise early. I tug on my canvas trousers, my boots, a Mumbai-style shirt edged with gold embroidery, and the jacket I inherited from Perpétue. I straighten the data pendant on its silver chain at my neck and check to be sure Perpétue's knife and my crow are secure in my belt. Then I kiss Miyole and Soraya good-bye over their tea, and take the train down to the shipyard to meet Rushil.

I'm shaky at first when I kick in the ship's burners and lift off from the yard, but by the time Navi Flightport patches in with our exit trajectory, my hands hold the push bars steady. Rushil perches on the edge of the passenger seat so he can take in the view of Mumbai fading to a jeweled thumb of land as the sky grows dark around us.

The winds bounce and jog us as we cross their streams.

"Better strap in," I say, eyes locked ahead. The break in the atmosphere looms before us, growing darker as the wisps of air sweep thin.

We burst through, into the cold stillness of space. Rushil takes in a breath. The stars burn steady, but none so bright as the Earth beneath us. I sneak a look at him.

"Is it how you thought?"

"It's so much more. . . ."

I reach for his hand and push us on to Bhutto station.

We make dock on the commerce tier. Rushil links his fingers through mine as we step down on the docking floor. His eyes fly everywhere, taking in the bustle of passengers from every corner of the world, the holograms and vendors, and the laborers trucking carts of goods through the tight-packed crowds.

"You okay?"

"Yeah." His eyes have a faraway, stunned look, like a bird that's flown into a window. "It's just so . . . so . . ."

"It takes some getting used to." I press my lips together, trying not to laugh.

He remembers to blink and turns to me. "I guess this is how you felt when you first got to Mumbai, huh?"

"Some." I smile up at him.

My crow pings at my belt. I look down at the time. "*Chaila*. My appointment's in fifteen minutes. You have the specs for those air scrubbers?"

Rushil pats his crow.

"I'll see about the shipping license, then," I say. The tremor in my voice is half fear, half excitement. "Wish me luck."

Rushil squeezes my hand tight and laughs. "Stop worrying, okay?" He kisses me quick. "You'll do fine."

"I know." I go up on tiptoe and kiss him back. "Meet me back here?"

"Two hours?"

I nod. "Two hours."

I stand outside the flight authority office, clutching my tablet to my chest. The forms are all done inside, only waiting to be transferred and accepted, along with a small bribe for the flight officials to keep things moving smoothly. When my turn comes, I step up to the window.

A square-jawed woman wearing the uniform of the Bhutto Station Authority stares dully out at me. I slide my tablet across the counter with the square of pay plastic on top. She pockets the plastic without looking up from my form. "Ava Parastrata?"

"Right so," I say.

"Ship's name?"

"The *Perpétue*." I've whispered it to myself so many times as I lay in bed at night or in the cold-fused protective insulation between the layers of the ship's hull, I can say it now without stumbling.

"Sign here." She flips the tablet around to face me and holds out a stylus.

I mark my first and last name, neat and even. No one would know I couldn't string together the letters a mere turn past.

The official scans my tablet, and a seal appears over the document on the screen. She stretches out a tired smile for me. "Congratulations, Captain. Make sure you upload that into your ship's identification signal. Good flying."

I can't help but smile back wide. I walk away through the thronging corridor, staring down at the seal on my screen. Captain Ava Parastrata. I could almost skip. Here I am, walking sure and fearless in a place I once thought would swallow me live. From now on, I choose where I want to go.

I don't notice the woman balancing a baby in one arm and a box in the other, standing in the middle of the corridor, until it's too late. I knock into her full speed. She manages to hold on to the baby but drops the box of thumb-sized

$CO_2$ cartridges. They clatter to the floor.

"Sorry, so missus." I drop to my knees and grab at them.

The woman doesn't move. "What did you call me?"

"So missus . . . ," I begin, and glance up.

A pair of ocean-blue eyes look down at me. She wears her black hair in a messy braid tucked behind her cocked-out ears. She and her baby are both cloud pale, with blue veins branching under their skin. She stares at me.

I stand. "Soli?"

She fixes on the pendant at my neck and frowns, then reaches out a hand to touch it. "Ava?"

"Right so." My eyes water. "Oh, Soli."

"Mercies." She pulls me close with her free arm, the cartridges forgotten. The baby squawks in protest.

She pulls back but keeps a tight grip on my arm. "We thought you were dead. We looked for you such a long time. And then your father said you *were* dead, that you had fallen down groundways—"

"My father?" I frown. "What are you doing out alone, Soli?"

"Oh, don't worry on that now." Soli's eyes are soft, but new-laid care lines fan out at their corners. She looks as if she's aged five turns in the time since I saw her last. "They'll want to see you."

"Who?"

Soli's smile creeps in with a touch of mischief. "You'll see." She repositions the baby on her hip and grabs my hand. "Everything is different now, Ava. Things have changed, ever since . . ." She closes her mouth as if she's thought better of what she was about to say.

I pull back. "Ever since what? Different how?"

"It's better if you see." She tugs at my hand. "Hurry on. Truly, Ava, they'll be so glad."

I shudder with a sudden thought. *Luck. Could he . . .*

*No. Luck is dead.* I can't start spinning wild fantasies, only to have them crushed again. I check my crow. Thirty minutes until I'm supposed to meet Rushil back at the sloop. Bare time, but some. Enough to see what Soli means.

"Right so," I agree, and Soli's face lights up.

I follow her through Bhutto station's corridors, my heart and steps quickening. She chatters on about her baby—Heart, a boy—and marriages and other crewe gossip, and all the while, her son peeks out at me from her shoulder. I remember my first glimpse of Soraya when I was a smallgirl, her certain step and unflinching gaze, how grand and strange she was. I give Heart a small smile. He buries his face against Soli's neck and stuffs his pudgy finger in his mouth, but then glances back and gives me a gap-toothed smile. We take the lift down to tier twelve and come to the big metal doors of a docking bay. Soli lets go of my hand to open the latchport.

I step back, suddenly flush with worry. What if things aren't so different? What if her crewemen still despise me? What if this whole thing is a trap meant to lure me back to justice? I watch Soli tap in a code and push the door open.

She glances back. "Come how, Ava? I promise, everything's fine."

I search her face, with its tired eyes and knitted brows. Soli would never betray me. No matter what else has changed, I know that. I step through the latchport.

No crowd meets us this time, but some of the crewemen and women stare warily after me as Soli leads me through the ship. *Earthborn. Filth. Unnatural.* I can almost hear them.

We veer off down one of the *Æther*'s looping cooridors. Another crewewoman passes us going the opposite way and gives me an undisguised scowl.

I hurry to match steps with Soli. "Where are we going?"

"The women's quarters." She shoots a look at my clothes. "I thought you might want to put on something more . . . presentable."

I stop short. *Presentable?*

Soli continues on a few paces before she realizes I've

stopped. She turns and frowns. “Come, Ava. Don’t you want to look nice?”

“Soli.” My mouth has gone dry, and my heart is beating high and tight. “What is this? Enough games. Tell me true.”

Soli sighs and sags her shoulders, then addresses the baby. “Your modrie Ava won’t let us have any fun, will she?”

“Modrie?” I echo. I can’t breathe. “Soli, what . . .” My crow pings at my side. I should be making my way back to the sloop now.

“Hurry on.” Soli doubles back the way we came, throwing her words over her shoulder. “But I’m telling it true. You have to see for yourself.”

I tap out a quick message to Rushil as we walk—RUNNING LATE. DON’T WORRY—and hurry to catch up with Soli. We arrive at the pair of doors closing off the captain’s quarters. Saeleas is still there in the wood, words scrolling out from her mouth, only now I can read them. *Women of the air* . . . The last time I stood here, I was soaking wet and shaking with fear and shame. An echo of that feeling flutters through me.

Soli raps her knuckles on the wood, and the doors open. I step inside with her, each of us holding tight to the other’s arm. Floor pillows and thick rugs still lap over each other in drifts, but the lights have been tuned brighter, and with only some dozen people gathered around the captain's dais, the room feels near naked. They stand as we draw near, and it clicks for me what's different. A few among the gathered are women. And one of them stands out more than the rest, with her clay-red hair and green eyes.

Llell. *What is Llell doing here?*

But then the man at the center of the group turns. My steps falter. A pair of ozone-blue eyes. Bruised half-moons of tired skin well beneath them. His dark hair has grown long enough to tuck behind his ears. The stiff, embroidered stole of the captaincy drapes heavy on his shoulders.

"Luck?" I can barely breathe the name.

He looks up. Confusion passes over his face as he looks from me to Soli, and then back again.

"It's her, Luck." Soli's voice shakes with excitement. "I found her."

Luck blinks. He sucks in a breath. "Ava?"

I nod. "Right so. It's me."

He steps down from the dais and closes the distance between us in a few heartbeat-quick steps.

"How . . . ," I start to say.

But Luck clutches me to him, as if he's been starved for me this whole time. "Thank the Mercies," he says into my hair.

My body locks to his with a force that shakes my bones. Luck, alive.

"I thought you were dead," I say into his shoulder.

He rocks me side to side, strokes my hair, kisses the crown of my head. "I'm not dead. I'm not dead," he repeats, as though trying to make himself believe it so much as me.

"But Llell said they . . . she said they bathed you for burial and everything."

"They did," I say. "But Iri helped me slip them, and I went down groundways to my blood modrie—"

"Your blood modrie?"

"Right so." There's so much to tell. I look around the room. Besides Llell and Soli, I don't recognize anyone, though the man with his arm around Soli's waist must be her husband, Ready. "Is Iri . . . ?"

Luck shakes his head. "When we went to bargain with your father, she was already long dead. Soli tried to talk on it with some of the women, but she said they wouldn't even speak her name."

Some part of me knew it would ravel up this way. I knew it the moment I saw her fall, but the blow of it still rings me through.

"You're bound to be weary," Luck says. "Come, we can sit and talk in my quarters. We have all the time we need, now."

*Rushil,* I think faintly, and glance down at my crow. *He'll be waiting for me.* But this is too important. This is the sort of thing what stops time.

"Right so," I hear myself say.

"Very good." Luck claps his hands to dismiss the small crowd around the dais. They all file out except Llell, who I mark now is wearing a flowing Æther-red dress, and Soli with her baby in her arms.

"Would you find some food and drink for our Ava?" he asks them.

"Course." Soli sends me a smile. Llell grimaces, but follows her without a word.

Luck steps back to look at me, gripping my arms as if he fears I'll ghost away. "When your father said you had gone off with that groundways woman, we counted you dead. We were sure she took you down to the Earth with her. None of us thought you'd be strong enough to bear up under it."

"I bore it." I swallow down the memory of the curling, bitter pain of my first few months down groundways. "It was none easy, but I bore it."

Luck pulls me to him again. "I'm sorry. On me and all my crewe, I'm sorry."

"I'm well." I move back a slip. "Well and healed."

I shake my head and wipe my eyes against my jacket shoulder. "But you, I thought they would have sent you out to meet the Void, same as me."

Luck nods. "My father was talking on it, but he wanted us clear of the spaceport first, so the station authority wouldn't interfere. Only it ends up some on our crewe thought he was taking too many brides, turning out too many boys. I s'pose it was some too much, what passed with you and me. They said it was my rightful time to take a firstwife, and he had tried to take her instead. So they mutinied. My mother and her brothers came and got me from the brig, and the rest . . . It was his body we sent out to the Void, not mine."

"You killed him?"

"Yes." Luck grips my hand. "I don't regret it. I thought he had killed you, Ava. I thought his hand brought about your death. So I took the captaincy from him."

"The captaincy?" I can barely keep pace with what Luck is saying.

"And I turned the ship around," he says. "Came back to claim you from the *Parastrata*, but you weren't there. They said at first they had put you out into the Void. But Llell . . ." He stops. "I knew something else had happened, only I couldn't fix on what until I talked your father into telling me."

"You talked my father into telling you? How?"

Luck smiles sheepishly and shrugs. "You know, the *Æther*'s some known for its rice-wine stills." He glances up to the door where Soli and Llell disappeared. A worried look flits across his face. "Among other things."

"Other things?" A twinge of unease spiders down my throat.

"I'm sorry." Luck kisses me hard on the top of my forehead. "Forgive me, Ava. I'm sorry I took their word you were dead. But I've found you, and I won't let anyone hurt you now. Not ever again."

His words curl around me, strong and warm like his arms and shoulders. And I want, oh, I want it to be true, that this man has the power to keep all hurt from me. For him to be the balm to all my cares . . .

"Luck, tell me." My throat stays tight. "What other things?"

At that moment, Soli and Llell return with a cold pitcher of rice wine and a tray stacked high with crisp cakes, soft cheese, and dried apricots.

"Does it matter?" Luck laughs. "Small things. Nothing to worry on. What's important is, I've hammered out a peace with your father's crewe again. We've written up new trade agreements, and now you're alive. You'll be my wife, Ava. Isn't that all we ever wanted?"

"Your wife." I roll the word around in my mouth. He's right, isn't he? It's what we wanted. But something isn't right. Crewes always seal a trade agreement with a marriage, and my betrayal with Luck was some gulf to overcome. It would have taken a grand gesture on his crewe's part to bridge it.

"Your firstwife, you mean?" I ask, to be sure.

Luck hesitates. His eyes go back to Soli and Llell. And then I see it. My heart stops. The subtle round of early pregnancy buds out from the waist of Llell's red dress. Her hair coils tight in marriage braids. She cuts her eyes up at me, and a tiny smirk twists the corners of her mouth.

"What . . ."

"Ava." Soli steps in, her voice low and gentle. "There wasn't any other way to seal the peace with your father. After everything that happened, Luck couldn't afford to lose the crewe's respect, not with his captaincy so new. And Llell helped us . . ."

Luck looks sick. "We can still make our life the way we talked," he says. "You can learn reading and figuring, and when you're not with child, you can be on Fixes. Or whatever duty you choose."

"I don't . . ." I frown.

I look at Heart in Soli's arms. For a moment, the image of me in an Æther-red dress flashes before my eyes, me lying in a birthing bed, a dark-haired child asleep on my chest, and Luck beside us, watching over us. But then I see my grandmother, young and pale, drunk on love, unaware of her own fast-approaching death or the fate the Mercies held for her daughter.

I take a deep breath. "I don't know if I want to be with child. . . ."

A troubled look crosses Luck's face, but he blinks it away. "I understand. You'll need some months healing after what you've been through. I can wait, Ava."

"No," I say more firmly. "That's not what I mean."

"Did something happen to you down there?" He straightens. "I don't care if the Earth made you barren, Ava. I want you still, no matter what."

"No," I manage. "It's only . . ." Luck's eyes search mine, and a part of me wants to collapse against him, give him everything, anything to make the hurt on his face go away. No matter that Llell is firstwife. He loves me. Isn't that all that matters?

*But Miyole and Soraya. And Rushil.*

I imagine him waiting by the sloop. Waiting and scanning the crowd, and me never coming. *You're beautiful like this, you know?* My old cord still tied around his wrist, the feel of his hands in my hair, our unhurried kisses, and nights under the Mumbai sky. How can I give up his love for Luck's? How can I give up Luck's for his? And smallones . . . my head skips back to the idea. It seems so much more a question now, not a certainty.

"I don't know if I want smallones at all," I say. "Not right now, anyway. Maybe when I'm some turns older."

Luck looks as though I've put fire to everything he holds dear.

"But later." He squeezes my hands in his. "You'll want them later?"

"I . . ." My throat closes up. What do I want? The *Æther* under Luck's captaincy is some freer, true. I can see that. But it's not so changed in all. At least, not so changed as me. Would I ever get to see those worlds, the ones I've only ever hovered above? Would my limbs and lungs grow weak again, deprived of gravity? Would my mind lose its hard-won sharpness? Would working on Fixes and having Luck's love make up for that?

Luck steps close so our heads rest together. "Are you worried about Llell?" He whispers. "You know you're the firstwife of my heart, Ava, always."

And I want, oh, I want to make him happy. I want to

give him everything he deserves—love and children and all the years of my life. But I can't.

"I . . ." How to make him understand? I move his hand from my cheek and take it in mine again. "I learned to pilot a ship, Luck. And figuring and reading. There's so much more . . . And Miyole and Soraya, what about them?"

"Who?" Luck furrows his brow.

"Soraya, my blood modrie. And Miyole, she's . . . she's some like a sister to me."

"I don't understand," Luck says. "Don't you want me? Don't you want to come home?"

*Home.* I close my eyes, and the image that flutters before me is of Rushil pretending to dump the whole sugar pot into Miyole's tea, singing alongside Ankur in Zarine's flat, Soraya poring over her lecture notes at the kitchen table, sneaking up the wobbling fire escape into the talkies, and my sloop skirting above the Mumbai skyline.

Sadness settles over me like burial finery. A life with Luck might swallow up some of my sorrows, but it would bring others, heavy as the ones it took away. I wouldn't be the last wife Luck took. I would be secondwife, and someday there would be a third, and maybe a fourth, and then we would be the ones leaving other women's children behind. The whole thing would start all over.

"Of course I love you," I say to Luck. I turn to Soli with Heart clutched in her arms, and to Llell, too. "All of you. But this life—I'm not made for it anymore."

"You're every bit as worthy to be a captain's wife as a girl who's never touched the ground," Luck says fiercely, gripping my hand.

"I know I am," I say simply. I lean against him, taking in his warmth and smell—of grass and handmade paper, oil and air.

He drops his head. "They'll forget all this, Ava. I'll make them. It'll be as though it never happened."

"For you," I say, and brush the dark bangs from his forehead. I look into his eyes and try to memorize their exact shade of blue. "But I can't pretend it never happened. What I want, that changed when I changed. What I want now would only hurt you."

"I don't care—"

"But you will," I say. "In a turn or two, when we have no smallones and the men are starting to mutter behind their hands. I'll cave to please you, or it'll eat you away. Then what will we have but guilt and regret?"

"Ava."

"Luck." I touch my forehead to his. "Promise me something."

"Anything," he says.

"Promise you won't leave any more of the boys behind."

Shame passes over his face.

"You know what I'm talking on," I say.

"I . . . I won't," he stammers. "I never wanted to."

"I know," I say.

"Then stay," he pleads. "Stay by my side. Help me remake this crewe."

"I can't." I am crying now, and true. "I will love you and love you. You'll always be my first love, but I can't. Not any more than you can give up the *Æther*."

"Ava . . ."

I turn away. Soli stands back, aghast, and even Llell looks shocked as I walk out through the great doors, head high, tears cutting bright lines down my cheeks.

I look back as the door starts to close behind me, and blink my tears away. Luck holds up his hand. *Good-bye.*

And I hold up mine. *Good-bye.*

And then I turn and make my way out to Bhutto station, back to Miyole and Soraya and Rushil and the *Perpétue*, and everything my life is yet to be.